WORLDS APART

WORLDS APART

an anthology of lesbian and gay science fiction and fantasy

edited by Camilla Decarnin, Eric Garber and Lyn Paleo

Boston · Alyson Publications, Inc.

This is a paperback original from Alyson Publications, Inc., 40 Plympton St., Boston, Mass. 02118. Distributed in Great Britain by GMP Publishers, PO Box 247, London, N16 6RW.

ISBN 0-932870-87-2

First Edition, first printing: July 1986

Library of Congress Cataloging-in-Publication Data

Worlds apart.

Contents: Harper Conan and Singer David / Edgar Pangborn — Houston, Houston, Do you read? / James Tiptree, Jr. — To keep the oath / Marion Zimmer Bradley — Do androids dream of electric love? / Walt Liebscher — [etc.]

1. Homosexuality—Fiction. 2. Science fiction, American. 3. Fantastic fiction, American. 4. American fiction—20th century. I. Decarnin, Camilla. II. Garber, Eric. III. Paleo, Lyn.

PS648.H57W67 1986 86-14125

813'.0876'08354

Contents

INTRODUCTION 7

Harper Conan and Singer David, EDGAR PANGBORN 11

Houston, Houston, Do You Read? JAMES TIPTREE, JR. 37

To Keep the Oath, MARION ZIMMER BRADLEY 95

Do Androids Dream of Electric Love? WALT LIEBSCHER 122

Lollipop and the Tar Baby, JOHN VARLEY 125

The Mystery of the Young Gentleman, JOANNA RUSS 149

The Gods of Reorth, ELIZABETH A. LYNN 175

Find the Lady, NICHOLAS FISK 196

No Day Too Long, JEWELLE GOMEZ 215

Full Fathom Five My Father Lies, RAND B. LEE 224

Time Considered as a Helix of Semi-Precious Stones, SAMUEL R. DELANY 243

ABOUT THE CONTRIBUTORS 284

Introduction

Though science fiction did not come into being as a genre until the 1920s, its roots reach back through ghost tales and vampire stories, fantastic travelogs and ancient myth. For much of this time, homosexuality was a forbidden topic, and therefore often appeared in the guise of androgynes, sex-changers and other sexual variants. By means of these creations, writers could place the taboo subject in the distant realm of the unknown, the undiscovered, the unreal. Their efforts revealed not only attitudes towards homosexual behavior, but also notions of roles and inherent gender traits current at the time of writing – notions sometimes very peculiar indeed.

When science fiction came into being it too incorporated common cultural stereotypes in its treatment of sexual variance. Homosexuals were portrayed as evil, demented, or at least spiritually weak. Gay men made convenient villains – traitors, slave owners, corrupt effeminates. Their characters were secondary to the plot and wholly one-dimensional. The lesbian character fared no better. She was sexually threatening, yet strangely magnetic, drawing young women in to ravish them. Or she was hard and masculine – more bent on destroying men than on seducing women; she often inhabited worlds in which men were being exterminated or had become extinct. The function of the lesbian character was complicated because she demonstrated not only attitudes toward lesbianism but feelings about the relationship between men and women as well.

After 30 years of stereotypes, Theodore Sturgeon's superb story, "The World Well Lost" (1953), jolted readers and writers of the supposedly forward-thinking genre awake to the potential for more positive approaches. Marion Zimmer Bradley, Thomas Burnett Swann, Edgar Pangborn and others quickly took advantage of the freer climate to introduce sympathetic lesbian and gay images.

A private distribution network developed among enthusiastic science fiction readers, known as fans, who published small, noncommercial "fanzines" for the purpose of communicating with each other. Lisa Ben's *Vice Versa* and Jim Kepner's *Toward Tomorrow*, surfacing within this network, were among the earliest publications in the U.S. to come from the lesbian and gay community. In the post-war, post-Kinsey United States, it was becoming possible for more lesbians and gay men to emerge not only in fiction but in real life.

As the 1960s merged into the 1970s, science fiction writers produced more and more of what science writer Ctein has called "Future Insulation," taking ideas from the cutting edge of sex-role exploration and incorporating them in stories in ways that readers could relate to with comprehension rather than fear. Sexual orientation issues were particularly central to the work of Joanna Russ and Samuel R. Delany, but were also important in the writing of many others – among them, Ursula K. LeGuin, Thomas M. Disch, Michael Moorcock, Marge Piercy and David Gerrold. In the late 70s there was a noticeable increase in stories with gay and lesbian themes. Among the writers who created this wave were James Tiptree, Jr., Suzy McKee Charnas, John Varley, Elizabeth A. Lynn, Tom Reamy and Sally M. Gearhart.

This spectacular surge has leveled off. Ordinary lesbians and gay men have joined the ranks of stock characters, used to demonstrate a social acceptance of minorities in fictional futures or to throw a new twist into the boy-meets-alien romance. Scarcely a cruel-lipped lesbian tyrant or effeminate evil space-baron is to be seen. Though the early attempts to show gays as sympathetic produced a disproportionately high number of tragic endings, it can't be denied that the image of "the homosexual" in science fiction has altered radically for the better.

Lesbians and gay men have continued to participate in "fandom" – the science fiction reader community. Gay programming is becoming a common feature at the hundreds of science fiction conventions held annually. Lesbian and gay fanzines are still being published. There has also arisen a fascinating sub-genre of fanzine fiction based on the "Star Trek" television characters; endless changes are rung on the premise that Captain Kirk and his trusted first officer Mr. Spock have fallen in love – with each other! Interestingly enough, of the hundreds of such stories that have appeared, nearly all are authored by heterosexual women. These "Kirk/Spock" stories cannot be published commercially, but are widely available in the non-profit fannish networks.

There is a great deal more quality lesbian and gay science fiction than we were able to include in this anthology. Seek it out. A good place to start is *Uranian Worlds: A Reader's Guide to Alternative Sexuality in Science Fiction and Fantasy.* Anthologies of gay and feminist interest include *Kindred Spirits, Aurora, Strange Bedfellows, Dangerous Visions,* the *Women of Wonder* series, and *Amazons.*

Science fiction has the power to create, as critic Douglas Barbour has written, "worlds out of words." As lesbian and gay readers, we can find reflections of our own dreams in the alternate societies that others have envisioned, supportive of our loves and worlds apart from the intolerance of the societies in which we actually live. There are adventures, romance, and excitement in these worlds, and maybe some genuine alternatives for the future.

Harper Conan & Singer David

Edgar Pangborn

Spring, as Edgar Pangborn describes it, the season "of strawberries, of June passions," is a good time to fall in love. Youthful love is one of Pangborn's favorite themes, included again and again in his pastoral visions of life after a 20th Century apocalypse.

Donsil village stands inland sixty miles from the Hudson Sea. About twenty families, a good inn at the four corners where West Road meets South, a green with an open market, a town hall and a church. Conan the Hunter, son of Evan, Master Silversmith, was born in this small hamlet. Binton Ruins, which Conan visited in later years – that's forty miles off down the West Road. Word of them – rumor, legend, gossip – had reached him in childhood, and they possessed their own dark place among the creations of his mind. When he learned to play the lyre his father made for him, one of the first of his own songs was a fantasy belonging to that place: his mind saw desolate ground, fields of tumbled rocks that had once formed the bones of houses, the stubs of once great buildings like blackened tree stumps after a fire; but since his eyes had never seen Binton Ruins, Conan's poem spoke of all ruins everywhere, all the loss of Old Time. Later, much later, when David led him into the neighborhood of the actual Binton Ruins in pursuit of a fabulous rumor, Conan understood the direction of the journey he was making. The west winds cooled his face; his hand was spread out on David's shoulder for communication, or it was grasped by David's hand; for at that time Conan the Hunter had become Harper Conan, and he was blind.

In his eighteenth summer, already well known for skill with bow and spear, for his endurance, and courage, and acute vision, Conan had gone on a bear hunt out of Donsil with three or four young and turbulent companions. It was the Month of Strawberries, of June passions. After the killing the young men rejoiced, and sang in the praise of the bear's bravery and for propitiation of his gods. They wrestled in the early summer air, and bathed in a pool where they found exciting diving from a high bank – delightful and treacherous diving. Since Conan was stronger than any of them, taller, perhaps more eager to discover and display the outer limits of his strength and skill, his last dive carried him out where a rock lurking under water cut his skull. Terrified and heartbroken – one of them had been daring him on – his friends got him out on the bank and found that he breathed, slowly and harshly. Breathing so but aware of nothing (so far as we know, so far as he could ever remember) he lay at home for ten days before recovering awareness of his surroundings, and then he was blind.

Evan the Silversmith, his father, was praying. Evan was a valued and formidable man in the village, his work known well beyond it: a proud and religious man, now frightened and humbled. "Deliver back to me, O God, my true beloved son who does not know me, whose soul is wandering the outer fields before the natural time! Deliver him back to me and I will offer up—"

"Father, I know your voice. I'm here. Will you light a candle?" Conan understood, by the smell and feel of things, that he was lying on the bearskin of his room at home.

"Now God be thanked! Oh, a thousand candles! I am answered. But look at us Conan! Look at your mother and me!"

"Why, I can't see you. Isn't it midnight?" The air stirred before his face. He knew his father's hand had passed in front of his eyes. He heard his mother weeping. Presently, his father's trembling embrace, and a long trouble of words. Midnight remained.

"Conan," his father said – weeks afterward, when the boy had begun to learn his way about in the dark country, to develop the careful, not quite heartbreaking art of seeing with his fingers and ears and nose – "Conan, son, it's not so great a thing to be a hunter. I was skillful in it once; I taught you. But when I learned the mystery of making good things from metals, I found I cared much less for other work. Of course I was pleased when you became the best of the hunters, but something else has been closer to my desires for a long time. There's something all good men do, and we call it making the most of what happens. I don't know whether that means accepting God's guidance or merely taking whatever comes and thinking about it, examining it, more deeply than a fool can do or a sorrowful man find the patience to do." He set in Conan's grasp a cool framework, of silver by the feel of it. Conan's exploring fingers found a base that could rest on his left arm, or on a table, and a mechanism that could be studied. Most admirable was the waiting presence of taut cords and wires, which murmured to his touch as though a god had said: *I am here to become a part of you.*

"This lyre I made," said Evan Silversmith, "under the guidance of Harper Donal of Brakabin. He tells me that one comes to the great harp later, after learning this. But one never abandons this first instrument, he says, if one has the fire for it, the voice to sing with it, the heart to speak through the song. Harper Donal came here once, and you won't have forgotten it. But I remember how even before then you made songs for yourself in childhood. I think your ear is true, though I'm no judge. You shall go live a while with Donal at Brakabin. It's arranged – he wishes it, he remembers the listening child you were. He's very old. You'll find ways of being useful to him in his feebleness, and he'll teach you all he can. You may not possess what he calls the fire: he will know."

"My father, if I haven't it I will find it."

"A brave saying, possibly an unwise one. Harper Donal spoke to me of the many who waste life trying to find it, only to learn it's not for them. And then, he says, it may blaze up in some who haven't the strength to bear it. Dangerous country, Conan."

"I must explore it. I think I can do that."

"Go then with my love and blessing. Learn to give people music as I give them the work of my hands."

Therefore, with the consent of Chief Councilman Oren and the other Elders, Conan went north and lived with Harper Donal at Brakabin for four years, learning first the art of singing with the lyre. Donal himself had learned this from one of the Waylands of Trempa, who may have learned it from Esau of Nupal, who could have learned it from a musician born in Old Time, whose name is lost. That legendary one survived the Red Plague and lived to a great age, traveling through Katskil and teaching music (also something called philosophy) to the children at Nuber, Cornal, elsewhere as far north as Gilba, as far south as Sofran. Some say the Old Time singer and visionary was one Aron of Penn. Others claim this legendary figure was a woman, Alma of Monsella, who composed the best of our hymns in praise of God and his Son and Prophet, Abraham. Look also on a bothersome contradiction that intrudes here: not one of the Old Time books we possess mentions the art of singing to the lyre in connection with that period they called the Twentieth Century. In other words we're in the habit of believing numerous lies, and nobody knows much, and every civilization has bloated itself on vanity, and most of them have died of it.

As he studied and grew, it appeared to Conan that although the fire burgeoned in his heart and hands, it was absent from his voice. His singing, in his own judgment, was good but never more than good, which is the devil of a thing – any artist will know what he meant. However, nobody can hear the timbre of his own voice. Harper Donal told him he sang rather well, which from Donal was next to the highest praise. (The old man's highest was to say that a student had done not too badly.) Then at the appropriate time, Donal taught him the handling of the great harp, which is to the art of the lyre as the ocean to a brook.

Conan took to this study with a brillance that dumbfounded his master. Harper Donal's maidservant, a kindly taciturn woman of Moha, noticed that because Conan could not see it, Harper Donal grew careless about his face, something she had not observed in thirty years of worshipful service. A teacher must maintain his mask of varied uses, but Donal's lessons with this boy were frequently illuminated by smiles, astonished frowning, starting of water to the old man's eyes. A marvel like Conan's rapid learning of the harp is not unheard of. Donal had taught many other fine players and singers; he remembered and loved them all, and followed their fortunes. Technique is in itself no mystery. Donal himself used to say so, and to him it was a commonplace. The mystery prevails in the mind and heart that bridle technique and ride it out beyond the morning mist.

A time came when Conan heard his teacher declare he was playing not badly. Moments later the maidservant touched Conan's shoulder. He was then playing, at Donal's request, the rowdy, joyful dance *Elderberry Time*, composed by Donal in his own youth. She told Conan his teacher had smiled, nodded, and ceased to breathe.

This was Harper Donal's passing, as Conan knew of it. No doubt there had been the usual sad small indignities of dying, while Harper Donal's own merry music was making nothing of them.

At the funeral Conan played and sang the laments and other traditional music, in the company of two or three others whom the Brakabin Town Council found fit for the honor. And at that time the Council told the blind youth that the will of Donal bequeathed him the golden harp thought to have once belonged to Alma of Monsella. Donal had already spoken of this intention to the boy, so he was prepared with acceptable words and able to speak them with the graciousness expected by the Council. They were old men, wise, kindly, and rather stuffy. But then – (etiquette required, by the way, that he ask the Council's permission; greater fires than grief were burning in Conan, and he just forgot it) – Conan played and sang his own lament for his ancient master. The golden harp was in his hands. Part of the *Lament for Donal* came as an impromptu, born that moment, and a few of his hearers were disturbed.

Donal is dead, who sang for the morning.
Out of the gray cavern his song bore us the glow,
the warmth of fruitful daytime.
Out of the stillness music he wakened;
out of the winter gloom his song brought us the green

and gold of fruitful springtime.
Sing for Donal as I cannot, waking birds!
Sing for Donal as I dare not, waking winds!
Sing for Donal, jonquils and violets delivered from
the snow!
Sing as I cannot,
for Donal is dead, who sang the morning.
I fear long life, knowing now that song perishes
and the earth lies still, unloved.

Donal is dead, who hymned the sunny roads,
sang for the sweet dimness, sang the tale of the
deer-paths,
the hush of summer clearings.
In loveless age the music of companions
rang in his song, telling of loyalty and love,
of summer journeying.
Sing for Donal as I cannot, wanderers!
Sing for Donal as I dare not, true companions!
Sing for Donal, lovers delivered by his music from
the dark!
Sing as I cannot,
for Donal is dead, who sang the high noon.
I fear great love, knowing now that song perishes
and the flesh lies still, unkissed.

Donal is dead, his melody the evening.
Out of day's melting his song draws on the stars
that stir in the harbor of the hills.
Out of the evening, music he wakened.
Out of the summer and the winter night his song
harbored beyond the Pleiades.
Sing for Donal as I cannot, constant stars!
Sing for Donal as I dare not, autumn winds!
Sing for Donal, mountains that knew him, streams
that cooled his feet!
Sing as I cannot,
for Donal is dead in the world's evening.

I will live and love, knowing that no song perishes while one soul lives to hear.

Certainly there were those whom the *Lament for Donal* disturbed. They believed, those nice old men, that blind Conan might have been more concerned with his conscious art than with his dead teacher. It never occurred to them how immensely this would have pleased Harper Donal himself, who might have snorted that he thought there was already grief enough on earth without the customers complaining about short measure. But the Council was generous, too, and gave the young musician a safe escort out of Brakabin, all the way home through the forest and hill country with his golden harp.

Thus Conan in his twenty-second year returned to his father's dwelling at Donsil. After four years in the house of Donal of Brakabin, this was one way of beginning his journey into the world. Evan the Silversmith, whose obscure talent for fatherhood amounted to genius, didn't ask the boy what he planned to do next.

Donsil enjoys the many annual festivals of music, and takes pride and pleasure in accommodating them. That inn at the four corners is rather large, several private houses, especially the communal types, also invite paying guests at festival times. Other visitors can camp a few nights in the town's groves that spread out from the green like wheel spokes, if they mind their manners. Since they have come for the music, they generally do, even to the extent of picking up their own trash and using the public latrines. A village of hospitality is worth a bit of kindness.

Donsil makes a good thing out of festival times financially, but that has little to do with the emotional climate of the place. History tells of a school of Old Time sociologists, safely extinct we may hope, to whom the dollar-value of the music festivals would have provided the full explanation of Donsil village. But good nature is one of the those stubborn activities of the mind and heart which can be made an end in itself – like love and honesty – if human people so choose and if circumstances aren't too persistently clobbering them. Having never heard of Twentieth Century sociology, and possessing a small enclave so far only moderately oppressed by a developing feudal tyranny from above, the Donsil villagers were free to be pleasant folk. Somehow, at least in this one little spot of the world, after the long dark of the Years of Confusion when savagery ruled and most remnants of civilization were forced to shelter behind wooden stockades relearning the primitive arts (and forgetting much) – somehow the sick money-greed of Old Time had diminished to a manageable intensity. Human beings were still as a rule greedy animals – of course. But the bloated hugeness of Old Time and its ghastly illusion of success, had favored piggishness at every turn, often openly making a virtue of it.

Since we create our own ends and purposes, whether or not we invent gods to blame them on, it would be astonishing if we didn't create plenty of stinkers. But a survival society, unless it is content with a pretty flabby and boring goal of day-to-day eating, security and copulation, actually cannot afford the perversion of piggishness. Donsil had discovered music.

The incursions of visitors at well spaced and predictable intervals had also encouraged, even driven Donsil's citizens into developing the art of composing to a remarkable degree of efficiency. In the best of human societies as well as the worst, one thing does lead to another, and we do all get to learn a few cute tricks. Culture, anthropologists call it.

To Donsil, several times, while Conan was away at Brakabin, had come the young singer David of Maplestock, at first with a traveling choir for the festival of Midsummer Eve, celebrated in this country on the fourth day of July. He did not sing alone that time. It was merely noted how brilliant the Maplestock choir sounded in the tenor section – too brilliant for the rest; in fact for that reason the famous choir only won second prize, nosed out of first place by the Nupal Glee. Later that year, before the Harvest Festival – not any special occasion but the will of his own wandering – David came to Donsil alone, and drew crowds to the green for three days before he moved on. He could have stayed another three and repeated his repertory; the crowds would not have diminished, for when something like that occurs, word goes around the countryside.

A wanderer by nature was David, at any rate he said so, claiming not to know where he was born. It might have been in a gyppo wagon heading north from Moha, for his first sure memories belonged to the deep forest and mountain country of Adirondack Island. He had adopted the name "of Maplestock," he said frankly, just because he'd lived in the town a couple of years and liked it well enough. His manner suggested that further questions weren't invited. The gyppo part of his tale was clearly absurd. He couldn't be a gyp with such fair hair and gray eyes, to say nothing of a touch of accent that sounded like Penn or even the southern country, and nobody around here nowadays believes those stories about the gyppos stealing babies.

He was ugly, some felt, with his pug nose, big flexible mouth that made his eyes appear small, a jagged scar on his left cheek that could have been acquired in a knife brawl, heavy shoulders and neck and chest seeming too big for the rest of his short frame. Now and then, though rarely, a quick smile revealed good nature, a quality Donsil village always recognized, and redeemed what some thought of as his ugliness. It was never a confiding smile, just a friendly way of saying: "Give me no trouble and I'll give you none; give me some and heaven help you." He possessed an unremarkable lyre with a light frame of bronze nicely polished, and he played it well enough to accompany himself, just respectably.

When he sang, nothing else existed — no crowd, no weather good or bad, only a surpassing voice that searched out and touched every element of response in the hearer's nature, as if the singer had studied and cherished that one particular person all his life. So clear and blessed was this illusion that some felt the presence of magic and made the sign of the Wheel over their hearts. Good magic of course. Any critic would have been torn apart if he chirped while they were under the spell: a significant hazard of the profession which has an indirect bearing on Darwinian natural selection.

David's voice was rich in the baritone, and spread through some not quite believable tenor range beyond two octaves — up to a treble C if you care to believe me; I am not by profession a liar.

Through that upper range the tenor quality was sustained; no hint of falsetto, no loss of power. C sharp, maybe. What mattered was not the tonal but the emotional range: no nerve of human experience that David of Maplestock could not touch.

Certainly, certainly it was magic, the magic not of hush-hush and spookery but of art, which grabs hold of any available science it needs as a carpenter reaches for a saw. It was the magic that derives from intense long labors toward a perfection admitted to be unattainable, carried on by one with adequate endowment for the art, the patience to endure, the vision to discover a goal and the road that runs there. At some early age, perhaps fifteen or sixteen, when all boys must start threading the obstacle course of booby traps that the community mindlessly dumps in their path, David had simply told himself: "I will make myself the best singer it is possible to be, given my body and my intelligence."

Councilman Oren of Donsil remarked, during those first three days when David of Maplestock visited Donsil alone, that when this young man was singing a person dying in agony of a mortal wound or illness would hold off death until the song ended. The Councilman was an honest old fellow not thought to be very imaginative, and since at that time he was suffering an illness that did prove mortal, his words were remembered with a bit of keenness.

Magic: one element is courage; another, strange though you find it, is good sense. If you happen on a genuine artist who is also a kook, that's for fun, or an accident, or because the public is in a mood to gobble it down and pay for it: under the fuss, somebody inside there knows what he's doing, otherwise the art itself would be of the sort that wilts on a second look. This form of magic was the only one possessed by Alma of Monsella, Donal of Brakabin, Conan himself.

David, by the way, was no sort of kook, just a rugged young man who minded his own business. He never tried to be flamboyant. As a matter of course he wore the mouse-brown shirt and loin-rag and sandals that have come to be like a uniform for itinerant minstrels. His singing inevitably drove women insane. In this matter he tried to conduct himself with good manners and kindness. What great singer could go to bed with all of them?

They don't make that kind of bed.

David was heard of from distant places, word drifting back on the tongues of other wanderers – from Moha, Vairmant, Conicut, the Bershar mountain land, even from Main. Yet he returned to Donsil – drawn to the town and its inn, he said, by Mam Selby's corn fritters, and he was indeed observed consuming those culinary poems with the vigor of a starved farmer. Donsil had come to expect David's frequent returns, and his name was much in the common talk on the spring days after Conan came home.

"He is truly one of the great singers, my father?"

"So far as I am a judge," said Evan the Silversmith. Others might, and did, make the dull error of belittling David of Maplestock with the notion of soothing the jealousy they imagined the blind youth to be feeling; not Evan. Conan since his homecoming had sung a little, and played, and his music was praised not on its merits (he felt) but merely because he was one of the town's own, originally Conan the Hunter. His singing, as he knew himself, was no great wonder; the power and strangeness and harmonic discoveries of his harp-playing seemed to be over their heads, and probably were; no one had told Donsil village that there was anything uncommon here to admire. He was just Evan's boy, and had made himself a fine harp-player – very nice. "When David of Maplestock sings," said Evan Silversmith, "one thinks and cares about nothing else except to hope that he will soon sing again."

"I can never become a singer of that kind. But I am a player of the harp. In another year or two I shall be a great one."

"And you compose new music."

"Not as I wish. One thing or two things. In the rest, so far, something's lacking, my father. I mean to learn what it is, and how to bring it into my music."

"Conan, I think I could find someone with the art of writing down your music. That ought to be done."

"Not yet. As for my songs, other singers remember them from hearing – we're trained to do so. The harp music – well, sometime, but not yet . . . this David of Maplestock will sing tomorrow?"

"He came to the inn today, they tell me, dusty and tired, and

Mam Selby restored him with corn fritters. Yes, he'll certainly be singing at the green tomorrow, if the day's fair."

"My father..." The Silversmith's hand on his arm told him to continue. "The fire is in me. Donal of Brakabin believed so. In the music of the harp, not in my voice, which can obey only so far as nature allows. Music is – a world in itself. I have no other way to explain it, maybe I need none. I am finding ways to explore that world, ways that I think no one has discovered, unless it was done in Old Time and then lost. New avenues. They open slowly."

Next day in that time of afternoon when the height of town hall and church hold the village green in comfortable shade, Conan with his father and mother went down the slope from the house of Evan the Silversmith to the village. Town folk and visitors were gathering; Evan described them for his blind son, who already sensed their presence. And as Conan's footsteps began to tell him of level ground, a song passed him on the air, one of the old airy love lyrics of Esau of Nupal, with the freshness of breeze and bird wings.

My love is fair like summer leaves,
like autumn fruit my love is fair.

But when this trifle of delight had gone on its way – one could only love the singer, without need of thought – Conan halted in astonishment, hearing the voice, to an unknown simple accompaniment of the lyre, sound a plangent outcry–

Donal is dead, who sang for the morning.
Out of the gray cavern–

Clearly someone who heard him at Brakabin had remembered, as the minstrels of today are expected to do. But David of Maplestock broke off the *Lament* after only a few lines. At Conan's side his mother exclaimed: "Why, he's coming to us Conan! Do you know him?"

"In a way I do, Mother."

Then his hand was grasped, the voice was coming to him with warmth and assurance: "I was afraid you might not be here,

Harper Conan." One doesn't use "Harper" as a title unless the person one speaks to is an acknowledged master; the silent, friendly-breathing crowd around them knew this. "Man, where's your harp? I must sing this with the music they heard at Brakabin and couldn't remember for me, the music none but you can play. At best I am only a singer." The crowd rumbled a bit of laughter, but Conan knew he had spoken with no thought of jesting. "Where's your harp?"

"I will bring it Singer David," said Evan of Donsil, Master Silversmith. Conan in his daze heard an unfamiliar happiness in his father's voice. Relief too, if that is the just word: the relief of one who sees the sun come out on a day that had promised gray sadness; for Evan was another of those incalculable eccentrics who do not build their lives on jealousy.

They played and sang together that afternoon, as wind and bright cloud belong together, or sea and sky, arm and hand. Some listeners later said that until that day they had scarcely been aware of their own man, Conan son of Evan. The quiet, the hushed, almost diffident quality of the crowd's reception, derived mainly from astonishment at what happened when these two musicians came together without rehearsal, without having even met before. The applause, though not loud, was persistent, entranced; it was long before the villagers permitted the music to end. Then Conan and David, allowed to be alone, walked across the fields together.

It may seem strange that a village noted for good nature should also excel in tact. Some of it the people might have picked up from Evan Silversmith and a few like him; but Donsil is an uncanny place in its own right. Not fantastic; not out of this world exactly. One dreads to use a term so long and bitterly abused as the word "civilized," but maybe there's no other.

"I twice heard you play alone," said David, "when you were with Harper Donal of Brakabin. It was at the student concerts he arranged so rarely. I was in the crowd and learned only that you were of Donsil. That's why I returned here several times – no reflection on Mam Selby's corn fritters: they drew me, too. There's a tree root here." As if he had performed such little services all his life, he touched Conan's arm and guided him past the obstruction.

"I wish you had spoken, at Brakabin."

"Harper Donal was rather peppery – maybe you knew – about others making contact with his students while they were in his charge. Afraid of patrons and such like taking them away before they had learned enough. And also, the listening crowd – what I wanted to say to you wasn't to be said in a crowd. It may surprise you, coming from a singer who's won a bit of popularity, but I'm a shy man, Conan. I suppose we all live too much in our skulls."

"Most of the time it's necessary, isn't it?"

"Yes, but not in this hour. Here's high sunny ground, let's sit a while. I must tell you first about a rumor that came to me less than a year ago – and God forgive me if I raise false hopes. It may be nothing but rumor – trash talk, deception. But I felt so much possibility of truth in it that, now we are friends, I must pass it on for what it's worth. It reached me when I was traveling the Twenyet Road, and I stopped overnight at an inn near Onanta, a dull place. One of the guests, a bright old man, was on his way to Skendy in northern Moha. I thought him sober and sensible. He was telling about his experience with a group of healers who have settled, it appears, right in the middle of Binton Ruins. You may already have heard something about them?"

"Not of any healers. Word might have reached Donsil, but I have been at Brakabin until only a short while ago, and Harper Donal, as you say, didn't want the world coming close to his students. Even here at Donsil news from the west is slow in reaching us. Most of our festival visitors come from the more civilized parts – Nuin, Conicut. I know of Binton Ruins, however. They say it's very desolate."

"It is. I've never gone inside the limits of the place, only skirted the fringes, and that's dreary. I went there from curiosity after meeting that old man at Onanta. From Skendy southwest to Binton Ruins, the way the roads twist, must be well over a hundred miles. The old man couldn't afford a litter for that. His back was in such continuous pain that he couldn't ride, and dreaded the jolting of a cart, the only vehicle he owned, more than the ordeal of struggling along on crutches. His wife and daughter and one old friend made the pilgrimage with him, so there was love to help him walk. If the healers had failed him, he told us, he would as lief have lain down and died there at Binton Ruins as anywhere else – the pain was that severe, and had been with him so long that it was shoving everything else out of his life. It disgusted him: he had no desire to exist as a creeping bag of pain . . . they healed him, Conan. As he told us the story the old boy kept getting up on his feet, grinning and proud, to show us how well he could walk."

"They healed him."

"Not long after this came the first time I heard you play, at Brakabin. It never occurred to me you were blind; no one told me. The second time, someone did, but I feared – oh, false hopes – and I may be raising them now, doing harm when I only wish–"

"Whatever comes from your heart is good, David of Maplestock."

"Conan – probably these strange people at Binton Ruins *can't* do anything for blindness. It's only a mad hope. All I know about them comes from what this old man said, and some – some talk I've picked up since then in my travels, bits and pieces that I don't really credit. I value the old man's story because he was so intelligent, because there seemed no doubt that they had cured him of a great trouble. But when it comes to – oh, curing the smallpox, making the dead walk – ach, who knows? For example, his wife and friend and daughter never talked directly with the healers, and they were convinced it was all a blessed magic, or maybe not so blessed, anyhow something they didn't want to inquire into closely. Rumors from other sources will have it that the healers are wizards of Old Time who've been living underground or off on a cloud somewhere, praise Abraham, amen – damned nonsense. They say the healers have something called a generator, a machine that creates the Old Time marvel of electricity, whatever that was. They say they can regenerate lost organs – arms, legs–"

"They say that?"

"Rumor does. They say, they say."

"But they did heal the old man's pain."

"Yes. According to what *he* said – and he'd talked with them, listened, asked questions that I'm sure were intelligent – according to him they don't even call themselves healers. They describe their work as inquiry, themselves as seekers. The old man said they have books of method and knowledge – neither he nor his family could read, by the way – and it seems to me they must have kept alive or rediscovered some of the wisdom of Old Time. They used no drugs on him except a little of one of the common harmless herbs – I forget which; all the cure-women and herb-women know it – marawan? – well, I don't remember. But he said they knew a great deal on that subject and talked with him freely about it, and about everything that they did for him, in a very clear, friendly way. None of the hocus-pocus and puff-puff show that most of our ordinary doctors make to conceal their bloody ignorance. They gave him massage – better than what a Skendy cure-woman had done for him, but the same kind, and they kept him a fairly long time in a cool quiet room with nice meals, and frequent visits from several of them, not very many from his family. All this right there in the middle of those haunted ruins, in a few of the Old Time buildings that they've been able to make useful. They have an area out near the fringe of the ruins where friends and relatives of sick people can camp, and food comes in from farms in the neighborhood. The old man lost count of the days. He had rest, and a few simple exercises, and in time the pain just faded out. They warned him it might return, and told him how to care for himself if it did. They inquired what he could afford to pay, and asked half of that . . . he said only one thing, Conan, that suggested a hint of the supernatural, and though it did so to him, it might not to you or me. He said their faces had a distant, close-listening look. But surely we've all seen that look on someone who's concentrating on a problem and needs to shut away the immediate surroundings. I suppose it was the circumstances, the coming out of his long time of pain, that made the old man find something remarkable in it. I believe the healers were just listening to their own thoughts as we all do."

"Will you go with me to this place, Singer David?"

"With all my heart, and we'll make music on the road."

"How can this be?" said the blind harper. But he spoke like one who says: *How strange that the sun rises!*

"Since I first heard you play, Harper Conan, I've desired to go with you, and be your eyes, my voice reminding you how the fields look under the sun, wherever you go and as long as we live. I am only a singer; I had never imagined the country you explore with your harp until you made it known to me: there you must be my guide. But if there were no music in the world, in a world of the deaf and blind, Conan, still I would love you."

The mother of Conan had been and still was a true believer in the near and constant presence of God, a faith that Evan's skepticism never attempted to assail, though now and then he used the defensive weapon of silence. Her faith made her vulnerable to bewilderment at the stark happening of her son's blindness; it had come on him so like God's punishment! – but what had he done so terrible as to deserve it? Surely, she knew all his sins great and small! And she would count them over and try to measure them against a lifetime of darkness – yet God cannot err – and so on and so on around a circle, with no result except that chronic bewilderment, embittered now by seeing how blithely Conan went down the road in the company of a stranger, when she had only just welcomed him back from the long absence at Brakabin. He walked with a swing of the shoulders she had not seen since the days of Conan the Hunter.

Except for this inevitable pain for which there was and is no healing even within the power of Evan the Silversmith, the young men were allowed to make a quiet departure. Just a bit of a westward journey (they said). They would practice making music together, and explore the countryside for the devil of it. Without even discussing it between themselves, neither mentioned Binton Ruins.

"How can you trust that – that Maplestock man so lightly, Evan? It isn't as if they *knew* each other. And if Conan's to go haring off like this at the first whim, how will he ever get himself a decent girl and settle down the way he must?"

"I don't know, Ella."

"You sit there. You sit there and say you don't know! Where do I find the patience?"

When the friends set out for Binton Ruins it was again the Month of Strawberries, a season that love must have for its own whatever the rest of the year may do in the way of sorrow and confusion.

Between Donsil and Binton Ruins the roads at their best are not much more than expanded deer trails, even where now and then some fragment of Old Time blacktop appears and runs a little way, not yet quite crumbled into lifeless black mud. The trails together with these bits of ancient road describe a shallow northward curve through a country of small hills, and turn again south toward Binton, serving on the way nothing larger than a few stockaded villages, surrounded by poorly protected fields of rye, wheat, buckwheat, corn and hay. Everywhere between these lonesome villages stands heavy forests. More pine and mixed growth, less hemlock here than in the hill country to the north, but Conan smelled the hemlock sometimes and felt its presence. Occasionally David found a spruce tree exuding a mild resinous gum that he liked to chew, finding it good for his singer's throat. These were warm days, of trust and pleasure and the making of music. David's most cherished burden was a thick sheaf of fine paper purchased long before in Maplestock, on which with quill pens and good oak gall ink he could capture his friend's harp-music and the new songs that were almost daily born of Conan's mind; thus in future time they might become known, played anywhere in the world, without the loss that we know occurs when memory, even the best, is the sole means of preservation. Whole worlds, in fact, have been lost that way. It is a pity.

I see the road where you part the branches
and run toward the sun's heart, yourself new gold
in the divided light.

I see the brook where you stand in beauty
and lift the bright stream to cool your flesh
in the still-shining day.

I see the night where you hold the shadows
around me like a shelter: your mouth is sweet
with deep-forest spices.

"Ah, Conan, who would know you were not singing of what your own eyes tell you?"

"As I shall be soon. As I shall be."

"But Conan, Conan— " There was great fear in David's voice, remaining when Conan told him not to be afraid; but Conan grasped his arms and wrestled him laughing to the ground and then nothing more was said that touched on the healers of Binton Ruins until a day when the two came out into open country drenched in sunlight, and Conan heard distant voices and clatter from the campsite at the border of the dead city. David said: "We have come to it. The camp is bigger than when I saw it less than a year ago. O Conan, remember—"

"That it may be useless, certainly. But here is no illusion," said Conan and kissed his cheek.

On the edge of a mighty field of rubble stood a three-story building of ancient style, stark and alone, a fragment of Old Time not quite submerged. From the structure a fence ran in both directions to the surrounding woods. Everywhere on the rubbled ground, among slowly disintegrating heaps of plaster, brick, metal that could not rust, indestructible plastic garbage and other rubbish of every sort, vegetation had found small footholds of available earth and declared the intention to live. Behind the fence the same sort of desolation continued until hidden by a rise of ground, but beyond that here and there the ruined upper parts of tall structures appeared, hazy and meaningless. All this David described to his friend. The fence, he remarked, looked sturdy and forbidding, while those shut out by it showed no resentment, no notion of defying it. The building looked like a place under invisible siege, asserting property rights to a section of the calamity of history. "When I came here before," said David, "only a few dozen people were camping here, and they were all relatives or friends of the sick, who were being cared for at some place deep in the ruins. Word must have been traveling, Conan. I remember this isolated house, but there was no fence then. Now, by the look of it, there must be two or three hundred in the camp, with many sick people among them, waiting."

"Then we must wait too." Conan smelled the crowd, a dull

stink of people who had scant facilities for washing or caring for themselves or disposing of their own pollutions. A little dog barked stupidly on and on – *ack-ack* – *ack-ack* – *ack-ack* – nerve-rasping and unappeasable. With the same persistence, a baby unanswerably wept.

Two men were posted at the entrance of the house, and a woman with a book. She sat at a desk. Since her face invited them, David led his friend to her. Casual and kind, she asked: "What is your trouble, sir?"

"I have far less trouble than most people," said Conan, "for I am a minstrel, and we rejoice in our work. Music comes to me, I love and am loved, my friend is a singer like no other. But it is true that my eyes are blind."

"Were you born blind, my dear?"

"No," said Conan, and he told her of his injury, of the ten days lost out of his life. Her friendly quietness made it easy to speak. When he had finished, the silence was long and thoughtful; David's hand on his arm counseled patience. The quality of the woman's voice had told Conan that she was of middle years, herself patient.

"Come," she said at last, and he heard her rise.

"My friend with me."

"Wherever he goes," David said, "I am his eyes until his own eyes are healed."

She hesitated, but then said: "Of course. I hope we can help you. If we can't – and there are many we can't help at all – you still have the greatest of all forces for healing."

They understood her. They followed her into the building and up a flight of stairs to a room at the rear which held a pleasant scent of dried herbs. Here the monotone discomfort of the crowd was hushed to a murmur no more intrusive than the sound of a waterfall off in the woods. A man's cordial voice exclaimed: "Why, Sara, surely nothing ails these handsome cubs? What a beautiful harp! They must have come to entertain the old man."

"Your voice isn't old, sir," Conan said.

"My voice – oh, I understand." Conan heard the woman Sara going away, and David guided him into a chair and stood by him, his hand on Conan's shoulder communicating in a language that had been growing wider and more fluent with every day that passed. The cordial voice continued: "I am Marcus of Ramapo. Do not call me doctor – it would have been fitting in Old Time; not now. Not healer either, as so many insist on calling us – there are too many we cannot heal. I am a member of our small society of inquiry. I have some knowledge of sickness and health, ancient and modern; not very much. Tell me who you are, so that I can look intelligent and write something in a big book."

"We are Harper Conan and Singer David."

"Singer David of Maplestock? Why, I heard you, sir. I heard you at Albani in Moha a year ago, but I was far out in the crowd and could hardly see your face, or I'd have recognized you. I have never forgotten it, Singer David."

"When you hear Harper Conan play, you'll never forget that, Marcus of Ramapo."

"I believe it. Well – now tell me what happened." And when Conan had done so he sighed, and Conan heard the soft tap of his fingers on the edge of his book. David's hand said only: *Be patient. I'm here with you.*

"Do you have headaches?" asked Marcus of Ramapo.

"Sometimes. Not always very bad, and when they pass all's well."

"When was the last one, as near as you remember?"

"It will have been the day after I came home from Brakabin, a little over two weeks before I met my friend, and we have been more that a week on the road, lazing along. We spent two days in a good place, not traveling at all. A month, say, since the last headache that was bad enough to remember."

"And before that one?"

"Two months, about."

"Headaches like that before your injury, too?"

"Why, in those days I scarcely knew what a headache was."

"Any suggestion of vision returning?"

"Not real vision. Flashes – like light, perhaps, but – well, like what anyone sees if he bumps his head or presses his eyeballs, only the flashes come with no cause like that."

"Nausea?"

"Nay, hardly ever. I eat like a hog."

"Like a thin hog," said David.

"Drowsiness when you should be wakeful?"

"Once in a while."

Marcus of Ramapo asked a number of other questions, his voice brooding and mild; and David later told his friend that the lean, sad, bearded face of Marcus had certainly shown a listening look – but as David had guessed it was the look of a man listening with all his powers to a thousand books and a thousand years, and the magic of it was the magic of a human mind reaching for light in darkness. At length Marcus of Ramapo said: "Gentlemen – I will not say that we can never help you. If you come to us again in a few years – who knows? Our knowledge is growing, very slowly. In a few years it just might be possible to attempt some of the simpler kinds of brain surgery that were practised in Old Time. We have some of the books – a few, never enough, but we search all the time. I myself have tried some easy surgical techniques on little forest monkeys and other animals – with not much success. Do you understand, gentlemen? There is no body of experience, no tradition to support us. Only what we can win from the books. No industry – no chemistry, physics, engineering, nothing at all of the great interdependent disciplines that Old Time medicine and surgery could take for granted as part of their environment. All gone down the drain, and so long ago! Two hundred years some say – I would guess more than that. We don't even understand asepsis enough to be successful with it – that's the technique of preventing infection; we know most of the principles and theory, but we haven't the chemistry or the practical experience. Look at the rubble out there and this one creaky building that somehow managed to stay upright long enough for us to come shore it up. A good monument it is to Old Time, a civilization wrecked apparently by the old, old union of politics and stupidity, plus the horror of misused science. Come, boys – I'd like to show you our – hospital and laboratory, let me call them; I suppose nobody will dispute my use of the nice old words. If you see what we are trying to do, perhaps a thought of it will come into your music now and then, Conan and David, and that way a little something of us will continue even if we fail altogether or are destroyed."

"Destroyed, sir?" said Conan. "Destroyed?"

"At least a third of those people out there hate us for not accomplishing the impossible. Oh, they would far better go to the famous shrines of the saints, and some would be cured, too, seeing how great a part imagination plays in it – I can say that to you because of what I see in your faces. Yes, we've been attacked by the angry once or twice – our reason for the fence. Harder is the desperate expectant staring of those who never get angry, but simply insist in their thought that somehow we must be able to lift a stick of magic called science, and heal some walking shell already half dead. Gentlemen, I am certainly talking too much – so seldom we meet anyone here who is fresh and brave. Seldom anyone even young, for that matter – except the mue babies, except the mue babies – oh, I talk too much!" But as he spoke he had lifted his book, with deliberate care to make no noise with it, and turned it outward so that David must read: *I recognise your love for him. He may have several years or only a few; or I may be mistaken. Never, never leave him.*

Then Conan and David left the building and followed Marcus across the rubbled area, up and over the rise of ground and into what must long ago have been the center of a large city. Endless blocks of houses, most of them fallen and covered with creeping vines but not all – some were upright, as very old men and women might lean into each other's shoulders if they were trying to stand against a wind. They crossed broad squares still partly paved and David was alert that Conan should not stumble. Once Marcus said: "Feeble attacks, hardly even mobs, you know, but soon they'll be around us in greater numbers. We live strangely, gentlemen. We heal a few, we learn – but then, how can you tell them not to spread the word? How could we make them understand that the recovery of wisdom takes a long time? I'll tell you something, knowing it will be safe with you. Our group – we are only fifteen – has decided to move again, this coming winter. Three times we've been driven out by hordes of the sick we could not heal, many of them hating us. We began in Penn, moved out to the edge of the wilderness country, moved again south, then here. After this month we'll admit no more to the hospital except those we could take with us. Seems harsh? Well, it's decided so. Next year we shall be near the coast of Adirondack Island. Come to us again, on the far chance that I shall have learned enough to help you, Conan. A small chance, but I shall work toward it."

"What brought the blindness on me, can you say?"

"Oh, the injury. Our eyes see through our brains. In some manner your injury damaged the connection of eye and brain. Sight may return – don't hope for it, I only say it may. I can do nothing now, Harper Conan – if I attempted it, you would die. But next year, or the next – who knows?"

"Then I will live with blindness," said Conan, "and I honor you for telling me the truth. It's not hard – I have my love and my music."

"This building was truly a hospital in Old Time," said Marcus, and they entered a place of stone walls and floors. "The old machines are all useless – depended on electricity. If there was iron in them, there's rust, and anything adaptable for a weapon or tool was long ago stolen." They passed some open doorway; Conan heard muted voices, and someone whimpering. "In here" – Marcus greeted someone passing and opened a squeaking door – "here we have a toy that we put together from an ancient book. I have crazy hopes about it, gentlemen – you know, in our group they sometimes laugh at me for hoping too much. The thing's called a generator. There's the remains of a big Old Time generator in the cellar, along with a thousand other gadgets, covered with dust – no fuel even if we knew how to repair and operate them." Something buzzed under his hand.

"Describe it for me, David." But David only made a harsh noise in his throat, startled by the contraption, Conan supposed.

"He's stepped over to the window," said Marcus, and touched Conan's arm peacefully. "Some things in this place are a bit grim for a newcomer. Well, this generator toy – God, the thing hardly has the power to galvanize the leg of a frog." The buzzing ceased. "And yet, Conan, an electric current no stronger than this was once made to do marvelous things. Believe this, I *know* it to be true: in Old Time there was a device for sending a tiny wire down through the great vein in the throat, as far as a heart that had ceased beating, and the light push of an electric current made that heart beat again, and sometimes the one who would have died lived for years afterward in quite fair health. Also" – but his voice sagged, and Conan felt his hand shiver as he took it away – "there's word in the writings of bringing about a regeneration of entire lost organs through the stimulus of a weak electric field. Experimental work was being done on that when the world blew up. Well, carry it in your imagination. Find a song in it, if songs are made that way – I don't know. I suppose I shouldn't take up your time with this any more. Your friend is disturbed because down the corridor we passed a room with some very sick patients, and the door was open."

"I'm all right," said David, returning. "Wasn't expecting it, that was all. They didn't look so bad."

"Are they too sick to enjoy a little music?"

"Oh," said Marcus – "no, they are not. Would you do that for us, Conan? David?"

David cleared his throat. "I am not disturbed, Marcus of Ramapo. I will sing and Conan will make music with me. Conan, let's give them *Jo Buskin's Wedding* and *Elderberry Time* – then your tarantella for the harp, and – and the new song I learned from you yesterday evening in the woods."

The legend says that Harper Conan and Singer David never played and sang as splendidly as they did that afternoon for the sick people in Binton Ruins. It is not known whether the two were able to come the following year to Adirondack Island; it is known that they traveled widely all over the eastern nations, and were loved. Since it was long ago, and all records confused, it is not known when Conan died. He may have lived a full lifetime: Marcus of Ramapo is said to have assured David that this well might happen, in a later moment when they spoke out of Conan's hearing; or that could be another story.

It is known (to some) that by dwelling in the present, conceding what is necessary to past and future but no more than is necessary, it is quite possible to live happily ever after.

By an interesting chance, one of the sick people in the

hospital at Binton Ruins was a musician, Luisa of Sortees, with a true minstrel's memory, and she recovered and returned to her good life; for this reason the new song Conan gave them is remembered by more than legend.

In sleep I could not find you—
only the winter blurs of dreaming
desolate, not you, not you.

My morning sought you
over the reddening hills
and down steep shadows.

You with summer breath
found me and restored the day,
and I am content.

One yellow leaf falls
unrescued, undefended:
evening is blameless.

Winter shall be our portion,
but in the flow of foreign voices
your music known sustains me.

Houston, Houston, Do You Read?

James Tiptree, Jr.

James Tiptree, Jr. is known for her exceptionally fine writing and her attention to feminist concerns. In this Hugo Award winning story, three macho NASA astronauts returning from the first circumsolar mission find that a few changes have taken place back home.

Lorimer gazes around the big crowded cabin, trying to listen to the voices, trying also to ignore the twitch in his insides that means he is about to remember something bad. No help; he lives it again, that long-ago moment. Himself running blindly – or was he pushed? – into the strange toilet at Evanston Junior High. His fly open, his dick in his hand, he can still see the grey zipper edge of his jeans around his pale exposed pecker. The hush. The sickening wrongness of shapes, faces turning. The first blaring giggle. *Girls*. He was in the *girl's can*.

He flinches now wryly, so many years later, not looking at the women's faces. The cabin curves around over his head, surrounding him with their alien things: the beading rack, the twins' loom, Andy's leather work, the damned kudzu vine wriggling everywhere, the chickens. So cosy . . . Trapped, he is. Irretrievably trapped for life in everything he does not enjoy. Structurelessness. Personal trivia, unmeaning intimacies. The claims he can somehow never meet. Ginny: *You never talk to me* . . . Ginny, love, he thinks involuntarily. The hurt doesn't come.

Bud Geirr's loud chuckle breaks in on him. Bud is joking with some of them, out of sight around a bulkhead. Dave is visible, though. Major Norman Davis on the far side of the cabin, his bearded profile bent toward a small dark woman Lorimer can't quite focus on. But Dave's head seems oddly tiny and sharp, in fact the whole cabin looks unreal. A cackle bursts out from the "ceiling" – the bantam hen in her basket.

At this moment Lorimer becomes sure he has been drugged.

Curiously, the idea does not anger him. He leans or rather tips back, perching cross-legged in the zero gee, letting his gaze go to the face of the woman he has been talking with. Connie. Constantia Morelos. A tall moon-faced woman in capacious green pajamas. He has never really cared for talking to women. Ironic.

"I suppose," he says aloud, "it's possible that in some sense we are not here."

That doesn't sound too clear, but she nods interestedly. She's watching my reactions, Lorimer tells himself. Women are natural poisoners. Has he said that aloud too? Her expression doesn't change. His vision is taking on a pleasing local clarity. Connie's skin strikes him as quite fine, healthy-looking. Olive tan even after two years in space. She was a farmer, he recalls. Big pores, but without the caked look he associates with women her age.

"You probably never wore make-up," he says. She looks puzzled. "Face paint, powder. None of you have."

"Oh!" Her smile shows a chipped front tooth. "Oh yes, I think Andy has."

"Andy?"

"For plays. Historical plays, Andy's good at that."

"Of course. Historical plays."

Lorimer's brain seems to be expanding, letting in light. He is understanding actively now, the myriad bits and pieces linking into patterns. Deadly patterns, he perceives; but the drug is shielding him in some way. Like an amphetamine high without the pressure. Maybe it's something they use socially? No, they're watching, too.

"Space bunnies, I still don't dig it," Bud Geirr laughs infectiously. He has a friendly buoyant voice people like; Lorimer still likes it after two years.

"You chicks have kids back home, what do your folks think about you flying around out here with old Andy, h'mm?" Bud floats into view, his arm draped around a twin's shoulders. The one called Judy Paris, Lorimer decides; the twins are hard to tell. She drifts passively at an angle to Bud's big body; a jut-breasted plain girl in flowing yellow pajamas, her black hair raying out. Andy's red head swims up to them. He is holding a big green spaceball, looking about sixteen.

"Old Andy." Bud shakes his head, his grin flashing under his thick dark mustache. "When I was your age folks didn't let their women fly around with me."

Connie's lips quirk faintly. In Lorimer's head the pieces slide toward pattern. I know, he thinks. Do you know I know? His head is vast and crystalline, very nice really. Easier to think. Women . . . No compact generalisation forms in his mind, only a few speaking faces on a matrix of pervasive irrelevance. Human, of course. Biological necessity. Only so, so . . . diffuse? Pointless? . . . His sister Amy, *soprano con tremolo: Of course women could contribute as much as men if you'd treat us as equals. You'll see!* And then marrying that idiot the second time. Well, now he can see.

"Kudzu vines," he says aloud. Connie smiles. How they all smile.

"How 'bout that?" Bud says happily, "Ever think we'd see chicks in zero gee, hey, Dave? Artits-stico. Woo-ee!" Across the cabin Dave's bearded head turns to him, not smiling.

"And ol' Andy's had it all to his self. Stunt your growth, lad." He punches Andy genially on the arm, Andy catches himself on the bulkhead. Bud can't be drunk, Lorimer thinks; not on that fruit cider. But he doesn't usually sound so much like a stage Texan either. A drug.

"Hey, no offense," Bud is saying earnestly to the boy, "I mean that. You have to forgive one underprilly, underprivileged brother. These chicks are good people. Know what?" he tells the girl, "You could look stupen-dous if you fix yourself up a speck. Hey, I can show you, old Buddy's a expert. I hope you don't mind my saying that. As a matter of fact you look real stupendous to me right now."

He hugs her shoulders, flings out his arm and hugs Andy too. They float upwards in his grasp, Judy grinning excitedly, almost pretty.

"Let's get some more of that good stuff." Bud propels them both toward the serving rack which is decorated for the occasion with sprays of greens and small real daisies.

"Happy New Year! Hey, Happy New Year, y'all!"

Faces turn, more smiles. Genuine smiles, Lorimer thinks, maybe they really like their new years. He feels he has infinite time to examine every event, the implications evolving in crystal facets. I'm an echo chamber. Enjoyable, to be the observer. But others are observing too. They've started something here. Do they realise? So vulnerable, three of us, five of them in this fragile ship. They don't know. A dread unconnected to action lurks behind his mind.

"By god we made it," Bud laughs. "You space chickies, I have to give it to you. I commend you, by god I say it. We wouldn't be here, wherever we are. Know what, I jus' might decide to stay in the service after all. Think they have room for old Bud in your space program, sweetie?"

"Knock that off, Bud," Dave says quietly from the far wall. "I don't want to hear us use the name of the Creator like that." The full chestnut beard gives him a patriarchal gravity. Dave is forty-six, a decade older than Bud and Lorimer. Veteran of six successful missions.

"Oh, my apologies, Major Dave old buddy." Bud chuckles intimately to the girl. "Our commanding ossifer. Stupendous guy. Hey, Doc!" he calls, "How's your attitude? You making out dinko?"

"Cheers," Lorimer hears his voice reply, the complex stratum of his feelings about Bud rising like a kraken in the moonlight of his mind. The submerged silent thing he has about them all, all the Buds and Daves and big, indomitable, cheerful, able, disciplined, slow-minded mesomorphs he has cast his life with. Mesoectos, he corrected himself; astronauts aren't muscleheads. They like him, he has been careful about that. Liked him well enough to get him on *Sunbird*, to make him the official scientist on the first circumsolar mission. That little Doc Lorimer, he's cool, he's on the team. No shit from Lorimer, not like those other scientific assholes. He does the bit well with his small neat build and his dead-pan remarks. And the years of turning out for the bowling, the volleyball, the tennis, the skeet, the skiing that broke his ankle, the touch football that broke his collarbone. Watch that Doc, he's a sneaky one. And the big men banging him on the back, accepting him. Their token scientist . . . The trouble is, he isn't any kind of scientist any more. Living off his postdoctoral plasma work, a lucky hit. He hasn't really been into the math for years, he isn't up to it now. Too many other interests, too much time spent explaining elementary stuff. I'm a half-jock, he thinks. A foot taller and a hundred pounds heavier and I'd be just like them. One of them. An alpha. They probably sense it underneath, the beta bile. Had the jokes worn a shade thin in *Sunbird*, all that year going out? A year of Bud and Dave playing gin. That damn exercycle, gearing it up too tough for me. They didn't mean it, though. We were a team.

The memory of gaping jeans flicks at him, the painful end part – the grinning faces waiting for him when he stumbled out. The howls, the dribble down his leg. Being cool, pretending to laugh, too. You shit-heads, I'll show you. I am not a girl.

Bud's voice rings out, chanting, "And a hap-pee New Year to you-all down there!" Parody of the oily NASA tone. "Hey, why don't we shoot'em a signal? Greetings to all you Earthlings, I mean all you little Lunies. Happy New Year in the good year whatsis." He snuffles comically. "There is a Santy Claus, Houston, ye-ew nevah saw nothin' like this! Houston, wherever you are," he sings out. "Hey Houston! Do you read?"

In the silence, Lorimer sees Dave's face set into Major Norman Davis, commanding.

And without warning he is suddenly back there, back a year ago in the cramped, shook-up command module of *Sunbird*, coming out from behind the sun. It's the drug doing this, he thinks as memory closes around him, it's so real. Stop. He tries to hang onto reality, to the sense of trouble building underneath.

–But he can't, he is *there*, hovering behind Dave and Bud in the triple couches, as usual avoiding his official station in the middle, seeing beside them their reflections against blackness in the useless port window. The outer layer has been annealed, he can just make out a bright smear that has to be Spica floating through the image of Dave's head, making the bandage look like a kid's crown.

"Houston, Houston, *Sunbird*," Dave repeats; "*Sunbird* calling Houston. Houston, do you read? Come in, Houston."

The minutes start by. They are giving it seven out, seven back; seventy-eight million miles, ample margin.

"The high gain's shot, that's what it is," Bud says cheerfully. He says it almost every day.

"No way." Dave's voice is patient, also as usual. "It checks out. Still too much crap from the sun, isn't that right, Doc?"

"The residual radiation from the flare is just about in line with us," Lorimer says. "They could have a hard time sorting us out." For the thousandth time he registers his own faint, ridiculous gratification at being consulted.

"Shit, we're outside Mercury." Bud shakes his head. "How we gonna find out who won the Series?"

He often says that too. A ritual, out here in eternal night. Lorimer watches the sparkle of Spica drift by the reflection of Bud's curly face-bush. His own whiskers are scant and scraggly, like a blond Fu Manchu. In the aft corner of the window is a striped glare that must be the remains of the port energy accumulators, fried off in the solar explosion that hit them a month ago and fused the outer layers of their windows. That was when Dave cut his head open on the sexlogic panel. Lorimer had been banged in among the gravity wave experiment, he still doesn't trust the readings. Luckily the particle stream has missed one piece of the front window; they still have about twenty degrees of clear vision straight ahead. The brilliant web of the Pleiades shows there, running off into a blur of light.

Twelve minutes . . . thirteen. The speaker sighs and clicks emptily. Fourteen. Nothing.

"*Sunbird* to Houston, *Sunbird* to Houston. Come in, Houston. *Sunbird* out." Dave puts the mike back in its holder. "Give it another twenty-four."

They wait ritually. Tomorrow Packard will reply. Maybe.

"Be good to see old Earth again," Bud remarks.

"We're not using any more fuel on attitude," Dave reminds him. "I trust Doc's figures."

It's not my figures, it's the elementary facts of celestial mechanics, Lorimer thinks; in October there's only one place for Earth to be. He never says it. Not to a man who can fly two-body solutions by intuition once he knows where the bodies are. Bud is a good pilot and a better engineer; Dave is the best there is. He takes no pride in it. "The Lord helps us, Doc, if we let Him."

"Going to be a bitch docking if the radar's screwed up," Bud says idly. They all think about that for the hundredth time. It will be a bitch. Dave will do it. That is why he is hoarding fuel.

The minutes tick off.

"That's it," Dave says – and a voice fills the cabin, shockingly.

"Judy?" It is high and clear. A girl's voice.

"Judy, I'm so glad we got you. What are you doing on this band?"

Bud blows out his breath; there is a frozen instant before Dave snatches up the mike.

"*Sunbird*, we read you. This is Mission *Sunbird* calling Houston, ah, *Sunbird One* calling Houston Ground Control. Identify, who are you? Can you relay our signal? Over."

"Some skip," Bud says. "Some incredible ham."

"Are you in trouble, Judy?" the girl's voice asks. "I can't hear, you sound terrible. Wait a minute."

"This is United States Space Mission *Sunbird One*," Dave repeats. "Mission *Sunbird* calling Houston Space Center. You are dee-exxing our channel. Identify, repeat identify yourself and say if you can relay to Houston. Over."

"Dinko, Judy, try it again," the girl says.

Lorimer abruptly pushes himself up to the Lurp, the Long-Range Particle Density Cumulator experiment, and activates its shaft motor. The shaft whines, jars; lucky it was retracted during the flare, lucky it hasn't fused shut. He sets the probe pulse on max and begins a rough manual scan.

"You are intercepting official traffic from the United States space mission to Houston Control," Dave is saying forcefully. "If you cannot relay to Houston get off the air, you are committing a federal offence. Say again, can you relay our signal to Houston Space Center? Over."

"You still sound terrible," the girl says. "What's Houston? Who's talking, anyway? You know we don't have much time." Her voice is sweet but very nasal.

"Jesus, that's close," Bud says. "That is close."

"Hold it." Dave twists around to Lorimer's improvised radar-scope.

"There." Lorimer points out a tiny stable peak at the extreme edge of the read-out slot, in the transcoronal scatter. Bud cranes too.

"A bogey!"

"Somebody else out here."

"Hello, hello? We have you now," the girl says. "Why are you so far out? Are you dinko, did you catch the flare?"

"Hold it," warns Dave. "What's the status, Doc?"

"Over three hundred thousand kilometers, guesstimated. Possibly headed away from us, going around the sun. Could be cosmonauts, a Soviet mission?"

"Out to beat us. They missed."

"With a *girl*?" Bud objects.

"They've done that. You taping this, Bud?"

"Roger-r-r." He grins. "That sure didn't sound like a Russky chick. Who the hell's Judy?"

Dave thinks for a second, clicks on the mike. "This is Major Norman Davis commanding United States spacecraft *Sunbird One*. We have you on scope. Request you identify yourself. Repeat, who are you? Over."

"Judy, stop joking," the voice complains. "We'll lose you in a minute, don't you realise we worried about you?"

"*Sunbird* to unidentified craft. This is not Judy. I say again, this is not Judy. Who are you? Over."

"What—" the girl says, and is cut off by someone saying, "Wait a minute, Ann." The speaker squeals. Then a different woman says, "This is Lorna Bethune in *Escondita*. What is going on here?"

"This is Major Davis commanding United States Mission

Sunbird on course for Earth. We do not recognise any spacecraft *Escondita*. Will you identify yourself? Over."

"I just did." She sounds older with the same nasal drawl. "There is no spaceship *Sunbird* and you're not on course for Earth. If this is an andy joke it isn't any good."

"This is no joke, madam!" Dave explodes. "This is the American circumsolar mission and we are American astronauts. We do not appreciate your interference. Out."

The woman starts to speak and is drowned in a jibber of static. Two voices come through briefly. Lorimer thinks he hears the words "*Sunbird* program" and something else. Bud works the squelcher; the interference subsides to a drone.

"Ah, Major Davis?" The voice is fainter. "Did I hear you say you are on course for Earth?"

Dave frowns at the speaker and then says curtly, "Affirmative."

"Well, we don't understand your orbit. You must have very unusual flight characteristics, our readings show you won't node with anything on your present course. We'll lose the signal in a minute or two. Ah, would you tell us where you see Earth now? Never mind the coordinates, just tell us the constellation."

Dave hesitates and then holds up the mike. "Doc."

"Earth's apparent position is in Pisces," Lorimer says to the voices. "Approximately three degrees from P. Gamma."

"It is not," the woman says. "Can't you see it's in Virgo? Can't you see out at all?"

Lorimer's eyes go to the bright smear in the port window. "We sustained some damage—"

"Hold it," snaps Dave.

"—to one window during a disturbance we ran into at perihelion. Naturally we know the relative direction of Earth on this date, October nineteen."

"October? It's March, March fifteen. You must—" Her voice is lost in a shriek.

"E-M front," Bud says, tuning. They are all leaning at the speaker from different angles, Lorimer is head-down. Space-noise wails and crashes like surf, the strange ship is too close to the coronal horizon. "—Behind you," they hear. More howls. "Band, try . . . ship . . . if you can, your signal—" Nothing more comes through.

Lorimer pushes back, staring at the spark in the window. It has to be Spica. But is it elongated, as if a second point-source is beside it? Impossible. An excitement is trying to flare out inside him, the women's voices resonate in his head.

"Playback," Dave says. "Houston will really like to hear this."

They listen again to the girl calling Judy, the woman saying she is Lorna Bethune. Bud holds up a finger. "Man's voice in there." Lorimer listens hard for the words he thought he heard. The tape ends.

"Wait till Packard gets this one." Dave rubs his arms. "Remember what they pulled on Howie? Claiming they rescued him."

"Seems like they want us on their frequency." Bud grins. "They must think we're fa-a-ar gone. Hey, looks like this other capsule's going to show up, getting crowded out here."

"If it shows up," Dave says. "Leave it on voice alert, Bud. The batteries will do that."

Lorimer watches the spark of Spica, or Spica-plus-something, wondering if he will ever understand. The casual acceptance of some trick or ploy out here in this incredible loneliness. Well, if these strangers are from the same mold, maybe that is it. Aloud he says, "*Escondita* is an odd name for a Soviet mission. I believe it means 'hidden' in Spanish."

"Yeah," says Bud. "Hey, I know what that accent is, it's Australian. We had some Aussie bunnies at Hickam. Or-stryle-ya, woo-ee! You s'pose Woomera is sending up some kind of combined do?"

Dave shakes his head. "They have no capability whatsoever."

"We ran into some fairly strange phenomena back there, Dave," Lorimer says thoughtfully. "I'm beginning to wish we could take a visual check."

"Did you goof, Doc?"

"No. Earth is where I said, if it's October. Virgo is where it would appear in March."

"Then that's it," Dave grins, pushing out of the couch. "You been asleep five months, Rip van Winkle? Time for a hand before we do the roadwork."

"What I'd like to know is what that chick looks like," says Bud, closing down the transceiver. "Can I help you into your space-suit, Miss? Hey, Miss, pull that in, psst-psst-psst! You going to listen, Doc?"

"Right." Lorimer is getting out his charts. The others go aft through the tunnel to the small day-room, making no further comment on the presence of the strange ship or ships out here. Lorimer himself is more shaken than he likes; it was that damn phrase.

The tedious exercise period comes and goes. Lunchtime: They give the containers a minimum warm to conserve the batteries. Chicken *à la* again; Bud puts ketchup on his and breaks their usual silence with a funny anecdote about an Australian girl, laboriously censoring himself to conform to *Sunbird's* unwritten code on talk. After lunch Dave goes forward to the command module. Bud and Lorimer continue their current task of checking out the suits and packs for a damage-assessment EVA to take place as soon as the radiation count drops.

They are just clearing away when Dave calls them. Lorimer comes through the tunnel to hear a girl's voice blare, "—dinko trip. What did Lorna say? *Gloria* over!"

He starts up the Lurp and begins scanning. No results this time. "They're either in line behind us or in the sunward quadrant," he reports finally. "I can't isolate them."

Presently the speaker holds another thin thread of sound.

"That could be their ground control," says Dave. "How's the horizon, Doc?"

"Five hours; Northwest Siberia, Japan, Australia."

"I told you the high gain is fucked up." Bud gingerly feeds power to his antenna motor. "Easy, eas-ee. The frame is twisted, that's what it is."

"Don't snap it," Dave says, knowing Bud will not.

The squeaking fades, pulses back. "Hey, we can really use this," Bud says. "We can calibrate on them."

A hard soprano says suddenly "—should be outside your orbit.

Try around Beta Aries."

"Another chick. We have a fix," Bud says happily. "We have a fix now. I do believe our troubles are over. That monkey was torqued one hundred forty-nine degrees. Woo-ee!"

The first girl comes back. "We see them, Margo! But they're so small, how can they live in there? Maybe they're tiny aliens! Over."

"That's Judy," Bud chuckles. "Dave, this is screwy, it's all in English. It has to be some U.N. thingie."

Dave massages his elbows, flexes his fists; thinking. They wait. Lorimer considers a hundred and forty-nine degrees from Gamma Piscium.

In thirteen minutes the voice from Earth says, "Judy, call the others, will you? We're going to play you the conversation, we think you should all hear. Two minutes. Oh, while we're waiting, Zebra wants to tell Connie the baby is fine. And we have a new cow."

"Code," says Dave.

The recording comes on. The three men listen once more to Dave calling Houston in a rattle of solar noise. The transmission clears up rapidly and cuts off with the woman saying that another ship, the *Gloria*, is behind them, closer to the sun.

"We looked up history," the Earth voice resumes. "There was a Major Norman Davis on the first *Sunbird* flight. Major was a military title. Did you hear them say 'Doc'? There was a scientific doctor on board, Doctor Orren Lorimer. The third member was Captain – that's another title – Bernhard Geirr. Just the three of them, all males of course. We think they had an early reaction engine and not too much fuel. The point is, the first *Sunbird* mission was lost in space. They never came out from behind the sun. That was about when the big flares started. Jan thinks they must have been close to one, you heard them say they were damaged."

Dave grunts. Lorimer is fighting excitement like a brush discharge sparking in his gut.

"Either they are who they say they are or they're ghosts; or they're aliens pretending to be people. Jan says maybe the disruption in those super-flares could collapse the local time dimension. Pluggo. What did you observe there, I mean the highlights?"

Time dimension . . . never came back . . . Lorimer's mind narrows onto the reality of the two unmoving bearded heads before him, refuses to admit the words he thought he heard: *Before the year two thousand.* The language, he thinks. The language would have to have changed. He feels better.

A deep baritone voice says, "Margo?" In *Sunbird,* eyes come alert.

"—like the big one fifty years ago." The man has the accent too. "We were really lucky being right there when it popped. The most interesting part is that we confirmed the gravity turbulence. Periodic but not waves. It's violent, we got pushed around some. Space is under monster stress in those things. We think France's theory that our system is passing through a micro-black-hole cluster looks right. So long as one doesn't plonk us."

"France?" Bud mutters. Dave looks at him speculatively.

"It's hard to imagine anything being kicked out in time. But they're here, whatever they are, they're over eight hundred kays outside us scooting out toward Aldebaran. As Lorna said, if they're trying to reach Earth they're in trouble unless they have a lot of spare gees. Should we try to talk to them? Over. Oh, great about the cow. Over again."

"Black holes," Bud whistles softly. "That's one for you, Doc. Was we in a black hole?"

"Not in one or we wouldn't be here." If we are here, Lorimer adds to himself. A micro-black-hole cluster . . . what happens when fragments of totally collapsed matter approach each other, or collide, say in the photosphere of a star? Time disruption? Stop it. Aloud he says, "They could be telling us something, Dave."

Dave says nothing. The minutes pass.

Finally the Earth voice comes back, saying that it will try to contact the strangers on their original frequency. Bud glances at Dave, tunes the selector.

"Calling *Sunbird One?*" the girl says slowly through her nose. "This is Luna Central calling Major Norman Davis of *Sunbird One.* We have picked up your conversation with our ship *Escondita.* We are very puzzled as to who you are and how you got here. If you really are *Sunbird One* we think you must have been jumped forward in time when you passed the solar flare." She pronounces it Cockney-style, "toime."

"Our ship *Gloria* is near you, they see you on their radar. We think you may have a serious course problem because you told Lorna you headed for Earth and you think it is now October with Earth in Pisces. It is not October, it is March fifteen. I repeat the Earth date—" she says "dyte" "—is March fifteen, time twenty hundred hours. You should be able to see Earth very close to Spica in Virgo. You said your window is damaged. Can't you go out and look? We think you have to make a big course correction. Do you have enough fuel? Do you have a computer? Do you have enough air and water and food? Can we help you? We're listening on this frequency. Luna to *Sunbird One*, come in."

On *Sunbird* nobody stirs. Lorimer struggles against internal eruptions. *Never came back. Jumped forward in time.* The cyst of memories he has schooled himself to suppress bulges up in the lengthening silence. "Aren't you going to answer?"

"Don't be stupid," Dave says.

"Dave. A hundred and forty-nine degrees is the difference between Gamma Piscium and Spica. That transmission is coming from where they say Earth is."

"You goofed."

"I did not goof. It has to be March."

Dave blinks as if a fly is bothering him.

In fifteen minutes the Luna voice runs through the whole thing again, ending "Please come in."

"Not a tape." Bud unwraps a stick of gum, adding the plastic to the neat wad back of the gyro leads. Lorimer's skin crawls, watching the ambiguous dazzle of Spica. Spica-plus-Earth? Unbelief grips him, rocks him with a complex pang compounded of faces, voices, the sizzle of bacon frying, the creak of his father's wheelchair, chalk on a sunlit blackboard, Ginny's bare legs on the flowered couch, Jenny and Penny running dangerously close to the lawnmower. The girls will be taller now, Jenny is already as tall as her mother. His father is living with Amy in Denver, determined to last till his son gets home. *When I get home.* This has to be insanity, Dave's right; it's a trick, some crazy trick. The language.

Fifteen minutes more; the flat, earnest female voice comes back and repeats it all, putting in more stresses. Dave wears a remote frown, like a man listening to a lousy sports program. Lorimer has the notion he might switch off and propose a hand of gin; wills him to do so. The voice says it will now change frequencies.

Bud tunes back, chewing calmly. This time the voice stumbles on a couple of phrases. It sounds tired.

Another wait; an hour now. Lorimer's mind holds only the bright point of Spica digging at him. Bud hums a bar of *Yellow Ribbons*, falls silent again.

"Dave," Lorimer says finally, "our antenna is pointed straight at Spica. I don't care if you think I goofed, if Earth is over there we have to change course soon. Look, you can see it could be a double light source. We have to check this out."

Dave says nothing. Bud says nothing but his eyes rove to the port window, back to his instrument panel, to the window again. In the corner of the panel is a polaroid snap of his wife, Patty; a tall, giggling, rump-switching red-head; Lorimer has occasional fantasies about her. Little-girl voice, though. And so tall . . . Some short men chase tall women: it strikes Lorimer as undignified. Ginny is an inch shorter than he. Their girls will be taller. And Ginny insisted on starting a pregnancy before he left, even though he'll be out of commo. Maybe, maybe a boy, a son – *stop* it. Think about anything. Bud . . . Does Bud love Patty? Who knows? He loves Ginny. At seventy million miles . . .

"Judy?" Luna Central or whoever it is says. "They don't answer. You want to try? But listen, we've been thinking. If these people really are from the past this must be very traumatic for them. They could be just realising they'll never see their world again. Myda says these males had children and women they stayed with, they'll miss them terribly. This is exciting for us but it may seem awful to them. They could be too shocked to answer. They could be frightened, maybe they think we're aliens or hallucinations even. See?"

Five seconds later the nearby girl says, "Da, Margo, we were into that too. Dinko. Ah, *Sunbird*? Major Davis of *Sunbird*, are you there? This is Judy Paris in the ship *Gloria*, we're only about a million kay from you, we see you on our screen." She sounds young and excited. "Luna Central has been trying to reach you, we think you're in trouble and we want to help. Please don't be frightened, we're people just like you. We think you're way off course if you want to reach Earth. Are you in trouble? Can we help? If your radio is out can you make any sort of signal? Do you know Old Morse? You'll be off our screen soon, we're truly worried about you. Please reply somehow if you possibly can, *Sunbird*, come in!"

Dave sits impassive. Bud glances at him, at the port window, gazes stolidly at the speaker, his face blank. Lorimer has exhausted surprise, he wants only to reply to the voices. He can manage a rough signal by heterodyning the probe beam. But what then, with them both against him?

The girl's voice tries again determinedly. Finally she says, "Margo, they won't peep. Maybe they're dead? I think they're aliens."

Are we not? Lorimer thinks. The Luna station comes back with a different, older voice.

"Judy, Myda here, I've had another thought. These people had a very rigid authority code. You remember your history, they peck-ordered everything. You notice Major Davis repeated about being commanding. That's called dominance-submission structure, one of them gave orders and the others did whatever they were told; we don't know quite why. Perhaps they were frightened. The point is that if the dominant one is in shock or panicked maybe the others can't reply unless this Davis lets them."

Jesus Christ, Lorimer thinks. Jesus H. Christ in colors. It is his father's expression for the inexpressible. Dave and Bud sit unstirring.

"How weird," the Judy voice says. "But don't they know they're on a bad course? I mean, could the dominant one make the others fly right out of the system? Truly?"

It's happened, Lorimer thinks; it has happened. I have to stop this. I have to act now, before they lose us. Desperate visions of himself defying Dave and Bud loom before him. Try persuasion first.

Just as he opens his mouth he sees Bud stir slightly and with immeasurable gratitude hears him say, "Dave-o, what say we take an eyeball look? One little old burp won't hurt us."

Dave's head turns a degree or two.

"Or should I go out and see, like the chick said?" Bud's voice is mild.

After a long minute Dave says neutrally, "All right . . . Attitude change." His arm moves up as though heavy; he starts methodically setting in the values for the vector that will bring Spica in line with their functional window.

Now why couldn't I have done that, Lorimer asks himself for the thousandth time, following the familiar check sequence. Don't answer . . . And for the thousandth time he is obscurely moved by the rightness of them. The authentic ones, the alphas. Their bond. The awe he had felt first for the absurd jocks of his school ball team.

"That's go, Dave, assuming nothing got creamed."

Dave throws the ignition safety, puts the computer on real time. The hull shudders. Everything in the cabin drifts sidewise while the bright point of Spica swims the other way, appears on the front window as the retros cut in. When the star creeps out onto clear glass Lorimer can clearly see its companion. The double light steadies there; a beautiful job. He hands Bud the telescope.

"The one on the left."

Bud looks, "There she is, all right. Hey Dave, look at that!"

He puts the scope in Dave's hand. Slowly, Dave raises it and looks. Lorimer can hear him breathe. Suddenly Dave pulls up the mike.

"Houston!" he says harshly. "*Sunbird* to Houston, *Sunbird* calling Houston. Houston, come in!"

Into the silence the speaker squeals, "They fired their engines – wait, she's calling!" And shuts up.

In *Sunbird's* cabin nobody speaks. Lorimer stares at the twin stars ahead, impossible realities shifting around him as the minutes congeal. Bud's reflected face looks downwards, grin gone. Dave's beard moves silently; praying, Lorimer realises. Alone of the crew Dave is deeply religious; at Sunday meals he gives a short dignified grace. A shocking pity for Dave rises in

Lorimer; Dave is so deeply involved with his family, his four sons, always thinking about their training, taking them hunting, fishing, camping. And Doris his wife so incredibly active and sweet, going on their trips, cooking and doing things for the community. Driving Penny and Jenny to classes while Ginny was sick that time. Good people, the backbone ... This can't be, he thinks. Packard's voice is going to come through in a minute, the antenna's beamed right now. Six minutes now. This will all go away. *Before the year two thousand* – stop it, the language would have changed. Think of Doris ... She has that glow, feeding her five men; women with sons are different. But Ginny, but his dear woman, his *wife*, his *daughters*, – grandmothers now? All dead and dust? *Quit that*. Dave is still praying ... Who knows what goes on inside those heads? Dave's cry ... Twelve minutes, it has to be all right. The second sweep is stuck, no, it's moving. Thirteen. It's all insane, a dream. Thirteen plus ... fourteen. The speaker hissing and clicking vacantly. Fifteen now. A dream ... or are those women staying off, letting us see? Sixteen...

At twenty Dave's hand moves, stops again. The seconds jitter by, space crackles. Thirty minutes coming up.

"Calling Major Davis in *Sunbird*?" It is the older woman, a gentle voice. "This is Luna Central. We are the service and communication facility for space flight now. We're sorry to have to tell you that there is no space center at Houston any more. Houston itself was abandoned when the shuttle base moved to White Sands over two centuries ago."

A cool dust-colored light enfolds Lorimer's brain, isolating it. It will remain so a long time.

The woman is explaining it all again, offering help, asking if they were hurt. A nice dignified speech. Dave still sits immobile, gazing at Earth. Bud puts the mike in his hand.

"Tell them, Dave-o."

.Dave looks at it, takes a deep breath, presses the send button.

"*Sunbird* to Luna Control," he says quite normally. (It's "Central," Lorimer thinks.) "We copy. Ah, negative on life support, we have no problems. We copy the course change suggestion and are proceeding to recompute. Your offer of computer assistance is appreciated. We suggest you transmit position data so we can get squared away. Ah, we are economising on transmission until we see how our accumulators have held up. *Sunbird* out."

And so it had begun.

Lorimer's mind floats back to himself now floating in *Gloria*, nearly a year, or three hundred years, later; watching and being watched by them. He still feels light, contented; the dread underneath has come no nearer. But it is so silent. He seems to have heard no voices for a long time. Or was it a long time? Maybe the drug is working on his time sense, maybe it was only a minute or two.

"I've been remembering," he says to the woman Connie, wanting her to speak.

She nods, "You have so much to remember. Oh, I'm sorry – that wasn't good to say." Her eyes speak sympathy.

"Never mind." It is all dreamlike now, his lost world and this other which he is just now seeing plain. "We must seem like very strange beasts to you."

"We are trying to understand," she says. "It's history, you learn the events but you don't really feel what the people were like, how it was for them. We hope you'll tell us."

The drug, Lorimer thinks, that's what they're trying. Tell them . . . how can he? Could a dinosaur tell how it was? A montage flows through his mind, dominated by random shots of Operations' north parking lot and Ginny's yellow kitchen telephone with the sickly ivy vines . . . Women and vines. . .

A burst of laughter distracts him. It's coming from the chamber they call the gym, Bud and the others must be playing ball in there. Bright idea, really, he muses: using muscle power, sustained mild exercise. That's why they are all so fit. The gym is a glorified squirrel-wheel, when you climb or pedal up the walls it revolves and winds a gear train, which among other things rotates the sleeping drum. A real Woolagong . . . Bud and Dave usually take their shifts together, scrambling the spinning gym like big pale apes. Lorimer prefers the easy rhythm of the women, and the cycle here fits him nicely. He usually puts in his shift with Connie, who doesn't talk much, and one of the Judys, who do.

No one is talking now, though. Remotely uneasy he looks around the big cylinder of the cabin, sees Dave and Lady Blue by the forward window. Judy Dakar is behind them, silent for once. They must be looking at Earth; it has been a beautiful expanding disk for some weeks now. Dave's beard is moving, he is praying again. He has taken to doing that, not ostentatiously, but so obviously sincere that Lorimer, a life atheist, can only sympathise.

The Judys have asked Dave what he whispers, of course. When Dave understood that they had no concept of prayer and had never seen a Christian Bible there had been a heavy silence.

"So you have lost all faith," he said finally.

"We have faith," Judy Paris protested.

"May I ask in what?"

"We have faith in ourselves, of course," she told him.

"Young lady, if you were my daughter I'd tan your britches," Dave said, not joking. The subject was not raised again.

But he came back so well after that first dreadful shock, Lorimer thinks. A personal god, a father-model, man needs that. Dave draws strength from it and we lean on him. Maybe leaders have to believe. Dave was so great; cheerful, unflappable, patiently working out alternatives, making his decisions on the inevitable discrepancies in the position readings in a way Lorimer couldn't do. A bitch. . .

Memory takes him again; he is once again back in *Sunbird*, gritty-eyed, listening to the women's chatter, Dave's terse replies. God, how they chattered. But their computer work checks out. Lorimer is suffering also from a quirk of Dave's, his reluctance to transmit their exact thrust and fuel reserve. He keeps holding out a margin and making Lorimer compute it back in.

But the margins don't help; it is soon clear that they are in big trouble. Earth will pass too far ahead of them on her next orbit, they don't have the acceleration to catch up with her before they cross her path. They can carry out an ullage manoeuver, they can kill enough velocity to let Earth catch them on the second go-by; but that would take an extra year and their life support would be long gone. The grim question of whether they have enough to enable a single man to wait it out pushes into Lorimer's mind. He pushes it back; that one is for Dave.

There is a final possibility: Venus will approach their trajectory three months hence and they may be able to gain velocity by swinging by it. They go to work on that.

Meanwhile Earth is steadily drawing away from them and so is *Gloria*, closer toward the sun. They pick her out of the solar interference and then lose her again. They know her crew now: the man is Andy Kay, the senior woman is Lady Blue Parks; they appear to do the navigating. Then there is a Connie Morelos, and the two twins, Judy Paris and Judy Dakar, who run the communications. The chief Luna voices are women too, Margo and Azella. The men can hear them talking to the *Escondita*, which is now swinging in toward the far side of the sun. Dave insists on monitoring and taping everything that comes through. It proves to be largely replays of their exchanges with Luna and *Gloria*, mixed with a variety of highly personal messages. As references to cows, chickens, and other livestock mutiply, Dave reluctantly gives up his idea that they are code. Bud counts a total of five male voices.

"Big deal," he says. "There were more chick drivers on the road when we left. Means space is safe now, the girlies have taken over. Let them sweat their little asses off." He chuckles. "When we get this bird down, the stars ain't gonna study old Buddy no more, no ma'm. A nice beach and about a zillion steaks and ale and all those sweet things. Hey, we'll be living history, we can charge admission."

Dave's face takes on the expression that means an inappropriate topic has been breached. Much to Lorimer's impatience, Dave discourages all speculation as to what may await them on this future Earth. He confines their transmissions strictly to the problem in hand; when Lorimer tries to get him at least to mention the unchanged-language puzzle Dave only says firmly, "Later." Lorimer fumes; inconceivable that he is three centuries in the future, unable to learn a thing.

They do glean a few facts from the women's talk. There have been nine successful *Sunbird* missions after theirs and one other casualty. And the *Gloria* and her sister ship are on a long-planned fly-by of the two inner planets.

"We always go along in pairs," Judy says. "But those planets are no good. Still, it was worth seeing."

"For Pete's sake Dave, ask them how many planets have been

visited," Lorimer pleads.

"Later."

But about the fifth meal-break Luna suddenly volunteers.

"Earth is making up a history for you, *Sunbird*," the Margo voice says. "We know you don't want to waste power asking, so we thought we'd send you a few main points right now." She laughs. "It's much harder than we thought, nobody here does history."

Lorimer nods to himself; he has been wondering what he could tell a man from 1690 who would want to know what happened to Cromwell – was Cromwell then? – and who had never heard of electricity, atoms or the U.S.A.

"Let's see, probably the most important is that there aren't as many people as you had, we're just over two million. There was a world epidemic not long after your time. It didn't kill people but it reduced the population. I mean there weren't any babies in most of the world. Ah, sterility. The country called Australia was affected least." Bud holds up a finger.

"And North Canada wasn't too bad. So the survivors all got together in the south part of the American states where they could grow food and the best communications and factories were. Nobody lives in the rest of the world but we travel there sometimes. Ah, we have five main activities, was industries the word? Food, that's farming and fishing. Communications, transport, and space – that's us. And the factories they need. We live a lot simpler than you did, I think. We see your things all over, we're very grateful to you. Oh, you'll be interested to know we use zeppelins just like you did, we have six big ones. And our fifth thing is the children. Babies. Does that help? I'm using a children's book we have here."

The men have frozen during this recital: Lorimer is holding a cooling bag of hash. Bud starts chewing again and chokes.

"Two million people and a space capability?" He coughs. "That's incredible."

Dave gazes reflectively at the speaker. "There's a lot they're not telling us."

"I gotta ask them," Bud says. "Okay?"

Dave nods. "Watch it."

"Thanks for the history, Luna," Bud says. "We really appreciate it. But we can't figure out how you maintain a space program with only a couple of million people. Can you tell us a little more on that?"

In the pause, Lorimer tries to grasp the staggering figures. From eight billion to two million . . . Europe, Asia, Africa, South America, America itself – wiped out. *There weren't any more babies.* World sterility, from what? The Black Death, the famines of Asia – those had been decimations. This is magnitudes worse. No, it is all the same: beyond comprehension. An empty world littered with junk.

"*Sunbird*?" says Margo, "Da, I should have thought you'd want to know about space. Well, we have only the four real spaceships and one building. You know the two here. Then there's *Indira* and *Pech*, they're on the Mars run now. Maybe the Mars dome was since your day. You had the satellite stations though, didn't you? And the old Luna dome, of course – I remember now, it was during the epidemic. They tried to set up colonies to, ah, breed children, but the epidemic got there too. They struggled terribly hard. We owe a lot to you really, you men, I mean. The history has it all, how you worked out a minimal viable program and trained everybody and saved it from the crazies. It was a glorious achievement. Oh, the marker here has one of your names on it. Lorimer. We love to keep it all going and growing, we all love travelling. Man is a rover, that's one of our mottoes."

"Are you hearing what I'm hearing?" Bud asks, blinking comically.

Dave is still staring at the speaker. "Not one word about their government," he says slowly. "Not a word about economic conditions. We're talking to a bunch of monkeys."

"Should I ask them?"

"Wait a minute . . . Roger, ask the name of their chief of state and the head of the space program. And – no, that's all."

"President?" Margo echoes Bud's query. "You mean like queens and kings? Wait, here's Myda. She's been talking about you with Earth."

The older woman they hear occasionally says, "*Sunbird*? Da, we realise you had a very complex activity, your governments.

With so few people we don't have that type of formal structure at all. People from the different activities meet periodically and our communications are good, everyone is kept informed. The people in each activity are in charge of doing it while they're there. We rotate, you see. Mostly in five year hitches, for example Margo here was on the zeppelins and I've been on several factories and farms and of course the, well, the education, we all do that. I believe that's one big difference from you. And of course we all work. And things are basically far more stable now, I gather. We change slowly. Does that answer you? Of course you can always ask Registry, they keep track of us all. But we can't, ah, take you to our leader, if that's what you mean." She laughs, a genuine jolly sound. "That's one of our old jokes. I must say," she goes on seriously, "it's been a joy to us that we can understand you so well. We make a big effort not to let the language drift, it would be tragic to lose touch with the past."

Dave takes the mike. "Thank you, Luna. You've given us something to think about. *Sunbird* out."

"How much of that is for real, Doc?" Bud rubs his curly head. "They're giving us one of your science fiction stories."

"The real story will come later," says Dave. "Our job is to get there."

"That's a point that doesn't look too good."

By the end of the session it looks worse. No Venus trajectory is any good. Lorimer reruns all the computations; same result.

"There doesn't seem to be any solution to this one, Dave," he says at last. "The parameters are just too tough. I think we've had it."

Dave massages his knuckles thoughtfully. Then he nods. "Roger. We'll fire the optimum sequence on the Earth heading."

"Tell them to wave if they see us go by," says Bud.

They are silent, contemplating the prospect of a slow death in space eighteen months hence. Lorimer wonders if he can raise the other question, the bad one. He is pretty sure what Dave will say. What will he himself decide, what will he have the guts to do?

"Hello, *Sunbird*?" the voice of *Gloria* breaks in. "Listen, we've been figuring. We think if you use all your fuel you could come back in close enough to our orbit so we could swing out and pick you up. You'd be using solar gravity that way. We have plenty of manoeuver but much less acceleration than you do. You have suits and some kind of propellants, don't you? I mean, you could fly across a few kays?"

The three men look at each other; Lorimer guesses he had not been the only one to speculate on that.

"That's a good thought, *Gloria*," Dave says. "Let's hear what Luna says."

"Why?" asks Judy. "It's our business, we wouldn't endanger the ship. We'd only miss another look at Venus, who cares. We have plenty of water and food and if the air gets a little smelly we can stand it."

"Hey, the chicks are all right," Bud says. They wait.

The voice of Luna comes on. "We've been looking at that too, Judy. We're not sure you understand the risk. Ah, *Sunbird*, excuse me. Judy, if you manage to pick them up you'll have to spend nearly a year in the ship with these three male persons from a *very different culture*. Myda says you should remember history and it's a risk no matter what Connie says. *Sunbird*, I hate to be so rude. Over."

Bud is grinning broadly, they all are. "Cave men," he chuckles. "All the chicks land preggers."

"Margo, they're human beings," the Judy voice protests. "This isn't just Connie, we're all agreed. Andy and Lady Blue say it would be very interesting. If it works that is. We can't let them go without trying."

"We feel that way too, of course," Luna replies. "But there's another problem. They could be carrying diseases. *Sunbird*, I know you've been isolated for fourteen months, but Murti says people in your day were immune to organisms that aren't around now. Maybe some of ours could harm you, too. You could all get mortally sick and lose the ship."

"We thought of that, Margo," Judy says impatiently. "Look, if you have contact with them at all somebody has to test, true? So we're ideal. By the time we get home you'll know. And how could we get sick so fast we couldn't put *Gloria* in a stable orbit where you could get her later on?"

They wait. "Hey, what about that epidemic?" Bud pats his hair elaborately. "I don't know if I want a career in gay lib."

"You rather stay out here?" Dave asks.

"Crazies," says a different voice from Luna. "*Sunbird*, I'm Murti, the health person here. I think what we have to fear most is the meningitis-influenza complex – they mutate so readily. Does your Doctor Lorimer have any suggestions?"

"Roger, I'll put him on," says Dave. "But as to your first point, madam, I want to inform you that at time of takeoff the incidence of rape in the United States space cadre was zero point zero. I guarantee the conduct of my crew provided you can control yours. Here is Doctor Lorimer."

But Lorimer can not of course tell them anything useful. They discuss the men's polio shots, which luckily have used killed virus, and various childhood diseases which still seem to be around. He does not mention their epidemic.

"Luna, we're going to try it," Judy declares. "We couldn't live with ourselves. Now let's get the course figured before they get any farther away."

From there on there is no rest on *Sunbird* while they set up and refigure and rerun the computations for the envelope of possible intersecting trajectories. The *Gloria*'s drive, they learn, is indeed low-thrust, although capable of sustained operation. *Sunbird* will have to get most of the way to the rendez-vous on her own if they can cancel their outward velocity.

The tension breaks once during the long session, when Luna calls *Gloria* to warn Connie to be sure female crew members wear concealing garments at all times if the men came aboard.

"Not suit-liners, Connie, they're much too tight." It is the older woman, Myda. Bud chuckles.

"Your light sleepers, I think. And when the men unsuit, your Andy is the only one who should help them. You others stay away. The same for all body functions and sleeping. This is very important, Connie, you'll have to watch it the whole way home. There are a great many complicated taboos. I'm putting an instruction list on the bleeper, is your receiver working?"

"Da, we used it for France's black hole paper."

"Good. Tell Judy to stand by. Now listen, Connie, listen carefully. Tell Andy he has to read it all. I repeat, *he* has to read every word. Did you hear that?"

"Ah, dinko," Connie answers. "I understand, Myda. He will."

"I think we just lost the ball game, fellas," Bud laments. "Old mother Myda took it all away."

Even Dave laughs. But later when the modulated squeal that is a whole text comes through the speaker, he frowns again. "There goes the good stuff."

The last factors are cranked in; the revised program spins, and Luna confirms them. "We have a pay-out, Dave," Lorimer reports. "It's tight but there are at least two viable options. Provided the main jets are fully functional."

"We're going EVA to check."

That is exhausting; they find a warp in the deflector housing of the port engines and spend four sweating hours trying to wrestle it back. It is only Lorimer's third sight of open space but he is soon too tired to care.

"Best we can do," Dave pants finally. "We'll have to compensate in the psychic mode."

"You can do it, Dave-o," says Bud. "Hey, I gotta change those suit radios, don't let me forget."

In the psychic mode . . . Lorimer surfaces back to his real self, cocooned in *Gloria*'s big cluttered cabin seeing Connie's living face. It must be hours, how long has he been dreaming?

"About two minutes," Connie smiles.

"I was thinking of the first time I saw you."

"Oh, yes. We'll never forget that, ever."

Nor will he . . . He lets it unroll again in his head. The interminable hours after the first long burn, which has sent *Sunbird* yawing so they all have to gulp nausea pills. Judy's breathless voice reading down their approach: "Oh, very good, four hundred thousand . . . Oh great, *Sunbird*, you're almost three, you're going to break a hundred for sure—" Dave has done it, the big one.

Lorimer's probe is useless in the yaw, it isn't until they stabilise enough for the final burst that they see the strange blip bloom and vanish in the slot. Converging, hopefully, on a theoretical near-intersection point.

"Here goes everything."

The final burn changes the yaw into a sickening tumble with the starfield looping past the glass. The pills are no more use and the fuel feed to the attitude jets goes sour. They are all vomiting before they manage to hand-pump the last of the fuel and slow the tumble.

"That's it, *Gloria*. Come and get us. Lights on, Bud. Let's get those suits up."

Fighting nausea they go through the laborious routine in the fouled cabin. Suddenly, Judy's voice sings out, "We see you, *Sunbird!* We see your light! Can't you see us?"

"No time," Dave says. But Bud, half-suited, points at the window. "Fellas, oh, hey, look at that."

Lorimer stares, thinks he sees a faint spark between the whirling stars before he has to retch.

"Father, we thank you," says Dave quietly. "All right, move it on, Doc. Packs."

The effort of getting themselves plus the propulsion units and a couple of cargo nets out of the rolling ship drives everything else out of mind. It isn't until they are floating linked together and stabilised by Dave's hand jet that Lorimer has time to look.

The sun blanks out their left. A few meters below them *Sunbird* tumbles empty, looking absurdly small. Ahead of them, infinitely far away, is a point too blurred and yellow to be a star. It creeps: *Gloria*, on her approach tangent.

"Can you start, *Sunbird*?" says Judy in their helmets. "We don't want to brake any more on account of our exhaust. We estimate fifty kay in an hour, we're coming out on a line."

"Roger. Give me your jet, Doc."

"Goodbye, *Sunbird*," says Bud. "Plenty of lead, Dave-o."

Lorimer finds it restful in a childish way, being towed across the abyss tied to the two big men. He has total confidence in Dave, he never considers the possibility that they will miss, sail by and be lost. Does Dave feel contempt? Lorimer wonders; that banked up silence, is it partly contempt for those who can manipulate only symbols, who have no mastery of matter? . . . He concentrates on mastering his stomach.

It is a long, dark trip. *Sunbird* shrinks to a twinkling light, slowly accelerating on the spiral course that will end her ultimately in the sun with their precious records that are three hundred years obsolete. With, also, the packet of photos and letters that Lorimer has twice put in his suit-pouch and twice taken out. Now and then he catches sight of *Gloria*, growing from a blur to an incomprehensible tangle of lighted crescents.

"Woo-ee, it's big," Bud says. "No wonder they can't accelerate, that thing is a flying trailer park. It'd break up."

"It's a space ship. Got those nets tight, Doc?"

Judy's voice suddenly fills their helmets. "I see your lights! Can you see me? Will you have enough left to brake at all?"

"Affirmative to both, *Gloria*," says Dave.

At that moment Lorimer is turned slowly forward again and he sees – will see forever: the alien ship in the starfield and on its dark side the tiny lights that are women in the stars, waiting for them. Three – no, four; one suit-light is way out, moving. If that is a tether it must be over a kilometer.

"Hello, I'm Judy Dakar!" The voice is close. "Oh, mother, you're big! Are you all right? How's your air?"

"No problem."

They are in fact stale and steaming wet; too much adrenalin. Dave uses the jets again and suddenly she is growing, is coming right at them, a silvery spider on a trailing thread. Her suit looks trim and flexible; it is mirror-bright, and the pack is quite small. Marvels of the future, Lorimer thinks; Paragraph One.

"You made it, you made it! Here, tie in. Brake!"

"There ought to be some historic words," Bud murmurs. "If she gives us a chance."

"Hello, Judy," says Dave calmly. "Thanks for coming."

"Contact!" She blasts their ears. "Haul us in, Andy! Brake, brake – the exhaust is back there!"

And they are grabbed hard, deflected into a great arc toward the ship. Dave uses up the last jet. The line loops.

"Don't jerk it," Judy cries. "Oh, I'm *sorry*." She is clinging on them like a gibbon, Lorimer can see her eyes, her excited mouth. Incredible. "Watch out, it's slack."

"Teach me, honey," says Andy's baritone. Lorimer twists and sees him far back at the end of a heavy tether, hauling them smoothly in. Bud offers to help, is refused. "Just hang loose, please," a matronly voice tells them. It is obvious Andy has done this before. They come in spinning slowly, like space fish. Lorimer finds he can no longer pick out the twinkle that is *Sunbird*. When he is swung back, *Gloria* has changed to a disorderly cluster of bulbs and spokes around a big central cylinder. He can see pods and miscellaneous equipment stowed all over her. Not like science fiction.

Andy is paying the line into a floating coil. Another figure floats beside him. They are both quite short, Lorimer realises as they near.

"Catch the cable," Andy tells them. There is a busy moment of shifting inertial drag.

"Welcome to *Gloria*, Major Davis, Captain Geirr, Doctor Lorimer. I'm Lady Blue Parks. I think you'll like to get inside as soon as possible. If you feel like climbing go right ahead, we'll pull all this in later."

"We appreciate it, Ma'm."

They start hand-over-hand along the catenary of the main tether. It has a good rough grip. Judy coasts up to peer at them, smiling broadly, towing the coil. A taller figure waits by the ship's open airlock.

"Hello, I'm Connie. I think we can cycle in two at a time. Will you come with me, Major Davis?"

It is like an emergency on a plane, Lorimer thinks as Dave follows her in. Being ordered about by supernaturally polite little girls.

"Space-going stews," Bud nudges him. "How 'bout that?" His face is sprouting sweat. Lorimer tells him to go next, his own LSP has less load.

Bud goes in with Andy. The woman named Lady Blue waits beside Lorimer while Judy scrambles on the hull securing their cargo nets. She doesn't seem to have magnetic soles; perhaps ferrous metals aren't used in space now. When Judy begins hauling in the main tether on a simple hand winch Lady Blue looks at it critically.

"I used to make those," she says to Lorimer. What he can see of her features looks compressed, her dark eyes twinkle. He has the impression she is part Black.

"I ought to get over and clean that aft antenna." Judy floats up. "Later," says Lady Blue. They both smile at Lorimer. Then the hatch opens and he and Lady Blue go in. When the toggles seat there comes a rising scream of air and Lorimer's suit collapses.

"Can I help you?" She has opened her faceplate, the voice is rich and live. Eagerly Lorimer catches the latches in his clumsy gloves and lets her lift the helmet off. His first breath surprises him, it takes an instant to identify the gas as fresh air. Then the inner hatch opens, letting in greenish light. She waves him through. He swims into a short tunnel. Voices are coming from around the corner ahead. His hand finds a grip and he stops, feeling his heart shudder in his chest.

When he turns that corner the world he knows will be dead. Gone, rolled up, blown away forever with *Sunbird*. He will be irrevocably in the future. A man from the past, a time traveller. In the future. . .

He pulls himself around the bend.

The future is a vast bright cylinder, its whole inner surface festooned with unidentifiable objects, fronds of green. In front of him floats an odd tableau: Bud and Dave, helmets off, looking enormous in their bulky white suits and packs. A few meters away hang two bare-headed figures in shiny suits and a dark-haired girl in flowing pink pajamas.

They are all simply staring at the two men, their eyes and mouths open in identical expressions of pleased wonder. The face that has to be Andy's is grinning, openmouthed like a kid at the zoo. He is a surprisingly young boy, Lorimer sees, in spite of his deep voice; blond, downy-cheeked, compactly muscular. Lorimer finds he can scarcely bear to look at the pink woman, can't tell if she really is surpassingly beautiful or plain. The taller suited woman has a shiny ordinary face.

From overhead bursts an extraordinary sound which he finally recognises as a chicken cackling. Lady Blue pushes past him.

"All right, Andy, Connie, stop staring and help them get their suits off. Judy, Luna is just as eager to hear about this as we are."

The tableau jumps to life. Afterwards Lorimer can recall mostly eyes, bright curious eyes tugging his boots, smiling eyes upside-down over his pack – and always that light, ready laughter. Andy is left alone to help them peel down, blinking at the fittings which Lorimer still finds embarrassing. He seems easy and nimble in his own half-open suit. Lorimer struggles out of the last lacings, thinking, a boy! A boy and four women orbiting the sun, flying their big junky ships to Mars. Should he feel humiliated? He only feels grateful, accepting a short robe and a bulb of tea somebody – Connie? – gives him.

The suited Judy comes in with their nets. The men follow Andy along another passage, Bud and Dave clutching at the small robes. Andy stops by a hatch.

"This greenhouse is for you, it's your toilet. Three's a lot, but you have full sun."

Inside is a brilliant jungle, foliage everywhere, glittering water droplets, rustling leaves. Something whirs away – a grasshopper.

"You crank that handle." Andy points to a seat on a large cross-duct. "The piston rams the gravel and waste into a compost process and it ends up in the soil core. That vetch is a heavy nitrogen user and a great oxidator. We pump CO_2 in and oxy out. It's a real Woolagong."

He watches critically while Bud tries out the facility.

"What's a Woolagong?" asks Lorimer dazedly.

"Oh, she's one of our inventors. Some of her stuff is weird. When we have a pluggy looking thing that works we call it a Woolagong." He grins. "The chickens eat the seeds and the hoppers, see, and the hoppers and iguanas eat the leaves. When a greenhouse is going darkside we turn them in to harvest. With this much light I think we could keep a goat, don't you? You didn't have any life at all on your ship, true?"

"No," Lorimer says, "not a single iguana."

"They promised us a Shetland pony for Christmas," says Bud, rattling gravel. Andy joins perplexedly in the laugh.

Lorimer's head is foggy; it isn't only fatigue, the year in *Sunbird* has atrophied his ability to take in novelty. Numbly he uses the Woolagong and they go back out and forward to *Gloria*'s big control room, where Dave makes a neat short speech to Luna and is answered graciously.

"We have to finish changing course now," Lady Blue says. Lorimer's impression has been right, she is a small light part-Negro in late middle age. Connie is part something exotic too, he sees; the others are European types.

"I'll get you something to eat," Connie smiles warmly. "Then you probably want to rest. We saved all the cubbies for you." She says "syved"; their accents are all identical.

As they leave the control room Lorimer sees the withdrawn look in Dave's eyes and knows he must be feeling the reality of being a passenger in an alien ship, not in command, not deciding the course, the communications going on unheard.

That is Lorimer's last coherent observation, that and the taste of the strange, good food. And then being led aft through what he now knows is the gym, to the shaft of the sleeping drum. There are six irised ports like dogdoors; he pushes through his assigned port and finds himself facing a roomy mattress. Shelves and a desk are in the wall.

"For your excretions." Connie's arm comes through the iris, pointing at bags. "If you have a problem stick your head out and call. There's water."

Lorimer simply drifts toward the mattress, too sweated out to reply. His drifting ends in a curious heavy settling and his final astonishment: the drum is smoothly, silently starting to revolve. He sinks gratefully onto the pad, growing "heavier" as the minutes pass. About a tenth gee, maybe more, he thinks, it's still accelerating. And falls into the most restful sleep he has known in the long weary year.

It isn't till next day that he understands that Connie and two others have been on the rungs of the gym chamber, sending it around hour after hour without pause or effort and chatting as they went.

How they talk, he thinks again floating back to real present time. The bubbling irritant pours through his memory, the voices of Ginny and Jenny and Penny on the kitchen telephone, before that his mother's voice, his sister Amy's. Interminable. What do they always have to talk, talk, talk of?

"Why, everything," says the real voice of Connie beside him now, "it's natural to share."

"Natural. . ." Like ants, he thinks. They twiddle their antennae together every time they meet. Where did you go, what did you do? Twiddle-twiddle. How do you *feel*? Oh, I feel this, I feel that, blah blah, twiddle-twiddle. Total coordination of the hive. Women have no self-respect. Say anything, no sense of the strategy of words, the dark danger of naming. Can't hold in.

"Ants, bee-hives," Connie laughs, showing the bad tooth. "You truly see us as insects, don't you? Because they're females?"

"Was I talking aloud? I'm sorry." He blinks away dreams.

"Oh, please don't be. It's so sad to hear about your sister and your children and your, your wife. They must have been wonderful people. We think you're very brave."

But he has only thought of Ginny and them all for an instant – what has he been babbling? What is the drug doing to him?

"What are you doing to us?" he demands, lanced by real alarm now, almost angry.

"It's all right, truly." Her hand touches his, warm and somehow shy. "We all use it when we need to explore something. Usually it's pleasant. It's a laevonoramine compound, a disinhibitor, it doesn't dull you like alcohol. We'll be home so soon, you see. We have the responsibility to understand and you're so locked in." Her eyes melt at him. "You don't feel sick, do you? We have the antidote."

"No. . ." His alarm has already flowed away somewhere. Her explanation strikes him as reasonable enough. "We're not locked in," he says, or tries to say. "We talk. . ." he gropes for a word to convey the judiciousness, the adult restraint. Objectivity, maybe? "We talk when we have something to say." Irrelevantly he thinks of a mission coordinator named Forrest, famous for his blue jokes. "Otherwise, it would all break down," he tells her. "You'd fly right out of the system." This isn't quite what he means; let it pass.

The voices of Dave and Bud ring out suddenly from opposite ends of the cabin, awakening the foreboding of evil in his mind. They don't know us, he thinks. They should look out, stop this. But he is feeling too serene, he wants to think about his own new understanding, the pattern of them all he is seeing at last.

"I feel lucid," he manages to say, "I want to think."

She looks pleased. "We call that the ataraxia effect. It's so nice when it goes that way."

Ataraxia, philosophical calm. Yes. But there are monsters in the deep, he thinks or says. The night side. The night side of Orren Lorimer, a self hotly dark and complex, waiting in leash. They're so vulnerable. They don't know we can take them. Images rush up: a Judy spread-eagled on the gym rungs, pink pajamas gone, open to him. Flash sequence of the three of them taking over the ship, the women tied up, helpless, shrieking, raped and used. The team – get the satellite station, get a shuttle down to Earth. Hostages. Make them do anything, no defense whatever . . . Has Bud actually said that? But Bud doesn't know, he remembers. Dave knows they're hiding something, but he thinks it's socialism or sin. When they find out . . .

How has he himself found out? Simply listening, really, all these months. He listens to their talk much more than the others; "fraternising," Dave calls it . . . They all listened at first, of course. Listened and looked and reacted helplessly to the female bodies, the tender bulges so close under the thin, tantalising clothes, the magnetic mouths and eyes, the smell of them, their electric touch. Watching them touch each other, touch Andy, laughing, vanishing quietly into shared bunks. *What goes on? Can I? My need, my need–"*

The power of them, the fierce resentment . . . Bud muttered and groaned meaningfully despite Dave's warnings. He kept needling Andy until Dave banned all questions. Dave himself was noticeably tense and read his Bible a great deal. Lorimer found his own body pointing after them like a famished hound, hoping to Christ the cubicles are as they appeared to be, unwired.

All they learn is that Myda's instructions must have been ferocious. The atmosphere has been implacably antiseptic, the discretion impenetrable. Andy politely ignored every probe. No word or act has told them what, if anything, goes on; Lorimer was irresistably reminded of the weekend he spent at Jenny's scout camp. The men's training came presently to their rescue and they resigned themselves to finishing their mission on a super-*Sunbird,* weirdly attended by a troop of Boy and Girl Scouts.

In every other way their reception couldn't be more courteous. They have been given the run of the ship and their own dayroom in a cleaned-out gravel storage pod. They visit the control room as they wish. Lady Blue and Andy give them specs and manuals and show them every circuit and device of *Gloria*, inside and out. Luna has bleeped up a stream of science texts and the data on all their satellites and shuttles and the Mars and Luna dome colonies.

Dave and Bud plunged into an orgy of engineering. *Gloria* is, as they suspected, powered by a fission plant that uses a range of Lunar minerals. Her ion drive is only slightly advanced over the experimental models of their own day. The marvels of the future seem so far to consist mainly of ingenious modifications.

"It's primitive," Bud tells him. "What they've done is sacrifice everything to keep it simple and easy to maintain. Believe it, they can hand-feed fuel. And the back-ups, brother! They have redundant redundancy."

But Lorimer's technical interest soon flags. What he really wants is to be alone a while. He makes a desultory attempt to survey the apparently few new developments in his field, and finds he can't concentrate. What the hell, he tells himself, I stopped being a physicist three hundred years ago. Such a relief to be out of the cell of *Sunbird*; he has given himself up to drifting solitary through the warren of the ship, using their excellent 400 mm telescope, noting the odd life of the crew.

When he finds that Lady Blue likes chess they form a routine of bi-weekly games. Her personality intrigues him; she has reserve and an aura of authority. But she quickly stops Bud when he calls her "Captain."

"No one here commands in your sense. I'm just the oldest." Bud goes back to "Ma'm."

She plays a solid positional game, somewhat more erratic than a man but with occasional elegant traps. Lorimer is astonished to find that there is only one new chess opening, an interesting queen-side gambit called the Dagmar. One new opening in three centuries? He mentions it to the others when they come back from helping Andy and Judy Paris overhaul a standby converter.

"They haven't done much anywhere," Dave says. "Most of your new stuff dates from the epidemic, Andy, if you'll pardon me. The program seems to be stagnating. You've been gearing up this Titan project for eighty years."

"We'll get there," Andy grins.

"C'mon Dave," says Bud. "Judy and me are taking on you two for the next chicken dinner, we'll get a bridge team here yet. Woo-ee, I can taste that chicken! Losers get the iguana."

The food is so good. Lorimer finds himself lingering around the kitchen end, helping whoever is cooking, munching on their various seeds and chewy roots as he listens to them talk. He even likes the iguana. He begins to put on weight, in fact they all do. Dave decrees double exercise shifts.

"You going to make us *climb* home, Dave-o?" Bud groans. But Lorimer enjoys it, pedalling or swinging easily along the rungs while the women chat and listen to tapes. Familiar music: he identifies a strange spectrum from Handel, Brahms, Sibelius, through Strauss to ballad tunes and intricate light jazz-rock. No lyrics. But plenty of informative texts doubtless selected for his benefit.

From the promised short history he finds out more about the epidemic. It seems to have been an air-borne quasi-virus escaped from Franco-Arab military labs, possibly potentiated by pollutants.

"It apparently damaged only the reproductive cells," he tells Dave and Bud. "There was little actual mortality, but almost universal sterility. Probably a molecular substitution in the gene code in the gametes. And the main effect seems to have been on the men. They mention a shortage of male births afterwards, which suggests that the damage was on the Y-chromosome where it would be selectively lethal to the male fetus."

"Is it still dangerous, Doc?" Dave asks. "What happens to us when we get back home?"

"They can't say. The birth rate is normal now, about two percent and rising. But the present population may be resistant. They never achieved a vaccine."

"Only one way to tell," Bud says gravely. "I volunteer."

Dave merely glances at him. Extraordinary how he still commands. Not submission, for Pete's sake. A team.

The history also mentions the riots and fighting which swept the world when humanity found itself sterile. Cities bombed, and burned, massacres, panics, mass rapes and kidnapping of women, marauding armies of biologically desperate men, bloody cults. The crazies. But it is all so briefly told, so long ago. Lists of honoured names. "We must always be grateful to the brave people who held the Denver Medical Laboratories—" And then on to the drama of building up the helium supply for the dirigibles.

In three centuries it's all dust, he thinks. What do I know of the hideous Thirty Years War that was three centuries back for me? *Fighting devastated Europe for two generations.* Not even names.

The description of their political and economic structure is even briefer. They seem to be, as Myda had said, almost ungoverned.

"It's a form of loose social credit system run by consensus," he says to Dave. "Somewhat like a permanent frontier period. They're building up slowly. Of course they don't need an army or air force. I'm not sure if they even use cash money or recognise private ownership of land. I did notice one favorable reference to early Chinese communalism," he adds, to see Dave's mouth set. "But they aren't tied to a community. They travel about. When I asked Lady Blue about their police and legal system she told me to wait and talk with real historians. This registry seems to be just that, it's not a policy organ."

"We've run into a situation here, Lorimer," Dave says soberly. "Stay away from it. They're not telling the story."

"You notice they never talk about their husbands?" Bud laughs. "I asked a couple of them what their husbands did and I swear they had to think. And they all have kids. Believe me, it's a swinging scene down there, even if old Andy acts like he hasn't found out what it's for."

"I don't want any prying into their personal family lives while we're on this ship, Geirr. None whatsoever. That's an order."

"Maybe they don't have families. You ever hear 'em mention anybody getting married? That has to be the one thing on a chick's mind. Mark my words, there's been some changes made."

"The social mores are bound to have changed to some extent," Lorimer says. "Obviously you have women doing more work outside the home, for one thing. But they have family bonds; for instance Lady Blue has a sister in an aluminum mill and another in health. Andy's mother is on Mars and his sister works in Registry. Connie has a brother or brothers on the fishing fleet near Biloxi, and her sister is coming out to replace her here next trip, she's making yeast now."

"That's the top of the iceberg."

"I doubt the rest of the iceberg is very sinister, Dave."

But somewhere along the line the blandness begins to bother Lorimer too. So much is missing. Marriage, love-affairs, children's troubles, jealousy squabbles, status, possessions, money problems, sicknesses, funerals even – all the daily minutiae that occupied Ginny and her friends seems to have been edited out of these women's talk. *Edited* . . . Can Dave be right, is some big, significant aspect being deliberately kept from them?

"I'm still surprised your language hasn't changed more," he says one day to Connie during their exertions in the gym.

"Oh, we're very careful about that." She climbs at an angle beside him, not using her hands. "It would be a dreadful loss if we couldn't understand the books. All the children are taught from the same original tapes, you see. Oh, there's faddy words we use for a while, but our communicators have to learn the old texts by heart, that keeps us together."

Judy Paris grunts from the pedicycle. "You, my dear children, will never know the oppression we suffered," she declaims mockingly.

"Judys talk too much," says Connie.

"We do, for a fact." They both laugh.

"So you still read our so-called great books, our fiction and poetry?" asks Lorimer. "Who do you read, H.G. Wells? Shakespeare? Dickens, ah, Balzac, Kipling, Brian?" He gropes; Brian had been a bestseller Ginny liked. When had he last looked at Shakespeare or the others?

"Oh, the historicals," Judy says. "It's interesting, I guess. Grim. They're not very realistic. I'm sure it was to you," she adds generously.

And they turn to discussing whether the laying hens are getting too much light, leaving Lorimer to wonder how what he supposes are the eternal verities of human nature can have faded from a world's reality. Love, conflict, heroism, tragedy – all "unrealistic"? Well, flight crews are never great readers; still, women read more . . . Something *has* changed, he can sense it. Something basic enough to affect human nature. A physical development perhaps; a mutation? What is really under those floating clothes?

It is the Judys who give him part of it.

He is exercising alone with both of them, listening to them gossip about some legendary figure named Dagmar.

"The Dagmar who invented the chess opening?" he asks.

"Yes. She does anything, when she's good she's great."

"Was she bad sometimes?"

A Judy laughs. "The Dagmar problem, you can say. She has this tendency to organise everything. It's fine when it works but every so often it runs wild, she thinks she's queen or what. Then they have to get out the butterfly nets."

All in present tense – but Lady Blue has told him the Dagmar gambit is over a century old.

Longevity, he thinks; by god, that's what they're hiding. Say they've achieved a doubled or tripled life span, that would certainly change human psychology, affect their outlook on everything. Delayed maturity, perhaps? We were working on endocrine cell juvenescence when I left. How old are these girls, for instance?

He is framing a question when Judy Dakar says, "I was in the creche when she went pluggo. But she's good, I loved her later on."

Lorimer thinks she has said "crash" and then realises she means a communal nursery. "Is that the same Dagmar?" he asks. "She must be very old."

"Oh no, her sister."

"A sister a hundred years apart?"

"I mean, her daughter. Her, her *grand*-daughter." She starts pedalling fast.

"Judys," says her twin, behind them.

Sister again. Everybody he learns of seems to have an extraordinary number of sisters, Lorimer reflects. He hears Judy Paris saying to her twin, "I think I remember Dagmar at the Creche. She started uniforms for everybody. Colors and numbers."

"You couldn't have, you weren't born," Judy Dakar retorts.

There is a silence in the drum.

Lorimer turns on the rungs to look at them. Two flushed cheerful faces stare back warily, make identical head-dipping gestures to swing the black hair out of their eyes. Identical . . . But isn't the Dakar girl on the cycle a shade more mature, her face more weathered?

"I thought you were supposed to be twins."

"Ah, Judys talk a lot," they say together – and grin guiltily.

"You aren't sisters," he tells them. "You're what we called clones."

Another silence.

"Well, yes," says Judy Dakar. "We call it sisters. Oh, mother! We weren't supposed to tell you, Myda said you would be frightfully upset. It was illegal in your day, true?"

"Yes. We considered it immoral and unethical, experimenting with human life. But it doesn't upset me personally."

"Oh, that's beautiful, that's great," they say together. "We think of you as different," Judy Paris blurts, "you're more hu – more like us. Please, you don't have to tell the others, do you? Oh, *please* don't."

"It was an accident there were two of us here," says Judy Dakar. "Myda *warned* us. Can't you wait a little while?" Two identical pairs of dark eyes beg him.

"Very well," he says slowly. "I won't tell my friends for the time being. But if I keep your secret you have to answer some questions. For instance, how many of your people are created artificially this way?"

He begins to realise he *is* somewhat upset. Dave is right, damn it, they are hiding things. Is this brave new world populated by subhuman slaves, run by master brains? Decorticate zombies, workers without stomachs or sex, human cortexes wired into machines, monstrous experiments rush through his mind. He has been naive again. These normal-looking women could be fronting for a hideous world.

"How many?"

"There's only about eleven thousand of us," Judy Dakar says. The two Judys look at each other, transparently confirming something. They're unschooled in deception, Lorimer thinks; is that good? And is diverted by Judy Paris exclaiming, "What we can't figure out is why did you think it was wrong?"

Lorimer tries to tell them, to convey the horror of manipulating human identity, creating abnormal life. The threat to individuality, the fearful power it would put in a dictator's hand.

"Dictator?" one of them echoes blankly. He looks at their faces and can only say, "Doing things to people without their consent. I think it's sad."

"But that's just what we think about you," the younger Judy bursts out. "How do you know who you *are*? Or who anybody is? All alone, no sisters to share with! You don't know what you can do, or what would be interesting to try. All you poor singletons, you – why, you just have to blunder along and die, all for nothing!"

Her voice trembles. Amazed, Lorimer sees both of them are misty-eyed.

"We better get this m-moving," the other Judy says.

They swing back into the rhythm and in bits and pieces Lorimer finds out how it is. Not bottled embryos, they tell him indignantly. Human mothers like everybody else, young mothers, the best kind. A somatic cell nucleus is inserted in an enucleated ovum and reimplanted in the womb. They have each borne two "sister" babies in their late teens and nursed them a while before moving on. The creches always have plenty of mothers.

His longevity notion is laughed at; nothing but some rules of healthy living have as yet been achieved. "We should make ninety in good shape," they assure him. "A hundred and eight, that was Judy Eagle, she's our record. But she was pretty blah at the end."

The clone-strains themselves are old, they date from the epidemic. They were part of the first effort to save the race when the babies stopped and they've continued ever since.

"It's so perfect," they tell him. "We each have a book, it's really a library. All the recorded messages. The Book of Judy Shapiro, that's us. Dakar and Paris are our personal names, we're doing cities now." They laugh, trying not to talk at once about how each Judy adds her individual memoir, her adventures and problems and discoveries in the genotype they all share.

"If you make a mistake it's useful for the others. Of course you try not to – or at least make a *new* one."

"Some of the old ones aren't so realistic," her other self puts in. "Things were so different, I guess. We make excerpts of the parts we like best. And practical things, like Judys should watch out for skin cancer."

"But we have to read the whole thing every ten years," says the Judy called Dakar. "It's inspiring. As you get older you understand some of the ones you didn't before."

Bemused, Lorimer tries to think how it would be, hearing the voices of three hundred years of Orren Lorimers. Lorimers who were mathematicians or plumbers or artists or bums or criminals, maybe. The continuing exploration and completion of self. And a dozen living doubles; aged Lorimers, infant Lorimers. And other Lorimers' women and children . . . would he enjoy it or resent it? He doesn't know.

"Have you made your records yet?"

"Oh, we're too young. Just notes in case of accident."

"Will we be in them?"

"You can say!" They laugh merrily, then sober. "Truly you won't tell?" Judy Paris asks. "Lady Blue, we have to let her know what we did. Oof. But *truly* you won't tell your friends?"

He hadn't told on them, he thinks now, emerging back into his living self. Connie beside him is drinking cider from a bulb. He has a drink in his hand too, he finds. But he hasn't told.

"Judys will talk." Connie shakes her head, smiling. Lorimer realises he must have gabbled out the whole thing.

"It doesn't matter," he tells her. "I would have guessed soon anyhow. There were too many clues . . . Woolagongs invent, Mydas worry, Jans are brains, Billy Dees work so hard. I picked up six different stories of hydroelectric stations that were built or improved or are being run by one Lala Singh. Your whole way of life. I'm more interested in this sort of thing than a respectable physicist should be," he says wryly. "You're all clones, aren't you? Every one of you. What do Connies do?"

"You really do know." She gazes at him like a mother whose child has done something troublesome and bright. "Whew! Oh, well, Connies farm like mad, we grow things. Most of our names are plants. I'm Veronica, by the way. And of course the creches, that's our weakness. The runt mania. We tend to focus on anything smaller or weak."

Her warm eyes focus on Lorimer, who draws back involuntarily.

"We control it." She gives a hearty chuckle. "We aren't all that way. There's been engineering Connies, and we have two young sisters who love metallurgy. It's fascinating what the genotype can do if you try. The original Constantia Morelos was a chemist, she weighed ninety pounds and never saw a farm in her life." Connie looks down at her own muscular arms. "She was killed by the crazies, she fought with weapons. It's so hard to understand . . . And I had a sister Timothy who made dynamite and dug two canals and she wasn't even an andy."

"*An* andy," he says.

"Oh, dear."

"I guessed that too. Early androgen treatments."

She nods hesitantly. "Yes. We need the muscle-power for some jobs. A few. Kays are quite strong anyway. Whew!" She suddenly stretches her back, wriggles as if she'd been cramped. "Oh, I'm glad you know. It's been such a strain. We couldn't even sing."

"Why not?"

"Myda was sure we'd make mistakes, all the words we'd have had to change. We sing a lot." She softly hums a bar or two.

"What kinds of songs do you sing?"

"Oh, every kind. Adventure songs, work songs, mothering songs, roaming songs, mood songs, trouble songs, joke songs — everything."

"What about love songs?" he ventures. "Do you still have, well, love?"

"Of course, how could people not love?" But she looks at him doubtfully.

"The love stories I've heard from your time are so, I don't

know, so weird. Grim and pluggy. It doesn't seem like love . . . Oh, yes, we have famous love songs. Some of them are partly sad too. Like Tamil and Alcmene O, they're fated together. Connies are fated too, a little." She grins bashfully. "We love to be with Ingrid Anders. It's more one-sided. I hope there'll be an Ingrid on my next hitch. She's so exciting, she's like a little diamond."

Implications are exploding all about him, sparkling with questions. But Lorimer wants to complete the darker pattern beyond.

"Eleven thousand genotypes, two million people: that averages two hundred of each of you alive now." She nods. "I suppose it varies? There's more of some?"

"Yes, some types aren't as viable. But we haven't lost any since early days. They tried to preserve all the genes they could, we have people from all the major races and a lot of small strains. Like me, I'm the Carib Blend. Of course we'll never know what was lost. But eleven thousand is a lot really. We all try to know every one, it's a life hobby."

A chill penetrates his ataraxia. Eleven thousand, period. That is the true population of Earth now. He thinks of two hundred tall olive-skinned women named after plants, excited by two hundred little bright Ingrids; two hundred talkative Judys, two hundred self-possessed Lady Blues, two hundred Margos and Mydas and the rest. He shivers. The heirs, the happy pallbearers of the human race.

"So evolution ends," he says somberly.

"No, why? It's just slowed down. We do everything much slower than you did, I think. We like to experience things *fully*. We have time." She stretches again, smiling. "There's all the time."

"But you have no new genotypes. It is the end."

"Oh but there are, now. Last century they worked out the way to make haploid nuclei combine. We can make a stripped egg-cell function like pollen," she says proudly. "I mean sperm. It's tricky, some don't come out too well. But now we're finding both Xs viable we have over a hundred new types started. Of course it's hard for them, with no sisters. The donors try to help."

Over a hundred, he thinks. Well. Maybe . . . But, "both Xs

viable," what does that mean? She must be referring to the epidemic. But he had figured it primarily affected the men. His mind goes happily to work on the new puzzle, ignoring a sound from somewhere that is trying to pierce his calm.

"It was a gene or genes on the X-chromosome that was injured," he guesses aloud. "Not the Y. And the lethal trait had to be recessive, right? Thus there would have been no births at all for a time, until some men recovered or were isolated long enough to manufacture undamaged X-bearing gametes. But women carry their lifetime supply of ova, they could never regenerate reproductively. When they mated with the recovered males only female babies would be produced, since the female carries two Xs and the mother's defective gene would be compensated by a normal X from the father. But the male is XY, he receives only the mother's defective X. Thus the lethal defect would be expressed, the male fetus would be finished . . . A planet of girls and dying men. The few odd viables died off."

"You truly do understand," she says admiringly.

The sound is becoming urgent; he refuses to hear it, there is significance here.

"So we'll be perfectly all right on Earth. No problem. In theory we can marry again and have families, daughters anyway."

"Yes," she says. "In theory."

The sound suddenly broaches his defenses, becomes the loud voice of Bud Geirr raised in song. He sounds plain drunk now. It seems to be coming from the main garden pod, the one they use to grow vegetables, not sanitation. Lorimer feels the dread alive again, rising closer. Dave ought to keep an eye on him. But Dave seems to have vanished too, he recalls seeing him go towards Control with Lady Blue.

"OH, THE SUN SHINES BRIGHT ON PRETTY RED WI-I-ING," carols Bud.

Something should be done, Lorimer decides painfully. He stirs; it is an effort.

"Don't worry," Connie says. "Andy's with them."

"You don't know, you don't know what you've started." He pushes off toward the garden hatchway.

"—AS SHE LAY SLE-EEPING, A COWBOY CRE-E-EEPING—"

General laughter from the hatchway. Lorimer coasts through into the green dazzle. Beyond the radial fence of snap-bean he sees Bud sailing in an exaggerated crouch after Judy Paris. Andy hangs by the iguana cages, laughing.

Bud catches one of Judy's ankles and stops them both with a flourish, making her yellow pajamas swirl. She giggles at him upside-down, making no effort to free herself.

"I don't like this," Lorimer whispers.

"Please don't interfere." Connie has hold of his arm, anchoring them both to the tool rack. Lorimer's alarm seems to have ebbed; he will watch, let serenity return. The others have not noticed them.

"Oh, there once was an Indian maid." Bud sings more restrainedly, "Who never was a-fraid, that some buckaroo would slip it up her, ahem, ahem," he coughs ostentatiously, laughing. "Hey, Andy, I hear them calling you."

"What?" says Judy, "I don't hear anything."

"They're calling you, lad. Out there."

"Who?" asks Andy, listening.

"*They* are, for Crissake." He lets go of Judy and kicks over to Andy. "Listen, you're a great kid. Can't you see me and Judy have some business to discuss in private?" He turns Andy gently around and pushes him at the bean-stakes. "It's New Year's Eve, dummy."

Andy floats passively away through the fence of vines, raising a hand at Lorimer and Connie. Bud is back with Judy.

"Happy New Year, kitten," he smiles.

"Happy New Year. Did you do special things on New Year?" she asks curiously.

"What we did on New Year's." He chuckles, taking her shoulders in his hands. "On New Year's Eve, yes we did. Why don't I show you some of our primitive Earth customs, h'mm?"

She nods, wide-eyed.

"Well, first we wish each other well, like this." He draws her to him and lightly kisses her cheek. "Kee-rist, what a dumb bitch," he says in a totally different voice. "You can tell you've been out too long when the geeks start looking good. Knockers, ahhh—" His hand plays with her blouse. The man is unaware, Lorimer realises. He doesn't know he's drugged, he's speaking his thoughts. I must have done that. Oh, god . . . He takes shelter behind his crystal lens, an observer in the protective light of eternity.

"And then we smooch a little." The friendly voice is back, Bud holds the girl closer, caressing her back. "Fat ass." He puts his mouth on hers; she doesn't resist. Lorimer watches Bud's arms tighten, his hands working on her buttocks, going under her clothes. Safe in the lens his own sex stirs. Judy's arms are waving aimlessly.

Bud breaks for breath, a hand at his zipper.

"Stop staring," he says hoarsely. "One fucking more word, you'll find out what that big mouth is for. Oh, man, a flagpole. Like steel . . . Bitch, this is your lucky day." He is baring her breasts now, big breasts. Fondling them. "Two fucking years in the ass end of noplace," he mutters, "shit on me will you? Can't wait, watch it – titty-titty-titties–"

He kisses her again quickly and smiles down at her. "Good?" he asks in his tender voice, and sinks his mouth on her nipples, his hand seeking in her thighs. She jerks and says something muffled. Lorimer's arteries are pounding with delight, with dread.

"I, I think this should stop," he makes himself say falsely, hoping he isn't saying more. Through the pulsing tension he hears Connie whisper back, it sounds like "Don't worry, Judy's very athletic." Terror stabs him, they don't know. But he can't help.

"Cunt," Bud grunts, "you have to have a cunt in there, is it froze up? You dumb cunt–" Judy's face appears briefly in her floating hair, a remote part of Lorimer's mind notes that she looks amused and uncomfortable. His being is riveted to the sight of Bud expertly controlling her body in midair, peeling down the yellow slacks. Oh god – her dark pubic mat, the thick white thighs – a perfectly normal woman, no mutation. Ohhh, god . . . But there is suddenly a drifting shadow in the way: Andy again floating over them with something in his hands.

"You dinko, Jude?" the boy asks.

Bud's face comes up red and glaring. "Bug out, you!"

"Oh, I won't bother."

"Jee-sus Christ." Bud lunges up and grabs Andy's arm, his legs still hooked around Judy. "This is man's business, boy, do I have to spell it out?" He shifts his grip. "Shoo!"

In one swift motion he has jerked Andy close and back-handed his face hard, sending him sailing into the vines.

Bud gives a bark of laughter, bends back to Judy. Lorimer can see his erection poking through his fly. He wants to utter some warning, tell them their peril, but he can only ride the hot pleasure surging through him, melting his crystal shell. Go on, more – avidly he sees Bud mouth her breasts again and then suddenly flip her whole body over, holding her wrists behind her in one fist, his legs pinning hers. Her bare buttocks bulge up helplessly, enormous moons. "Ass-s-s," Bud groans. "Up you bitch, ahhh-hh–" He pulls her butt onto him.

Judy gives a cry, begins to struggle futilely. Lorimer's shell boils and bursts. Amid the turmoil ghosts outside are trying to rush in. And something *is* moving, a real ghost – to his dismay he sees it is Andy again, floating toward the joined bodies, holding a whirring thing. Oh, no – a camera. The fools.

"Get away!" he tries to call to the boy.

But Bud's head turns, he has seen. "You little pissass." His long arm shoots out and captures Andy's shirt, his legs still locked around Judy.

"I've had it with you." His fist slams into Andy's mouth, the camera goes spinning away. But this time Bud doesn't let him go, he is battering the boy, all of them rolling in a tangle in the air.

"Stop!" Lorimer hears himself shout, plunging at them through the beans. "Bud, stop it! You're hitting a woman."

The angry face comes around, squinting at him.

"Get lost Doc, you little fart. Get your own ass."

"Andy is a *woman*, Bud. You're hitting a girl. She's not a man."

"Huh?" Bud glances at Andy's bloody face. He shakes the shirt-front. "Where's the boobs?"

"She doesn't have breasts, but she's a woman. Her real name is Kay. They're all women. Let her go, Bud."

Bud stares at the androgyne, his legs still pinioning Judy, his penis poking the air. Andy puts up his/her hands in a vaguely combative way.

"A dyke?" says Bud slowly. "A goddam little bull dyke? This I gotta see."

He feints casually, thrusts a hand into Andy's crotch.

"No balls!" he roars, "No balls at all!" Convulsing with laughter he lets himself tip over in the air, releasing Andy, his legs letting Judy slip free. "Na-ah," he interrupts himself to grab her hair and goes on guffawing. "A dyke! Hey, dykey!" He takes hold of his hard-on, waggles it at Andy. "Eat your heart out, little dyke." Then he pulls up Judy's head. She has been watching unresisting all along.

"Take a good look, girlie. See what old Buddy has for you? Tha-a-at's what you want, say it. How long since you saw a real man, hey, dog-face?"

Maniacal laughter bubbles up in Lorimer's gut, farce too strong for fear. "She never saw a man in her life before, none of them has. You imbecile, don't you get it? There aren't any other men, they've all been dead three hundred years."

Bud slowly stops chuckling, twists around to peer at Lorimer.

"What'd I hear you say, Doc?"

"The men are all gone. They died off in the epidemic. There's nothing but women left alive on Earth."

"You mean there's, there's two million women down there and no men?" His jaw gapes. "Only little bull dykes like Andy . . . Wait a minute. Where do they get the kids?"

"They grow them artificially. They're all girls."

"Gawd . . ." Bud's hand clasps his drooping penis, jiggles it absently. It stiffens. "Two million hot little cunts down there, waiting for old Buddy. Gawd. The last man on Earth . . . You don't count, Doc. And old Dave, he's full of crap."

He begins to pump himself, still holding Judy by the hair. The motion sends them slowly backward. Lorimer sees that Andy – Kay – has the camera going again. There is a big star-shaped smear of blood on the boyish face; cut lip, probably. He himself feels globed in thick air, all action spent. Not lucid.

"Two million cunts," Bud repeats. "Nobody home, nothing but pussy everywhere. I can do anything I want, any time. No more shit." He pumps faster. "They'll be spread out for miles begging for it. Clawing each other for it. All for me, King Buddy . . . I'll have strawberries and cunt for breakfast. Hot buttered boobies, man. 'N' head, there'll be a couple little twats licking whip cream off my cock all day long . . . Hey, I'll have contests! Only the best for old Buddy now. Not you, cow." He jerks Judy's head. "Li'l teenies, tight li'l holes. I'll make the old broads hot 'em up while I watch." He frowns slightly, working on himself. In a clinical corner of his mind Lorimer guesses the drug is retarding ejaculation. He tells himself that he should be relieved by Bud's self-absorption, is instead obscurely terrified.

"King, I'll be their god," Bud is mumbling. "They'll make statues of me, my cock a mile high, all over . . . His Majesty's sacred balls. They'll worship it . . . Buddy Geirr, the last cock on Earth. Oh man, if old George could see that. When the boys hear that they'll really shit themselves, woo-ee!"

He frowns harder. "They can't all be gone." His eyes rove, find Lorimer. "Hey, Doc, there's some men left someplace, aren't there? Two or three, anyway?"

"No." Effortfully Lorimer shakes his head. "They're all dead, all of them."

"Balls." Bud twists around, peering at them. "There has to be some left. Say it." He pulls Judy's head up. "*Say it*, cunt."

"No, it's true," she says.

"No men," Andy/Kay echoes.

"You're lying." Bud scowls, frigs himself faster, thrusting his pelvis. "There has to be some men, sure there are . . . They're hiding out in the hills, that's what it is. Hunting, living wild . . . Old wild men, I knew it."

"Why do there have to be men?" Judy asks him, being jerked to and fro.

"Why, you stupid bitch." He doesn't look at her, thrusts furiously. "Because, dummy, otherwise nothing counts, that's why . . . There's some men, some good old buckaroos – Buddy's a good old buckaroo–"

"Is he going to emit sperm now?" Connie whispers.

"Very likely," Lorimer says, or intends to say. The spectacle is of merely clinical interest, he tells himself, nothing to dread. One of Judy's hands clutches something: a small plastic bag. Her other hand is on her hair that Bud is yanking. It must be painful.

"Uhhh, ahh," Bud pants distressfully, "fuck away, fuck–"

Suddenly he pushes Judy's head into his groin, Lorimer glimpses her nonplussed expression.

"You have a mouth, bitch, get working! . . . Take it for shit's sake, *take* it! Uh, uh–" A small oyster jets limply from him. Judy's arm goes after it with the bag as they roll over in the air.

"*Geirr!*"

Bewildered by the roar, Lorimer turns and sees Dave – Major Norman Davis – looming in the hatchway. His arms are out, holding back Lady Blue and the other Judy.

"Geirr! I said there would be no misconduct on this ship and I mean it. Get away from that woman!"

Bud's legs only move vaguely, he does not seem to have heard. Judy swims through them bagging the last drops.

"You, what the hell are you doing?"

In the silence Lorimer hears his own voice say, "Taking a sperm sample, I should think."

"Lorimer? Are you out of your perverted mind? Get Geirr to his quarters."

Bud slowly rotates upright. "Ah, the reverend Leroy," he says tonelessly.

"You're drunk, Geirr. Go to your quarters."

"I have news for you, Dave-o," Bud tells him in the same flat voice. "I bet you don't know we're the last men on Earth. Two million twats down there."

"I'm aware of that," Dave says furiously. "You're a drunken disgrace. Lorimer, get that man out of here."

But Lorimer feels no nerve of action stir. Dave's angry voice has pushed back the terror, created a strange hopeful stasis encapsulating them all.

"I don't have to take that any more . . ." Bud's head moves back and forth, silently saying no, no, as he drifts toward Lorimer. "Nothing counts any more. All gone. What for, friends?" His forehead puckers. "Old Dave, he's a man. I'll let him have some. The dummies . . . Poor old Doc, you're a creep but you're better'n nothing, you can have some too . . . We'll have places, see, big spreads. Hey, we can run drags, there has to be a million good old cars down there. We can go hunting. And then we find the wild men."

Andy, or Kay, is floating toward him, wiping off blood.

"Ah, no you don't!" Bud snarls and lunges for her. As his arm stretches out Judy claps him on the triceps.

Bud gives a yell that dopplers off, his limbs thrash – and then he is floating limply, his face suddenly serene. He is breathing, Lorimer sees, releasing his own breath, watching them carefully straighten out the big body. Judy plucks her pants out of the vines, and they start towing him out through the fence. She has the camera and the specimen bag.

"I put this in the freezer, dinko?" she says to Connie as they come by. Lorimer has to look away.

Connie nods. "Kay, how's your face?"

"I felt it!" Andy/Kay says excitedly through puffed lips, "I felt physical anger, I wanted to hit him. Woo-ee!"

"Put that man in my wardroom," Dave orders as they pass. He has moved into the sunlight over the lettuce rows. Lady Blue and Judy Dakar are back by the wall, watching. Lorimer remembers what he wanted to ask.

"Dave, do you really know? Did you find out they're all women?"

Dave eyes him broodingly, floating erect with the sun on his chestnut beard and hair. The authentic features of man. Lorimer thinks of his own father, a small pale figure like himself. He feels better.

"I always knew they were trying to deceive us, Lorimer. Now that this woman has admitted the facts I understand the full extent of the tragedy."

It is his deep, mild Sunday voice. The women look at him interestedly.

"They are lost children. They have forgotten He who made them. For generations they have lived in darkness."

"They seem to be doing all right," Lorimer hears himself say. It sounds rather foolish.

"Women are not capable of running anything. You should know that, Lorimer. Look what they've done here, it's pathetic. Marking time, that's all. Poor souls." Dave sighs gravely. "It is not their fault. I recognise that. Nobody has given them any guidance for three hundred years. Like a chicken with its head off."

Lorimer recognises his own thought; the structureless, chattering, trivial, two-million-celled protoplasmic lump.

"The head of the woman is the man," Dave says crisply. "Corinthians one eleven three. No discipline whatsoever." He stretches out his arm, holding up his crucifix as he drifts toward the wall of vines. "Mockery. Abominations." He touches the stakes and turns, framed in the green arbor.

"We were sent here, Lorimer. This is God's plan. *I* was sent here. Not you, you're as bad as they are. My middle name is Paul," he adds in a conversational tone. The sun gleams on the cross, on his uplifted face, a strong, pure, apostolic visage. Despite some intellectual reservations Lorimer feels a forgotten nerve respond.

"Oh Father, send me strength," Dave prays quietly, his eyes closed. "You have spared us from the void to bring Your light to this suffering world. I shall lead Thy erring daughters out of the darkness. I shall be a stern but merciful father to them in Thy name. Help me to teach the children Thy holy law and train them in the fear of Thy righteous wrath. Let the women learn in silence and all subjection; Timothy two eleven. They shall have sons to rule over them and glorify Thy name."

He could do it, Lorimer thinks, a man like that really could get life going again. Maybe there is some mystery, some plan. I was too ready to give up. No guts . . . He becomes aware of women whispering.

"This tape is about through." It is Judy Dakar. "Isn't that enough? He's just repeating."

"Wait," murmurs Lady Blue.

"And she brought forth a man child to rule the nations with a rod of iron, Revelations twelve five," Dave says, louder. His eyes are open now, staring intently at the crucifix. "*For God so loved the world that he sent his only begotten son.*"

Lady Blue nods; Judy pushes off toward Dave. Lorimer understands, protest rising in his throat. They mustn't do that to Dave, treating him like an animal for Christ's sake, a man—

"Dave! Look out, don't let her get near you!" he shouts.

"May I look, Major? It's beautiful, what is it?" Judy is coasting close, her hand out toward the crucifix.

"She's got a hypo, watch it!"

But Dave has already wheeled round. "Do not profane, woman!"

He thrusts the cross at her like a weapon, so menacing that she recoils in mid-air and shows the glinting needle in her hand.

"Serpent!" He kicks her shoulder away, sending himself upward. "Blasphemer. All right," he snaps in his ordinary voice, "there's going to be some order around here starting now. Get over by that wall, all of you."

Astounded, Lorimer sees that Dave actually has a weapon in his other hand, a small grey handgun. He must have had it since Houston. Hope and ataraxia shrivel away, he is shocked into desperate reality.

"Major Davis," Lady Blue is saying. She is floating right at him, they all are, right at the gun. Oh god, do they know what it is?

"Stop!" he shouts at them. "Do what he says, for god's sake. That's a ballistic weapon, it can kill you. It shoots metal slugs." He begins edging toward Dave along the vines.

"Stand back." Dave gestures with the gun. "I am taking command of this ship in the name of the United States of America under God."

"Dave, put that gun away. You don't want to shoot people."

Dave sees him, swings the gun around. "I warn you, Lorimer, get over there with them. Geirr's a man, when he sobers up." He looks at the women still drifting puzzledly toward him and understands. "All right, lesson one. Watch this."

He takes deliberate aim at the iguana cages and fires. There is a pinging crack. A lizard explodes bloodily, voices cry out. A loud mechanical warble starts up and overrides everything.

"A leak!" Two bodies go streaking toward the far end, everybody is moving. In the confusion Lorimer sees Dave calmly pulling himself back to the hatchway behind them, his gun ready. He pushes frantically across the tool rack to cut him off. A spray canister comes loose in his grip, leaving him kicking in the air. The alarm warble dies.

"You will stay here until I decide to send for you," Dave announces. He has reached the hatch, is pulling the massive lock door around. It will seal off the pod, Lorimer realises.

"Don't do it, Dave! Listen to me, you're going to kill us all." Lorimer's own internal alarms are shaking him, he knows now what all that damned volleyball has been for and he is scared to death. "Dave, listen to me!"

"Shut up." The gun swings toward him. The door is moving. Lorimer gets a foot on solidity.

"Duck! It's a bomb!" With all his strength he hurls the massive cannister at Dave's head and launches himself after it.

"Look out!" And he is sailing helplessly in slow motion, hearing the gun go off again, voices yelling. Dave must have missed him, overhead shots are tough – and then he is doubling downwards, grabbing hair. A hard blow strikes his gut, it is Dave's leg kicking past him but he has his arm under the beard, the big man bucking like a bull, throwing him around.

"Get the gun, get it!" People are bumping him, getting hit. Just as his hold slips a hand snakes by him onto Dave's shoulder and they are colliding into the hatch door in a tangle. Dave's body is suddenly no longer at war.

Lorimer pushes free, sees Dave's contorted face tip slowly backward looking at him.

"Judas–"

The eyes close. It is over.

Lorimer looks around. Lady Blue is holding the gun, sighting down the barrel.

"Put that down," he gasps, winded. She goes on examining it.

"Hey, thanks!" Andy – Kay – grins lopsidedly at him, rubbing her jaw. They are all smiling, speaking warmly to him, feeling themselves, their torn clothes. Judy Dakar has a black eye starting, Connie holds a shattered iguana by the tail.

Beside him Dave drifts breathing stertorously, his blind face pointing at the sun. *Judas . . .* Lorimer feels the last shield break inside him, desolation flooding in. *On the deck my captain lies.*

Andy-who-is-not-a-man comes over and matter-of-factly zips up Dave's jacket, takes hold of it and begins to tow him out. Judy Dakar stops them long enough to wrap the crucifix chain around his hand. Somebody laughs, not unkindly, as they go by.

For an instant Lorimer is back in that Evanston toilet. But

they are gone, all the little giggling girls. All gone forever, gone with the big boys waiting outside to jeer at him. Bud is right, he thinks. *Nothing counts any more.* Grief and anger hammer at him. He knows now what he has been dreading: not their vulnerability, his.

"They were good men," he says bitterly. "They aren't bad men. You don't know what bad means. You did it to them, you broke them down. You made them do crazy things. Was it interesting? Did you learn enough?" His voice is trying to shake. "Everybody has aggressive fantasies. They didn't act on them. Never. Until you poisoned them."

They gaze at him in silence. "But nobody does," Connie says finally. "I mean, the fantasies."

"They were good men," Lorimer repeats elegiacally. He knows he is speaking for it all, for Dave's Father, for Bud's manhood, for himself, for Cro-Magnon, for the dinosaurs too, maybe. "I'm a man. By god yes, I'm angry. I have a right. We gave you all this, we made it all. We built your precious civilisation and your knowledge and comfort and medicines and your dreams. All of it. We protected you, we worked our balls off keeping you and your kids. It was hard. It was a fight, a bloody fight all the way. We're tough. We had to be, can't you understand? Can't you for Christ's sake understand that?"

Another silence.

"We're trying," Lady Blue sighs. "We are trying, Doctor Lorimer. Of course we enjoy your inventions and we do appreciate your evolutionary role. But you must see there's a problem. As I understand it, what you protected people from was largely other males, wasn't it? We've just had an extraordinary demonstration. You have brought history to life for us." Her wrinkled brown eyes smile at him; a small, tea-colored matron holding an obsolete artifact.

"But the fighting is long over. It ended when you did, I believe. We can hardly turn you loose on Earth, and we simply have no facilities for people with your emotional problems."

"Besides, we don't think you'd be very happy," Judy Dakar adds earnestly.

"We could clone them," says Connie. "I know there's people who would volunteer to mother. The young ones might be all right, we could try."

"We've been *over* all that." Judy Paris is drinking from the water tank. She rinses and spits into the soil bed, looking worriedly at Lorimer. "We ought to take care of that leak now, we can talk tomorrow. And tomorrow and tomorrow." She smiles at him, unselfconsciously rubbing her crotch. "I'm sure a lot of people will want to meet you."

"Put us on an island," Lorimer says wearily. "On three islands." That look; he knows that look of preoccupied compassion. His mother and sister had looked just like that the time the diseased kitten came in the yard. They had comforted it and fed it and tenderly taken it to the vet to be gassed.

An acute, complex longing for the women he has known grips him. Women to whom men were not simply – irrelevent. Ginny . . . dear god. His sister Amy. Poor Amy, she was good to him when they were kids. His mouth twists.

"Your problem is," he says, "if you take the risk of giving us equal rights, what could we possibly contribute?"

"Precisely," says Lady Blue. They all smile at him relievedly, not understanding that he isn't.

"I think I'll have that antidote now," he says.

Connie floats toward him, a big, warm-hearted, utterly alien woman. "I thought you'd like yours in a bulb." She smiles kindly.

"Thank you." He takes the small, pink bulb. "Just tell me," he says to Lady Blue, who is looking at the bullet gashes, "what do you call yourselves? Women's World? Liberation? Amazonia?

"Why, we call ourselves human beings." Her eyes twinkle absently at him, go back to the bullet marks. "Humanity, mankind." She shrugs. "The human race."

The drink tastes cool going down, something like peace and freedom, he thinks. Or death.

To Keep the Oath
Marion Zimmer Bradley

Marion Zimmer Bradley has been a favorite of lesbians and gay men since her early appearances in The Ladder and The Mattachine Review. Many of her positive portrayals of same-sex love take place on the imaginary planet of Darkover, where technology is based on applied parapsychological talents. "To Keep the Oath" is part of Bradley's Darkover cycle.

The red light lingered on the hills; two of the four small moons were in the sky, green Idriel near to setting, and the tiny crescent of Mormallor, ivory-pale near the zenith. The night would be dark. Kindra n'ha Mhari did not, at first, see anything strange about the little town. She was too grateful to have reached it before sunset – shelter against the rainswept chill of a Darkovan night, a bed to sleep in after four days of traveling, a cup of wine before she slept.

But slowly she began to realize that there was something wrong. Normally, at this hour, the women would be going back and forth in the streets, gossiping with neighbors, marketing for the evening meal, while their children played and squabbled in the street. But tonight there was not a single woman in the street, nor a single child.

What was wrong? Frowning, she rode along the main street toward the inn. She was hungry and weary.

She had left Dalereuth many days before with a companion,

bound for Neskaya Guild-house. But unknown to either of them, her companion had been pregnant; she had fallen sick of a fever, and in Thendara Guild-house she had miscarried and still lay there, very ill. Kindra had gone alone to Neskaya; but she had turned aside three days' ride to carry a message to the sick woman's oath-mother. She had found her in a village in the hills, working to help a group of women set up a small dairy.

Kindra was not afraid of traveling alone; she had journeyed in these hills at all seasons and in all weathers. But her provisions were beginning to run low. Fortunately, the innkeeper was an old acquaintance; she had little money with her, because her journey had been so unexpectedly prolonged, but old Jorik would feed her and her horse, give her a bed for the night and trust her to send money to pay for it – knowing that if she did not, or could not, her Guild-house would pay, for the honor of the Guild.

The man who took her horse in the stable had known her for many years, too. He scowled as she alighted. "I don't know where we shall stable your horse, and that's certain, *mestra*, with all these strange horses here . . . will she share a box stall without kicking, do you suppose? Or shall I tie her loose at the end?" Kindra noticed that the stable was crammed with horses, two dozen of them and more. Instead of a lonely village inn, it looked like Neskaya on market-day!

"Did you meet with any riders on the road, *mestra*?"

"No, none," Kindra said, frowning a little. "All the horses in the Kilghard Hills seem to be here in your stable – what is it, a royal visit? What is the matter with you? You keep looking over your shoulder as if you expect to find your master there with a stick to beat you – where is old Jorik, why is he not here to greet his guests?"

"Why, *mestra*, old Jorik's dead," the old man said, "and Dame Janella trying to manage the inn alone with young Annelys and Marga."

"Dead? Gods preserve us," Kindra said. "What happened?"

"It was those bandits, *mestra*, Scarface's gang; they came here and cut Jorik down with his apron still on," said the old groom. "Made havoc in the town, broke all the ale-pots, and when the menfolk drove 'em off with pitchforks, they swore they'd be back and fire the town! So Dame Janella and the elders put the cap round and raised copper to hire Brydar of Fen Hills and all his men to come and defend us when they come back; and here Brydar's men have been ever since, *mestra*, quarreling and drinking and casting eyes on the women until the townfolk are ready to say the remedy's worse than the sickness! But go in, go in, *mestra*, Janella's ready to welcome you."

Plump Janella looked paler and thinner than Kindra had ever seen her. She greeted Kindra with unaccustomed warmth. Under ordinary conditions, she was cold to Kindra, as befitted a respectable wife in the presence of a member of the Amazon Guild; now, Kindra supposed, she was learning that an innkeeper could not afford to alienate a customer. Jorik, Kindra knew, had not approved of the Free Amazons either; but he had learned from experience that they were quiet guests who kept to themselves, caused no trouble, did not get drunk and break bar-stools and ale-pots, and paid their reckoning promptly. *A guest's reputation*, Kindra thought wryly, *does not tarnish the color of his money*.

"You have heard, good *mestra*? Those wicked men, Scarface's fellows, they cut my good man down, and for nothing – just because he flung an ale-pot at one of them who laid rough hands on my little girl, and Annelys not fifteen yet! Monsters!"

"And they killed him? Shocking!" Kindra murmured, but her pity was for the girl. All her life, young Annelys must remember that her father had been killed in defending her, because she could not defend herself. Like all the women of the Guild, Kindra was sworn to defend herself, to turn to no man for protection. She had been a member of the Guild for half her lifetime; it seemed shocking to her that a man should die defending a girl from advances she should have known how to ward off herself.

"Ah, you don't know what it's like, *mestra*, being alone without the goodman. Living alone as you do, you can't imagine!"

"Well, you have daughters to help you," Kindra said, and Janella shook her head and mourned. "But they can't come out among all those rough men, they are only little girls!"

"It will do them good to learn something of the world and its ways," Kindra said, but the woman sighed, "I wouldn't like them too learn too much of that."

"Then, I suppose, you must get you another husband," Kindra said, knowing that there was simply no way she and Janella could communicate. "But indeed I am sorry for your grief. Jorik was a good man."

"You can't imagine how good, *mestra*," Janella said plaintively. "You women of the Guild, you call yourselves free women, only it seems to me I have always been free, until now, when I must watch myself night and day, lest someone get the wrong idea about a woman alone. Only the other day, one of Brydar's men said to me – and that's another thing, these men of Brydar's. Eating us out of house and home, and just look, *mestra*, no room in the stable for the horses of our paying customers, with half the village keeping their horses here against bandits, and those hired swords drinking up my good old man's beer day after day– " Abruptly she recalled her duties as landlord. "But come into the common-room, *mestra*, warm yourself, and I'll bring you some supper; we have a roast haunch of *chervine*. Or would you fancy something lighter, rabbithorn stewed with mushrooms, perhaps? We are crowded, yes, but there's the little room at the head of the stairs, you can have that to yourself, a room fit for a fine lady, indeed Lady Hastur slept here in that very bed, a few years gone. Lilla! Lilla! Where's that simpleminded wench gone? When I took her in, her mother told me she was lack-witted, but she has wits enough to hang about talking to that young hired sword, Zandru scratch them all! Lilla! Hurry now, show the good woman her room, fetch her wash-water, see to her saddlebags!"

Later, Kindra went down to the common-room. Like all Guild-women, she had learned to be discreet when traveling alone; a solitary woman was prey to questions, at least, so they usually journeyed in pairs. This subjected them to raised eyebrows and occasional dirty speculations, but warded off the less palatable approaches to which a lone woman traveling on Darkover was subject. Of course, any woman of the Guild could protect herself if it went past rude words, but that could cause trouble for all the Guild. It was better to conduct oneself in a way that minimized the possibility of trouble. So Kindra sat alone in a tiny corner near the fireplace, kept her hood drawn around her face – she was neither young nor particularly pretty – sipped her wine and warmed her feet, and did nothing to attract anyone's attention. It occurred to her that at this moment she, who called herself a Free Amazon, was considerably more constrained than Janella's young daughters, going back and forth, protected by their family's roof and their mother's presence.

She finished her meal – she had chosen the stewed rabbithorn – and called for a second glass of wine, too weary to climb the stairs to her chamber and too tired to sleep if she did.

Some of Brydar's hired swords were sitting around a long table at the other end of the room, drinking and playing dice. They were a mixed crew; Kindra knew none of them, but she had met Brydar himself a few times, and had even hired out with him, once to guard a merchant caravan across the desert to the Dry Towns. She nodded courteously to him, and he saluted her, but paid her no further attention. He knew her well enough to know that she would not welcome even polite conversation when she was in a roomful of strangers.

One of the younger mercenaries, a young man, tall, beardless and weedy, ginger hair cut close to his head, rose and came toward her. Kindra braced herself for the inevitable. If she had been with two or three other Guild-women, she would have welcomed harmless companionship, a drink together and talk about the chances of the road, but a lone Amazon simply did NOT drink with men in public taverns, and damn it, Brydar knew it as well as she did.

One of the older mercenaries must have been having some fun with the green boy, needling him to prove his manhood by approaching the Amazon, amusing themselves by enjoying the rebuff he'd inevitably get.

One of the men looked up and made a remark Kindra didn't hear. The boy snarled something, a hand to his dagger. "Watch yourself, you ______!" He spoke a foulness. Then he came to Kindra's table and said, in a soft, husky voice, "A good evening to you, honorable mistress"

Startled at the courteous phrase, but still wary, Kindra said, "And to you, young sir."

"May I offer you a tankard of wine?"

"I have had enough to drink," Kindra said, "but I thank you for the kind offer." Something faintly out of key, almost effeminate, in the youth's bearing, alerted her; his proposition, then, would not be the usual thing. Most people knew that Free Amazons took lovers if and when they chose, and all too many men interpreted that to mean that any Amazon could be had, at any time. Kindra was an expert at turning covert advances aside without ever letting it come to question or refusal; with ruder approaches, she managed with scant courtesy. But that wasn't what this youngster wanted; she knew when a man was looking at her with desire, whether he put it into words or not, and although there was certainly interest in this young man's face, it wasn't sexual interest! What did he want with her, then?

"May I – may I sit here and talk to you for a moment, honorable dame?"

Rudeness she could have managed. This excessive courtesy was a puzzle. Were they simply making game of a woman-hater, wagering he would not have the courage to talk to her? She said neutrally, "This is a public room; the chairs are not mine. Sit where you like."

Ill at ease, the boy took a seat. He was young indeed. He was still beardless, but his hands were calloused and hard, and there was a long-healed scar on one cheek; he was not as young as she thought.

"You are a Free Amazon, *mestra*?" He used the common, and rather offensive term; but she did not hold it against him. Many men knew no other name.

"I am," she said, "but we would rather say: I am of the oath-bound–" The word she used was *Comhi-Letzii* – "A Renunciate of the Sisterhood of Freed Women."

"May I ask – without giving offense – why the name Renunciate, *mestra*?"

Actually, Kindra welcomed a chance to explain. "Because, sir, in return for our freedom as women of the Guild, we swear an oath renouncing those privileges that we might have by choosing to belong to some man. If we renounce the disabilities of being property and chattel, we must renounce, also, whatever benefits there may be; so that no man can accuse us of trying to have the best of both choices."

He said gravely, "That seems to me an honorable choice. I have never yet met a – a – a Renunciate. Tell me, *mestra*–" His voice suddenly cracked high. "I suppose you know the slanders that are spoken of you – tell me, how does any woman have the courage to join the Guild, knowing what will be said of her?"

"I suppose," Kindra said quietly, "for some women, a time comes when they think that there are worse things than being the subject of public slanders. It was so with me."

He thought that over for a moment, frowning. "I have never seen a Free – er – a Renunciate traveling alone before. Do you not usually travel in pairs, honorable dame?"

"True. But need knows no mistress," Kindra said, and explained that her companion had fallen sick in Thendara.

"And you came so far to bear a message? Is she your *bredhis*?" the boy asked, using the polite word for a woman's freemate or female lover; and because it was the polite word he used, not the gutter one, Kindra did not take offense. "No, only a comrade."

"I – I would not have dared speak if there had been two of you–"

Kindra laughed. "Why not? Even in twos and threes we are not dogs to bite strangers."

The boy stared at his boots. "I have cause to fear – women–" he said, almost inaudibly. "But you seemed kind. And I suppose, *mestra*, that whenever you come into these hills, where life is so hard for women, you are always seeking out wives and daughters who are discontented at home, to recruit them for your Guild?"

Would that we might! Kindra thought, with all the old bitterness; but she shook her head. "Our charter forbids it," she said. "It is the law that a woman must seek us out herself, and formally petition to be allowed to join us. I am not even allowed to tell women of the advantages of the Guild, when they ask. I may only tell them of the things they must renounce, by oath." She tightened her lips and added, "If we were to do as you say, to seek out discontented wives and daughters and lure them away to the Guild, the men would not let any Guild-house stand in the Domains, but would burn our houses about our ears." It was the old injustice; the women of Darkover had won this concession, the charter of the Guild, but so hedged about with restrictions that many women never saw or spoke with a Guild-sister.

"I suppose," she said, "that they have found out that we are not whores, so they insist that we are all lovers of women, intent on stealing out their wives and daughters. We must be, it seems, one evil thing or the other."

"Are there no lovers of women among you, then?"

Kindra shrugged. "Certainly," she said. "You must know that there are some women who would rather die than marry; and even with all the restrictions and renunciations of the oath, it seems a preferable alternative. But I assure you we are not all so. We are free women – free to be thus or otherwise, at our own will." After a moment's thought, she added carefully, "And if you have a sister you may tell her so from me."

The young man started, and Kindra bit her lip; again she had let her guard down, picking up hunches so clearly formed that sometimes her companions accused her of having a little of the telepathic gift of the higher castes; *laran*. Kindra, who was, as far as she knew, all commoner and without either noble blood or telepathic gift, usually kept herself barricaded; but she had picked up a random thought, a bitter thought from somewhere, *My sister would not believe* . . . a thought quickly vanished, so quickly that Kindra wondered if she had imagined the whole thing.

The young face across the table twisted into bitter lines.

"There is none, now, I may call my sister."

"I am sorry," Kindra said, puzzled. "To be alone, that is a sorrowful thing. May I ask your name?"

The boy hesitated again, and Kindra knew, with that odd intuition that the real name had almost escaped the taut lips; but he bit it back.

"Brydar's men call me Marco. Don't ask my lineage; there is none who will claim kin to me now – thanks to those foul bandits under Scarface." He twisted his mouth and spat. "Why do you think I am in this company? For the few coppers these village folk can pay? No, *mestra*. I too am oath-bound. To revenge."

Kindra left the common-room early, but she could not sleep for a long time. Something in the young man's voice, his words, had plucked a resonating string in her own mind and memory. Why had he questioned her so insistently? Had he a sister or kinswoman, perhaps, who had spoken of becoming a Renunciate? Or was he, an obvious effeminate, jealous of her because she could escape the role ordained by society for her sex and he could not? Did he fantasy, perhaps, some such escape from the demands made upon men? Surely not; there were simpler lives for men than that of a hired sword! And men had a choice of what lives they would live – more choice, anyhow, than most women. Kindra had chosen to become a Renunciate, making herself an outcast among most people in the Domains. Even the innkeeper only tolerated her, because she was a regular customer and paid well, but he would have equally tolerated a prostitute or a traveling juggler, and would have had fewer prejudices against either.

Was the youth, she wondered, one of the rumored spies sent out by *cortes*, the governing body in Thendara, to trap Renunciates who broke the terms of their charter by proselytizing and attempting to recruit women into the Guild? If so, at least she had resisted the temptation. She had not even said, though tempted, that if Janella were a Renunciate she would have felt competent to run the inn by herself, with the help of her daughters.

A few times, in the history of the Guild, men had even tried to infiltrate them in disguise. Unmasked, they had met with summary justice, but it had happened and might happen again. At that, she thought, he might be convincing enough in women's clothes; but not with the scar on his face or those calloused hands. Then she laughed in the dark, feeling the calluses on her own fingers. Well, if he was fool enough to try it, so much the worse for him. Laughing, she fell asleep.

Hours later she woke to the sound of hoofbeats, the clash of steel, yells and cries outside. Somewhere women were shrieking. Kindra flung on her outer clothes and ran downstairs. Brydar was standing in the courtyard, bellowing orders. Over the wall of the courtyard she could see a sky reddened with flames. Scarface and his bandit crew were loose in the town, it seemed.

"Go, Renwal," Brydar ordered. "Slip behind their rear-guard and set their horses loose, stampede them, so they must stand to fight, not strike and flee again! And since all the good horses are stabled here, one of you must stay and guard them lest they strike here for ours . . . the rest of you come with me, and have your swords at the ready—"

Janella was huddled beneath the overhanging roof of an outbuilding, her daughters and serving women like roosting hens around her. "Will you leave us all here unguarded, when we have housed you all for seven days and never a penny in pay? Scarface and his men are sure to strike here for the horses, and we are unprotected, at their mercy—"

Brydar gestured to the boy Marco. "You. Stay and guard horses and women—"

The boy snarled, "No! I joined your crew on the pledge that I should face Scarface, steel in hand! It is an affair of honor — do you think I need your dirty coppers?"

Beyond the wall all was shrieking confusion. "I have no time to bandy words," Brydar said quickly. "Kindra — this is no quarrel of yours, but you know me a man of my word; stay here and guard the horses and these women, and I will make it worth your while!"

"At the mercy of a woman? A woman to guard us? Why not set a mouse to guard a lion!" Janella's shrewish cry cut him off. The boy Marco urged, eyes blazing, "Whatever I have been promised for this foray is yours, *mestra*, if you free me to meet my sworn foe!"

"Go; I'll look after them," Kindra said. It was unlikely Scarface would get this far, but it was really no affair of hers; normally she fought beside the men, and would have been angry at being left in a post of safety. But Janella's cry had put her on her mettle. Marco caught up his sword and hurried to the gate, Brydar following him. Kindra watched them go, her mind on her own early battles. Some turn of gesture, of phrase had alerted her. *The boy Marco is noble,* she thought. *Perhaps even Comyn, some bastard of a great lord, perhaps even a Hastur. I don't know what he's doing with Brydar's men, but he's no ordinary hired sword!*

Janella's wailing brought her back to her duty.

"Oh! Oh! Horrible," she howled. "Left here with only a woman to look after us. . ."

Kindra said tersely,"Come on!" She gestured. "Help me close

that gate!"

"I don't take orders from one of you shameless women in breeches—"

"Let the damned gate stay open, then," Kindra said, right out of patience. "Let Scarface walk in without any trouble. Do you want me to go and invite him, or shall we send one of your daughters?"

"Mother!" remonstrated a girl of fifteen, breaking away from Janella's hand."That is no way to speak – Lilla, Marga, help the good *mestra* shove this gate shut!" She came and joined Kindra, helping to thrust the heavy wooden gate tightly into place, pull down the heavy cross-beam. The women were wailing in dismay; Kindra singled out one of them, a young girl about six or seven moons along in pregnancy, who was huddled in a blanket over her nightgear.

"You," she said, "take all the babies and the little children upstairs into the strongest chamber, bolt the doors, and don't open them unless you hear my voice or Janella's." The woman did not move, still sobbing, and Kindra said sharply, "Hurry! Don't stand there like a rabbithorn frozen in the snow! Damn you, move, or I'll slap you senseless!" She made a menacing gesture and the woman started, then began to hurry the children up the stairs; she picked up one of the littlest ones, hurried the others along with frightened, clucking noises.

Kindra surveyed the rest of the frightened women. Janella was hopeless. She was fat and short of breath, and she was staring resentfully at Kindra, furious that she had been left in charge of their defense. Furthermore, she was trembling on the edge of a panic that would infect everyone; but if she had something to do, she might calm down. "Janella, go into the kitchen and make up some hot wine punch," she said. "The men will want it when they come back, and they'll deserve it too. Then start hunting out some linen for bandages, in case anyone's hurt. Don't wory," she added "they won't get you while we're here. And take that one with you," she added, pointing to the terrified simpleton Lilla, who was clinging to Janella's skirt, round-eyed with terror, whimpering. "She'll only be in our way."

When Janella had gone, grumbling, the lackwit at her heels,

Kindra looked around at the sturdy young women who remained.

"Come, all of you, into the stables, and pile heavy bales of hay around the horses, so they can't drive the horses over them or stampede them out. No, leave the lantern there; if Scarface and his men break through, we'll set a couple of bales afire; that will frighten the horses, and they might well kick a bandit or two to death. Even so, the women can escape while they round up the horses; contrary to what you may have heard, most bandits look first for horses and rich plunder, and women are not the first item on their list. And none of you have jewels or rich garments they would seek to strip from you." Kindra herself knew that any man who laid his hand on her, intending rape, would quickly regret it; and if she was overpowered by numbers she had been taught ways in which she could survive the experience undestroyed; but these women had had no such teaching. It was not right to blame them for their fears.

I could teach them this. But the laws of our charter prevent me and I am bound by oath to obey those laws; laws made, not by our own Guild-mothers, but by men who fear what we might have to say to their women!

Well, perhaps, at least they will find it a matter for pride that they can defend their home against invaders! Kindra went to lend her own wiry strength to the task of piling up the heavy bales around the horses; the women worked, forgetting their fears in hard effort. But one grumbled, just loud enough for Kindra to hear, "It's all very well for *her!* She was trained as a warrior and she's used to this kind of work! I'm not!"

It was no time to debate Guild-house ethics; Kindra only asked mildly, "Are you proud of the fact that you have not been taught to defend yourself, child?" But the girl did not answer, sullenly hauling at her heavy hay-bale.

It was not difficult for Kindra to follow her thought; if it had not been for Brydar, each man of the town could have protected each one his own women! Kindra thought, in utter disgust, that this was the sort of thinking that laid villages in flames, year after year, because no man owed loyalty to another, or would protect any household but his own! It had taken a threat like Scarface to get these village men organized enough to buy the services of a few hired swords, and now their women were grumbling because their men could not stand, each at his own door, protecting his own woman and hearth!

Once the horses had been barricaded, the women clustered together nervously in the courtyard. Even Janella came to the kitchen door to watch. Kindra went to the barred gate, her knife loose in its scabbard. The other girls and women stood under the roof of the kitchen, but one young girl, the same who had helped Kindra to shut the gate, bent and tucked her skirt resolutely up to her knees, then went and brought back a big wood-chopping hatchet and stood with it in her hand, taking up a place at the gate beside Kindra.

"Annelys!" Janella called. "Come back here! By me!"

The girl cast a look of contempt at her mother and said "If any bandit climbs these walls, he will not get his hands on me, or on my little sister, without facing cold steel! It's not a sword, but I think even in a girl's hands this blade would change his mind in a hurry!" She glanced defiantly at Kindra and said, "I am ashamed for all of you, that you would let one lone woman protect us! Even a rabbithorn doe protects her kits!"

Kindra gave the girl a companionable grin. "If you have half as much skill with that thing as you have guts, little sister, I would rather have you at my back than any man. Hold the axe with your hands close together, if the time comes to use it, and don't try anything fancy, just take a good hard chop at his legs, just like you were cutting down a tree. The thing is, he won't be expecting it, see?"

The night dragged on. The women huddled on hay-bales and boxes, listening with apprehension and occasional sobs and tears as they heard the clash of swords, cries and shouts. Only Annelys stood grimly beside Kindra, clutching her axe. After an hour or so, Kindra said, settling herself down on a hay-bale, "You needn't clutch it like that, you'll only weary yourself for an attack. Lean it against the bale, so you can snatch it up when the need comes."

Annelys asked in an undertone, "How did you know so well what to do? Are all the Free Amazons – you call them something else, don't you? – how do the Guild-women learn? Are they all fighting women and hired swords?"

"No, no, not even many of us," Kindra said. "It is only that I have not many other talents; I cannot weave or embroider very well, and my skill at gardening is only good in the summertime. My own oath-mother is a midwife, that is our most respected trade; even those who despise the Renunciates confess that we can often save babes alive when the village healer-women fail. She would have taught me her profession; but I had no talent for that, either, and I am squeamish about the sight of blood—" She looked down suddenly at her long knife, remembering her many battles, and laughed; and Annelys laughed with her, a strange sound against the frightened moaning of the other women.

"You are afraid of the sight of blood?"

"It's different," Kindra said. "I can't stand suffering when I can't do anything about it, and if a babe is born easily they seldom send for the midwife; we come only when matters are desperate. I would rather fight with men, or beasts, than for the life of a helpless woman or baby . . ."

"I think I would too," said Annelys, and Kindra thought: *Now, if I were not bound by the laws of the Guild, I could tell her what we are. And this one would be a credit to the Sisterhood . . .*

But her oath held her silent. She sighed and looked at Annelys, frustrated.

She was beginning to think the precautions had been useless, that Scarface's men would never come here at all, when there was a shriek from one of the women, and Kindra saw the tassel of a coarse knitted cap come up over the wall; then two men appeared on top of the wall, knives gripped in their teeth to free their hands for climbing.

"So here's where they've hidden it all, women, horses, all of it—" growled one. "You go for the horses, I'll take care of — oh, you would," he shouted as Kindra ran at him with her knife drawn. He was taller than Kindra; as they fought, she could only defend herself, backing step by step toward the stables. Where were the men? Why had the bandits been able to get this far? Were they the last defense of the town? Behind her, out of the corner of her eye she saw the other bandit coming up with his sword; she circled, backing carefully so she could face them both.

Then there was a shriek from Annelys, the axe flashed once,

and the second bandit fell, howling, his leg spouting blood. Kindra's opponent faltered at the sound; Kindra brought up her knife and ran him through the shoulder, snatching up his knife as it fell from his limp hand. He fell backward, and she leaped on top of him.

"Annelys!" she shouted. "You women! Bring thongs, rope, anything to tie him up – there may be others–"

Janella came with a clothesline and stood by as Kindra tied the man, then, stepping back, looked at the bandit, lying in a pool of his own blood. His leg was nearly severed at the knee. He was still breathing, but he was too far gone even to moan, and while the women stood and looked at him, he died. Janella stared at Annelys in horror, as if her young daughter had suddenly sprouted another head.

"You killed him," she breathed. "You chopped his leg off!"

"Would you rather he had chopped off mine, mother?" Annelys asked, and bent to look at the other bandit. "He is only stabbed through the shoulder, he'll live to be hanged!"

Breathing hard, Kindra straightened, giving the clothesline a final tug. She looked at Annelys and said "You saved my life, little sister."

The girl smiled up at her, excited, her hair coming down and tumbling into her eyes. There was a cold sleet beginning to fall in the court; their faces were wet. Annelys suddenly flung her arms around Kindra and the older woman hugged her, disregarding the mother's troubled face.

"One of our own could not have done better. My thanks, little one!" Damn it, the girl had *earned* her thanks and approval, and if Janella stared at them as if Kindra were a wicked seducer of young women, then so much the worse for Janella! She let the girl's arm stay around her shoulders as she said, "Listen; I think that is the men coming back."

And in a minute they heard Brydar's hail, and they struggled to raise the great crossbeam of the gate. His men drove before them more than a dozen good horses, and Brydar laughed, saying, "Scarface's men will have no more use for them; so we're well paid! I see you women got the last of them?" He looked down at the bandit lying in his gore, at the other tied with Janella's clothesline. "Good work, *mestra*, I'll see you have a share in the booty!"

"The girl helped," Kindra said. "I'd have been dead without her."

"One of them killed my father," the girl said fiercely, "so I have paid my just debt, that is all!" She turned to Janella and ordered, "Mother, bring our defenders some of that wine-punch, at once!"

Brydar's men sat all over the common-room, drinking the hot wine gratefully. Brydar set down the tankard and rubbed his hands over his eyes with a tired "Whoosh!" He said, "Some of my men are hurt, dame Janella; have any of your women skill with leech-craft? We will need bandages, and perhaps some salves and herbs. I—" He broke off as one of the men beckoned him urgently from the door, and he went at a run.

Annelys brought Kindra a tankard and put it shyly into her hand. Kindra sipped; it was not the wine punch Janella had made, but a clear, fine, golden wine from the mountains. Kindra sipped it slowly, knowing the girl had been telling her something. She sat across from Kindra, taking a sip now and then of the hot wine in her own tankard. They were both reluctant to part.

Damn that fool law that says I cannot tell her of the Sisterhood! She is too good for this place and for that fool mother of hers; the idiot Lilla is more what her mother needs to help run the inn, and I suppose Janella will marry her off to some yokel at once, just to have help in running this place! Honor demanded she keep silent. Yet, watching Annelys, thinking of the life the girl would lead here, she wondered, troubled, what kind of honor it was, to require that she leave a girl like this in a place like this.

Yet she supposed it was a wise law; anyway, it had been made by wiser heads than hers. She supposed, otherwise, young girls, glamored for the moment with the thought of a life of excitement and adventure, might follow the Sisterhood without being fully aware of the hardships and the renunciations that awaited them. The name Renunciate was not lightly given; it was not an easy life. And considering the way Annelys was looking at her, Annelys might follow her simply out of hero-worship. That wouldn't do. She sighed and said, "Well, the excitement is over for tonight, I suppose. I must be away to my bed; I have a long way to ride tomorrow. Listen to that racket! I didn't know any of Brydar's men were seriously hurt—"

"It sounds more like a quarrel than men in pain," Annelys said, listening to the shouts and protests. "Are they quarreling over the spoils?"

Abruptly the door thrust open and Brydar of Fen Hills came into the room. "*Mestra*, forgive me, you are wearied—"

"Enough," she said, "but after all this hullabaloo I am not like to sleep much; what can I do for you?"

"I beg you – will you come? It is the boy – young Marco; he is hurt, badly hurt, but he will not let us tend his wounds until he has spoken with you. He says he has an urgent message, very urgent, which he must give before he dies..."

"Avarra's mercy," Kindra said, shocked. "Is he dying, then?"

"I cannot tell, he will not let us near enough to dress his wound. If he would be reasonable and let us care for him – but he is bleeding like a slaughtered *chervine*, and he has threatened to slit the throat of any man who touches him. We tried to hold him down and tend him willy-nilly, but it made his wounds bleed so sore as he struggled that we dared not wait – will you come, *mestra*?"

Kindra looked at him with question – she had not thought he would humor any man of his band so. Brydar said defensively, "The lad is nothing to me; not foster-brother, kinsman, nor even friend. But he fought at my side, and he is brave; it was he who killed Scarface in single combat. And may have had his death from it."

"Why should he want to speak to me?"

"He says, *mestra*, that it is a matter concerning his sister. And he begs you in the name of Avarra the pitiful that you will come. And he is young enough, almost, to be your son."

"So," Kindred said at last. She had not seen her own son since he was eight days old and he would, she thought, be too young to bear a sword. "I cannot refuse anyone who begs me in the name of the Goddess," she said, and rose, frowning; young Marco had said he had no sister. No; he had said that there was none, now, that he could call sister. Which might be a different thing.

On the stairs she heard the voice of one of Brydar's men, expostulating, "Lad, we won't hurt ye, but if we don't get to that wound and tend to it, you could die, do y'hear?"

"Get away from me!" The young voice cracked. "I swear by Zandru's hells, and, by the spilt tripes of Scarface out there dead, I'll shove this knife into the throat of the first man who touches me!"

Inside, by torchlight, Kindra saw Marco half-sitting, half-lying on a straw pallet; he had a dagger in his hand, holding them away with it; but he was pale as death, and there was icy sweat on his forehead. The straw pallet was slowly reddening with a pool of blood. Kindra knew enough of wounds to know that the human body could lose more blood than most people thought possible without serious danger; but to any ordinary person it looked most alarming.

Marco saw Kindra and gasped, "*Mestra*, I beg you – I must speak with you alone–"

"That's no way to speak to a comrade, lad," said one of the mercenaries kneeling behind him, as Kindra knelt beside the pallet. The wound was high on the leg, near the groin; the leather breeches had broken the blow somewhat, or the boy would have met the same fate as the man Annelys had struck with the axe.

"You little fool," Kindra said. "I can't do half as much for you as your friend can."

Marco's eyes closed for a moment, from pain or weakness. Kindra thought he had lost consciousness, and gestured to the man behind him. "Quick, now, while he is unconscious–" she said swiftly, but the tortured eyes flicked open.

"Would you betray me, too?" He gestured with the dagger, but so feebly that Kindra was shocked. There was certainly no time to be lost. The best thing was to humor him.

"Go," she said, "I'll reason with him, and if he won't listen, well, he is old enough to take the consequences of his folly." Her mouth twisted as the men went away. "I hope what you have to tell me is worth risking your life for, you lackwitted simpleton!"

But a great and terrifying suspicion was born in her as she knelt on the bloody pallet. "You fool, do you know this is likely to be your deathwound? I have small skill at leechcraft; your comrades could do better for you."

"It is sure to be my death unless you help me," said the hoarse, weakening voice. "None of these men is comrade enough that I could trust him . . . *mestra*, help me, I beg you, in the name of the merciful Avarra – I am a woman."

Kindra drew a sharp breath. She had begun to suspect – and it was true, then. "And none of Brydar's men knows–"

"None. I have dwelt among them for half a year and I do not think any man of them suspects – and I fear women even more. But you, you I felt I might trust–"

"I swear it," Kindra said hastily. "I am oath-bound never to refuse aid to any woman who asks me in the name of the Goddess. But let me help you now, my poor girl, and pray Avarra you have not delayed too long!"

"Even if it was so–" the strange girl whispered – "I would rather die as a woman, than – disgraced and exposed. I have known so much disgrace–"

"Hush! Hush, child!" But she fell back against the pallet; she had really fainted, this time, at last; and Kindra cut away the leather breeches,looking at the serious cut that sliced through the top of the thigh and into the pubic mound. It had bled heavily, but was not, Kindra thought, fatal. She picked up one of the clean towels the men had left, pressed heavily against the wound; when it slowed to an ooze, she frowned, thinking it should be stitched. She hesitated to do it – she had little skill at such things, and she was sure the man from Brydar's band could do it more tidily and sure-handed; but she knew that was exactly what the young woman had feared, to be handled and exposed by men. Kindra thought: *If it could be done before she recovers consciousness, she need not know* . . . But she had promised the girl, and she would keep her promise. The girl did not stir as she stepped out into the hall.

Brydar came halfway up the stairs. "How goes it?"

"Send young Annelys to me," Kindra said. "Tell her to bring linen thread and a needle; and linen for bandages, and hot water and soap." Annelys had courage and strength; what was more, she was sure that if Kindra asked her to keep a secret, Annelys would do so, instead of gossiping about it.

Brydar said, in an undertone that did not carry a yard past

Kindra's ear, "It's a woman – isn't it?"

Kindra demanded, with a frown, "Were you listening?"

"Listening, hell! I've got the brains I was born with, and I was remembering a couple of other little things. Can you think of any other reason a member of my band wouldn't let us get his britches off? Whoever she is, she's got guts enough for two!"

Kindra shook her head in dismay. Then all the girl's suffering was useless, scandal and disgrace there would be in any case. "Brydar, you pledged this would be worth my while. Do you owe me, or not?"

"I owe you," Brydar said.

"Then swear by your sword that you will never open your mouth about this and I am paid. Fair enough?"

Brydar grinned. "I won't cheat you out of your pay for that," he said. "You think I want it to get round these hills that Brydar of Fen Hills can't tell the men from the ladies? Young Marco rode with my band for half a year and proved himself the man. If his foster-sister or kinswoman or cousin or what you will chooses to nurse him herself, and take him home with her afterward, what's it to any of my men? Damned if I want my crew thinking some girl killed Scarface right under my nose!" He put his hand to sword-hilt. "Zandru take this hand with the palsy if I say any word about this. I'll send Annelys to you," he promised and went.

Kindra returned to the girl's side. She was still unconscious; when Annelys came in, Kindra said curtly, "Hold the lamp there; I want to get this stitched before she recovers consciousness. And try not to get squeamish or faint; I want to get it done quick enough so we don't have to hold her down while we do it."

Annelys gulped at the sight of the girl and the gaping wound, which had begun to bleed again. "A woman! Blessed Evanda! Kindra, is she one of your Sisterhood? Did you know?"

"No, to both questions. Here, hold the light–"

"No," Annelys said. "I have done this many times; I have steady hands for this. Once when my brother cut his thigh chopping wood, I sewed it up, and I have helped the midwife, too. You hold the light."

Relieved, Kindra surrendered the needle. Annelys began her work as skillfully as if she were embroidering a cushion; halfway through the business, the girl regained consciousness; she gave a faint cry of fright, but Kindra spoke to her, and she quieted and lay still, her teeth clamped in her lip, clinging to Kindra's hand. Halfway through, she moistened her lip and whispered, "Is she one of you, *mestra*?"

"No. No more than yourself, child. But she is a friend. And she will not gossip about you, I know it," Kindra said confidently.

When Annelys had finished, she fetched a glass of wine for the woman, and held her head while she drank it. Some color came back into the pale cheeks, and she was breathing more easily. Annelys brought one of her own nightgowns and said, "You will be more comfortable in this, I think. I wish we could carry you to my bed, but I don't think you should be moved yet. Kindra, help me to lift her." With a pillow and a couple of clean sheets she set about making the woman comfortable on the straw pallet.

The stranger made a faint sound of protest as they began to undress her, but was too weak to protest effectively. Kindra stared in shock as the undertunic came off. She would never have believed that any woman over fourteen could successfully pose as a man among men; yet this woman had done it, and now she saw how. The revealed form was flat, spare, breastless; the shoulders had the hardened musculature of any swordsman. There was more hair on the arms that most women would have tolerated without removing it somehow, with bleach or wax. Annelys stared in amazement, and the woman, seeing that shocked look, hid her face in the pillow. Kindra said sharply, "There is no need to stare. She is *emmasca*, that is all; haven't you ever seen one before?" The neutering operation was illegal all over Darkover, and dangerous; and in this woman it must have been done before, or shortly after puberty. She was filled with questions, but courtesy forbade any of them.

"But – but–" Annelys whispered. "Was she born so or made so? It is unlawful – who would dare–"

"Made so," the girl said, her face still hidden in the pillow. "Had I been born so, I would have had nothing to fear . . . and I chose this so that I might have nothing more to fear!"

She tightened her mouth as they lifted and turned her; Annelys gasped aloud at the shocking scars, like the marks of whips across the woman's back; but she said nothing, only pulled the merciful concealment of her own nightgown over the frightful revelation of those scars. Gently, she washed the woman's face and hands with soapy water. The ginger-pale hair was dark with sweat, but at the roots Kindra saw something else; the hair was beginning to grow in fire-red there.

Comyn. The telepath caste, red-haired . . . this woman was a noblewoman, born to rule in the Domains of Darkover!

In the name of all the Gods, Kindra wondered, who can she be, what has come to her? How came she here in this disguise, even her hair bleached so none can guess at her lineage? And who has mishandled her so? She must have been beaten like an animal...

And then, shocked, she heard the words forming in her mind, not knowing how.

Scarface, said the voice in her mind. *But now I am avenged. Even if it means my death*...

She was frightened; never had she so clearly perceived; her rudimentary telepath gift had always, before, been a matter of quick intuition, hunch, lucky guess. She whispered aloud, in horror and dismay, "By the Goddess! Child, who are you?"

The pale face contorted in a grimace which Kindra recognized, in dismay, was intended for a smile. "I am – no one," she said. "I had thought myself the daughter of Alaric Lindir. Have you heard the tale?"

Alaric Lindir. The Lindir family were a proud and wealthy family, distantly akin to the Aillard family of the Comyn. Too highly born, in fact, for Kindra to claim acquaintance with any of that kin; they were of the ancient blood of the Hastur-kin.

"Yes, they are a proud people," whispered the woman. "My mother's name was Kyria, and she was a younger sister to Dom Lewis Ardais – not the Ardais Lord, but his younger brother. But still, she was high-born enough that when she proved to be with child by one of the Hastur lords of Thendara, she was hurried away and married in haste to Alaric Lindir. And my father – he that I had always believed my father – he was proud of his red-haired daughter; all during my childhood, I heard how proud he was of me, for I would marry into Comyn, or go to one of the

Towers and become a great and powerful sorceress or Keeper. And then – then came Scarface and his crew, and they sacked the castle, and carried away some of the women, just as an afterthought, and by the time Scarface discovered who he had as his latest captive – well, the damage was done, but still he sent to my father for ransom. And my father, that selfsame Dom Alaric who had not enough proud words for his red-haired beauty who should further his ambition by a proud marriage into the Comyn, my father–" She choked, then spat the words out. "He sent word that if Scarface could guarantee me – untouched – then he would ransom me at a great price; but if not, then he would pay nothing. For if I was – was spoilt, ravaged – then I was no use to him, and Scarface might hang me or give me to one of his men, as he saw fit."

"Holy Bearer of Burdens!" Annelys whispered. "And this man had reared you as his own child?"

"Yes – and I had thought he loved me," the woman said, her face twisting. Kindra closed her eyes in horror, seeing all too clearly the man who had welcomed his wife's bastard – but only while she could further his ambition!

Annelys' eyes were filled with tears. "How dreadful! Oh, how could any man–"

"I have come to believe any man would do so, for Scarface was so angry at my father's refusal that he gave me to one of his men to be a plaything, and you can see how he used me. *That* one I killed while he lay sleeping one night, when at last he had come to believe me beaten into submission – and so made my escape, and back to my mother, and she welcomed me with tears and with pity, but I could see in her mind that her greatest fear, now, was that I should shame her by bearing the child of Scarface's bastard; she feared that my father would say to her, *like mother, like daughter,* and my disgrace would revive the old story of her own. And I could not forgive my mother – that she should continue to love and to live with that man who had rejected me and given me over to such a fate. And so I made my way to a *leronis,* who took pity on me – or perhaps she, too, wanted only to be certain I would not disgrace my Comyn blood by becoming a whore or a bandit's drab – and she made me *emmasca,* as you see. And I took service with Brydar's men, and so I won my revenge—"

Annelys was weeping; but the girl lay with a face like stone. Her very calm was more terrible than hysteria; she had gone beyond tears, into a place where grief and satisfaction were all one, and that one wore the face of death.

Kindra said softly, "You are safe now; none will harm you. But you must not talk any more; you are weary and weakened with loss of blood. Come, drink the rest of this wine and sleep, my girl." She supported the girl's head while she finished the wine, filled with horror. And yet, through the horror, was admiration. Broken, beaten, ravaged, and then rejected, this girl had won free of her captors by killing one of them; and then she had survived the further rejection of her family, to plot her revenge, and to carry it out, as a noble might do.

And the proud Comyn rejected this woman? She has the courage of any two of their menfolk! It is this kind of pride and folly that will one day bring the reign of the Comyn crashing down into ruin! And she shuddered with a strange premonitory fear, seeing with her wakening telepathic gift a flashing picture of flames over the Hellers, strange sky-ships, alien men walking the streets of Thendara clad in black leather. . .

The woman's eyes closed, her hands tightening on Kindra's. "Well, I have had my revenge," she whispered again, "and so I can die. And with my last breath I will bless you, that I die as a woman, and not in this hated disguise, among men. . ."

"But you are not going to die," Kindra said. "You will live, child."

"No." Her face was set stubbornly in lines of refusal, closed and barriered. "What does life hold for a woman friendless and without kin? I could endure to live alone and secret, among men, disguised, while I nursed the thought of my revenge to strengthen me for the — the daily pretense. But I hate men, I loathe the way they speak of women among themselves, I would rather die than go back to Brydar's band, or live further among men."

Annelys said softly, "But now you are revenged, now you can live as a woman again."

Again the nameless woman shook her head. "Live as a woman, subject to men like my father? Go back and beg shelter from my mother, who might give me bread in secret so I would not disgrace them further by dying across her doorstep, and keep me hidden away, to drudge among them hidden, sew or spin, when I have ridden free with a mercenary band? Or shall I live as a lone woman, at the mercy of men? I would rather face the mercy of the blizzard and the banshee!" Her hand closed on Kindra's. "No," she said. "I would rather die."

Kindra drew the girl into her arms, holding her against her breast. "Hush, my poor girl, hush, you are over-wrought, you must not talk like that. When you have slept you will not feel this way," she soothed, but she felt the depth of despair in the woman in her arms, and her rage overflowed.

The laws of her Guild forbade her to speak of the Sisterhood, to tell this girl that she could live free, protected by the Guild Charter, never again to be at the mercy of any man. The laws of the Guild, which she might not break, the oath she must keep. And yet, on a deeper level, was it not breaking the oath to withhold from this woman, who had risked so much and who had appealed to her in the name of her Goddess, the knowledge that might give her the will to live?"

Whatever I do, I am forsworn; either I break my oath by refusing this girl my help, or I break it by speaking when I am forbidden by the law to speak.

The law! The law made by men, which still hemmed her in on every side, though she had cast off the ordinary laws by which men forced women to live! And she was doubly damned if she spoke of the Guild before Annelys, though Annelys had fought at her side. The just law of the Hellers would protect Annelys from this knowledge; it would make trouble for the Sisterhood if Kindra should lure away a daughter of a respectable innkeeper, whose mother needed her, and needed the help her husband would bring to the running of her inn!

Against her breast, the nameless girl had closed her eyes. Kindra caught the faint thread of her thoughts; she knew that the telepath caste could will themselves to die . . . as this girl had willed herself to live, despite everything that had happened, until she had had her cherished revenge.

Let me sleep so . . . and I can believe myself back in my

mother's arms, in the days when I was still her child and this horror had not touched me . . . Let me sleep so and never wake . . .

Already she was drifting away, and for a moment, in despair, Kindra was tempted to let her die. *The law forbids me to speak.* And if she should speak, then Annelys, already struck with hero-worship of Kindra, already rebelling against a woman's lot, having tasted the pride of defending herself, Annelys would follow her, too. Kindra knew it, with a strange, premonitory shiver.

She let the rage in her have its way and overflow. She shook the nameless woman awake, knowing that already she was willing herself to death.

"Listen to me! Listen! You must not die," she said angrily. "Not when you have suffered so much! That is a coward's way, and you have proven again and again that you are no coward!"

"Oh, but I am a coward," the woman said. "I am too much a coward to live in the only way a woman like me can live – through the charity of women such as my mother – or the mercy of men like my father, or like Scarface! I dreamed that when I had my revenge, I could find some other way. But there is no other way."

And Kindra's rage and resolution overflowed. She looked despairing over the nameless woman's head, into Annelys's frightened eyes. She swallowed, knowing the seriousness of the step she was about to take.

"There – there might be another way," she said, still temporizing. "You – I do not even know your name, what is your name?"

"I am nameless," the woman said, her face like stone. "I swore I would never again speak the name given me by the father and the mother who rejected me. If I had lived, I would have taken another name. Call me what pleases you."

And with a great surge of wrath, Kindra made up her mind. She drew the girl against her.

"I will call you Camilla," she said, "for from this day forth, I swear it, I shall be mother and sister to you, as was the blessed Cassilda to Camilla; this I swear. Camilla, you shall not die," she said, pulling the girl upright. Then, with a deep resolute breath, clasping Camilla's hand in one of hers, and stretching the other to Annelys, she began.

"My little sisters, let me tell you of the Sisterhood of Free Women, which men call Free Amazons. Let me tell you of the ways of the Renunciates, the Oath-bound, the *Comhi-Letzii*..."

One of the major characters in this story also appears in Bradley's later Darkover novel, Sharra's Exile, where it is made clear that she is in fact a lesbian.

Do Androids Dream of Electric Love?

Walt Liebscher

Technology surrounds us. Machines are assuming more and more functions in our daily lives. They process our food, manage our money, and provide our entertainment. But there will always be things a machine can't do for us. Or will there?

The psychodroid walked into the room and stopped several feet from its patient.

"I'm here to help you," it said.

"No one can help me," said the patient, turning his face to the sterile, white walls of the hosprison cell.

"Please let me try. For all practical purposes I'm completely human. However, a small part of me is still machine. That part just might understand." The android settled into a chair.

"No matter, understanding. I know they are going to convert me." The human sighed.

"That might depend on me."

"You! You are nothing but another mind-sucking machine. I told my story to one of your brothers. Sisters? Cohorts? What in the hell does one machine call another?" He paused for a moment and added, "No offense meant."

"I know, I can tell when you are lying."

"That sophisticated?"

"State psychiatrist Model II, Mark III. I'm the latest and the best."

The man laughed at the almost haughty statement, then asked, "Can you cry?"

The question seemed to have no effect. "I can feel like crying, but I'm not set up to produce tears. What psychiatrist is?"

"I like you," said the man. "How about a game of chess, or is game-playing confined to the theradroids?"

"Usually, but I'm programmed for all kinds of therapeutic play. Anything that will make you more comfortable, or less tense. Tell you what. Trade you a game of chess for a statement, or story, or whatever you might want to tell me."

"Is your chess-playing infallible?"

"It could be, but it won't. I know your IQ and reasoning quotient. I will make it even by adjusting myself to your level."

"Downward or upward?"

"Don't be facetious," said the android.

The human roared with laughter. When he finished the outburst, the android's usually expressionless face was smiling.

"Don't look so damned smug," said the man. "So I laughed for the first time in weeks. Pleased with yourself?"

"I like laughter. I wish I could do it."

The man thought for a moment, then said, "OK, Hal, sing 'Daisy, Daisy.'"

The android shook for a moment, and grinned broadly. "That was quite pleasant."

The man was pleased. "I thought I could do it."

"Now it's my turn to tell you not to be so damned smug. So you made me laugh. Big deal."

"We're even," said the man. "Let's forget the chess game. It was only a ploy anyway. What can I tell you?"

"Everything."

"Well, to begin, I suppose you know why I'm here?"

"Because you ostensibly committed an act that even in this enlightened age was considered, shall we say, way out."

"That's enough for a starter." And the man told his story.

When he finished, the android stared at the man for a long,

long while. "That's quite a story, and if you don't mind my saying so, I found it exceedingly sexy."

"Thanks. But the pertinent point is do you believe me?"

"I told you I could tell when you were lying. However, under the circumstances it really doesn't, or won't, matter. You will be exonerated."

"Simple as that, is it?"

"Very simple. Ostensibly I'm a machine with no feelings. I will have no difficulty convincing them of your innocence. The fact that I find you provocatively desirable won't matter."

With that the android rose and started to leave the room. "I'll certainly be seeing you again."

"One more question," said the startled man.

"Yes."

"Are androids equipped—? I mean do you have gender?"

"That's for you to figure out," the android said impishly. Then it turned and sashayed out the door and down the hall.

Lollipop and the Tar Baby

John Varley

In John Varley's "Eight Worlds" stories, intergalactic Invaders have brought a wealth of technological advancement. Body alterations and sex changes are as simple as having a dress made, and cloning techniques have been perfected. This sophisticated technology has opened new frontiers to both outer space and human intimacy.

"Zzzzello. *Zzz.* Hello. Hello." Someone was speaking to Xanthia from the end of a ten-kilometer metal pipe, shouting to be heard across a roomful of gongs and cymbals being knocked over by angry giant bees. She had never heard such interference.

"Hello?" she repeated. "What are you doing on my wavelength?"

"Hello." The interference was still there, but the voice was slightly more distinct. "Wavelength. Searching, searching wavelength . . . get best reception with . . . Hello? Listening?"

"Yes, I'm listening. You're talking over . . . my radio isn't even. . ." She banged the radio panel with her palm in the ancient ritual humans employ when their creations are being balky. "My goddamn *radio* isn't even on. Did you know that?" It was a relief to feel anger boiling up inside her. Anything was preferable to feeling lost and silly.

"Not necessary."

"What do you mean, not – who *are* you?"

"Who. Having . . . *I'm*, pronoun, yes, I'm having difficulty. Bear with. Me? Yes, pronoun. Bear with me. I'm not who. What. *What* am I?"

"All right. *What* are you?"

"Spacetime phenomenon. I'm gravity and causality-sink. Black hole."

Xanthia did not need black holes explained to her. She had spent her entire eighteen years hunting them, along with her clone-sister, Zoetrope. But she was not used to having them talk to her.

"Assuming for the moment that you really are a black hole," she said, beginning to wonder if this might be some elaborate trick played on her by Zoe, "just taking that as a tentative hypothesis – how are you able to talk to me?"

There was a sound like an attitude thruster going off, a rumbling pop. It was repeated.

"I manipulate spacetime framework . . . no, please hold line . . . *the* line. I manipulate the spacetime framework with controlled gravity waves projected in narrow . . . a narrow cone. I direct at the speaker in your radio. You hear. Me."

"What was that again?" It sounded like a lot of crap to her.

"I elaborate. I will elaborate. I cut through space itself, through – hold the line, hold the line, reference." There was a sound like a tape reeling rapidly through playback heads. "This is the BBC," said a voice that was recognizably human, but blurred by static. The tape whirred again. "gust the third, in the year of our Lord nineteen fifty-seven. Today in–" Once again the tape hunted.

"chelson-Morley experiment disproved the existence of the ether, by ingeniously arranging a rotating prism–" Then the metallic voice was back.

"Ether. I cut through space itself, through a – hold the line." This time the process was shorter. She heard a fragment of what sounded like a video adventure serial. "Through a spacewarp made through the ductile etheric continuum–"

"Hold on there. That's not what you said before."

"I was elaborating."

"Go on. Wait, what were you doing? With that tape business?"

The voice paused, and when the answer came the line had cleared up quite a bit. But the voice still didn't sound human. Computer?

"I am not used to speech. No need for it. But I have learned your language by listening to radio transmissions. I speak to you through use of indeterminate statistical concatenations. Gravity waves and probability, which is not the same thing in a causality singularity, enables a nonrational event to take place."

"Zoe, this is really you, isn't it?"

Xanthia was only eighteen Earth-years old, on her first long orbit into the space beyond Pluto, the huge cometary zone where space is truly flat. Her whole life had been devoted to learning how to find and capture black holes, but one didn't come across them very often. Xanthia had been born a year after the beginning of the voyage and had another year to go before the end of it. In her whole life she had seen and talked to only one other human being, and that was Zoe, who was one hundred and thirty-five years old and her identical twin.

Their home was the *Shirley Temple*, a fifteen thousand tonne fusion-drive ship registered out of Lowell, Pluto. Zoe owned *Shirley* free and clear; on her first trip, many years ago, she had found a scale-five hole and had become instantly rich. Most hole hunters were not so lucky.

Zoe was also unusual in that she seemed to thrive on solitude. Most hunters who made a strike settled down to live in comfort, buy a large company or put the money into safe investments and live off the interest. They were unwilling or unable to face another twenty years alone. Zoe had gone out again, and a third time after the second trip had proved fruitless. She had found a hole on her third trip, and was now almost through her fifth.

But for some reason she had never adequately explained to Xanthia, she had wanted a companion this time. And what better company than herself? With the medical facilities aboard *Shirley* she had grown a copy of herself and raised the little girl as her daughter.

Xanthia squirmed around in the control cabin of *The Good Ship Lollipop*, stuck her head through the hatch leading to the aft exercise room, and found nothing. What she had expected, she didn't know. Now she crouched in midair with a screwdriver, attacking the service panels that protected the radio assembly.

"What are you doing by yourself?" the voice asked.

"Why don't *you* tell *me*, Zoe?" she said, lifting the panel off and tossing it angrily to one side. She peered into the gloomy interior, wrinkling her nose at the smell of oil and paraffin. She shone her pencil-beam into the space, flicking it from one component to the next, all as familiar to her as neighborhood corridors would be to a planet-born child. There was nothing out of place, nothing that shouldn't be there. Most of it was sealed into plastic blocks to prevent moisture or dust from getting to critical circuits. There were no signs of tampering.

"I am failing to communicate. I am not your mother, I am a gravity and causality—"

"She's not my mother," Xanthia snapped.

"My records show that she would dispute you."

Xanthia didn't like the way the voice said that. But she was admitting to herself that there was no way Zoe could have set this up. That left her with the alternative: she really was talking to a black hole.

"She's not my mother," Xanthia repeated. "And if you've been listening in, you *know* why I'm out here in a lifeboat. So why do you ask?"

"I wish to help you. I have heard tension building between the two of you these last years. You are growing up."

Xanthia settled back in the control chair. Her head did not feel so good.

Hole hunting was a delicate economic balance, a tightrope walked between the needs of survival and the limitations of mass. The initial investment was tremendous and the return was undependable, so the potential hole hunter had to have a line to a source of speculative credit or be independently wealthy.

No consortium or corporation had been able to turn a profit at the business by going at it in a big way. The government of Pluto maintained a monopoly on the use of one-way robot probes, but they had found over the years that when a probe succeeded in finding a hole, a race usually developed to see who would reach it and claim it first. Ships sent after such holes had a way of disappearing in the resulting fights, far from law and order.

The demand for holes was so great that an economic niche remained which was filled by the solitary prospector, backed by people with tax write-offs to gain. Prospectors had a ninety per cent bankruptcy rate. But as with gold and oil in earlier days, the potential profits were huge, so there was never a lack of speculators.

Hole hunters would depart Pluto and accelerate to the limits of engine power, then coast for ten to fifteen years, keeping an eye on the mass detector. Sometimes they would be half a lightyear from Sol before they had to decelerate and turn around. Less mass equalled more range, so the solitary hunter was the rule.

Teaming of ships had been tried, but teams that discovered a hole seldom came back together. One of them tended to have an accident. Hole hunters were a greedy lot, self-centered and self-sufficient.

Equipment had to be reliable. Replacement parts were costly in terms of mass, so the hole hunter had to make an agonizing choice with each item. Would it be better to leave it behind and chance a possibly fatal failure, or take it along, decreasing the range, and maybe miss the glory hole that is sure to be lurking just one more AU away? Hole hunters learned to be handy at repairing, jury-rigging, and bashing, because in twenty years even fail-safe triplicates can be on their last legs.

Zoe had sweated over her faulty mass detector before she admitted it was beyond her skills. Her primary detector had failed ten years into the voyage, and the second one had begun to act up six years later. She tried to put together one functioning detector with parts cannibalized from both. She nursed it along for a year with the equivalents of bobby pins and bubblegum. It was hopeless.

But *Shirley Temple* was a palace among prospecting ships. Having found two holes in her career, Zoe had her own money. She had stocked spare parts, beefed up the drive, even included that incredible luxury, a lifeboat.

The lifeboat was sheer extravagance, except for one thing. It had a mass detector as part of its astrogational equipment. She had bought it mainly for that reason, since it had only an eighteen-month range and would be useless except at the beginning and end of the trip, when they were close to Pluto. It made extensive use of plug-in components, sealed in plastic to prevent tampering or accidents caused by inexperienced passengers. The mass detector on board did not have the range or accuracy of the one on *Shirley*. It could be removed or replaced, but not recalibrated.

They had begun a series of three-month loops out from the mother ship. Xanthia had flown most of them earlier, when Zoe did not trust her to run *Shirley*. Later they had alternated.

"And that's what I'm doing out here by myself," Xanthia said. "I have to get out beyond ten million kilometers from *Shirley* so its mass doesn't affect the detector. My instrument is calibrated to ignore only the mass of this ship, not *Shirley*. I stay out here for three months, which is a reasonably safe time for the life systems on *Lollipop*, and time to get pretty lonely. Then back for refueling and supplying."

"The *Lollipop*?"

Xanthia blushed. "Well, I named this lifeboat that, after I started spending so much time on it. We have a tape of Shirley Temple in the library, and she sang this song, see—"

"Yes, I've heard it. I've been listening to radio for a very long time. So you no longer believe this is a trick by your mother?"

"She's *not* . . ." Then she realized she had referred to Zoe in the third person again.

"I don't know what to think," she said, miserably. "Why are you doing this?"

"I sense that you are still confused. You'd like some proof that I am what I say I am. Since you'll think of it in a minute, I might as well ask you this question. Why do you suppose I haven't yet registered on your mass detector?"

Xanthia jerked in her seat, then was brought up short by the straps. It was true, there was not the slightest wiggle on the dials of the dectector.

"All right, why haven't you?" She felt a sinking sensation. She was sure the punchline came now, after she'd shot off her mouth about *Lollipop* – her secret from Zoe – and made such a point of the fact that Zoe was not her mother. It was her own private rebellion, one that she had not had the nerve to face Zoe with. Now she's going to reveal herself and tell me how she did it, and I'll feel like a fool, she thought.

"It's simple," the voice said. "You weren't in range of me yet. But now you are. Take a look."

The needles were dancing, giving the reading of a scale-seven hole. A scale seven would mass about a tenth as much as the asteroid Ceres.

"Mommy, what *is* a black hole?"

The little girl was seven years old. One day she would call herself Xanthia, but she had not yet felt the need for a name and her mother had not seen fit to give her one. Zoe reasoned that you needed two of something before you needed names. There was only one other person on *Shirley*. There was no possible confusion. When the girl thought about it at all, she assumed her name must be Hey, or Darling.

She was a small child, as Zoe had been. She was recapitulating the growth Zoe had already been through a hundred years ago. Though she didn't know it, she was pretty: dark eyes with an oriental fold, dark skin, and kinky blond hair. She was a genetic mix of Chinese and Negro, with dabs of other races thrown in for seasoning.

"I've tried to explain that before," Zoe said. "You don't have the math for it yet. I'll get you started on spacetime equations, then in about a year you'll be able to understand."

"But I want to know now." Black holes were a problem for the child. From her earliest memories the two of them had done nothing but hunt them, yet they never found one. She'd been doing a lot of reading – there was little else to do – and was wondering if they might inhabit the same category where she had tentatively placed Santa Claus and leprechauns.

"If I try again, will you go to sleep?"

"I promise."

So Zoe launched into her story about the Big Bang, the time

in the long-ago when little black holes could be formed.

"As far as we can tell, all the little black holes like the ones we hunt were made in that time. Nowadays other holes can be formed by the collapse of very large stars. When the fires burn low and the pressures that are trying to blow the star apart begin to fade, gravity takes over and starts to pull the star in on itself." Zoe waved her hands in the air, forming cups to show bending space, flailing out to indicate pressures of fusion. These explanations were almost as difficult for her as stories of sex had been for earlier generations. The truth was that she was no relativist and didn't really grasp the slightly incredible premises behind black-hole theory. She suspected that no one could really visualize one, and if you can't do that, where are you? But she was practical enough not to worry about it.

"And what's gravity? I forgot." The child was rubbing her eyes to stay awake. She struggled to understand but already knew she would miss the point yet another time.

"Gravity is the thing that holds the universe together. The glue, or the rivets. It pulls everything toward everything else, and it takes energy to fight it and overcome it. It feels like when we boost the ship, remember I pointed that out to you?"

"Like when everything wants to move in the same direction?"

"That's right. So we have to be careful, because we don't think about it much. We have to worry about where things are because when we boost, everything will head for the stern. People on planets have to worry about that all the time. They have to put something strong between themselves and the center of the planet, or they'll go down."

"Down." The girl mused over that word, one that had been giving her trouble as long as she could remember, and thought she might finally have understood it. She had seen pictures of places where down was always the same direction, and they were strange to the eye. They were full of tables to put things on, chairs to sit in, and funny containers with no tops. Five of the six walls of rooms on planets could hardly be used at all. One, the "floor," was called on to take all the use.

"So they use their legs to fight gravity with?" She was yawning now.

"Yes. You've seen pictures of the people with the funny legs. They're not so funny when you're in gravity. Those flat things on the ends are called feet. If they had peds like us, they wouldn't be able to walk so good. They always have to have one foot touching the floor, or they'd fall toward the surface of the planet."

Zoe tightened the strap that held the child to her bunk, and fastened the velcro patch on the blanket to the side of the sheet, tucking her in. Kids needed a warm snug place to sleep. Zoe preferred to float free in her own bedroom, tucked into a fetal position and drifting. "G'night, Mommy."

"Good night. You get some sleep, and don't worry about black holes."

But the child dreamed of them, as she often did. They kept tugging at her, and she would wake breathing hard and convinced that she was going to fall into the wall in front of her.

"You don't mean it? I'm rich!"

Xanthia looked away from the screen. It was no good pointing out that Zoe had always spoken of the trip as a partnership. She owned *Shirley* and *Lollipop*.

"Well, you too, of course. Don't think you won't be getting a real big share of the money. I'm going to set you up so well that you'll be able to buy a ship of your own, and raise little copies of yourself if you want to."

Xanthia was not sure that was her idea of heaven, but said nothing.

"Zoe, there's a problem, and I . . . well, I was—" But she was interrupted again by Zoe, who would not hear Xanthia's comment for another thirty seconds.

"The first data is coming over the telemetry channel right now, and I'm feeding it into the computer. Hold on a second while I turn the ship. I'm going to start decelerating in about one minute, based on these figures. You get the refined data to me as soon as you have it."

There was a brief silence.

"What problem?"

"It's talking to me, Zoe. The hole is talking to me."

This time the silence was longer than the minute it took the radio signal to make the round trip between ships. Xanthia furtively thumbed the contrast knob, turning her sister-mother down until the screen was blank. She could look at the camera and Zoe wouldn't know the difference.

Damn, damn, she thinks I've flipped. But I *had* to tell her.

"I'm not sure what you mean."

"Just what I *said*. I don't understand it, either. But it's been talking to me for the last hour, and it says the *damnedest* things."

There was another silence.

"All right. When you get there, don't do anything, repeat, *anything*, until I arrive. Do you understand?"

"Zoe, I'm not crazy. I'm *not*."

Then why am I crying?

"Of course you're not, baby, there's an explanation for this and I'll find out what it is as soon as I get there. You just hang on. My first rough estimate puts me alongside you about three hours after you're stationary relative to the hole."

Shirley and *Lollipop*, traveling parallel courses, would both be veering from their straight-line trajectories to reach the hole. But Xanthia was closer to it; Zoe would have to move at a more oblique angle and would be using more fuel. Xanthia thought four hours was more like it.

"I'm signing off," Zoe said. "I'll call you back as soon as I'm in the groove."

Xanthia hit the off button on the radio and furiously unbuckled her seatbelt. Damn Zoe, damn her, damn her, *damn her*. Just sit tight, she says. I'll be there to explain the unexplainable. It'll be all right.

She knew she should start her deceleration, but there was something she must do first.

She twisted easily in the air, grabbing at braces with all four hands, and dived through the hatch to the only other living space in *Lollipop:* the exercise area. It was cluttered with equipment that she had neglected to fold into the walls, but she didn't mind; she liked close places. She squirmed through the maze like a fish gliding through coral, until she reached the wall she was looking for. It had been taped over with discarded manual pages, the only paper she could find on *Lollipop*. She started ripping at the paper, wiping tears from her cheeks with one ped as she worked. Beneath the paper was a mirror.

How to test for sanity? Xanthia had not considered the question; the thing to do had simply presented itself and she had done it. Now she confronted the mirror and searched for . . . what? Wild eyes? Froth on the lips?

What she saw was her mother.

Xanthia's life had been a process of growing slowly into the mold Zoe represented. She had known her pug nose would eventually turn down. She had known what baby fat would melt away. Her breasts had grown just into the small cones she knew from her mother's body and no farther.

She hated looking in mirrors.

Xanthia and Zoe were small women. Their most striking feature was the frizzy dandelion of yellow hair, lighter than their bodies. When the time had come for naming, the young clone had almost opted for Dandelion until she came upon the word *xanthic* in a dictionary. The radio call-letters for *Lollipop* happened to be X-A-N, and the word was too good to resist. She knew, too, that Orientals were thought of as having yellow skin, though she could not see why.

Why had she come here, of all places? She strained toward the mirror, fighting her repulsion, searching her face for signs of insanity. The narrow eyes were a little puffy, and as deep and expressionless as ever. She put her hands to the glass, startled in the silence to hear the multiple clicks as the long nails just missed touching the ones on the other side. She was always forgetting to trim them.

Sometimes, in mirrors, she knew she was not seeing herself. She could twitch her mouth, and the image would not move. She could smile, and the image would frown. It had been happening for two years, as her body put the finishing touches on its eighteen-year process of duplicating Zoe. She had not spoken of it, because it scared her.

"And this is where I come to see if I'm sane," she said aloud, noting that the lips in the mirror did not move. "Is she going to start talking to me now?" She waved her arms wildly, and so did Zoe in the mirror. At least it wasn't that bad yet; it was only the details that failed to match: the small movements, and especially the facial expressions. Zoe was inspecting her dispassionately and did not seem to like what she saw. That small curl at the edge of the mouth, the almost brutal narrowing of the eyes. . .

Xanthia clapped her hands over her face, then peeked out through the fingers. Zoe was peeking out, too. Xanthia began rounding up the drifting scraps of paper and walling her twin in again with new bits of tape.

The beast with two backs and legs at each end writhed, came apart, and resolved into Xanthia and Zoe, drifting, breathing hard. They caromed off the walls like monkeys, giving up their energy, gradually getting breath back under control. Golden, wet hair and sweaty skin brushed against each other again and again as they came to rest.

Now the twins floated in the middle of the darkened bedroom. Zoe was already asleep, tumbling slowly with that total looseness possible only in free fall. Her leg rubbed against Xanthia's belly and her relative motion stopped. The leg was moist. The room was close, thick with the smell of passion. The recirculators whined quietly as they labored to clear the air.

Pushing one finger gently against Zoe's ankle, Xanthia turned her until they were face to face. Frizzy blonde hair tickled her nose, and she felt warm breath on her mouth.

Why can't it always be like this?

"You're not my mother," she whispered. Zoe had no reaction to this heresy. "You're *not.*"

Only in the last year had Zoe admitted the relationship was much closer. Xanthia was now fifteen.

And what was different? Something, there had to be something beyond the mere knowledge that they were not mother and child. There was a new quality in their relationship, growing as they came to the end of the voyage. Xanthia would look into those eyes where she had seen love and now see only blankness, coldness.

"Oriental inscrutability?" she asked herself, half-seriously. She knew she was hopelessly unsophisticated. She had spent her life in a society of two. The only other person she knew had her own face. But she had thought she knew Zoe. Now she felt less confident with every glance into Zoe's face and every kilometer passed on the way to Pluto.

Pluto.

Her thoughts turned gratefully away from immediate problems and toward that unimaginable place. She would be there in only four more years. The cultural adjustments she would have to make were staggering. Thinking about that, she felt a sensation in her chest that she guessed was her hert leaping in anticipation. That's what happened to characters in tapes when they got excited, anyway. Their hearts were forever leaping, thudding, aching, or skipping beats.

She pushed away from Zoe and drifted slowly to the viewport. Her old friends were all out there, the only friends she had ever known, the stars. She greeted them all one by one, reciting childhood mnemonic riddles and rhymes like bedtime prayers.

It was a funny thought that the view from her window would terrify many of those strangers she was going to meet on Pluto. She'd read that many tunnel-raised people could not stand open spaces. What it was that scared them, she could not understand. The things that scared her were crowds, gravity, males, and mirrors.

"Oh, damn. Damn! I'm going to be just *hopeless*. Poor little idiot girl from the sticks, visiting the big city." She brooded for a time on all the thousands of things she had never done, from swimming in the gigantic underground disneylands to seducing a boy.

"To *being* a boy." It had been the source of their first big argument. When Xanthia had reached adolescence, the time when children want to begin experimenting, she had learned from Zoe that *Shirley Temple* did not carry the medical equipment for sex changes. She was doomed to spend her critical formative years as a sexual deviate, a unisex.

"It'll stunt me forever," she had protested. She had been reading a lot of pop psychology at the time.

"Nonsense," Zoe had responded, hard-pressed to explain why

she had not stocked a viro-genetic imprinter and the companion Y-alyzer. Which, as Xanthia pointed out, *any* self-respecting home surgery kit should have.

"The human race got along for millions of years without sex changing," Zoe had said. "Even after the Invasion. We were a highly technological race for hundreds of years before changing. Billions of people lived and died in the same sex."

"Yeah, and look what they were like."

Now, for another of what seemed like an endless series of nights, sleep was eluding her. There was the worry of Pluto, and the worry of Zoe and her strange behavior, and no way to explain anything in her small universe which had become unbearably complicated in the last years.

I wonder what it would be like with a man?

Three hours ago Xanthia had brought *Lollipop* to a careful rendezvous with the point in space her instruments indicated contained a black hole. She had long since understood that even if she ever found one she would never see it, but she could not restrain herself from squinting into the starfield for some evidence. It was silly; though the hole massed ten to the fifteenth tonnes (the original estimate had been off one order of magnitude) it was still only a fraction of a millimeter in diameter. She was staying a good safe hundred kilometers from it. Still, you ought to be able to sense something like that, you ought to be able to *feel* it.

It was no use. This hunk of space looked exactly like any other.

"There is a point I would like explained," the hole said. "What will be done with me after you have captured me?"

The question surprised her. She still had not got around to thinking of the voice as anything but some annoying aberration like her face in the mirror. How was she supposed to deal with it? Could she admit to herself that it existed, that it might even have feelings?

"I guess we'll just mark you, in the computer, that is. You're too big for us to haul back to Pluto. So we'll hang around you for a week or so, refining your trajectory until we know precisely where you're going to be, then we'll leave you. We'll make some maneuvers on the way in so no one could retrace our path and find out where you are, because they'll know we found a big one when we get back."

"How will they know that?"

"Because we'll be renting . . . well, *Zoe* will be chartering one of those big monster tugs, and she'll come out here and put a charge on you and tow you . . . say, how do you feel about this?"

"Are you concerned with the answer?"

The more Xanthia thought about it, the less she liked it. If she really was not hallucinating this experience, then she was contemplating the capture and imprisonment of a sentient being. An innocent sentient being who had been wandering around the edge of the system, suddenly to find him or herself. . .

"Do you have a sex?"

"No."

"All right, I guess I've been kind of short with you. It's just because you *did* startle me, and I *didn't* expect it, and it was all a little alarming."

The hole said nothing.

"You're a strange sort of person, or whatever," she said.

Again there was a silence.

"Why don't you tell me more about yourself? What's it like being a black hole, and all that?" She still couldn't fight down the ridiculous feeling those words gave her.

"I live much as you do, from day to day. I travel from star to star, taking about ten million years for the trip. Upon arrival, I plunge through the core of the star. I do this as often as is necessary, then I depart by a slingshot maneuver through the heart of a massive planet. The Tunguska Meteorite, which hit Siberia in 1908, was a black hole gaining momentum on its way to Jupiter, where it could get the added push needed for solar escape velocity."

One thing was bothering Xanthia. "What do you mean, 'as often as is necessary'?"

"Usually five or six thousand passes is sufficient."

"No, no. What I meant is *why* is it necessary? What do you get out of it?"

"Mass," the hole said. "I need to replenish my mass. The

Relativity Laws state that nothing can escape from a black hole, but the Quantum Laws, specifically the Heisenberg Uncertainty Principle, state that below a certain radius the position of a particle cannot be determined. I lose mass constantly through tunneling. It is not all wasted, as I am able to control the direction and form of the esaping mass, and to use the energy that results to perform functions that your present-day physics says are impossible."

"Such as?" Xanthia didn't know why, but she was getting nervous.

"I can exchange inertia for gravity, and create energy in a variety of ways."

"So you can move yourself."

"Slowly."

"And you eat . . ."

"Anything."

Xanthia felt a sudden panic, but she didn't know what was wrong. She glanced down at her instruments and felt her hair prickle from her wrists and ankles to the nape of her neck.

The hole was ten kilometers closer than it had been.

"How could you *do* that to me?" Xanthia raged. "I trusted you, and that's how you repaid me, by trying to sneak up on me and . . . and—"

"It was not intentional. I speak to you by means of controlled gravity waves. To speak to you at all, it is necessary to generate an attractive force between us. You were never in any danger."

"I don't believe that," Xanthia said angrily. "I think you're doubletalking me. I don't think gravity works like that, and I don't think you really tried very hard to tell me how you talk to me, back when we first started." It occurred to her now, also, that the hole was speaking much more fluently than in the beginning. Either it was a very fast learner, or that had been intentional.

The hole paused. "This is true," it said.

She pressed her advantage. "Then why did you do it?"

"It was a reflex, like blinking in a bright light, or drawing one's hand back from a fire. When I sense matter, I am attracted to it."

"The proper cliché would be 'like a moth to a flame.' But you're not a moth, and I'm not a flame. I don't believe you. I think you could have stopped yourself if you wanted to."

Again the hole hesitated. "You are correct."

"So you were trying to . . . ?"

"I was trying to eat you."

"Just like *that*? Eat someone you've been having a conversation with?"

"Matter is matter," the hole said, and Xanthia thought she detected a defensive note in its voice.

"What do you think of what I said we're going to do with you? You were going to tell me, but we got off on that story about where you came from."

"As I understand it, you propose to return for me. I will be towed to near Pluto's orbit, sold, and eventually come to rest in the heart of an orbital power station, where your species will feed matter into my gravity well, extracting power cheaply from the gravitational collapse."

"Yeah, that's pretty much it."

"It sounds ideal. My life is struggle. Failing to find matter to consume would mean loss of mass until I am smaller than an atomic nucleus. The loss rate would increase exponentially, and my universe would disappear. I do not know what would happen beyond that point. I have never wished to find out."

How much could she trust this thing? Could it move very rapidly? She toyed with the idea of backing off still further. The two of them were now motionless relative to each other, but they were both moving slowly away from the location she had given Zoe.

It didn't make sense to think it could move in on her fast. If it could, why hadn't it? Then it could eat her and wait for Zoe to arrive – Zoe, who was helpless to detect the hole with her broken mass detector.

She should relay the new vectors to Zoe. She tried to calculate where her twin would arrive, but was distracted by the hole speaking.

"I would like to speak to you now of what I initially contacted you for. Listening to Pluto radio, I have become aware of certain facts that you should know, if, as I suspect, you are not already aware of them. Do you know of Clone Control Regulations?"

"No, what are they?" Again, she was afraid without knowing why.

The genetic statutes, according to the hole, were the soul of simplicity. For three hundred years, people had been living just about forever. It had become necessary to limit the population. Even if everyone had only one child – the Birthright – population would still grow. For a while, clones had been a loophole. No more. Now, only one person had the right to any one set of genes. If two possessed them, one was excess, and was summarily executed.

"Zoe has prior property rights to her genetic code," the hole concluded. "This is backed up by a long series of court decisions."

"So I'm–"

"Excess."

Zoe met her at the airlock as Xanthia completed the docking maneuver. She was smiling, and Xanthia felt the way she always did when Zoe smiled these days: like a puppy being scratched behind the ears. They kissed, then Zoe held her at arm's length.

"Let me look at you. Can it only be three months? You've *grown*, my baby."

Xanthia blushed. "I'm not a baby anymore, Mother." But she was happy. Very happy.

"No, I should say not." She touched one of Xanthia's breasts, then turned her around slowly. "I should say not. Putting on a little weight in the hips, aren't we?"

"And the bosom. One inch while I was gone. I'm almost there." And it was true. At sixteen, the young clone was almost a woman.

"Almost there," Zoe repeated, and glanced away from her twin. But she hugged her again, and they kissed, and began to laugh as the tension was released.

They made love, not once and then to bed, but many times, feasting on each other. One of them remarked – Xanthia could not remember who because it seemed so accurate that either of them might have said it – that the only good thing about these three-month separations was the homecoming.

"You did very well," Zoe said, floating in the darkness and sweet exhausted atmosphere of their bedroom many hours later. "You handled the lifeboat like it was part of your body. I watched the docking. I *wanted* to see you make a mistake, I think, so I'd know I still have something on you." Her teeth showed in the starlight, rows of lights below the sparkles of her eyes and the great dim blossom of her hair.

"Ah, it wasn't that hard," Xanthia said, delighted, knowing full well that it *was* that hard.

"Well, I'm going to let you handle it again the next swing. From now on, you can think of the lifeboat as *your* ship. You're the skipper."

It didn't seem like the time to tell her that she already thought of it that way. Nor that she had christened the ship.

Zoe laughed quietly. Xanthia looked at her.

"I remember the day I first boarded my own ship," she said. "It was a big day for me. My own ship."

"This is the way to live," Xanthia agreed. "Who needs all those people? Just the two of us. And they say hole hunters are crazy. I . . . wanted to . . ." The words stuck in her throat, but Xanthia knew this was the time to get them out, if there ever would be a time. "I don't want to stay too long at Pluto, Mother. I'd like to get right back out here with you." There, she'd said it.

Zoe said nothing for a long time.

"We can talk about that later."

"I love you, Mother." Xanthia said, a little too loudly.

"I love you, too, baby," Zoe mumbled. "Let's get some sleep, okay?"

She tried to sleep, but it wouldn't happen. What was *wrong*?

Leaving the darkened room behind her, she drifted through the ship, looking for something she had lost, or was losing, she wasn't sure which. What had happened, after all? Certainly nothing she could put her finger on. She loved her mother, but all she knew was that she was choking on tears.

In the water closet, wrapped in the shower bag with warm water misting around her, she glanced in the mirror.

*

"Why? Why would she do a thing like that?"

"Loneliness. And insanity. They appear to go together. This is her solution. You are not the first clone she has made."

She had thought herself beyond shock, but the clarity that simple declarative sentence brought to her mind was explosive. Zoe had always needed the companionship Xanthia provided. She needed a child for diversion in the long, dragging years of a voyage; she needed someone to talk to. *Why couldn't she have brought a dog?* She saw herself now as a shipboard pet, and felt sick. The local leash laws would necessitate the destruction of the animal before landing. Regrettable, but there it was. Zoe had spent the last year working up the courage to do it.

How many little Xanthias? They might even have chosen that very name; they would have been that much like her. Three, four? She wept for her forgotten sisters. Unless . . .

"How do I know you're telling me the truth about this? How could she have kept it from me? I've seen tapes of Pluto. I never saw any mention of this."

"She edited those before you were born. She has been careful. Consider her position: there can be only one of you, but the law does not say which it has to be. With her death, you become legal. If you had known that, what would life have been like in *Shirley Temple*?"

"I don't believe you. You've got something in mind, I'm sure of it."

"Ask her when she gets here. But be careful. Think it out, all the way through."

She had thought it out. She had ignored the last three calls from Zoe while she thought. All the options must be considered, all the possibilities planned for. It was an impossible task; she knew she was far too emotional to think clearly, and there wasn't time to get herself under control.

But she had done what she could. Now *The Good Ship Lollipop*, outwardly unchanged, was a ship of war.

Zoe came backing in, riding the fusion torch and headed for a point dead in space relative to Xanthia. The fusion drive was too dangerous for *Shirley* to complete the rendezvous; the rest of the maneuver would be up to *Lollipop.*

Xanthia watched through the telescope as the drive went off. She could see *Shirley* clearly on her screen, though the ship was fifty kilometers away.

Her screen lit up again, and there was Zoe. Xanthia turned her own camera on.

"There you are," Zoe said. "Why wouldn't you talk to me?"

"I didn't think the time was ripe."

"Would you like to tell me how come this nonsense about talking black holes? What's gotten into you?"

"Never mind about that. There never was a hole, anyway. I just needed to talk to you about something you forgot to erase from the tape library in the *Lol* . . . in the lifeboat. You were pretty thorough with the tapes in *Shirley,* but you forgot to take the same care here. I guess you didn't think I'd ever be using it. Tell me, what are Clone Control Regulations?"

The face on the screen was immobile. Or was it a mirror, and was she smiling? Was it herself, or Zoe she watched? Frantically, Xanthia thumbed a switch to put her telescope image on the screen, wiping out the face. Would Zoe try to talk her way out of it? If she did, Xanthia was determined to do nothing at all. There was no way she could check out any lie Zoe might tell her, nothing she could confront Zoe with except a fantastic story from a talking black hole.

Please say something. Take the responsibility out of my hands. She was willing to die, tricked by Zoe's fast talk, rather than accept the hole's word against Zoe's.

But Zoe was acting, not talking, and the response was exactly what the hole had predicted. The attitude control jets were firing, *Shirley Temple* was pitching and yawing slowly, the nozzles at the stern hunting for a speck in the telescope screen. When the engines were aimed, they would surely be fired, and Xanthia and the whole ship would be vaporized.

But she was ready. Her hands had been poised over the thrust controls. *Lollipop* had a respectable acceleration, and every gee of it slammed her into the couch as she scooted away from the danger spot.

Shirley's fusion engines fired, and began a deadly hunt.

Xanthia could see the thin, incredibly hot stream playing around her as Zoe made finer adjustments in her orientation. She could only evade it for a short time, but that was all she needed.

Then the light went out. She saw her screen flare up as the telescope circuit became overloaded with an intense burst of energy. And it was over. Her radar screen showed nothing at all.

"As I predicted," the hole said.

"Why don't you shut up?" Xanthia sat very still, and trembled.

"I shall, very soon. I did not expect to be thanked. But what you did, you did for yourself."

"And you, too, you . . . you *ghoul!* Damn you, damn you to hell." She was shouting through her tears. "Don't think you've fooled me, not completely, anyway. I know what you did, and I know how you did it."

"Do you?" The voice was unutterably cool and distant. She could see that now the hole was out of danger, it was rapidly losing interest in her.

"Yes, I do. Don't tell me it was coincidence that when you changed direction it was just enough to be near Zoe when she got here. You had this planned from the start."

"From much further back than you know," the hole said. "I tried to get you both, but it was impossible. The best I could do was take advantage of the situation as it was."

"Shut up, shut up."

The hole's voice was changing from the hollow, neutral tones to something that might have issued from a tank of liquid helium. She would never have mistaken it for human.

"What I did, I did for my own benefit. But I saved your life. She was going to try to kill you. I maneuvered her into such a position that, when she tried to turn her fusion drive on you, she was heading into a black hole she was powerless to detect."

"You *used* me."

"You used me. You were going to imprison me in a power station."

"But you said you wouldn't *mind!* You said it would be the perfect place."

"Do you believe that eating is all there is to life? There is more to do in the wide universe than you can even suspect. I am slow. It is easy to catch a hole if your mass detector is functioning; Zoe did it three times. But I am beyond your reach now."

"What do you mean? What are you going to do? What am *I* going to do?" That question hurt so much that Xanthia almost didn't hear the hole's reply.

"I am on my way out. I converted *Shirley* into energy; I absorbed very little mass from her. I beamed the energy very tightly, and am now on my way out of your system. You will not see me again. You have two options. You can go back to Pluto and tell everyone what happened out here. It would be necessary for scientists to rewrite natural laws if they believed you. It has been done before, but usually with more persuasive evidence. There will be questions asked concerning the fact that no black hole has ever evaded capture, spoken, or changed velocity in the past. You can explain that when a hole has a chance to defend itself, the hole hunter does not survive to tell the story."

"I will. I *will* tell them what happened!" Xanthia was eaten by a horrible doubt. Was it possible there had been a solution to her problem that did not involve Zoe's death? Just how badly had the hole tricked her?

"There is a second possibility," the hole went on, relentlessly. "Just what *are* you doing out here in a lifeboat?"

"What am I . . . I told you, we had . . ." Xanthia stopped. She felt herself choking.

"It would be easy to see you as crazy. You discovered something in *Lollipop's* library that led you to know you must kill Zoe. This knowledge was too much for you. In defense, you invented me to trick you into doing what you had to do. Look in the mirror and tell me if you think your story will be believed. Look closely, and be honest with yourself."

She heard the voice laugh for the first time, from down in the bottom of its hole, like a voice from a well. It was an extremely unpleasant sound.

Maybe Zoe had died a month ago, strangled or poisoned or slashed with a knife. Xanthia had been sitting in her lifeboat, catatonic, all that time, and had constructed this episode to justify the murder. It *had* been self-defense, which was certainly a good excuse, and a very convenient one.

But she knew. She was sure, as sure as she had ever been of anything, that the hole was out there, that everything had happened as she had seen it happen. She saw the flash again in her mind, the awful flash that had turned Zoe into radiation. But she also knew that the other explanation would haunt her for the rest of her life.

"I advise you to forget it. Go to Pluto, tell everyone that your ship blew up and you escaped and you are Zoe. Take her place in the world, and never, *never* speak of talking black holes."

The voice faded from her radio. It did not speak again.

After days of numb despair and more tears and recriminations than she cared to remember, Xanthia did as the hole had predicted. But life on Pluto did not agree with her. There were too many people, and none of them looked very much like her. She stayed long enough to withdraw Zoe's money from the bank and buy a ship, which she named *Shirley Temple*. It was massive, with power to blast to the stars if necessary. She had left something out there, and she meant to search for it until she found it again.

The Mystery of the Young Gentleman
Joanna Russ

Many women live their whole lives without being able to reveal who they really are. The Woman in Disguise is not a new theme for Joanna Russ; frequently she demonstrates the advantages of at least being aware of one's own play-acting. But she also demonstrates that as long as disguises are necessary for women's survival, no woman will be truly free, and no man will ever know much more about women than the hapless, pompous little doctor of this tale.

> No sooner had Eliza entered her Dungeon than the first thought which occurred to her, was how to get out of it again.
>
> She went to the Door; but it was locked. She looked at the Window; but it was barred with iron; disappointed in both her expectations, she despaired of effecting her Escape, when she fortunately perceived in the Corner of her Cell, a small saw and a ladder of ropes . . .
>
> –*Henry and Eliza*, Jane Austen

June 6, 1885 – embarking on the *S.S. President Hayes*, London to New York, I have been reading Charcot and chuckling – the things these people manage to invent when they try to explain one another! – but know you will want all the physical science and economic theory you can get and so have sent ahead the proceedings of the Royal Society, the *Astronomical Journal*, recent issues of *The Lancet*, etc. and a very interesting new volume called *Capital*, which I think you will find useful. Maria-Dolores has submitted with decent civility to the necessity of skirts, petticoats, and boots, and luckily for me has discovered in herself a positive liking for bonnets; otherwise only her incapacity for proper English prevents her from the worst excesses of which she's capable. Having a fifteen-year-old from the slums of Barcelona registered as one's daughter is a tricky way to make the passage, especially since I have also my living to earn, as usual. I will continue to write to you in my spare time during the crossing; if this is mailed in New York, it will reach Denver before us. In any event the scribbling can do no harm – I will keep the stuff locked up and can use the practice in this odd skill, though it is no substitute for the real thing, as you and I (in my misery!) both know. It helps keep one's mind off the ship: one huge din only beginning to become separated from the infinitely more vast roar of London itself, which has got almost beyond bearing the last few weeks. I have bought a great many dime novels on which Maria-Dolores can practice her English; if these fail, I will concentrate on her manners, which are abominable. (The last few weeks have been given over entirely to lessons in Eating: Not Reaching, Not Using One's Fingers, Not Swearing, and so on.)

Clatter clatter bang-bang! (Maria Dolores coming down the companionway. Next will be Walking.)

"*Mamacita!*" (Loudly present in her cabin, which adjoins mine.)

I correct her automatically. "*Papá.*"

She turns red. "*Papá.*" Then, in Spanish, coming in to where I am sitting, writing: "I hate these shoes. I cannot remove them."

I reach into the tiny desk, withdraw the button hook, and show it to her, out of her reach. She says, "But they pain me, *Papá.*" She then instructs her boots, in Spanish, to fuck themselves, whereupon I lock the button hook up again. She is a good little soul and clings to me, half-erotically, pouting: "Papa, may I have dinner with you and the Captain tonight?" I slap her hand away; she is not to steal the key. I say, "You have twelve years,

Maria-Dolores. Behave so."

"*Tu madre!*" says she. I am trying not to feel those wild bare feet shut up in a London bootmaker's fantasy for little girls. I say in English, "Maria-Dolores, a gentleman cannot travel with a young woman of fifteen, however short and small. Nor can he eat with her until she learns how to behave. Now lie down and read your books. The feet will heal."

"Next time I will be your son," says Maria-Dolores, limping unnecessarily into her cabin. But I see her see *Miner Ned, Stories of the West*, and the others; there is the thrill, the rush, the heart-stopping joy. She thinks: *these* books! and throws herself down on the bed without a pain; I get up and go in to where I have a view of her white-kid calves and her child's dress.

I say, "Maria-Dolores, I am your father and you have forgotten to thank me."

She turns around, baffled. We're alone.

I say, "If you always behave in private as you must in public, then you will never forget the proper behavior in public."

I have put some force into this and she gets up off the bed, her feelings hurt. You understand, much of this is still mysterious to her. She curtseys, as I taught her. *"Gracias, papá."*

"In English, now," I say.

"Thank you, papa, for the books. I am sure to be pleased with them."

"Good," I say; "Much better. Now read," and instantly she is worlds away, her long black hair hanging over the edge of the bed. What they would make of us at the Salpêtrière! – but luckily Europe is now far enough away to be out of the range of my worry. England also. There is no extraordinary intelligence on board among the first-class passengers, although an elderly physician down the corridor has been observing the two of us from the first hour of boarding, with an "acute," thoroughly amateurish attention I find both exasperating and excruciatingly funny. I will have to keep an eye on him nonetheless; as they say in the mountains, even a goose can walk from Leadville to Kansas, given enough time. (There are some remarkable minds in steerage, but they are not preoccupied with us.) Joe Smith of Colorado then dresses for dinner: a diamond ring flat-cut, gold nuggets fastening the shirt-front, a gold watch, solid gold tobacco-case, the pearl-handled derringer, hair brushed back from a central parting with the mahogany-backed brushes Maria-Dolores took such a fancy to in the shop window in the Rue de Rivoli two weeks ago. Coming out into the corridor I have the very great pleasure of meeting the doctor's displeasure, so I stop, causing him to stop, roll my own, and light up. Instantly the dubious Italian with the little mistress becomes a young Western gentleman: well-off, tall, lean, still deeply sun-burnt. One must be careful, speaking: it's too easy to answer questions that haven't been asked. I say only, "Good evening, Doctor."

"How—"

I smile. "I overheard you speaking to another passenger. Not voluntary on my part, I assure you. And if I may take the liberty of answering the inevitable question, the accent is what you fellows call 'mid-Atlantic.' I was educated at __________."

His university, his college. We talk about that. He's looking for flaws but of course finds none. He bumbles a bit (rather obviously) about "the young lady" but when I swear and say she's an awful nuisance, makes me feel desperately awkward, needs a woman's care, unexpected wardship, aunt in Denver, second cousin fiancée, so on, it's all right. There is, in all this, a strong pull towards me and I wonder for a moment if there's going to be real trouble, but it's only usual confusion and mess. We are chatting. I think I have located the poker game. The doctor asks me to dine with him and I assent, would look odd not to. He takes a deep breath and pushes out his chest, saying authoritatively, "It will be a mild crossing." This is to impress me. At table are two married women, temporarily husbandless, whom I try to stay away from, an old man absorbed in his debts, and the ruin of his business, and a mother-daughter pair of that helpless-hopeless kind in which enforced misery breeds enforced hatred, all this made by the locking together, the real need of one for the other. There is an enormous amount of plumes, flounces, pillowings, corsets, tight boots. (Maria-Dolores, stealing rabbits, was luckier.) There are cut flowers at the center of the table (the first night), too much food, heavy monogrammed glasses, heavy monogrammed cutlery and china and a vague generalized appreciation of all this that is not pleasure but a kind of abstract sense of gratification. (Look up "wealth.") Everything coarsened and simplified for reasons of commerciality and the possibility of rough weather. No one notices the waiter (who is a union organizer). I make my escape after dinner but only to an interlude with the younger of the married women. We are all charming – you, I, Maria-Dolores – we have to be, we can't turn off; and in this situation and class there are approaches to which a gentleman must give in, despite the rules. ("What a beautiful night, Mr. Smith. Do you like stars?") She can't go anywhere in the evening without a companion. So we walk doggedly round and round the deck, Mrs. ________ making most of the conversation – "So you own a silver mine in Leadville, Mr. Smith?" "My father does, ma'am" – until that topic gives out. Maria-Dolores is a bad excuse for leaving, as Mrs. ________ will "take an interest" in and want to "form" her. That dull, perpetual, coerced lack she has been taught to call "love," which a gentleman's arm, a gentleman's face, a gentleman's conversation, so wonderfully soothes. It's a deadly business. I get away, finally, to the poker game in the gentlemen's lounge – that is, one of the gentlemen's lounges – where the problem is not to win but to keep from winning too much. I always lose, as a matter of rule, on the first night.

"A new man! What's your name?"

"Joseph Smith, Colorado."

Unoriginal jokes about Mormons, lots of nervous laughter, bragging, forceful shaking of hands. Then they talk about women. None over thirty but one older professional I'm going to have to watch out for. I allow a bit of Leadville in my speech, what they expect: Not playing with you folks, of course, just thought I'd watch.

The serious game. The fear of death, of failure. Risking fate, surviving it. One leaves, secretly in tears, saying casually "I'm cleaned out." I balance what I see, what I "should" see, what they think I see. It's a hot little room. I lose a little, win a little more, then lose again, then drop pretty catastrophically, more than three hundred pounds.

"You'll want to get that back," says the professional, who's clever enough to know I'm no novice. He's also been marking the deck, which makes things easier. I lose again – some – and he lets me win back about a third. Winks: "Quit while you're ahead." I go on and lose again. Which is time to leave, mentioning the rich dad and moral objections.

"I thought you fellows were born with a deck of cards in your hands!"

A promise – (embarrassed).

"What's wrong with a bit of fun?" (pretending to be aggrieved).

He says, confident, "See you tomorrow night."

So that's done. Maria-Dolores is asleep. Old Doctor Bumble passes me in the hall, beams and bows, delighted, unaware that his young friend is going to the dogs. I unlock the door to my state-room, waking Maria-Dolores, who calls, "Come talk to me." This means exactly what it says: I'm lonely, I'm curious, I like you, I want a little chat. She is, like most of us at that age, surprisingly transparent.

She says honestly, "Papá, what makes the ship go?"

"Engines," I say. "Great big ones. Down there." (Pointing to the floor.) "They burn coal."

"At night, too?" Amusing to see her trying to imagine this phenomenon; she knows only a coal stove.

"Men shovel coal into them," I say. "All night long."

She wakes up. "*Now?*"

"Yes, right now."

A vivid picture in her mind of a vast cave with doors about it and flame within. "It must be exciting."

"Not to them," I say.

She is surprised.

"Because," I say, to answer her, "It's very hot. And very, very hard. And they want badly to sleep."

She tries to think why they do it, and then solves the puzzle: "If they make the ship go, they decide where it goes."

"No," I say. "Someone else. Not the Captain, the Board of Directors – No not wood. Men."

She thinks sleepily, embroidering the furnace room (which I can see, hear, smell, touch from a dozen vantages) into Aladdin's cave, "They are paid *very* well. They are making their fortunes."

"Later," I say. She can join the argument about how much to

help the others after we get home. The answer is in the books she has been reading, but books don't count; they aren't real. Only Barcelona has poor people. And even Barcelona has been kind to orphaned Maria-Dolores. Not like scowling, skinny Maria-Elena, who worked sixteen hours a day making matches and lost the feeling in her hands, or pretty, frightened Maria-Theresa, sold and pregnant at thirteen, or ugly, hungry, limping Maria-Mercedes with the sores on her face, whose mamà beat her. Half the little girls in the Spanish slums are named after the Virgin; their twinkling, bare legs run like mice in Maria-Dolores's dreams. Asleep now. Something has always protected this mouse, warned her, led her, warmed her. Something has kept her safe and happy, even at fifteen.

Like you. Like me.

June 7 – An arch note from Mrs. __________, so I become ill, stay in the cabin in my dressing gown all day, and drill Maria-Dolores in manners. She gets madder and madder and towards evening begins to pester me:

"Next time I travel as your son!"

Once we get into the mountains, I tell her, she can travel as anything she likes. Even a hoppy-toad.

"I want *that*" – picture in a book of a young lady in full sail. Can she dress like that when we get home? Part of this is merely for nuisance's sake, but she is really fed up with being a twelve-year-old. I say yes, we'll send to Denver for it.

"Well, can I dress like a man?"

"Like this?" (pointing to myself) "Of course."

She says, being a real pest, "I bet there are no women in the mountains."

"That's right," I tell her. (She's also in real confusion.)

"But *me!*" she says.

"When you get there, there will still be no women."

"But you – Is it all *men?*"

"There are no men. Maria-Dolores, we've been over and over this."

She gives up, exasperated. Her head, like all the others', is full of *los hombres y las mujeres* as if it were a fact of nature: ladies with behinds inflated as if by bicycle pumps, gentlemen with handlebar mustachios who kiss the ladies' hands. If I say *las hombres y los mujeres*, as I once did and am tempted to do again, she will kick me.

"I'm bored!" She wanders to the porthole, looks out, reflecting that there's nothing interesting out there, and a whole world of people on the ship, but I am keeping her away from them.

There's something more. I have, I think, been lying to myself, as is so easy out here; she's too old; we have been together too long. I have been as cold to her as I dared, fearing this. I turn my back, put on my dinner jacket, tie my tie; she raises her eyes. An electric shock, an unbearable temptation. As when things rush together in a new form in someone's mind. Oh my dear, what will I do? What will I say? This is a real human being; this is one of ours.

She says, "You know everything. So why even ask? I've done it before. With girls too; girls do it with girls and boys with boys; everybody knows that."

She gets out softly, after a moment's struggle, "I like you."

I say, without expression, "Close the outer door." When she has: "Sit down. No, no on the other side of the room." Then:

"You are thinking how nice it would be, aren't you? You are thinking of it right now."

The resulting wave almost knocks me over. I continue as if it had not happened: "No. It would not be nice at all.

"Look, Maria-Dolores, we have talked about this before, about the difference and how, when you are a baby, you shut it off. Well, it isn't something you can choose to turn on or off, as you close or open your eyes. One loses one's sense of oneself at first; it is like being hammered to death. With so much clamor all around you, either you will shut again so fast that nothing will ever get you open or you will go crazy, like a mouse shut up in clockwork. And I must get doctors to put you to sleep with morphia for weeks to come — and this is bad for your health and very expensive and worst of all it will bring a great deal of suspicion down on me, which neither of us can afford. Do you want them to take you away from me and shut you up somewhere forever?" (Or all the other things!)

Well, she has been following this, but she has also been taking considerable pleasure in watching my lips move; I have to hold on rather hard to the writing desk. She says, "But why—" and then stops, understanding finally that I know. "Because," I say, "this is how it happens when one is young," and knowing so much more than she, sit down, knees giving away, with my face in my hands. The two mirrors so placed that they reflect each other to infinity, as you see in a barbershop, each knowing what the other feels. That remembered fusion which opens everything, even minds. So lost that I literally do not know she has crossed the little cabin until I hear her breathing. I smelled her hair and body before I saw her. She says, "Can we do it later?" and I nod. Somewhere in Kansas, miles from anyone! She says, very moved, "Oh, give me one kiss to show you don't hate me!" and I manage to say, "I don't hate you, Maria-Dolores, leave me alone, please," but cannot any longer trust myself with the act of speaking. She's planning to kiss me, little liar, and after that it will be really impossible, a wonderful impossible whirling descent from which I really cannot move. But manage to get up somehow and out into the corridor without touching her – fatal! – and the door shut and locked, which helps, as you would expect, not at all. So I did deliberately what I last did involuntarily fifteen years ago, confronted with my first town (three hundred souls) and no matter that old Bumble is ambling around the bend of the corridor: first things first.

Shut it all out.

The smell of orange blossoms, which becomes pungent and choking: sal ammoniac. Bumble withdraws, turning his back on me. I'm lying on something, not in my own cabin, and for a blurred moment can't see anything of him but his broad back. As helpless as any of them. He says, "I thought it best not to alarm the young lady."

I find myself coughing uncontrollably, sitting up on the edge of his berth, bed, what-do-you-call-it. I'm awake. He really is extraordinarily stupid. He says, "You seem to have cracked a rib." Having had, you understand, perhaps ninety seconds to get his first really good look at me, he has put two and two together and got five: *Uranian. Invert. Onanist.* (These are words they make up; you will find them in medical texts.) It may surprise you that this kind of thing does not happen often, but the division is so strong, so elaborate, so absolute, so much trained into them as habit, that within reasonable limits they see, generally, more or less what they expect to see, especially if one wears the mask of the proper behavior. His mistake has been made before, but those who make it usually do not speak out, either from the concern of fellowship or simply lack of interest. This one is that fatal combination: kindness and curiosity. For under the surface indignation he is pitying and embarrassed and would really like to say, Look here, dear fellow, let's forget all this, pretend it never happened, eh? and we'll both be so much happier. But he is fascinated too. He is even, unknown to himself, attracted. He has, you see, the genuine fixing on the female body, but there is also its dirtiness, its repulsiveness, its profound fearfulness, which as a doctor, he must both acknowledge and feel more strongly (and believes, because he is a doctor, that his confusions have the status of absolute truth), and then, worst of all, there is the terrible dullness of the business, which comes with the half-disillusionment of old age: women, the silliness of women, the perpetual disappointments of the act (no wonder!), the uncleanliness of the whole business, and finally the sullying and base suspicion that it's merely "propagation," one of the nasty cheats of an impersonal and soulless Nature, unless one is fool enough to sentimentalize it. (He sums all this up by saying from time to time, "I'm too old for all that; let the young men make fools of themselves!")

He harrumphs. Bumbles. Fudges. Peeks at me. Out of the welter comes:

"You – you ought to have that rib looked at, you know." (Thinks of himself investigating under the taping, greedy old pussycat!)

I say, "Thank you, I have. Immobility's not the thing, I'm told."

"Accident?"

"No, fight." He thinks he knows about what. He tiptoes about me mentally with all the elaborate skill of old Rutherford B. Hayes trying to catch a squirrel, fumbling with the tools in his medical bag as if he had something else to put back there, coughing, arranging and rearranging his stethoscope – and there is such a resemblance between the two that I cannot forbear imagining the doctor caught under the corner of our front porch at home and having to be pulled out yowling, his tail lashing, his fur erect, his sense of autonomy irretrievably shattered and pieces of dust and cobweb stuck on his elderly ginger whiskers (which they both have). He says:

"You ought to . . . lead a more active life. Open-air exercise, you know. Build yourself up."

I say, "I live on a ranch, Doctor."

He bursts out, "My dear fellow, you mustn't – it is quite obvious – you owe it to your father – and that poor child–"

I say dryly, "She is a good deal safer with me than with you, surely." This is calculated to enrage him. I admit the logic of the matter is hard to follow, but at its base you will find a remarkable confusion of ideas: heredity, biological causation, illness, choice, moral contamination, and some five or six other notions that have not quite got settled. There is also the backhanded compliment to the virility of a man of sixty. Why does old Rutherford B. Hayes, an hour after his ignominious handling by one of us, dimly convince himself that he has been rescued by an adorer and leap to one's bosom in gratitude, demanding liver? The cases are not unlike. Bumble is not only stupid, as I have said, but his stupidity is actually the principal cause of his kindliness. I don't mean this as cruelly as it sounds; let's say only that he has a genuine innocence, something fresh that his "ideas" don't affect, still less his "decency," which is (as is usual with them) the worst thing about him. My remark takes a moment to activate the mechanism; then drawing himself up – for I ought to have the "decency" to be disgusted at myself, that's the worst of it – he levels the most damning accusation he can, poor old soul: "Damn it, sir, you know what you are!"

Let him stew a bit. I re-stud my shirt, slowly, and fasten the cuffs, feel for my tie. Adjust the artfully tailored dinner jacket. I have come out without the derringer, or Bumble would remember it and he doesn't. What would he have made of it? He is beginning to be ashamed of himself, so now is the time to speak. I say steadily:

"Doctor, I am what my nature has made me. It was not my choice and I deserve neither blame nor credit in the business. I have done nothing in the whole of my life of which I need be ashamed, and I hope you will pardon me if I observe that, in my case, that has been of necessity a much lonelier and more bitter business than it has in yours." Here I take from his bedside stand the elaborately gold-framed photograph of his dead wife, saying, "I assume, sir, that this lady is some near kin to you?"

He nods, already remorseful. Says gruffly, "My wife."

I put it down. "Children?"

He nods. "Grown now, of course." Better to leave comparison unspoken. I merely say, "You may be sure, sir, that my little Spanish cousin is as morally safe with me as if she were in church. A married sister of mine in Denver wishes to give her a home. That is where I am taking her."

Not too thick. Leave quickly. We talk a bit more, about my sister, one Mrs. Butte, and the nieces and nephews – his preconceived notions of what the family is like are a trouble to me as they're rather strong and I have to work some not to match him too closely – and by then he is so pleased with himself for having been so very generous and good – and so lucky, too, in comparison with you-know-who – that he offers me a drink. I say:

"No, sir. I am no abstainer; I take wine with my dinner as you have seen, but otherwise I do not indulge."

He pooh-poohs.

I shake my head. "Not hard liquor, Doctor. Our frontier offers too many bad examples. In the mining camps I have seen so many ruined that way – good, normal young fellows whom I envied. Those tragedies have helped to keep me straight. What is only a temptation to you is poison to me, sir."

He says, solicitous, "But the pain of that rib–"

I shake my head.

He's very moved.

So am I.

Then off to the poker game, with a poker face, to win back two hundred and fifty pounds. This is how it's done: Lose spectacularly but win little by little and pocket some from time to time so that you don't seem to have won too much. This takes only a very moderate sleight-of-hand when others' attention is elsewhere.

But the card sharp knows.

June 9 – Two days' bad weather, seasickness, almost all the passengers down. To avoid puking my guts out because of the bombardment of others' misery, I must mesmerize myself more lightly than for sleep, but heavily enough to put everything into a comfortable, drunken blur. (In this condition, the novels I have bought for Maria-Dolores actually make a kind of sense.) That young lady, unaffected, eating heartily and in an ecstasy of freedom, is running alone about the almost unpeopled first class deck and dining room. The list of rules: Not to speak or understand English, swear, take her boots off, show her bottom, make obscene gestures, go anywhere but first class, and so on. She laughed, hearing it. Somone's saying authoritatively – somewhere in the ship – that the weather will let up tomorrow; we are skirting the edge of something-or-other. But I did not catch most of it.

June 10 – That old tomcat has been *writing up my case*, as he calls it: names, dates, details, everything that must never get into print! He even plans to bribe the steward to find out if there are women's clothes in my steamer trunk, a piece of idiocy that will land us both in an instant mess. I've explained to Maria-Dolores, who merely shrugged, bored to death, poor soul, and violently moody from having to restrain her feelings about me. She says, "Go tear it up."

"No," I say, "*he* must tear it up. Otherwise–" and I point significantly to the porthole.

She remarks that he is probably too fat to go through, opining that the English are all mad anyway. Her judgment of *maricons* is that (a) they're all over the place and (b) who cares (a view to which I certainly wish the good doctor would subscribe) and (c) please, please, please, can she go outside if only for a little before she goes mad herself?

"Yes," I say. "Yes, now you must." She whoops into the other room. For I know how – now – and will tell her, although like Mrs. H.B. Carrington, whose *Mystery of the Stolen Bride* (8 vo., boards, illus.) Maria-Dolores is now about to fling out the port-hole she has got open – I have to shout "Stop that at once!" – I won't tell you. They never do in their books; that makes the story more lifelike for them, I suppose. So you may pretend you are one of them now, and don't skip.

I'm going to brand him. So badly that he will never write a word about me – or want to think it, either. I think you can guess. Not nice, but easier than drowning, and safer (in these crowds.)

Now he is writing in a burst of inspiration – this very minute – that the only influence that has saved me from the "fate" of my "type" (lace stockings, female dress, self-pollution, frequenting low haunts, unnatural acts, drunkenness, a love of cosmetics, inevitable moral degeneration , eventual insanity, it goes on for pages, it is really the most dreadful stuff) *is my healthy outdoor life in the manly climate of the American West!*

Maria-Dolores has just popped her head in to know why I'm laughing so hard. Memories of the mining camps, I tell her. Bumble, you deserve it, you deserve it all.

After much thought, he proudly puts down the title: "A Hitherto Unconsidered Possibility: The Moral Invert."

June 14 – First class is commodes and red plush everywhere. A new dress every day. The moral fogginess, bad enough here, takes a sharp rise two levels down – out of simple desperation – then drops to something approaching limited realism as you enter steerage. (Not that anyone really sees much more than one rung above or below them on the ladder; the rest fades into mist.) Afternoons Mrs. ______, the doctor, and I make up a party with Maria-Dolores as its supposed center; at dinner, Maria-Dolores gone, everyone eats uncontrollably (as they've been doing all day), and Mrs. ______, flushed with the day's victories, makes a very determined set at me over the wine. I dodge. Bumble, outwardly approving, nonetheless manages always to claim his young friend for the evening somehow, and then the two of us spend the next few hours in little secret orgies of sentimentality by the rail watching the stars: "My dear fellow, a lovely woman like that!" – "But, Doctor, how can I honestly – and married –" Well, he didn't mean. He didn't really. Smokes. Sighs. Points out constellations. Discusses God. His substitute for emotion (all on Mrs. ______'s account, mind you). Not that any young fellow would arouse anything but wrath by attacking Bumble on the surface, as it were. But slowly, solemnly, he asks. Solemnly, tragic and shamed I answer. And slowly, slowly, I begin to talk *at* him, as one may say, smoke *at* him, look *at* him, from the turn of the head to the smile, to the slouch, the drawl, the hands in the pockets, until one of us would know – even stone blind – what is going on. Bumble, who is not one of us – he has not a trace of the pattern – doesn't, though it's all tailored to him. From him: suppressed memories of secondary school, memories of his wife. We have been staying up later and later, which cuts into my time at cards, so I sleep later and later but never too late for the all-important staying in shape – Maria-Dolores, at my ever-sleepier push-ups and workings-out: "Ugh. What *for*?"

Later: five-card draw. If you want the technical details, look about you; I've been at it too long to consider them anything but a complete bore. The company, somewhat reduced by now, is made up largely of young men, very free and easy in their manners but in fact deferring markedly to what I will call The Old Fake, the grizzled old professional with muttonchop whiskers, the usual rank-and-hierarchy business, so it will be no hard matter to shift their allegiance if only I can get the other things to work right. Having eaten all day, they now eat more; food and drink arriving periodically, bring nothing useful to me but a little fresh air. One's lungs are at risk.

I come in late, nod, sit down. The O.F, who has an arrangement with one of the waiters, calls for an unopened deck, which is brought in with more food, more whiskey, all in amounts I haven't the heart to describe. (There is, especially, a tray of bratwurst that is almost enough to propel one out of the room.)

T.O.F.:"Mr. Smith doesn't indulge?"

Someone makes a joke about Mrs. ______.

At this one just smiles; that's best.

Play. More play. We go on, everyone smoking ferociously.

The deck is marked. The Old Fake is being careful not to win too openly, so when he decides not to take a hand, I (if at all possible) do. It's a great convenience. It also begins to look uncanny, which is good.

Nobody wants to comment, because you know what *that* means. T.O.F., understanding that I've broken his code, drops back cautiously.

I make a pile.

Then Fake, outwardly grinning, suggests that we switch our games, poker to women; the waiter can bring anything. (He does have it arranged; there are women who work this crossing, as in every other.)

I say that when I play cards, playing cards is what I do.

Now the hardest thing in the world is to wait for something that will make you look surprised. T.O.F. – he's fifty-five and all he's done for the last twenty years is eat and sit – keeps me staring at the table-top an unconsionable, trying time. Then he says that of course Mr. Smith doesn't crave the new game; he has all he wants of that without paying for it.

Then he makes a joke about Maria-Dolores.

Well, I can't turn pale, of course, but there's a reaonable-looking way to impersonate the effect of this, done mostly with muscles and a fixed gaze, so that's what I do. I get up slowly and slowly I draw – no, not the derringer, not tonight; someone might, after all, get hold of it – but the Bowie (shoulder holster) and the room goes electric.

I say slowly, *turning pale*, "Why, you God-damned skunk!"

Then the knife, extremely sharp point first, driven deep into the polished surface of the table – see, I won't use it! – all very stupid and out of the kind of thriller you-know-who spends her nights reading. T.O.F., across the table from me, seated almost against the wall, rises, expecting that I'll circle – he's worried and planning to back off, protesting he meant no harm – but it's easy, you see, when you're aware what the other's going to do before he does it. Even before he knows it. The table's bolted to the floor and is pretty solid, too, so one can vault over it as over a fence, using one arm as a lever, and skidding a bit, really, feet first into poor Fake, that tub of lard (they all get like that at his age), staggering the poor old thing crash! against the wall. Then a couple of punches for show; he's had the wind knocked out of him already.

(And that, child, is *why*. She once poked my chest and said "But how do you breathe?" Me: "From my belly, like you.")

Breathing a little hard – no it's *not* enough, even for one raised at eleven thousand feet – and getting up into the marvelous scandal:

"Gentlemen, this deck is marked."

Now that is serious. I say to one of the young 'uns, "Jones, pick a card," and call it. And again. And again. And then again. Several begin, aghast, "But–" with a mental sniff-and-point at T.O.F. whom I now leave prudently on his side of the table. (And how much will damaging the furniture add to tonight's bill? Oh, Lord!)

I say, "Who ordered the deck?"

Turmoil. Nobody's sure. One bursts out: "But I did! I asked Mr. ______" (follows hand over mouth and he *does* turn pale).

Now everyone believes. Sensation. Thrill. Real horror. These are their "standards." This is their "code." I say, spreading out what I've won, "Gentlemen, if you remember your losses. . .?

"This has been no fair game," I say, "and I have no taste for further play," and go out leaving a great deal of money and a lot of conflicting feelings behind me, the latter being the direct result of the former. (Let them straighten it out.)

So now *I* am head faker. You see? And can stretch my luck a little for the next few nights. I will clear, I think, some two thousand pounds before we land, with luck.

What a species.

Still, even blind–!

June 15 – This is how it happens:

A fine, balmy night, the doctor standing at the rail smoking his cigar and looking out over the sea. I'm facing him, having rolled a cigarette (no anatomical comparisons, please!): two friends under the stars. Time is pressing and the doctor very uneasy. He wants to be away from the lights, so the women who drift slowly past, in pairs or accompanied by gentlemen, are recognizable only in silhouette, the dim shape of sleeves and skirt, the massed hair and hat, the gleam of an earring. The doctor is at sea and memories are disturbing him, all the more that he's not quite sure what they are. He's also a little drunk. We've been talking ever more confidentially: his school days, his friends, then the past few days on shipboard, then his wife, their meeting, our meeting, our talks, until all have fallen together in confusion; he feels the same nostalgia for all of them. He finds this troubling. Finally I lean closer, for all must happen under water now, dream-slow, dream-fast, and I say, somehow too close although still barely half-seen, hands in pockets, leaning against the rail, a low voice out of the darkness:

Bumble, your companionship and your example have meant a great deal to me these past few days.

The slight stammer excites him, the slouch, the soft precise wording, the lifted chin. All memorable, all unidentifiable. He mutters something self-deprecatory and turns to leave, extremely uncomfortable, but I'm in his way, looking more like *it* than ever. It says:

I cannot say, Doctor, how much I admire you, how much I look up to you.

He protests.

It says: *I would put this in stronger terms, but there's no need. Surely you know.*

Bumble begins to drown. I am close enough to take his arm now or he would bolt; he feels the grip and the heat through his clothes, almost as if they were gone; almost, his hand is being held. *It* says, a disembodied voice, a hard, hot touch on his arm – and this time there is warm breath on his neck–

As you told me yourself, there is an instinct in such things which can never be mistaken.

In a moment he'll go under; mermaids will tickle his ears with streams of bubbles: Who am I? Do I remind you of someone? They'll be playing with his hair, tweaking his ears. He'll be picked bones in a moment. The cylindrical people, the flounced and puffed people, pass by, a world away.

It says in his wife's voice, with the odd, light break between the syllables, which he feels as the tip of a tongue: *Ed-ward*. . .?

Bumble is pulling at my arm. He's in a panic. He's about to drop his cigar and top hat and won't know it. They can't stand two kinds of knowledge that don't mix – not knowing the secret – but then he finds the way out for himself and I wish you could see it – even Bumble! – like a switchback on a train ride: jerk! jerk! jerk! and the new track is there, shiny and straight, as convinced as if I had said it myself.

"You're a woman!"

I do nothing. I say nothing. I don't have to, you see, I have only to smile, all sex in my smile. He will do it all himself, from "My dear girl, why didn't you tell me!" to "But you mustn't walk alone, oh dear, no, you mustn't go alone to your cabin!" He remembers my face on a playbill (though the name eludes him) – must be an actress, of course, have to be an actress; we have to learn such things for the stage, don't we? Special dress, altered voice, dye on the skin – but nothing injurious, he hopes, nothing that will mar, eh? Don't want to spoil that complexion, not when one needs it for one's work, not when one's famous for it (still searching). And what a clever little woman, to pull it off, when otherwise they'd be all about me, spoiling my trip with their interviews and their publicity.

He babbles: *He* knew. Doctors *know*, you know. Little hands, little feet, smooth face, delicate features, slender body! Quite obvious. Quite, quite obvious. Trying to remember what he said to the gentleman that he oughtn't to have said to the lady – but actresses are different, don't you know – free-thinking – though nothing indelicate – and he was only playing along, you understand, being a little free in his language, but nothing sensible, only gabble, only a lot of nonsense–

In my cabin, not quite remembering how he got there, it all happened so fast. Another drink. He remembers kissing my hands in the corridor. He's in the one armless chair, drink in hand, skittish, embarrassed, giddy with relief and desire, all the dizzy recklessness of a man just made it off a collapsing bridge – when suddenly the little actress is straddling his knees, facing him (a position which would strike him as queer if he were sober) but her face close enough to kiss. Which he does.

I whisper in his ear, "Dear Edward. Dearest, dearest Edward!"

He tries greedily to get at my jacket buttons and can't; I have placed his arms outside mine, behind my back, the two boiled shirt-fronts crackling like armor-plate between us. He tries to get up and so I give him another kiss, a slow one with biting in it. The position bothers him but it's what I need, so I whisper, "Not yet. Let me," and reaching down, undo, to his indescribable shock and utter, helpless delight, the buttons of his trousers. Actresses *are* different. I fish for and play with his pretty thing and kiss his neck and mouth and tell him about the female form divine, which he will see in just a moment: the cushioned hips and swelling bosom and buttocks, and secret, round moist parts, all the upholstery that stiffens him and makes him push and pant. The liquor's slowing him but it also makes things possible, I mean the doubleness of dreams: right words, wrong smells (tobacco, men's hair-pomade), the armor between us, the lingering confusion about who's who, the sudden reasonless satisfacion with a stranger who knows exactly what fondling he wants, and the magic shameful words his wife never knew, and handles his secret self, as she never would, or put her tongue in his ear, an appalling, hideously exciting novelty. So he abandons himself to the dream, poor silky old sweet tom, which is suddenly happening much too soon – and straining me close and rigid (but my arms are in the way), he heroically tries to stop, I whisper "Shoot me!" and he spends himself freely over my hands and my second-best pair of evening trousers. For a moment he comes back to himself to see his wife – no, the Colorado gambler – no, the actress – in one dim, ambiguous person. He dozes.

He sits, snoring, trousers open. Poor old animal. Maria-Dolores stirs in her next-door sleep. Then, through Bumble's dreaming rag-bag of a mind, goes the overpowering glory of telling the whole story from start to finish: wonders, admirations, successes. He'll do it. He's incorrigible. And will wake up and want more – later tonight, tomorrow night, and so there's nothing else for it. I harden my heart.

He wakes. What is the dear girl doing?

I am, having washed my hands, sitting at my writing desk, cleaning a Smith and Wesson forty-five, with canvas over the desk-top to protect it. Also hides the Bowie. The doctor says gruffly, to an unidentifiable back, tears in his eyes, "So you fancied the old fellow, eh?"

Then, "My dear, couldn't you – that is, we're alone – something more natural?"

I say, without turning around, "It's all costume."

He chuckles. "Jewelry!" he says archly (the shirt studs, the diamond.)

I say, "They're worth money. I don't collect pound notes for the sound the paper makes, either."

Then I add, "Do you know, I'm quite sure that someone saw us in the corridor."

He can't remember. I say, "You were kissing my hands." He chuckles again, turning red. Hands! He says, "My dear, if you'd only turn–" So I do and he sees what I'm doing. Very puzzling, but there is some good reason, no doubt. I say:

"Doctor, have you read Krafft-Ebing's *Psycopathia Sexualis*?"

He hasn't. He's blank.

"The German medical specialist," I say, "is less generous than you in his view of the male invert. He writes that such people have no morality; they wish only to possess the generative organ of another man by any means, fair or foul; it is their sole object; and they take delight in spreading the contagion of their moral disease, especially when they find the germs of it hidden in an apparently normal man."

No connection, Bumble is slow.

I say "The German specialist is correct, Doctor. There is, as you yourself told me, an instinct in such matters that warns against contagion – if we desire to be warned. You, for example, did not desire to be warned."

Have you ever seen a man turn really pale? The color goes like a dropped window shade; it's most impressive. But the old creature is admirable, in his way; even buttoning his pants (an act not usually considered dignified among them) he can give a good impersonation of choleric indignation: "Sir – I will – I will expose–"

I say evenly, "In that case your own behavior will hardly bear examination. Remember, we were seen."

"You lied!" he cries, desperate and sincere.

"Did I?" (and I feel for the knife, just in case Bumble decides to try some first-hand research on my person). "Why I don't remember that. What I do remember is saying nothing at all while you made the whole story up yourself; you seemed very eager to believe it. An actress? Half a head taller than yourself? Where in Europe, on what possible stage? And this business of dye for the skin – which doesn't smell, won't wash off, and can't be detected even in the most intimate contact, not even by a medical man? Come! You lied because you wanted to. And you're still lying."

I add, more softly, "Don't make me dislike you." And then, in *its* voice, "Keep my secret and I'll keep yours, eh?"

Bumble will launch. Bumble has to be stopped by the sight of the Bowie, better than the heel of my hand under his chin and so on. Then Bumble has his inspiration; I did not lie. I was telling the truth, but I am lying *now*. Reasons? None at all, but he says flatly, folding his trembling arms across his chest to indicate unshakable belief:

"You are a woman."

The stupidity. The absolute unconquerable stupidity! Like the best swordsman in the world beaten by a jackass. I walk round him, searching, to Maria-Dolores's door. Say, "Have you heard what happened at cards last night? Yes, that's me; that is how I get my living; the nonsense about Colorado helps. Well, I knocked down a man fifty pounds heavier than myself; ask about it tomorrow."

Bumble is trembling.

I turn and flip the knife point-first across the cabin and into the door to the corridor – why is it that acts of manliness always involve damage to the furniture? – which is, you must understand, *something a woman cannot do.* That's faith. I repeat: What a woman cannot do.

Logic also. I say:

"If I am lying now, what is the purpose of my lie? To drive you away? The little actress would not want to drive you away, not after having gone to all the trouble of acquiring you! Why confess she's a woman unless she wanted you? And why should I lie? For fear you'll expose me? I can expose you. I could blackmail you if I wanted; we were seen, you know. To drive you away? I don't want to; I like you – although I don't fancy being attacked and having to knock you down or throttle you as I did to the other gentleman at the game last night – and why on earth, if I wanted to drive you away, should I have taken such trouble to – well, we won't name it. But it's perfect nonsense, my dear fellow, a woman pretending to be a man who pretends he's a woman in order to pretend to be a man? Come, come, it won't work! A female invert might want to dress and live as a man, but to confess she's a woman – which would defeat her purpose – and then be intimate with you – which she would find impossibly repulsive – in order to do what, for heaven's sake? Where's the sense to it? No, there's only one possibility, and that's the truth: that I have been deceiving nobody, including you, but that you, my poor dear fellow, have been for a very long time deceiving yourself. Why not stop now, eh? Right now?"

And with a smile, I touch my fingertips to the stain beginning to dry on the front of my trousers and put the fingers in my mouth. Havoc indescribable. This is not nice, not nice at all. If only Bumble does not drop dead this minute, in which case, Maria-Dolores – who has just come in, in her nightgown – and I must put him through the porthole anyhow.

She sees us, imitates alarm, and darts behind the door. Her head peeps out.

Poor grey old man whispers, "Child, has this man ever – has he ever–"

"Maria-Dolores," I say, "this man wants to know if I have ever kissed or touched you. Tell him the truth."

She knows, of course. She says dubiously, "You kiss me good night on the forehead."

"Have I touched you?"

She nods reluctantly, troubled. "You *push* me."

"Push?" says Bumble, grasping at straws.

"When uncle is reading at his desk or busy," says Maria-Dolores, "he *push* me. On the shoulder. He say, 'Go away.' It make me sad. It's happen many time."

Bumble says, "Your uncle – is – is – is he–"

She watches unblinking, as if it were a perfectly normal occurrence for strange old men to twitch and stammer in my cabin long past midnight. I say:

"This gentleman, for reasons I shall not explain to you, wants to know something about me. He wants to know whether I am a man or a woman. Tell him."

She does incredulous surprise much better than I do. Bumble, distressingly, starts to speak; I cut him short: "Not my clothes, Maria-Dolores, and not my behavior. He wants to know the rest of it. Do you understand me? He wants to know what's under the clothes. Tell him you're as ignorant as you ought to be, and you can go back to bed."

She droops, barely audible, "You'll get vexed."

I assure her that I won't.

She says quickly, ashamed and starting to cry, "I did not know. I thought you were away so I came in. You were in the bath they bring in, I ran right out. I will never do it again!"

"Child," says Bumble, "I am sorry to – I don't wish –"

"*Es muy hombre,*" says Maria-Dolores, with a sketchy gesture at her crotch and by some miracle of acting manages to turn bright red. She adds, looking very embarrassed, "Yes, is a man."

"But do you know, " says Bumble unexpectantly coherent, "what a man *is*, child? Do you truly know?"

"Yes, of course," says Maria-Dolores in genuine surprise. Then she looks interested. "Why? Don't you?"

Back to his cabin in a hurry to vomit into the commode, tear up his notes and essay, and burn the pieces in the washbasin.

So that's done.

June 16 – Somewhere west of Denver we'll camp for the night, miles from anyone. There in the high country, under the splendid million stars, I'll let down her black hair. Maria-Dolores giggles; she's done it with girls, too. "Joe Smith" of "Colorado" slides his hands under the little girl's shirt – a process I'm sure he could describe very well – but his face will never be reflected in her eyes. She shivers, partly from the cold, whispers, "I want to do things for you, too." I smile Yes, remembering Joe-Bob's lion silkiness and the first surprise of your wiry hair. As I bend slowly down to the nubbiness, the softness, the mossy slipperiness, the heat, that familiar reflection begins back and forth between us, a sudden scatter shot along the nerves, its focusing on the one place, the echoes in neck and palms and lips, the soles of her feet, her breasts. Maria-Dolores is breathless; "Don't stop!" forgetting that I know. She closes her eyes, sobs, grabs inside, clutches my head with her hand: overwhelming! And sees me, all I remember, all I feel, all I know: overwhelming! And then, out of the things I know – and can't help knowing – she sees the one thing as strange and terrible to her as the dark side of the moon: herself.

And that's done.

But not yet. I'm imagining in words, as they do out here. Odd, in a language that would fade from me in half a year if I didn't continually get it from outside. (And to you, you will know Polish and Yiddish only when I get back!) Maria-Dolores, innocent of either, is asleep in the next cabin, cranky at having to have so many times of the month in a month (and so irregularly too) "ridiculous even at fifteen, let alone twelve, " she says to me in eloquent Spanish, in her dream. Bumble, snoring, was lively enough today to have instantly annexed Mrs. ______, not only out of self defense but quite distinctly for revenge. I told Maria-Dolores and she said "That doesn't make sense." I said when did Bumble ever make sense. So I will seal this up and mail it in a few days?

But how to end? (It's a custom here.) Why, in the style of Maria-Dolores's books. There are only three left, since she's taken to deliberately heaving the ones she's tired of out the porthole when I'm not around. And I really haven't the heart to quarrel with her; they *are* bad! Here's the first one, a little oddly written, *The Mystery of Nevada* which is lying open under her bed.

Funny, them McCabes, don't look like a fambly even though ther's suthin' you can't put a name on that sets 'em apart from other folks. An' they got hired hands from all over; Chinks an' niggers, (that's you, pulling the apron off of me when someone comes, half-speaking, half-laughing, "Quick, gal!") *even Injuns. And why they stay up in them mountains all by their lonesome, God only knows.*

The second, very florid and lurid (it's called *Mystery of Captain Satan*), has been kicked, closed, into a corner of the room (on the floor):

O reader, how can we contemplate this disordered soul without horror? Gifted with a knowledge of self and others few mortals possess, he nevertheless ran the gamut of vice! Living like a parasite, cheating at cards, refusing to aid the very race that bred him but instead inflicting elaborate mental tortures on an elderly gentleman who strongly resembled his deceased papa, and using his kind's incapability for parenthood (I told Maria-Dolores this; she merely shrugged, not in the least interested.) *as an excuse for indulging in unnatural – and what is worse, even some natural – lusts! What doom is stored up in Heaven for these hard-hearted men and women, diabolically disguised as men and women or vice-versa and therefore invisible to our eyes, speaking the language of anyone in the room, which is dreadfully confusing because you can't tell what degenerate nation (or race) they may come from, and worst of all,* PRETENDING TO BE HUMAN BEINGS? WHEN IN FACT THEY ARE??? (it goes on.)

And here's the last, honorably placed on the table by her bed. It's a remarkably quiet and gentle one (all things considered) and she rather likes it. She's going to keep it. It's called *The Mystery of the Young Gentleman* (he's a not-so-young lady, we find out) and it ends accurately and simply, in a very old tradition:

They lived happily ever after.

The Gods of Reorth
Elizabeth A. Lynn

Since the earliest civilizations, complex pantheons of deities have been envisioned as overseeing life on this planet. Some of these immortals are said to have walked among us in human form. Elizabeth A. Lynn brings her usual sensitivity to this goddess-worship story.

This is the story of a goddess Who had once been a woman named Jael, and what She did.

She lived in a cave on an island. Around Her island of Mykneresta lay others: Kovos and Nysineria, Hechlos, Dechlas, and larger, longer, fish-shaped Rys, where the Fire God lived within his fuming, cone-shaped house. She was the Goddess. From Her cave sprang the vines and grains that women and men reaped from the fertile ground; from the springs of Her mountain welled the clear water that made the ground fertile, and gave life. Her mountain towered over the land. When She grew angry the lightning tore from the skies over Her cave, and the goats went mad on the mountainsides. *"Hard as frost, indolent as summer rain, spare us, spare us. O Lady of the Lightning,"* Her poets sang. Sometimes the music appeased Her, and then She smiled, and the skies smiled clear and purple-blue, as some said Her eyes must be. But they were not: they were dark and smoky-green, like the color in the heart of a sunlit pool, touched to movement by a summer shower.

They smoked now. Above Her cave lightning reached webbed fingers to the stars. "The Lady is angry," whispered the villagers.

Inside the vast cavern that was Her home She stood staring at a pulsing screen. It burned and leaped with pinpoints of light. She read the message from the screen as easily as a scribe reads writing, and Her fingers sent a rapid reply out to the waiting stars.

WHY DO THE MEN OF RYS ARM FOR WAR?
MYKNERESTA IS A PEACEFUL AND FRUITFUL PLACE.

A moment passed, and the patterns answered, scrolling lines of amber fire on the dark, metallic screen.

PROBABILITIES PROJECT RYS AN EMPIRE.
THIS IS DESIRABLE. DO NOT IMPEDE.

Jael stared at the fading pattern, and swept a fierce hand across the board. The message vanished; above the cave's roof, fireballs rolled and then disappeared down the sides of the mountain.

This is desirable. In her mind, the silent screen retained a voice, a cool, sardonic, male voice. War! She scowled across the room. An ugly, evil thing she knew it was — though she had never seen a war. She did not desire war on Mykneresta. Yet it was "desirable" that Rys become an empire. Were the worshippers of the Fire God to rule, eventually, all of the planet Methys? She snorted. The Fire God had once been only a man, named Yron. Long ago, when they had been much younger, they had used the lumenings, the lightscreens, to talk with one another across the planet. But that had been an age ago, it seemed. She did not want to talk to Yron now.

Are you jealous, she asked herself, because his children will rule a world, and yours will not? She caught herself thinking it, and laughed. What nonsense to be feeling, that she, who had seen five worlds, and governed four, should care who or what ruled on a little planet round a little sun, whirling on an arm of a vast galaxy, a galaxy ruled by Reorth. Yet — Methys was important. Long-term assignments to undeveloped planets were not made unless they were important. Somewhere on a probability-line Methys was a key, a focus of power. Somewhere on Reorth, in the great block-like towers that held their machines, a technician had seen this world matched to a time within a nexus of possibilities, and had decided that, changed thus and so, moved in this or that direction. Methys could matter. *Do not impede.* Reorth wants a war.

Jael stepped away from the cavern which held the lumenings, the spyeyes, and all the other machines that made her Goddess. She walked along passageways, grown with fungus that glowed as she passed it, and ducked through a door cut into the rock. Now she was outside. Above her the night sky gleamed, thick with stars. Wind whipped round the granite crags with words hidden in its howls. She rubbed her arms with her hands, suddenly cold. It was autumn, drawing close to winter. I wonder how Yron likes living in his volcano, she thought, all smoke. That made her smile. With the bracelets on her slim wrists she drew a cloak of warmth around herself, and sent ahead of her, along the hard ground, a beam of yellow light. Slowly she walked down the mountainside, listening, smelling, tasting the life that roamed in the darkness. Once a cougar leaped to pace beside her, great head proud. She reached to stroke it. It sprang away, regarding her with widened eyes. She could compel it back – but even as she thought it, she rejected the thought. It was part of the night, with the wind and the starlight. Let it run free.

She came at last to the path which led to the villages – a worn and hidden path it was, and even she could not remember when it first was made. One bright star shone through the tree trunks. She stared at its flickering yellow light. It was not a star, but flame. Curious, she dimmed the light from her bracelets and walked toward it. Who would dare to come so far up the mountainside? It was almost a sacrilege. Perhaps it was a poet; they did strange things sometimes. Perhaps some traveler, lost and tired and unable to go on, had dared to build a small fire almost at Her door, praying Her to spare him in his hour of need.

But it was more substantial than that; it was a house, a rough-hewn cabin, and at the side of the house was a rain barrel, and there was a yellow curtain at the window. Marveling a little, Jael went up to the curtain and put her eye to the gap where it flapped.

She saw a small room, with a neat pallet on the floor, a table, a chair near the hearth, a candle on the table. From the low rafters, like bats, hung bunches and strings of herbs, roots, leaves, a witchwoman's stock. A woman sat on the chair, bending forward, poking at the fire with a long forked stick.

Jael understood. This was a woman who had chosen, as was her right, to live alone; to take no man and bear no children; to be, instead, wise-woman, healer, barren yet powerful in her choice, for did not the Goddess honor those who chose to be lonely in Her service? She watched. The woman rose. She went to a chest beside the bed, took out a sheepskin cape, and began to pick the burrs from it.

Suddenly she turned toward the window. Jael drew back instinctively, and then caught herself and used the bracelets to blur the air around her, so that she could stand still and not be seen. Gray eyes seemed to look right into hers; gray eyes like smoke, framed by the smoke of long dark hair.

Then the dark head bowed and was covered by the cloak's hood. She walked to the door. Jael blurred herself wholly to human eyes and waited as the witchwoman opened the door and closed it behind her. She wondered (even She) where, on the Lady's mountain, even a witch would dare to go.

She walked along the path that followed the stream bed. Jael followed behind her, hidden and silent. At the pool by the waterfall, she knelt. Jael smiled. This was one of Her places; it was not so long ago that She had showed Herself, under the glare of a harvest moon, to an awed crowd. Now the stream bed was clogged with fallen leaves, but it was still a holy place. The waterfall was a small but steady drip over the lip of rock to the clear dark pool below.

The witchwoman knelt on the flat stones that ringed the pool's edge, staring into the fecund depth of water. Her face was grave and still. At last she rose, and made her way to the path. Her silent homage made Jael hesitate. But she decided not to follow the witchwoman to her cabin. Instead, she returned to her cave. Stalking to the lumenings, she lit them with a wave of her hand, and then, irresolute, stood thinking what to say.

She decided.

EXPLAIN NEED FOR EMPIRE AT THIS TIME.

The lights pulsed and went dim. She waited. No answer appeared. Oh well – they might answer another time. The question would surprise them. Jael remembered years of famine, of drought, of blight. Once She had sent a plague. It had hurt, watching the inexorable processes of disease and death sweep over Her people. She had not asked reasons for that.

War is different, she thought.

But how can I know that? I have never seen a war. Perhaps it is just like a plague. But plague is natural, she thought. War is made by men.

What's this? she asked herself. That plague was not "natural," *you* made it, with your training and your machines. What makes this different? Woman of Reorth, she said sternly, naming herself in her own mind, as she rarely did, how are *you* different from a war?

The next day brought no answer from the lumenings, nor did the one after that, nor the one after that.

Autumn began the steep slide into winter. Round the Lady's mountain it rained and rained, gullying the fields, now stripped of grain, and washing the last leaves from the thin trees. The waterfall sang strongly for a time.

Then one morning the ground was white and cold and hard, and ice spears tipped the trees and fences, and hung from the eaves. Village children drove their herds into barns, whooping and shouting, snapping willow switches from the dead branches of the willow trees. Men gathered wood; women counted over the apples and dried ears of corn that filled the storerooms, and prayed to the Goddess for a gentle winter. Mountain goats watched the stooping wood gatherers with disdainful eyes, their coats grown shaggy and long, for in winter the hunting stopped. In Rys and allied Hechlos, the mining ceased. Only in the smithies the men worked, forging swords and knives and shields and spears and arrowheads. In the smithies it stayed warm.

Sometime during the winter procession of ice, snow, and thaw, Reorth answered. The lumenings lit, held a pattern for a few moments, and then went dark.

It was the outline of a machine, sketched in light. For weeks

Jael could not think what it might mean. She had decided to dismiss it as a misdirected transmission, meant for someone, when one night she dreamed. It was a dream of Reorth, of home. She woke, weeping for a world she had not seen in three hundred years, and, in the darkness of her cave, heard herself say aloud the name of the machine.

It was a chronoscope, one of the great machines that scanned the timelines. She had not seen one in – in – she could not remember how long. Rage filled her. Was she a child, to be answered with pictures? The contemptuousness of the response brought her in haste to the screen, fingers crooked, ready to scorch the sky with lightning.

But she caught her hands back in mid-reach. The folk who had sent her here would not be impressed with her anger. The answer was plain, as they had meant it. The need is there, seen in the timelines. You know your job. Do as you are told.

Do not impede.

The year moved on. The waterfall over the pool froze into fantastic sculpted shapes, thawed, fell, froze again. The pool did not freeze. Only its color changed, deepening under stormy skies to black. The villagers did not visit it, but the witchwoman, Akys, did, coming to kneel on the icy, slippery stones once or twice each week.

The witchwoman's cabin by the streambed was as far up the Lady's mountain as the villagers would venture. They came reluctantly, drawn by need: a sick child, a sick cow, an ax wound. The women came first, and then the men. This was as it should be, for men had no place on Her mountain.

More rarely, the witchwoman went to the villagers, down the steep pathway from her home to the rutted village streets. How the knowledge came she was never sure, save that it did come, like a tugging within her head, a warning that something was amiss in wood or village. Once it was a girl who had slipped gathering kindling and wedged her legs between two rocks. Akys had gone down to the village to fetch the villagers and bring them to the child. Once a fire started in a storeroom; they never discovered how. Had Akys smelled the smoke? She could not tell, but with knowledge beating like the blood in her temples against her brain, she came scrambling down the path to call the villagers out from sleep, and helped them beat the flames out in the icy, knife-edged wind.

In the thick of the winter, trying to gather twigs on the stony slope, the witchwoman would find firewood outside her door, or apples, cider, even small jugs of wine, to warm her when the ashes gave no warmth, and the wind thrust its many-fingered hands through her cabin's myriad chinks. After the fire they left her a haunch of venison. She was grateful for it, for the hares and sparrows grew trapwise, and her snares often sat empty.

To pass the shut-in days in the lonely hut, the witchwoman cut a flute from a tree near the Lady's pool, and made music. It floated down the hillside, and the village children stopped their foraging to listen to the running melodies.

Jael heard them, too. They drew her. The quavering pure tones seemed to her to be the voice of winter, singing in the ice storms. Sometimes, on dark nights, she would throw on her cloak of green cloth – a cloak made on Reorth – and go past the pool, up to the shuttered window of the witch's house, to listen.

The music made her lonely.

On impulse one night, she shifted the lumenings to local and called across the islands to Yron. She called and called. Then she called Reorth.

YRON DOES NOT ACKNOWLEDGE TRANSMISSION

The reply came at once.

YRON RECALLED 20 YEARS AGO, LOCAL TIME.
NEW ASSIGNMENT ACCEPTED. COORDINATES FOLLOW.

There was a pause. Then a set of planetary coordinates flashed across the screen.

Jael shrugged. The transmission continued.

YOUR RECALL UNDER CONSIDERATION.
WOULD YOU ACCEPT REASSIGNMENT?
TAKE YOUR TIME.

Akys did not know when she first began to sense the presence of a stranger near her home. It came out of nowhere, like the gift of warning in her head. Especially it came at night, when clouds hid the moon and stars. At first she thought it was the wild things of the mountain, drawn by her music. But beasts leave signs that eyes can read. This presence left no sign – save, once, what might have been the print of a booted foot in snow.

On a day when the sun at noon was a copper coin seen through cloud, she heard a knock at her door. She thought, Someone in trouble? Her gift had given her no warning. She stood, laying the flute aside, moving slowly with weariness and hunger, for her snares had shown empty for three days. She went to the door and opened it.

A woman stood under the icicled eaves. She wore a long green cloak, trimmed with rich dark fur. From her fingers dangled two partridges.

"Favor and grace to you," she said. Her voice was low and gentle. "My name is Jael. We are neighbors on the mountain. I have heard your music in the evenings; it gives me much delight. I wished to bring you a gift." She held out the birds. Her hair, escaping from its hood, was the bright auburn of a harvest moon.

Akys stepped back. "Will you come inside? It's cold on the doorstep."

"Gladly," said the stranger. She dropped her hood back, and stepped into the small, smoky house.

Taking the birds from the slim hands, Akys said, "I didn't know I had any neighbors."

Her quick eyes caught the tint of gold as the cape shifted. Who was this woman, dressed so richly and strangely, who called her "neighbor" and brought her food?

"My name is Jael," said Jael again. "I am new come to this place. I lived before in" – she seemed to hesitate – "Cythera, west of here. Now I live near the Lady's well."

"I do not know that place, Cythera," said the witchwoman. She began to strip the feathers from the birds. "Are you alone?" she murmured.

Jael nodded. "I have no man," she said.

"Then will you eat with me tonight?" said Akys. "It is hard to come to a new home alone, especially in winter. And they are your birds, after all."

Jael came to the hearth, where Akys sat cleaning the birds. Kneeling, she stretched our her hands to the warmth. Her fingers were slender, unscarred by work. On her wrists wire bracelets shone gold in the firelight. The flame seemed to leap toward them.

She glanced up, into Akys' gray eyes. "Forgive my silence," she said. "I may not speak of my past. But I mean you no harm."

"I can see that," said Akys. "I accept your gift and your silence." She has a vow, she thought. Perhaps she has left wealth and family behind, to serve the Lady. That is noble in one so beautiful and young.

She picked up the bellows and blew the fire up, and dropped the cleaned partridge in the pot. "I am alone, too," she said matter-of-factly.

"So I see," said Jael, looking around at the one room with its narrow pallet, and single chair. "You've not much space."

Akys shrugged. "It's all I need. Though I never thought to have visitors. I might get another chair."

Jael tucked her feet beneath her and settled beside the fire. "Another chair," she agreed quietly, "for visitors – or a friend."

Through the rest of the short, severe winter the two women shared food: birds, coneys, dried fruits, nuts, and clear water. In the thaws, when the snow melted and the streams swelled, they made hooks and lines to catch fish. They hunted the squirrels' stores from the ground, and gathered wood for the hearth. Jael's hands and cheeks grew brown, chapped by wind and water.

"Akys!" she would call from the house, flinging wide the door.

And Akys, kneeling by the stream, water bucket in hand, felt her heart lift at that clear, lovely call. "Yes!"

"Can I stuff quail with nuts?"

"Have we enough?"

"I think so."

"Slice them thin." She brought the bucket to the house. Jael was chopping chestnuts into bits. She watched warily over Jael's shoulder, wondering as she watched how the younger woman had managed, alone. She did not know the simplest things. "Be careful with that knife."

"If I dull it," Jael said, "you'll have to get the smith to sharpen it for you again."

"I don't want you to cut yourself," said Akys.

Jael smiled. "I never do," she said, "do I?"

"No."

Jael set the knife down and pushed the sliced nuts into the cavity. She trussed the bird with cord, held it, hefted it. "It's a big one. I'm glad you got that new pot from the village."

"I hate asking for things," said Akys.

Jael said, "I know. But you can't build an iron pot the way you can a chair." Crossing the room, she dumped the bird into the cauldron. "And tomorrow I want to fish. I'll bring some metal hooks with me when I return in the morning."

Akys said, quietly, "Why don't you stay the night?"

Jael shook her head.

During the days she became a human woman. She learned, or relearned, for surely she had known these skills before, to chop wood, to skin, clean and cook animals, to fish, with coarse strings of hemp she had twisted herself, and a willow pole. She got cold and wet, went hungry when Akys did, and climbed to her cave tired and footsore. But she always went back at night. Fidelity had made her set the lumenings to Record, and she turned them on each evening, awaiting – what? Sometimes she told herself she was waiting for her recall. Touching her machines, she was once more the Goddess. But in the morning, when she went back down the slope to Akys, the reality of Reorth receded in her mind, and all its designs became bits of a dream, known only at night, and she did not think of recall.

Akys never asked questions. The brief tale told at their first meeting remained unembroidered, and Jael had half-forgotten it. She felt no need to have a past. Sometimes Akys looked at her with a stir of inquiry in her gray eyes. But if questions roiled her mind, they never reached her tongue.

Spring broke through winter like water breaking through a dam. They measured time by the rise and fall of the river. In spring the fish came leaping upstream, and if you held out a net –

ah, if you just held out your hands – they would leap to the trap, bellies iridescent in the sunshine. In the white rapids they looked like pieces cut from rainbow.

"I want to bathe in the river!" cried Jael.

"It's too cold now," said practical Akys. "You'll freeze."

"Then I want summer to come," Jael pouted. "Why does the year move so slowly?" she demanded, flinging her arms wide.

Yet in the cavern at night, she saw the year moving swiftly, and wished that her power extended to the movement of the planet in its course around its sun.

The spyeyes set to Rys told her that armies and ships were gathering. They will be coming in the fall, she thought. They will be ready then. Spykos, king of Rys, was drawing men from all his cities and from the cities of nearby Dechlas. He cemented his alliance with Hechlos by marrying his daughter to Hechlos' king's son, and the goddess within Jael-the-woman raged, that these men could see women as so many cattle, bought and bred to found a dynasty. Spykos raided the harbor towns of Nysineria and Kovos – in winter! – distracting them, frightening them, keeping them busy and off guard. Jael watched the raids with a drawn face. It hurt, to see the villages burn.

What will you do?

This was the question she did not allow herself to hear. If she heard it, she would have to answer it. It kept her wakeful at night, walking through her caverns, staring at the dark, unspeaking lumenings.

Akys scolded her. "What's wrong with you? Your eyes have pits under them. Are you sleeping?"

"Not very well."

"I can give you a drink to help you sleep."

"No."

"Won't you stay here? It tires you, going home at night."

Jael shook her head.

Summer came to the mountain with a rush of heat. The children herded the beasts up to the high pastures again. The crags echoed to their whistles and calls and to the barking of the dogs. The heavy scents of summer filled meadows and forests: honeysuckle, clover, roses, wet grass steamy after a rainstorm.

Akys said, "You could bathe in the river now."

They went to the river, now strong and swift in its bed. Jael flung off her clothes. Her body was slim, hard and flat, golden-white except where weather had turned it brown. She dipped a toe in the rushing stream. "Ah, it's cold!" She grinned at Akys. "I'm going to dive right off this rock!"

Akys sat on the bank, watching her, as she ducked beneath the flowing, foamy water, playing, pretending to be a duck, a salmon, an otter, a beaver, an eel. Finally, the cold turned her blue. She jumped out. Akys flung a quilt around her. She wrapped up in it, and rolled to dry. The long grass, sweet with the fragrance of summer, tickled her neck. She sat up.

"Hold still," said Akys. "You've got grass all over your hair." She picked it out with light, steady fingers.

Jael butted her gently. "Why don't you go in?"

"Too cold for me," said Akys. "Besides, I'd scare the fish." She looked at Jael. "I'm clumsy."

Jael said, "That's not true. You move like a mountain goat; I've watched you climbing on the rocks. And you're never clumsy with your hands. You didn't pull my hair, once."

Akys said, "Yes, but – you look like a merwoman in the water. I'd look like an old brown log."

Jael said, "I'm younger than you. I haven't had to work as hard."

"How old are you?" Akys asked.

Jael struggled to see her face through timebound eyes. "Twenty," she lied.

"I'm thirty-two," said Akys. "If I had had children, my body would be old by now, and I would be worrying about their future, and not my own."

Jael let the ominous remark pass. "Are you sorry that you have no children?" she said.

"No. A promise is a promise. For the beauty I lack – a little."

"Don't be silly," Jael bent forward and caught Akys' hands between her own. The quilt slid from her shoulders. "You *are* beautiful. You cannot see yourself, but I can see you, and I know. Do you think you need a man's eyes to find your beauty? Never say such nonsense to me again! You are strong, graceful, and wise."

She felt Akys' fingers tighten on her own. "I – I thank you."

"I don't want your thanks," said Jael.

That night, Jael lay in Akys' arms on the narrow, hard, straw-stuffed pallet, listening to rain against the roof slats, pat, pit-pat. The hiss of fire on wet wood made a little song in the cabin.

"Why are you awake still," murmured Akys into her hair. "Go to sleep."

Jael let her body relax. After a while Akys' breathing slowed and deepened. But Jael lay wakeful, staring at the dark roof, watching the patterns thrust against the ceiling by the guttering flames.

Autumn followed summer like a devouring fire. The leaves and grasses turned gold, red, brown, and withered; the leaves fell. Days shortened. The harvest moon burned over a blue-black sky. The villagers held Harvest Festival. Like great copper-colored snakes the lines with torches danced through the stripped fields, women and children first, and then the men.

Smoke from the flaring torches floated up the mountainside to the cabin. Akys played her flute. It made Jael lonely again to hear it. It seemed to mock the laughter and singing of the dancers, and, as if the chill of winter had come too soon, she shivered.

Akys pulled the winter furs from her chest, and hung them up to air out the musty smell. She set a second quilt at the foot of the pallet.

"We don't need that yet," said Jael.

"You were shivering," said the witchwoman. "Besides, we will."

One night they took the quilt out and lay in the warm dry grass to watch the stars blossom, silver, amber, red, and blue. A trail of light shot across the sky. "A falling star!" cried Akys. "Wish."

Jael smiled grimly, watching the meteor plunge through the atmosphere. She imagined that it hit the sea, hissing and boiling, humping up a huge wave, a wall of water thundering through the harbors, tossing the Rysian ships like wood chips on the surface of a puddle, smashing them to splinters against the rocks. I wish I could wish for that, she thought.

"What are you thinking . . . ?" said Akys.

"About Rys."

"The rumors . . ."

"Suppose," said Jael carefully, "suppose they're true."

Akys lifted on an elbow. "Do you think they are?"

"I don't know. They frighten me."

"We're inland, a little ways anyways, and this village is so close to Her mountain. They wouldn't dare come here."

Jael shivered.

"You dream about it, don't you?" said Akys. "Sometimes you cry out, in your sleep."

Later she said, "Jael, could you go back home?"

"What?"

"To that place you came from, in the west. I forget its name."

"Cythera."

"Yes. Could you go back there? You'd be safer there, if the men of Rys do come."

"No," said Jael, "I can't go back. Besides, I know you won't leave this place, and I won't leave you."

"That makes me happy and sad at the same time," said Akys.

"I don't want to make you sad."

"Come close, then, and make me happy."

They made love, and then slept, and woke when the stars were paling. The quilt was wet beneath them. They ran through the dewy grass to the cabin, and pulled the dry quilt around them.

Jael went back to the cave the next night.

This is madness, she told herself on the way. You cannot be two people like this; you cannot be both the Goddess and Akys' lover. But around her the dark forest gave no answer back, except the swoop of owls and the cry of mice, and the hunting howl of a mountain cat.

She went first to the lumenings, but they were dark. In all the months she had stayed away, no messages had come. Next she checked the spyeyes. Ships spread their sails across the water like wings, catching the wind, hurrying, hurrying, their sails dark against the moonlit sea. She calculated their speed. They would reach the coast of Mykneresta in, perhaps, four days. She contemplated sending a great fog over the ocean. Let them go blundering about on reefs and rocks. If not a fog, then a gale, a western wind to blow them back to Rys, an eastern wind to rip their sails and snap their masts, a northern wind to ice their decks . . . She clenched her teeth against her deadly dreaming.

She waited out a day and a night in the cave, and then went back to Akys.

The witchwoman was sitting at her table with a whetstone, sharpening her knives.

"You have some news," said Jael. "What have you heard?"

Akys tried to smile. Her lips trembled. "The runner came yesterday, while you were gone. They have sighted ships, a fleet. The villages are arming." Her face had aged overnight, but her hands were steady. "I walked down to the forge and asked the smith for a sharpening stone. I have never killed a man, but I know it helps to have your knife sharp."

"Maybe they will not come here," said Jael.

"Maybe." Akys laid down one knife, and picked up another. "I went to the Lady's pool yesterday, after I heard the news."

"And?"

"There was nothing, no sign. The Lady does not often speak, but this time I thought She might . . . I was wrong."

"Maybe She is busy with the fleet."

Akys said, "We cannot live on maybes."

"Have you had anything to eat today?" said Jael.

Akys stayed her work. "I can't remember."

"Idiot. I'll check the snares. You make a fire under the pot."

"I don't think I set the snares."

Jael kissed her. "You were thinking of other things. Don't worry, there'll be something. Get up now." She waited until Akys rose before leaving the little hut.

She checked the snares; they had not been set. I should never have stayed away, she thought. She stood beside a thicket, listening for bird sounds, keening her senses. When she heard the flutter of a grouse through grass she called it to her. Trusting, it came into her outstretched hands, and with a quick twist she wrung its neck.

She brought the bird to the table and rolled up her sleeves. Akys was poking up the fire. "I chased a fox from a grouse," Jael said. "Throw some herbs into the water."

In bed, under two quilts, they talked. "Why do men go to war?" said Akys.

"For wealth, or power, or lands," said Jael.

"Why should anyone want those things?"

"Why are you thinking about it? Try to sleep."

"Do you think She is angry with us, Jael, for something we have done, or not done?"

"I do not know," Jael answered. She was glad of the darkness, glad that Akys could not see her face.

"They have a god who lives in fire, these men of Rys."

"How do you know?"

"The smith told me. He must like blood, their god."

"Hush," said Jael.

Finally Akys wept herself into an exhausted sleep. Jael held her tightly, fiercely, keeping the nightmares away. So Akys had held her, through earlier nights.

In the morning they heard the children shrilling and calling to the herds. "What are they doing?" wondered Akys.

"Taking the cattle to the summer pasture."

"But why, when it is so late – ah. They'll be safer higher up. Will the children stay with them?"

Jael didn't know.

That night, when she wrapped her cloak around her, Akys stood up as if to bar the door. "No, Jael, you can't go back tonight. What if they come, and find you alone?"

Jael said, "They won't find me."

"You are young, and beautiful. I am old, and a witch, and under Her protection. Stay with me."

Under her cloak Jael's hands clenched together. "I must go," she said. "I'll come back in the morning. They won't come at night, Akys, when they can't see, not in strange country. They'll come in daylight, if they come at all. I'll come back in the morning."

"Take one of the knives."

"I don't dare. I'd probably cut myself in the dark."

"Don't go," pleaded Akys.

"I must."

At last she got away.

At the cave, she would not look at the spyeyes. She had told Akys the truth, they would not come at night, she was sure of that. But in the morning . . . She twisted her hands together until her fingers hurt. What have you chosen, woman of Reorth?

She couldn't sleep. She sat in the cavern with her machines, banks of them. With them she could touch anyplace on Methys, she could change the climate, trouble the seas, kill . . . The bracelets on her wrists shimmered with power. She dulled them. If only she could sleep. She rose. Slowly, she began to walk, pacing back and forth, back and forth, from one side of the cave to the other, chaining herself to it with her will.

You may not go out, she commanded herself. Walk. You may *not* go out. It became a kind of delirium. Walk to that wall. Now turn. Walk to *that* wall. Turn. Do not impede. Walk. This is desirable. Walk. Turn. You may not go out.

In the morning, when the machines told her the sun was up and high, she left the cave.

She went down the path toward the hut. The smell of smoke tormented her nostrils. She passed the pool, went through the trees that ringed it, and came out near the river. The cabin seemed intact. She walked toward it, and saw what she had not seen at first: the door, torn from its hinges, lying flat on the tramped-down, muddied grass.

She went into the cabin. Akys lay on the bed, on her side. There was blood all around her, all over the bed and floor. She was naked, but someone had tossed her sheepskin cloak across her waist and legs. Jael walked to her. Her eyes were open, her expression twisted with determination and pain. Her stiff right arm had blood on it to the elbow. Jael's foot struck something. She bent to see what it was. It was a bloody knife on the stained floor.

Jael looked once around the cabin. The raiders had broken down the door, to find a dead or dying woman, and had left. It was kind of them not to burn or loot the tiny place, she thought.

She walked from the hut. Smoke eddied still from the village below. She went down the path. She smelled charred meat. The storehouses were gone. They had come burning and hacking in the dawnlight. She wondered if they had killed everyone. There was a body in the street. She went to look at it; it was a ewe-goat with its throat slit. A man came out of a house, cursing and crying. Jael blurred Herself to human eyes. She went in through the broken door. There were dead women in here, too: one an old lady, her body a huddled, smashed thing against the wall, like a dead moth, the other a young woman who might have once been beautiful. One could not tell from the things they had done.

Had they killed only women, then? She left the house. No, there was a man. He lay against the wall, both hands holding his belly, from which his entrails spilled. Flies buzzed around his hands.

Around Her the sounds of weeping rose and fell.

She walked the length of the street, and then turned, and walked back again, past the dead man, the dead ewe, the granaries smoking in the sunlight. They had left enough people alive in the village to starve through the winter. She followed the river past the cabin, past the pool. Just below the cabin She hesitated, drawn by a change in the mutter of the stream. The raiders had tossed a dead body into the clear water, and wedged it between two big rocks, defiling it.

She returned to the cave.

She lit it with a wave of Her hand. The light flamed and stayed, as if the stone walls had incandesced. Surrounded by bright, bare, burning stone, Jael walked to Her machines. She flung a gesture at the lumenings: the points of light whirled crazily, crackled, and died. The screen went blank. She passed Her hand over it; it stayed blank, broken, dead.

She smiled.

She turned to a machine, setting the controlling pattern with deft fingertips. She had not used this instrument since the plague time, when She had had to mutate a strain of bacteria. Meticulously She checked the pattern, and then tuned it finer still. When She was wholly satisfied, She turned the machinery on.

It hummed softly. A beam went out, radiation, cued to a genetic pattern. It touched Spykos of Rys, where he lay in his war tent outside the walls of Mykneresta's capitol, the city of Ain, with a twelve-year-old captive daughter of that city whose home and street his soldiers were busy burning to ash. It touched the guard outside his door. It touched the soldiers pillaging the city. It touched the little bands of raiders raping and killing in the countryside.

It touched the nobles of Rys. It touched Araf, Hechlos' king, where he lay with his third wife, and Asch, his son, where *he* lay with a slave girl whose looks he'd admired, that morning. His new wife slept alone. It touched the nobles of Hechlos, the high families of Dechlas.

It touched every male human being over fourteen on the six islands. It did not kill, but when it encountered the particular genetic pattern to which it had been cued, it sterilized. The men of Kovos, Nysineria, and Mykneresta it ignored. But on Rys, Hechlos, and Dechlas, and wherever it found men of that breed, it lingered. No seed, no children; no children, no dynasty; no dynasty, no empire; no empire, no war.

At last She shut it off. Around Her the stones still burned with light. She looked once around the cave that had been Her home for three hundred years. Then, using the bracelets, She set a protective shield around Herself, and summoned the patient lightning from the walls.

To the remaining villagers who saw it, it seemed as if the whole of the Lady's mountain exploded into flame. Balls of fire hurtled down the mountainside; fire-wisps danced on the crags like demented demons. Stones flaked and crumbled. "It is the Fire God of Rys," the villagers whispered. "He has come to vanquish the Lady." All through the night they watched the fires burn. By morning the flames seemed gone. That day some brave women crept up the path. Where the Lady's pool had been was a rushing stream, scored by the tips of jagged rocks like teeth. Above it the mountaintop was scoured into bare, blue ash. The Lady had fled. The grieving women stumbled home, weeping.

No seed, no children.

With the coming of the first snow, word came to Mykneresta, carried by travelers. "The women of Rys are barren," they said. "They bear no children." And in the villages they wondered at this news.

But in the spring, the singers one by one came from their winter homes, to take their accustomed ways along the roads. They told the news a different way. "The Fire God's seed is ash," they cried, "He burns but cannot beget," and they made up songs to mock Him, and sang them throughout the marveling countryside. No children, no dynasty. The sang them under the walls of the brand new palace that Spykos of Rys had built in Ain. But no soldiers emerged to punish them for this temerity, for the brand new palace was empty, save for the rats. No dynasty, no empire. There was war in Rys over the succession, and Spykos had gone home.

It was the women who brought the truth. They came from Rys, from Hechlos, from Dechlas. Leaving lands, wealth, and kin, they came to the islands their men had tried to conquer. They came in boats, wives of fishermen, and in ships, wives of nobles. Wives of soldiers and merchants, kings and carpenters, they came. "Our men give us no children," they said. "We bear no sons for our fields, no daughters for our hearths. We come for children. Have pity on us, folk of Mykneresta; give us children, and our daughters will be your daughters, and our sons, your sons." No empire, no war.

Then the whole world knew. The poets sang it aloud: "The Lady is with us still, and She has taken vengeance for us." In Ain they rebuilt Her altar, and set Her statue on it, and they made Her hair as red as fire, and set hissing, coiling snakes about Her wrists, so real that one could almost see them move. Even on Rys the poets sang, and under the Harvest Moon the people danced for Her, keeping one eye on the Fire God's mountain. But it stayed silent and smokeless.

On Mykneresta the trees and bushes grew back on the Lady's mountain. One day in late summer, when the streams were dry, some rocks slid and fell. After the rain a pool formed, and it stayed. The old women went up the path to look. "She has returned," they said.

In spring the next year a woman came to the village. Her face was worn and weathered, but her back was straight, and though her red hair was streaked with gray, she walked as lightly as a young girl. "I am vowed to the Lady," she told the villagers, and she showed them the bracelets, like coiled snakes, on her slim brown wrists. "I am a healer. I have been in many lands, I have even been to Rys, but now I must come home. Help me build a house."

So the villagers built her a cabin by the curve of the stream, below the Lady's pool. They brought her meat and fruit and wine, when they had it, and she tended their sickness and healed their wounds. They asked her name, and she said, "My name is Jael."

"Have you really been to Rys?" they asked her.

"I have," she said. And she told them stories, about cities of stone, and tall men with golden hair, and ships with prows like the beaks of eagles, and streets with no children.

The children of the village asked, "Is it true they killed their king, because they thought he brought the Lady's Curse?"

"It's true," she said. "Camilla of Ain rules in Rys, and she is a better ruler than Spykos ever was or ever could be."

"Will they ever come again?"

"No, they never will."

A girl with brown braids and a small, serious face, asked, "Why did they come before?"

"Who knows? Now, be off with you, before night comes."

The children ran, save for the brown-haired girl. She lingered by the door. "Jael, aren't you ever afraid, so close to her holy place?"

"How could I be?" said the healer. "This is my home, and She is good. Go on now, run, before the light goes."

"May I come back tomorrow?" said the girl.

"Why?" said Jael.

"I – I want to learn. About herbs, and healing, and the Lady."

"Come then," said Jael.

The girl smiled, like a coal quickening in the darkness, and waved, and ran like a deer down the path beside the stream. Jael watched her go. Above her the clouds spun a net to catch the moon. She stood in the cabin doorway for a long time. At last the cold wind blew. Turning from the night, she pulled her green cloak close about her throat, and closed the cabin door against the stars.

Find the Lady

Nicholas Fisk

These days people who behave like "stereotypical" lesbians or gay men are often snubbed within their own communities as well as by heterosexuals. Why does such stereotypical behavior upset people? How far does surface behavior really define the person underneath? Such questions hover just behind the raised eyebrows at this different slant on a War of the Worlds situation.

The scarred metal grab reached out and touched the little wooden writing desk. Mitch, feeling the giggles rising in him, clutched Eugene's arm. Eugene glared, but it only made things worse.

"Ooop! – ooo! – ooop!" went Mitch.

"Shut up! Oh, do shut *up!*"

"Ooop! Oh dearie me, I'll die!"

"Silly pouf. Shut up!"

"Don't call me that name–"

"Shut UP! They'll hear."

The metal grab protuded a metal claw. It made a tiny puncture in the ginger wood and wihtdrew. A hundred feet or so away in the grab's parent body, a message was received. There was a lacklustre spurt of messages – a dim buzzing and clicking and whirring echoing up and down the extensible limb.

The metal grab, with surprising delicacy, again protruded its claw and began tracing the outlines and surfaces of the desk. It was what had been known as a Davenport. It had a tooled-leather inclined lid with storage space beneath it, supported on a body containing a multiplicity of drawers, sliding boxes and trite gadgetry. The claw explored.

"God save us," wheezed Eugene, "when it gets to the *legs* . . ." The giggles were fighting through again. The legs! "The *legs!*" groaned Mitch, clutching himself.

They were too absurd, the legs. Once, the Davenport must have been possessed of two respectable curlicued fretwork legs – or perhaps two faked wooden pillars with capitals. They had long gone. Filled with joyous spite, Mitch and Eugene had replaced them with two rusty chromium-plated tubes they had found in the rubble. The effect was lunatic: the grandiose little ginger Davenport had somehow become a desk of easy virtue. They had danced round it, shouting at it.

"Harlot!"

"Strumpet!"

"Wicked thing!"

"Dirty French whore, showing your legs!"

"Soiled dove!"

"Naughty saucy beastly dirty DAVENPORT!"

Then they had staggered in helpless laughter, holding each other up; two aging queers, delirious with malice and joy.

"Bet you They buy it!"

"Bet you They don't!"

"Don't be such a sillybilly, you *know* They will! They'll *leap* on it! They'll *lust* for it! Our dirty Davenport!"

"Just because They bought the telephone and the King George the Fifth biscuit tin doesn't mean They'll – "

"It does, it must! They'll simply *coo* over it! They've simply no *taste* – "

"They don't understand *nice* things, *pretty* things – "

"They've no *feelings* – "

"Well, how could They, the poor loves? I mean, just *look* at Them! *Gaze* upon Them!"

They had both turned their heads and gazed upon Them. There was nothing much else to look at. What had been a country town was now a plain of reddish dust. What had been trees were now fungus-pocked stains on that dust. What had been railway lines were rusty traces of another red. Even the sky was tainted with the same glowering, indelible redness. The dust was everywhere.

Not that They stirred it. For five years They had stood sentinel, ringing the area of the town center. They seldom moved. The reddened sun glanced off their opaque bodies – fused glass which sometimes emitted winks and rays and subdued noises, but more often not. The metallic legs, 250 feet or so high at full extension, seldom shifted their articulated, raft-like feet, which might be embedded for months on end in the compound of brick dust, vegetable dust and human bonemeal. Lichens and fungi grew over the feet, and once Eugene swore he had seen a rat. But never an insect or a bird. Dead five years.

But now, at this very moment, the claw was tracing the lines and textures of the Davenport and Mitch and Eugene clasped hands, shaken by suppressed and holy glee. The *legs!* The claw solemnly examined them, the clumsy grab moving on hidden articulations of silken perfection.

"OK," said the grab. It spoke in an approximation of the town's mayor – a voice five years silent.

"OK. Will take genuine antique. Genuine. Or kill. OK?"

"OK," whispered Eugene, the giggles suddenly gone.

"OK antique!" said Mitch. "Genuine. No kill. OK. *Hon*estly."

"*Ask!*" hissed Eugene.

"No, you!"

"It's your turn–"

"Fat pouf! You know it's your turn to ask–"

"Pouf yourself!"

"Bedwetter! Queer! Stinkpants! *Ask* it!"

But Mitch began helplessly to cry, so Eugene had to ask.

"What will you give us? Something good, OK?"

No answer. Messages ran up and down the grab's arm. Then the voice in the grab answered.

"More food. More bricks. More alcohol. More water. More lamp oil. OK."

"Yes, but – *how* much more? *Much* more this time, OK?"

Again a long pause; then, "OK." The grab retracted with a soft whirr, carrying the Davenport as if on a platform. The machine's legs twitched and moved and a great metal foot knocked the top off the humans' hovel, then guiltlessly crushed its way, hayfoot, strawfoot, across the dust to resume station.

"Oh, and *now* look what They've done!" wept Mitch. "Clumsy beasts! I hate Them! I loathe Them! Big silly *cows!*"

"Come and help me put it all *back* –"

"You called me *names*, you're always calling me *names* –"

"I didn't mean it, you know I didn't mean it. Do be a dear and *help.*"

"If I'm what you called me, so are you and worse. Worse! Sometimes I think I hate you, you're so cruel, so mean, you've given me my pain again –"

"Come and *help.*"

"My pain –"

"Oh, do please, please, please SHUT UP."

They put the hovel together and crawled into it. It grew darker. Quite soon, the only light would be the dim blue chain of beams linking Them. You could not pass this chain. Nobody had tried now for four years and eleven months. The powdery marks of disintegrated bodies had of course long since disappeared.

Two hours later, Mitch and Eugene were giggling mad again.

"Do stop!" gasped Mitch. "You're killing me! I'm quite *damp!*"

But Eugene wouldn't stop. "I'm one of THEM!" he chanted. "One of THEM!" He had pulled a broken plastic bucket over his head; the remains of two squeegee floor mops served as Their legs and feet. He jerked and slithered grotesquely. Then, inspired, he picked up an oil lamp and hung it over his backside.

"Deathray!" he shouted. "You can't get past! Oh no, you can't! I've got a deathray in my bottie!"

In the corner, the alcohol dripped from the still. Tonight was a good night. Tommorrow, They would bring more of life's little luxuries. Life was good.

Life was awful. Most of those who had lived past Their coming had died more or less voluntarily. There was nothing to live for.

It had all been very simple. One day, you were a barber or a butcher or a baby or a businessman or a beautician. You said "Good morning" or kept yourself to yourself. You ordered lamb chops, put the cat out, mowed the lawn, tinkered with the car, watched TV, played bingo, distributed leaflets for the council elections.

Next day, They came and you were dead.

The TV was dead, the telephone was dead, the neighbors were dead, the flowers in your garden were dead, the cat was dead, the baby was dead, the municipal county council was dead. All without a whimper. All inside one violet-flashing, flesh-eating, matter-consuming millisecond.

All except those who were actually under and within the areas covered by Them and Their machines. For those, if their hearts did not burst with the shock, there was life of a sort. Not that anyone understood what sort. Consider Eugene and Mitch.

They had been the scandal of the little town. As they walked together, their waved hair and their glittering slave bangles caught the sun. Their staggeringly tight jeans displayed rolling hips and twitching buttocks as they walked. Under the broad straps of their sandals peeped the lacquered toenails, now crimson, now silver-pearl. No hairs showed on their toes; they plucked them out with tweezers.

They touched each other incessantly as they walked. A manicured hand would find a sunlamp-bronzed forearm and rest there to stress a point. They were always stressing points. The waved heads would converge and nod and shake, the sibilant whispers would be exchanged, the eyes would roll and pop; then the heads would be thrown back and shrill whinnying laughter would bounce off the Georgian brickwork of the high street, tinkle against the curved glass of the slenderly framed and elegantly proportioned windows, desecrate the war memorial.

They simply adored the town, it was too utterly winsome and tender.

The town blackly hated them.

They ran the antique shop. Or seemed to do so. For no townsman would ever visit it. Perhaps Eugene and Mitch lived on legacies; perhaps they supplied the big, important antique dealers in the cities; no one knew how they lived or what they lived on. It was enough of an affront that they lived at all, a disgrace to the whole community.

Not that they had any part in the community. They lived in their own little tinkling pagoda of a world, primping their hair in the sweetly darling Regency mirror by the Adam mantel (but could one be sure it was really, truly Adam?) and pouting naughtily when it was their turn to make the Lapsang Souchong, or pursing lips in concentration when trying out new drapes (*not* the voile, Mitchie love, something more *floating* and *ethereal*) to hang on the great fourposter they were said to share . . . They needed no one but each other.

It was on one of those ordinary, halcyon days that Mitch said, "Oh, but Eugene, do *listen!*"

"I won't, I simply won't. I'm stopping my ears. There!"

"But Eugene, hear you must, hear you shall! It's a com*plete*ly genuine and *quite* ridiculous earthenware water filter thing, something from the Crimean *war*, I dare promise, and it's lying in a *field* not a mile from here and we could fill it with potpourri—"

"I despise the very sound of it."

"But if only you'd come with me and look at it with me and help me carry it, you'd make me the happiest boy in the *world*—"

"Really, Mitch, how camp can you get! 'The happiest boy in the world'!"

"Well, *will* you or *won't* you help me carry it?"

That evening, they had minced briskly down the main street and were soon out in the fields. The water filter, a great ceramic thing bespattered with relief plaques saying NONPAREIL and PATENTED and so on, lay in a ditch. As they bent over to lift it, the strange shadows darkened the ground. It was Them, one of Their machines, directly overhead.

A second later, the world ended.

"But did it?" Eugene asked. "I mean, who are They? I mean, is it the machines—"

"H.G. Wells hardware, that's all the machines are!"

"Well, what and where are They?"

"Grotty littls *insect* men, with colds in their heads. Or delicious hairy, bug-eyed monsters. *Do* you remember that *blissful* horror film, with that too utterly *ghoulish*—"

"Oh, do make an *effort*. I mean, at *most* fifty people survived in our town. We're probably the last people alive. And They took the mayor, do you remember . . . Why the mayor? Did They *know* he was the mayor? They can't have done, such a *plebeian* little man, you could never have told—"

"I can't see why They bothered to let *anyone* survive. I suppose we're merely specimens, and They keep us alive just to *gloat*."

"But the darlings do fancy our antiques."

"Oh, yes, we've always got that. Well, for a few weeks, anyhow."

"Anyhow, we're obviously not the last people alive, there's Adam and Madam and Crazy Annie. Oh, no, she's dead now, isn't she? *Poor* old faggot."

In a hovel some hundreds of feet from theirs had lived a crazy old woman called Annie. She had been crazed enough, God knows, before They came. Latterly she had rooted in the dust like a hen, scratching at nothing in particular with horny fingers and mouthing filth when Their machines came with supplies. Mitch and Eugene had been afraid of her. Not for what she *was*, but for what she represented: themselves, later. . .

Farther away, there was Adam something-or-other. He was dark, unpleasant, disgruntled and musical. He shared his hovel with a girl who had worked in the greengrocer's shop when there had been a greengrocer's shop. Then, she had been a nice little miniskirted, pony-tailed, blond piece. Now she was a nasty, gross, sacking-skirted virago and the blond had grown out. Her name was Lucy. This was the couple that Mitch and Eugene called Madam and Adam. But the two couples had seldom spoken to each other. Burying crazy old Annie had brought the four of them together.

Adam and Madam made musical instruments out of bits of tubing, and played and sang. They played very softly, for they were afraid of Them. They might hear and take away the instruments.

Possibly there were other people here or there, but there were reasons for not finding out. As Eugene and Mitch agreed, "We might seem a little odd, but we're used to being thought odd, aren't we? And we've got each other, while all Adam and Madam have got is a hatchet to *kill* you with, or a kinky tin whistle to *bore* you with . . . I mean, they're not really people any more. They've nothing to live for."

But then, only too often Eugene and Mitch would have a little spat and say things they didn't mean – or worse, things they did mean – and see each other as they really were. They would weep and accuse and even slap and scratch, and end by sobbing, "What are we living for? Why do we go on?"

One reason was the cellars. The Davenport had come from a cellar. Shortly, the Davenport would be transmuted into food, warmth and comfort. They knew this from experience. They had already offered Them oddments from various cellars and each time had been rewarded. It was rather like the old days when they ran the antique shop. Only now it was a matter of survival.

That was why they were so pleased with the pickaxe. Mitch had found it in the Davenport cellar; with it, they could open up more cellars. The pickaxe was their key to capitalism.

Almost immediately, it opened up a treasure-trove.

In a freshly opened cellar, they found a birdcage, a settee covered in brown plush and a wind-up gramophone.

As they were about to dig up more treasure, they heard the noise they should have anticipated: Their machine. It was shuffling about in the near distance outside their hovel. It was saying, "OK. Come out. OK. Bricks, lamp oil, food, alcohol, water. OK. OK, come out."

"Jesus H. *Christ,*" whispered Mitch. "If They knew we were here –"

"Oh, do be *quiet!* Walk, do not run, to your nearest hovel –"

"If it ever suspected –"

"Well, let's take it something. Distract it."

"Not the birdcage, it's *too* precious—"

"The gramophone, then. Quickly!"

The two of them slid through the hole in the cellar wall, Eugene carrying the gramophone. In seconds they were back in the hovel.

"Where you were?" said the grab.

"Call of nature, dear. OK?"

"Not OK," said the grab. "Perhaps kill."

"You don't have them, calls of nature, do you? Lucky old you!"

"Perhaps kill."

"Got its needle stuck, poor love," whispered Mitch.

"Oo, what a good idea! Show it the gramophone!" said Eugene.

"Look, dear!" said Mitch to the grab. "Lovely gramophone! *Ever* so genuine antique, worth goodness *knows* how much!"

"How much?" said the grab. Its messages had started up.

"Oh, lots and lots of *everything*. You see, gramophones are *quite priceless*—"

"Better even than Davenports with chromium-plated legs—"

"What is for?" said the grab.

"Ah," said Mitch, "I'm glad you asked me that. Well, no, I'm not. You see, it's ever so – complicated . . . Particularly," he added aside, "when you've got no bleeding records to play."

"What is for?" said the grab's voice, dourly.

"Like I said, dear, it's a gramophone—"

Messages started going back and forth within the grab's arm.

"Do be careful, Mitch, They take it all down and look it up in something," whispered Eugene.

"Gramophone OK," said the grab.

"OK? It's simply *fabulous*. Particularly these very super-delicious ones with the *doggies* on them—"

"Gramophone," said the grab. "What is for?"

"Well, as I was saying, this is a *round-and-rounder* type gramophone. You wind it up like this" – Eugene wound the dismally creaking handle – "and you turn the lever *so*, and there you are! Round and round! *Too* enchanting!"

"Not OK," said the grab. "Perhaps kill. Incomplete. Not OK.

Perhaps take away oil, water, food—"

"Don't let's be hasty!" said Eugene, horrified. "Mitch, for heaven's sake get back down there and look for *records.*"

"Don't be so *crass.* They musn't find out about the *cellar*—"

"Oh, dear. Listen, love," said Eugene brightly to the grab. "My friend and I will just riffle through our little treasures while you trot off and have a lovely rest. Your poor *feet* . . ."

"And come back before it's dark and perhaps we'll have a *surprise* for you!" said Mitch.

More messages; then the machine lumbered away.

"Cheeribye!" cried Mitch.

"Drop dead! Turn blue! Perhaps kill!" added Eugene, quietly.

It was gone, back in station with the others.

"Please God," sighed Eugene, "we'll find some records."

They found them. Old 78s in a sort of hatbox.

"Deanna Durbin!" breathed Mitch. "How too *utterly,* in*tox*icatingly, de*lir*iously mirth-provoking!"

"'I love to climb an apple-tree, but apples disagree with me—'"

"'And I'll be sick as sick can be—'"

"Perhaps kill, OK?"

They pranced with joy and put the record on. For a moment, the voice from the past clutched at some soft and vulnerable and half-forgotten soft centre inside them. But they were tougher than they knew. Soon their mocking falsettos blended with the scratchy soprano from the gramophone. They sorted through the records.

"Duke Ellington! 'The Mooche'! Whatever happens, we'll keep that, and *bother* Them!"

"Nothing *really* my style here, except one Peggy Lee."

"What's the good of records if we give Them the gramophone—"

"Oh, do *look,* I can't believe it. A Benny Goodman quintet! 'Seven Come—'"

"Not 'Seven Come Eleven'! Utter bliss! Throw darling Deanna away and let's get *in the groove,* as one said!"

They were dancing together, Eugene leading, to the strains of

"I'll be loving you, always" when suddenly they became aware that Their machine was standing looming over them. They broke apart and Mitch made to switch off the gramophone.

"OK," said the grab. "Continue. Don't stop."

"Well, actually, dear," said Mitch, "that was the last waltz and Mummy will be furious if I'm not home by midnight." He switched the gramophone off.

"Don't stop!" said the grab, loudly and instantly.

"In a *trice,* all our lovely clothes turn into *rags* –"

"Again," said the grab.

"– And Prince Charming will do his *lot!*"

"Again," said the grab, menacingly. The messages thrummed.

"Give him Deanna," said Mitch. "Don't waste Peggy Lee on old Tin-ear."

"'Ave Maria'!" announced Eugene. "*Wholly* holy." Deanna Durbin's voice warbled. The grab was still. The needle went "Grrk" at the end of the track. There was silence.

Then messages started running up and down, furiously.

"Again!" said the grab.

"That's all for now, there isn't any more," said Mitch.

"If you liked us, tell your friends," added Eugene. "If you don't like us, turn blue."

"Again!" said the grab.

"*Goodies,*" said Eugene blandly. "*Lots* of goodies. Oil, water, alcohol, everything – *lots* of everything. Then we play it again, OK?"

Messages percolated. "OK!" said the grab. "Again. Now."

"Okay, toots. One more time, Deanna baby – and make it *swing.*"

"Aaaaaaaaah ... vay ... MaREEEEE–EEEEE–aaah..." began the record. The music poured over the derelict landscape like treacle over iron filings.

"*Too* grotesque!" murmured Eugene. "*Too* puke-provoking."

"Look!" whispered Mitch.

"What? Where?"

"The *grab! Look* at it!"

Eugene looked. His eyes and mouth made Os of amazement.

The grab was swaying in time with the music.

Mitch swilled the Médoc round his teeth, swallowed, considered, and said, "No. Positively and irrevocably NO."

"Well, I think it's very fair for a 1962. And it must have been utter *agony* for them to find anything at *all*—"

"*Not* a nice wine. Not nice *at all.* If they can find that very acceptable Riesling, they can find something better in Médocs. I will *not* be put off with this dis*gus*ting, *spe*cious, hydrochloric-acid Médoc. Not after all the music we've played them."

"I suppose we'll have to pass the Médoc on to Adam and Madam. Though they couldn't care *less* what they drink. . ."

"They wouldn't notice the difference between python's pee and Piesporter. All I'm saying is, up with this I will not put. I shall tell our little metal chum when he comes: *could do better if tried harder.* I shall tell him, go and find some better red wines – *preferably* château-bottled – or it's *Smackbottomsville.*"

"And no Golden Hour of Melody tonight."

But of course there was a Golden Hour of Melody. There had to be. It was the GHM that bought the rugs, the unlimited lamp oil, the bottled chicken breasts, the spring mattress. It was the GHM that had turned the hovel into what Eugene and Mitch called the Mixed Blessing – a home filled with extraordinarily assorted furniture and fittings, but a home for all that.

For music had, to put it mildly, caught on with Them. It had infected Them, almost enslaved Them. They had to have their music. They had to pay for it with untold diggings and burrowings, by uncovering God knows what mounds of rotting horrors. The grabs would thrust and gouge through shreds of decaying scalp, through pavements and pelvises, through Old Masters or a stockpile of suppositories . . . The spoils would be laid before Eugene and Mitch: a doll's head, a belly dancer's nipple cover, a pack of cards, a garnet brooch, a German dictionary, a set of dentures – nearly, but not all, broken, decayed, crushed, torn, mouldering, useless, horrible; grist to the music mill, grist to the Mixed Blessing.

Adam and Madam arrived, dour, half-drunk, bickering,

stupid, smelly and uncouth.

"*Darlings!*" said Mitch, advancing on them, then recoiling from their stench. "All tuned up, are we? Ready to play?"

"Ur."

"How *very* fetching that sacking looks, Lucy. But now I *insist* you wet your little whistles with some of this too-scrumptious Médoc – the wine of France, the very latest consignment from our shippers, specially for *you*. Eugene, foaming beakers, *if* you please."

"With beaded bubbles winking at the *brim*, loves. Ladies first."

"Ur."

"The true, the blushful Hippocrene."

"Grr."

On the whole, though, the party was going very well. Adam and Madam tuned their by no means unsophisticated instruments – the grabs had worked overtime to find guitar strings, tuning heads, pieces of wind instruments, even a flute in working order – and, whatever their social failings, Adam and Madam played and sang rather well. Even more important, both had an excellent ear. Between the four of them, they could produce an almost endless anthology of words and music, containing anything from "Greensleeves" and harmonized fragments of operatic arias to soldiers' songs of unspeakable filthiness.

"Tonight, I *rather* thought," said Mitch, "we could oblige with a *soupçon* of the hey-nonny-no stuff. 'There was a lover and his lass,' perhaps. Then a nice slow rendition of 'Danny Boy,' very *pathetic*. Then – but do let's agree on the words – that rather *malodorous* song of yours, Adam, 'I've got a bulldog called Big Ben.'"

"Ur."

"'Eats like nine and' – oh dear! – '*defecates* like ten.' I *can't* bring myself to utter it. But They seem *so* to enjoy it–"

"They're coming," said Eugene. "Now, are we all in tune? *Goodness*, at least a quarter tone flat. How one *longs* for something that doesn't need tuning with a *spanner*. . ."

"They're here."

And there They were (three of them!) with grabs extended. "Like Oliver Twists," murmured Eugene, preparing to enjoy himself. He was Master of Ceremonies and as such felt himself licensed to be amusing at Their expense.

"Ladies, Gentlemen, and assorted Hardware," he began. "This evening, we celebrate the *umpteenth* Golden Hour of Melody – an occasion of *particular* significance, as you will readily agree – with the rendition of a deliriously auspicious conglomeration of polyphonic exuberances – in short, something for everyone. Something old, something new, something borrowed – yes, and something *blue* to set those turgid old circuits tingling–"

"Hurry *up.*"

"Don't *pull* at me. But before commencing our programme – which will begin with that stirring and ever-popular anthem in praise of our staunch four-footed friend, the bulldog – I will ask you to show your appreciation for the artistes in the accustomed manner. In short, *clap,* you bleeders! Rattle your puddies!"

"Good and *loud!*" muttered Mitch, leaning forward expectantly. This was the only part of the concert he really enjoyed – Their obligatory applause beforehand, the grating, rattling noise that the grabs had been taught to make. Applause! Well, after all, it represented some small victory or other...

"Let's hear it for the melody makers!" said Mitch in his DJ voice.

But there was no applause. No applause! The grabs were motionless. Mitch and Eugene looked at each other. Adam and Madam grumbled an uneasy "Ur." Eugene faced Them.

"The *usual* thing, the *polite* thing, before a concert is a nice cosy round of *applause*–" he began.

A grab moved, ominously. It came toward them. *"Sing!"* shouted Eugene. They sang. The grab kept moving forward and lifted to the height of their heads. Then higher. The song tailed off.

The grab kept moving. Now it was poised above the Mixed Blessing.

"Don't you *dare*–" yelled Mitch.

The grab slammed down. The Mixed Blessing bulged, leaked, crumpled, puffed red dust and flattened. Then the grab went up and down, slowly and rhythmically and deafeningly pounding the Mixed Blessing into the ground.

Mitch had stopped yelling and started blubbering. Eugene just looked, wide-eyed and expressionless. Adam and Madam formed a pyramid, leaning against each other. They looked merely bovinely interested, but tears trickled down the girl's face.

"They'll 'ave our place next," she snivelled.

She was right. The grab, leaking red silt, snaked away on its apparently infinite flexible arm, reached the hovel, smashed it at a blow, and turned over the debris as if with a spade. Madam began to howl, "*Ooooooo!*" and Adam growled.

Shattered, the little party stood there. The grab snaked back. An almost visible question mark hovered over the bowed human heads.

The question was answered.

"Your music," announced a grab, "no good. We kill."

"Natch," said Eugene, bravely flippant.

"Not OK music," said the grab. "We learn all you know. More. Listen."

There was a click, and it started. Their music. The music of Them. Music vast in amplitude—

A mother was bathing her baby one night,
'Twas the youngest of ten and a delicate mite,

They sang. The massed choir was so loud that dust trembled. The hooting orchestra was so sweet that teeth ached.

The mother was poor and the baby was thin,
'Twas only a skellington wrapped up in skin . . .

"Skellington . . ." murmured Mitch. "How bleeding, bloody *funny.*"

The mother looked round for the soap on the rack,
'Twas only a moment, but when she looked back—

Divine harmonies fluttered and swooped, twittered and burped. "*Crinoline* ladies, can't you *see* them!" said Mitch. "And we taught them. *We* taught them *this* . . ."

My baby has gorn down the plug 'ole!
My baby has fell down the plug!

bellowed the grab, in a maelstrom of bathos.

The pore little thing
Was so skinny and thin
It oughter been washed in a jug–

("– in a jug," echoed a million metal voices through a million metal noses.)

My baby has gone down the plug 'ole
It won't need a bath any more,
My baby has gone down the plug 'ole–
Not lost – but gone – beeeefore.

("Oh, gone, be–fore!" echoed the choir, its vibrato a whole tone wide, its pathos as wide as the ocean and as deep as an ink stain.)

The song ended. The silence was deafening. The game was up.

"You poor, silly, po-faced, stinking, bleeding, boneless, gutless, soulless, mindless *tin turds,*" said Eugene at last, and began to laugh. Soon the four of them were laughing. They laughed until they cried, cried until they hiccupped, hiccupped till they choked. Then were silent again.

"Now kill," said the grab.

"OK, kill," said Eugene. "Big deal."

"And so, as the sun sinks in the west, we bid a reluctant 'Farewell' to lovable old Mother Earth and her dirty denizens," recited Mitch, shakily.

"Kill," said the grab. The other two machines had already plodded back and resumed station. The blue beams were linked.

"Not with a bang, but a whimper," said Eugene. "We could be

the *very last four left!* On this whole planet! It gives one *furiously* to think." He began to weep, quietly.

"Fuck Them!" said Adam, indistinctly.

"Oh, *don't* do that for God's sake, I do *beseech.* There's enough of Them already," said Eugene, hysterically.

"Kill now," said the grab.

"How are you going to do it? Smash us flat?"

"Through the beams," said the grab. "Walk. Kill now."

"Bags I not go first!" said Mitch, flightily.

Adam bent down and picked up their pack of cards out of the dust.

"Cut," he said. "Go on, cut the cards. Loser goes first." They cut, cut again, and cut again. But it could not last.

"Now! Kill now!" said the grab. "Walk."

It lithely glided behind them, shepherding them. They walked.

"So ri*di*culous!" said Mitch. "The last! The very last! We could be the very last people in all the world! I mean, there was Jesus Christ and Fabergé and Socrates and the Unknown Soldier and poor Oscar and Queen Victoria and that boy in Corfu and George Washington – everyone–"

"–and the pyramids and spacecraft and men on the moon and Cleopatra on the Nile and soldiers dying from phosgene gas . . . Then us. Pitiful us. Oh, Mitch, pitiful, pitiful, *pitiful!*"

"First you see it, now you don't," said Adam unexpectedly. "The bloody end. Like this!" He spat in the red dust. They were very close now to the blue rays and death.

"First you see it, now you don't!" said Mitch. He was sniffling and at the same time doing a card trick. "First you see it" – and there was the card between two fingers – "now you don't." A flick of the wrist, a turn of the fingers.

They were at the perimeter. They stopped.

"Walk," said the grab. "Walk."

Eugene crumpled at the knees and sat down, legs straight out like a doll's. "It's no good, I just *can't!*" he sobbed. "Not like *this* . . . I'm *me, me!* It's not *fitting,* it's not *seemly,* it's too *hideous*–"

The girl sat down too. "I bleeding won't!" she said.

The grab sidled up and scooped them to their feet. "Kill now," it remarked. "Walk."

She began to run, away from the perimeter. She ran and ran, stumbled and fell, got up and ran again. The grab smoothly wove its way after her but when she stumbled, overshot. Mitch sniggered hysterically. "Find the lady!" he shouted. "Now you see her, now you don't!"

In the end she was shepherded back by the grab. No one could bear to look at her face; no one could keep their eyes from it. Desperately, Mitch shouted, "Come on then, you lucky lads! Find the lady, win a fiver! I place three cards, so! – Acey-deucy, King, and last *but* not least, the lady – the Queen! *Face* down, on the ground, positively no deception! You want a second look, lady? Right you are – Ace, King, Queen. Positively no deception! Now, keep your peepers on the *Queen*, that's all you've got to do! On the Queen. On the lady!"

His hands swept over the three cards, fluttering and magical. Yet it was easy enough to see through the trick. There was the Queen! Now there! Still there! Now over there, on the left! Child's play.

"All right!" shouted Mitch. "Now – *find the lady!*"

Adam spat disgustedly. Lucy looked at nothing through her swamped, defeated eyes. Eugene – But the grab pushed him aside, hovered over the three cards, extended its metal claw, and said, "Lady."

"Do I hear you aright, sir? *Here*, sir? *This* card, sir? You're quite *sure*, my dear sir?"

"Lady!" The metal claw tapped.

Mitch turned over the card: the King.

Messages tinkled, swelled, hummed.

"Again," said the grab.

The sun was lower, lower still.

"Again," said the grab.

The lamps, Their lamps, blazed under the night sky.

"Take a card. Any card! That is your choice? Excellent. Commit it to memory. . ." Mitch shuffled gaudily and kept up the patter. "Now, you, sir, as I instantly discerned, are no mere acolyte at the shrine of prestidigitation, but a veritable *adept*. So when I ask you once again to select a card—"

Dawn.

"Again," said the grab.

"Again," said the grabs.

No Day Too Long

Jewelle Gomez

Traditionally, in vampire stories, sexual passion is thinly disguised by considering the vampire's desire as hunger, not sex. What happens to the character of the vampire when sexual attraction may be explicitly described?

Gilda left the party, sure that the young girl, Effie, had been flirting with her. Although Gilda often went to the parties that the young women gave, she accepted that her life was separate from theirs. It had been too long since she had loved anyone.

While she sat at the piano, playing and singing, the girl stood across the room not moving or turning her eyes from Gilda. It did not matter how long she had been away from love, the look was unmistakable.

Gilda cherished singing for those enchanting women who were so full of energy. It fulfilled her in a way different from the nights on a bandstand singing to clouds of smoke and noisy ice cubes. The checks from the clubs in the Village or casinos in New Jersey never enriched her as much as their tender hands on her back or the dazzling smiles they showered on her when she sat among them singing to them alone.

The heels of Gilda's boots were silent and swift as she descended the marble steps of the large old apartment building, and on the sidewalk outside. She sped quickly down Riverside Drive toward her apartment in Chelsea. The October air was brisk and fresh on her face. She glanced at the New Jersey skyline as she side-stepped the memory of Effie.

Gilda felt an almost imperceptible change in the air as the sun's rays began to push dawn into the sky. She looked to the east then hurried along, becoming visible to the few who sat on parkside benches, anticipating the morning.

Once inside her apartment she bolted the doors and undressed for a shower. She looked around the small space that was so peculiarly hers. Her piano stood in one corner, its niche barely carved out of the mountain of books surrounding it. Bright cloth draped the ceiling and walls, hiding the fake wood panelling the realtor had mistakenly thought was a good selling point. Heavy blue velvet curtains covered the windows, whose panes were painted over with city scenes.

The Eiffel Tower adorned the top half of one, the market place in Accra enlivened another. Boston's Beacon Hill wound its way up the glass door which led to the back garden. She pulled the drapes around the rooms and dropped her clothes on the armchair.

She stood, not so tall without her boots, before the full-length mirror, while the steam from the shower filled the bathroom. She looked at her body, marvelling at its fineness. Her black skin shone like a polished stone. The rounded stomach and full legs were unchanged from those of her ancestors. Her teeth gleamed against soft lips and through the fog her dark eyes looked back at her as alive and sparkling as they had been when Gilda first saw herself in a looking glass 150 years before.

She washed her thoughts away from her as she lathered the rose scented soap over her body, rinsed clean and turned her mind to sleep. She unlocked the small room where she would lie. The full platform bed was covered with satin sheets and a comforter that rested on warm Mississippi soil.

Gilda locked the door behind her and lay down, naked except for the juju bracelets that had adorned her arm since she was a young girl. She lay still on her back looking at the shadowless ceiling for a few minutes. Then she closed her eyes, resolved not to think of the girl, Effie. Locked in and safe, she slept the sleep of the dead.

Saturdays were too often the same. Saturday nights had to be special and this Saturday the women were coming. They had secured a van and journeyed to New Jersey to hear her sing.

In the cubicle the management called her dressing room, Gilda sipped red wine. The sharp and sweet sound of the jazz trio on the bandstand was in the same room with her. It washed around her and relaxed her. The rhythms between her and other musicians created a family for her. Playing and singing had become the only constant joys in her long life. Now sharing this with the other women had raised the risk of discovery but still she held them to her. She refused to recall the number of times she had fled a city or friends, afraid they would demand too much of her.

Now whatever barrier she thrust between them dissolved when they laughed or called her name. They respected her whims or most obvious fabrication. Still when she arose at dusk and opened the mail there was always an invitation from one of them. They completed a circle of family that Gilda was desperate not to break.

She went to the side of the bandstand for the group's last number. She saw the women sitting there, attentive, but impatient for her to appear. There was Kaaren, the sleek, with her red nail polish and high heeled shoes. She sat next to her lover, Chris, whose serious face was softened by curls falling over her forehead. Ayeesha sat slightly apart. Her thick dreadlocks tied up in a richly colored strip of Kente cloth. When she opened her mouth in a smile the light played off the tantalizing gap in her teeth. Cynthia, next to her, was tiny and brown, like an exquisite museum miniature of a Nigerian work of art. Lavern sat tall, her long legs apologetically sprawled into the narrow aisle between the tiny tables pushed together for them. She was surprised and pleased to see Alberta out with the group.

"Good for her," Gilda thought as she listened to the applause for the musicians. Her friends were a good audience. Most of them were clapping and stomping their feet. Marian applauded politely, reluctant to give a man anything. Her eyes darted around the room, looking for danger or an exit. Her face remained a mask. There was Effie! She applauded loudly, bouncing youthfully in her seat and looking around at the same time.

Gilda heard the pianist introduce her before he left the bandstand. She blinked several times, drawing her face into the opened eyes smile that her fans expected from her. She stood on stage and looked down at her friends and sang a cappella, "I love you for sentimental reasons. I hope you do believe me. I've given you my heart."

For a moment they were hushed by the ringing quality of her voice alone, then they applauded wildly. When she sat at the piano it was only she and they again as it had been so often before. She looked out into the room unable to see them clearly over the lights which shone down on her.

"I want to sing a song I wrote that I haven't sung for anyone before tonight. It's dedicated to someone, of course, but I'm not sure who yet," she said wryly.

Her long fingers danced over the keys, gathering the rhythms and melodies of many ancient worlds. The notes cut through the smoky air silencing the random conversation. When she sang, her voice came out softly, caressing the air before slipping into the microphone.

> My love is the blood that enriches this ground
> The sun is a star denied you and me.
> But you are the life I've searched for and found
> And the moon is our half of the dream.
>
> No day is too long nor night too free
> Just come and be here with me.

The applause surrounded and engulfed her, a long awaited embrace. Each song brought her closer to them. Only in these moments did she feel at peace with the world. She kissed the air around her before she stepped down from the bandstand, exhausted. Even as she revelled in her success, she calculated how she would weaken the tide of their adoration. It was the only way she could go on luxuriating in the pleasure the singing gave her and still avoid the steady attention which would make her secret life come under suspicion. She must soon again become one of those many singers who blazed brilliantly then disappeared, a name no one quite remembered.

She put those thoughts off until later, now she joined her friends at their table. She signalled the bartender and he sent over the bottles of champagne she had ordered. The waiter poured freely and they all laughed and kissed each other, exultant at their discovery of this precious gem.

"Your new song is too good, girl. Why've you been keeping it to yourself?" Ayeesha said. Her penchant for organizing and promoting was barely hidden.

By the time the women had finally reached their boroughs, Gilda had been sitting in the back alley garden behind her apartment for over an hour. She looked up at the tenements rising around her and listened to the noises that lay in the air above her: babies sleeping in their cribs, Ismael Miranda singing through the speakers of a cheap stereo, and the low sounds of lovers.

She felt Effie trying to reach her through the night. Somewhere the girl lay alone in her bed, her body moving in rhythm with her quickened pulse and Gilda's name on her lips. Gilda withdrew from the night and returned to her room. She sat before her mirror bathed in candlelight, watching her eyes for some resolve to her confusion.

The evening played before her. She pushed backwards into her past, going far. There had been other friends, whose love she'd shared, whose graves she'd adorned with flowers. She looked into the history she knew and saw the angry words, secret looks, passion, jealousy, treachery and love. The machinations that make the world go around.

The light flickered around her memories as she sifted through them. Still, she found no counsel. She snuffed out the candle and crawled beneath the silken comforter, finding no comfort there. The ceiling remained a blank before her eyes. She could project no images except the face of the girl. She was young and hummed the tunes as if she knew them all.

Gilda turned over onto her side, unused to having rest elude her. More often it waited impatiently for her, eager to take her into its folds and protect her from harm. This morning she drew her knees up close to her chest and curled her toes, trying to recall what it had been like to be a child. Shortly before the first rays of morning sun began to tap unsuccessfully against her painted windows, she slept. This day she dreamed.

Before she dressed the following evening, Gilda sat at her piano in the corner nearest the window. She played the shadow game. The sun stole across the sky falling past the Hudson into the west. As it passed across an open alley opposite her rooms the fading yellow rays reflected through the opaque gold on her window panes. The painted Eiffel Tower turned into a beacon and refracted light cast shadows on the floor. She watched from the piano bench, poised like a cat, taut and confident, unseen by its prey. She tried to spin a world from that drop of light. She imagined it bathing the park and children sweating as they played beneath it. Before she could fix the picture in her mind the light was gone and evening had begun.

That night she sang in Queens, in a nightclub that embraced the small homeowners and winners from Belmont. The songs came easily but did not wipe the horrible memory from her mind. The blood she'd taken this evening had almost taken a life. She'd come upon a man, black and sure, smoking on a bench by the river. From his back she could see that he was strong, so she had no fear that he would miss the few ounces of life she drained from him.

She had slipped her arms around him, holding him immobile as she sprang over the bench and caught his gaze. The terror in his eyes was quelled by her tranquilizing stare. She sliced a small opening behind his ear and drank slowly. She held him to her breast so that anyone happening by would see them as lovers enraptured with each other. As his blood flowed into her she felt the spark that is all life rekindle inside of her. The blood was warm and soothing throughout her body. She closed her eyes and for a moment she was distracted by her thoughts. She took too much.

His fluttering lids over unseeing eyes startled her. She was angry at her indulgence and carelessness. There were others she knew who enjoyed the moment of death of their victims and revelled in satiation. Gilda did not need to kill, nor did she ever want to enjoy it. Unless it was her deliberate purpose.

When she lay him down on the bench, she measured his pulse and was relieved. She stepped away quickly and ran her tongue over her unpainted mouth clearing the least vestige of red and found her performance smile.

Her songs that night were sung savagely, filled with the anger she still felt. She spit them out at the smiling faces and somehow they took her pain as love. They applauded her anguish and congratulated her on her despair.

Through her second set she still could not clear the incident from her mind. She did not remember his face but the feel of his body filled her with revulsion. The unmistakable weight of death had made his body sag in her arms and she could not dispel the sensation. When the evening was over she hurried from the club, leaving through the back door. The rancid odor of garbage and decay filled the alleyway along with the sound of scurrying animals. Her footsteps were silent among them. She returned to the park and walked past the bench. He was gone.

She raced downtown, eager for the night to end. The Manhattan streets were alive with people returning home. The city was perfect for Gilda, living in the night was not unusual and her neighbors never noticed that she was rarely about during the day. They too were locked into their own coffins: offices, shops and factories, each one waiting for release into the freedom of night.

She turned the corner onto her empty street, relieved to be at home again. She took the two steps that led down to her door. As she opened it she heard a noise behind her and turned sharply.

"Gilda?" The girl, Effie, stood above her on the step.

She was startled by her abrupt appearance. Her mind ran in confusion through the excuses she could use to send her away.

"I've been waiting for you to return. I hope you don't mind."

"No, I'm happy to see you." The words came honestly to Gilda.

"May I come in for a moment?"

Gilda noticed the slight trace of an accent she could not identify and had not noticed before. Effie looked so tall standing on the steps and the shadows hid her youthful face.

Gilda opened the door and stood aside to let Effie enter first.

Gilda turned on the lamp which glowed a dull red beside the one overstuffed armchair.

"May I offer you something to drink, wine or a cup of tea?"

"No, thank you. I just wanted to talk to you."

Effie removed her short jacket and sat in the chair. Gilda paced the room, uncomfortable. She washed her hands in the bathroom, trying to think of conversation. When she finally sat down on the small trunk in front of her, Effie spoke immediately.

"I know that you are avoiding me and that makes me very sad. I think you know that. . ." the girl faltered a moment and her words trailed off into the thick quiet. She glanced around the rooms seeking reassurance from the shadows, then went on.

"You know what I feel for you but I had to face you with it. You must say that you do not love me, then I will leave."

Gilda sat frozen on the trunk, watching the girl's face. Her dark skin was shining under the glow of the lamp and her lips were pressed firmly together holding back the tears that followed her burst of courage. Gilda's fingers played mindlessly with the studs that lined the edge of the trunk. Under its lid lay the few treasures that made up her inheritance: the dress she'd worn in the fields before she had run away from the plantation, a caning knife she'd stolen on the night she escaped. She'd used it only once, to kill the white man who'd discovered her hidden in the tack house. Beside it lay the rusted metal cross her mother had made for her and a brown leaf journal that had belonged to the woman in Louisiana who had found her. She had taken Gilda to a fancy house and hidden her. She'd taken Gilda's life and returned it to her, making Gilda a creature of the night like herself.

"Old memories are so empty when they cannot be shared," Effie said softly, watching Gilda's surprise.

"What do you mean?" Gilda asked as she rose from the trunk and walked over to the piano as if seeking its protection.

"Your coolness is a device to push me away, when I know it is not what you want. You are scampering around inside of your own thoughts when you should be joining with mine."

Gilda turned to face her. She looked directly into Effie's eyes for the first time. The lamplight swirled hypnotically and she felt herself being drawn inside. This girl, Effie, was a woman centuries older than she! In a brief moment Effie's history unfolded behind her eyes and Gilda saw a girl both young and old, who had lived longer than any other Gilda had ever met. There was no reason for Gilda to run away from her.

Gilda's heart pounded wildly and her body trembled. Effie was there holding Gilda in her arms too quickly for her movement to be seen. They stood in the dark room holding each other for a moment. The words to Gilda's song rang in their minds.

> My love is the blood that enriches this ground
> The sun is a star denied you and me.
> But you are the life I've searched for and found
> And the moon is our half of the dream.
>
> No day is too long nor night too free
> Just come and be here with me.

Gilda locked the doors behind them and the two women slipped under the comforter. They slept easily in each other's arms, the morning light kept safely at bay.

Full Fathom Five My Father Lies

Rand B. Lee

Every human society has rules and regulations which dictate the behavior of its members. But what constitutes these social expectations and taboos can vary greatly from society to society, as demonstrated by the following story.

I buried my father at dawn, in the deep place beyond the reef, where the water sinks down until its blue becomes so black that the creatures living there have no word for light within them. My son Porran helped me bury him. We loaded his body onto the boat, Porran weeping, I not. We pushed the boat away from the shore. We paddled with our hands until we reached the hole in the grey reef's girdle, then used our staves. It is difficult to pass the reef at any time, but it is especially difficult in the early morning. Porran used the flat blade of his stave, *slap, slap!*, against the somber water, *slap, slap!*, like Greeter's hands at the Gate of the Newborn. I pushed against the guardian-weed with my stave. For a moment the green tubes resisted. Porran slapped the harder, crying "Would you hinder the dead?" in his deep voice. The watchers on the shore heard and sighed. The weed heard as well. It relaxed, and the boat slipped through the sudden hole in the girdle and out the other side, where the water lay bloody with the early morning and underneath, black.

We laid down our staves and resumed paddling with our hands. There was no more weed. Sea-Knower says that the weed cannot grow outside the reef just as the ploaters cannnot mate beyond the springtime. It was because Sea-Father and Plant-Father had appointed the weed guardian and a guardian does not leave its post. I think rather it may be that the water is too deep beyond the reef for the weed to grow; I do not say this. I am Plant-Knower, but the sea changes things. Perhaps Sea-Knower is right.

My father's grave is eighty strokes of the arm straight out from the reef-hole, fourteen strokes of the arm to the right of the reef-hole as a man's back is turned. I counted aloud, which is the custom. Porran, whose task it was to witness the counting so proper testimony could be given Death-Knower later, kept making small suppressed weeping sounds which distracted me. Once I nearly lost count. When we reached the place I stopped counting.

We worked quickly, for it is cold outside the reef in Ploater-month and of course we wore no clothing. Porran handed to me my father's stave. Our hands met briefly on its smoothness, its wood that does not grow. It looked different in the dawn. Before this morning, I had seen it only once in the open, away from the shadows of the lodge wall where it had always hung. I took it from Porran and raised it high, resting its base between my thighs and pointing its shaft toward the low red sun. I thought as I noticed the sun, *Bad weather today*. It is strange what people think when they are drowning.

To my father I said, "To Sky-Father, O my father, to Earth-Father, O my father, to Sea-Father, O my father, to these make your way."

"Through the dark make your way," said Porran at my side.

That is all there is. I wished for more as I sat there with my father's stave between my thighs, but I could think of nothing more, and after a time Porran whispered, "Hurry," so I lowered the stave and placed it in the boat. My own stave I took and placed upon my father's chest and belly. Porran tied it to him with ropes. I looked upon his face and the need to say something pressed against my temples. Instead, I took his head and kissed his eyes and then his mouth.

"Hurry," whispered Porran.

Hating him, I put my hands under my father's shoulders.

Porran had already grasped his legs. Slowly we lowered him over the side of the boat. The water touched his buttocks, pooled at his groin. He was bone against it. We let go of him and he sank. At once we turned away our eyes, for it is not lucky to view the beginnings of another's journey, especially the journey that is the last. We waited until we were certain that enough time had passed for him to have journeyed beyond reach of the light; then I glanced at the grave. Its surface was a lodge-wall, and there was nothing in its depths.

We paddled back to the shore. Again the slap of the paddle, only this time it was I who beat the guardians, to let them know that the stave of my father had returned as the stave of his son. The weed resisted us only a little, the warming sun having softened it. By noon it would be flaccid as the brittle leaf we use to scour our pots. We passed through the reef-hole and made our way in the red dawn toward the ones who waited on the bank.

I did not behave well. I walked past Death-Knower's comfort, past all the faces and the hands, with Porran at my heels urging me to stop. My father's stave I held on my shoulder, and it was as heavy as Earth-Father on Sky-Father's back. Not only did I not speak, I did not weep. When I came to the lodge I replaced my father's stave in its cleft, and I stood gazing upon it. Porran stood dark in the doorway.

"You are a shame to me," he said.

"I am sorry" I said. I did not turn to him. His feet scratched on the floor. He pressed his body against mine, from behind. He did not dare to place his hands upon me, but rested his chin on my shoulder. We stood in this way while I gazed upon my father's stave until something that had curled up within me uncurled. I found myself weak as a ploater-chick, weak as drizzle. I sat down on the floor of the lodge and beat my head against the hearth-stone and shrieked.

My father had told me what it had been like for him to lose his father, in the landslide before I had outgrown the Pool. In the worst agonies of my nights I had never imagined it to be as difficult as it was for me that morning. I heard the others enter the lodge, their hard feet; I heard them settle, and knew that they were seating themselves in semi-circle behind me; I heard my voice, rising and breaking and falling and rising; I even heard the ploaters calling to one another outside. I saw nothing and felt nothing but anger. I had never been so angry. My father had described it as a burning. It was worse, for a flame burns until its fuel is consumed. This needed no fuel.

It was loathsome. I thought it would not end. It did, of course. It ebbed, then withdrew in a rush, like the tide. I felt myself like the sands uncovered by the tide, littered with stinking, detestable things. So close as to have been at my side, a ploater scolded his child. I began to weeping. A glad sound passed through the others, a breaking of tension. My weeping was quiet. Porran came over and knelt directly behind me. He put his arms around me and laid his chin on my hair. I reached up and gripped his hands. "Now you are not a shame to me," he whispered.

Death-Knower was before me in the dimness. I let go of Porran's hands; he kept his arms around me. I looked up at Death-Knower. Above his sandy flank, beyond the farrow-hide skirt and the necklace of ploater-skulls, above his pale beard, his eyes stood. I felt fear. "Forgive me," I said. He spoke not to me but to Porran.

"Was the grave well-found?" he asked. His voice was the voice of the lightless shoals. Porran's arms tightened.

"It was well-found," he said. "Eighty strokes and fourteen."

Death-Knower grunted. His eyes held mine. I became aware of the closeness of his body. The smell of him, old, and the small brown smell of the farrow skins, came to me. All at once I knew he would not curse me. My father and he had been young together. I said to him, "It was well-found." He held my gaze a moment longer, then blinked, then nodded. Squatting, he reached for me; Porran nearly fell in his haste to escape Death-Knower's touch. The old one embraced me, very strong. We swayed, and the semi-circle of watchers swayed also.

Song-Knower began to sing a song of Fathers. We joined our voices to his, filling the lodge. It is strange, this song; it is the most strange to me of all their songs. Perhaps it is how the voice must form the tune, how it must pace like an old man restless for death-journey. Song-Knower, who knows as much about the hidden things of the First Fathers as Pool-Knower, says that this song is the only song that remains from the time before the Exile, when the First Fathers began their long crawl up Sky-Father's spine. It is a song a son sings sitting in his boat near his father's grave.

"Full fathom five my father lies," sang Song-Knower,
"Of his bones are coral made;
Those are pearls that were his eyes,
Nothing of him that doth fade
    but doth suffer a sea-change
Into something rich and strange.
Sea-bells hourly ring his knell;
Hark, now I hear them; hark, now I hear them;
Ding, dong, bell."

And we sang:

"Ding dong, ding, dong, bell;
Ding dong, ding, dong, bell;
Ding, dong, ding, dong, bell."

There are many words in the songs we do not understand, but we understand *sea*, and how it changes those who descend into it.

Afterward, we all sat together, under my father's stave, only it was not my father's stave any longer; it was mine. I talked of how my father had lived and how he had died. The others said the usual things. Porran sat close, thinking of my death. When it came his turn to speak, he said, "He-who-journeys planted for me a scion of the blue earlyvine that bloomed near the cave. Today it flowers for the first time near our lodge."

They murmured and nodded: *A smile from Plant-Father*. I was not grateful. The anger had left, and the weeping had cleansed me of the stinking things, and the song of Fathers had steadied me, but still there was a wrongness. Outside, the wind had changed, and there was a warning note in the calls of the ploaters.

Finally Death-Knower said, "It is well." He rose; we all looked up at him. "He-who-journeys is far beyond the reach of evil. As yet we are not. The storm that comes must be prepared for." Alone, for of course the Death-Knower has no son, he passed from among us and the lodge door opened. We did not turn until we heard the door close. Immediately the others rose, some stretching, some conversing. They were kind. They spoke to me and to Porran, each of them, Sea-Knower and his son, Sand-Knower and his son; Net-Knower and his son who had lost an eye, and all the rest. Some touched me on the shoulder as they departed. I smiled but I did not rise, nor did Porran. When all of them had gone, still we sat.

My father's stave hung in silence. I looked at my son: he was tense; his shoulders bunched in little hills. My father and he had been close. I said, "I know. It is as though someone had stolen the hearth from the lodge. Though it were summer, and there were no need for fire to warm us, still we would feel robbed."

"Yes," he said, deep in his throat like me.

"It is as hard for me, my son."

"I understand," he said. Of course he did not understand. He will not understand until he and his son lower me into the darkness beyond the reef with his stave strapped to my chest and belly.

I said, "We must go now to the Pool."

I took his hand and rose; his arm went with me, his body did not. Then it did. We walked outside. There were many clouds, and a wet smell to the air. Although the morning had far advanced, it was as dark as it had been at dawn. My stave I carried on my shoulder. Those who saw us glanced away, obeying the custom. It is said that the gods hid their faces and wept when the First Fathers turned their backs toward Exile, and that is why we do not look upon the faces of those who journey. We walked over the sand between the lodges and out of the village.

The Pool lies in the white lodge at the edge of the inlet. Porran tensed when we came within sight of it, for of course he had never been there. I had been there, once. It looked the same. Ploaters shrilled, and farrows scattered at the sound of our feet on the hard path. Pool-Knower Morras and his son Yavan were waiting for us at the entrance to the lodge. Morras raised his stave. "Who are you that approach?" he demanded.

When I had last been to the lodge, it had been his father who had challenged my father, and he who had stood to his father's left, watching politely.

"It is Jun Plant-Knower," I replied formally, "with Porran his son."

"Proffer your staves." We did this. Morras made a show of examining them, although he could tell at a glance by the symbols painted on them to whom they belonged. I grew impatient; the wind was rising, tossing Porran's black hair. Finally he said, "Pool-Knower greets Plant-Knower and his son. The Pool is prepared. It is well?"

"It is," I said.

"It is," said Porran, slowly. I glanced at him. His face was guarded. Morras's son Yavan was looking at him. I remembered how nervous I had felt with my father. Morras stepped aside, clearing the entrance to the lodge. I stepped forward, Porran trailing. The door to the lodge moved aside. I entered; Porran followed. I turned to help him, to guide him before me; I saw Yavan's expression, like disease. Morras came after us and closed the door behind him, shutting out his son.

It was exactly the same. The Pool lay in the white glow as though it were expecting something. The time-weed had not grown, or perhaps it had been trimmed; the Pool-Knowers do not tell. We passed the high banks and the god-letters only Pool-Knowers can read. We came to the edge. The clear shell that protected the surface of the Pool was open. We stood together as fathers and sons have always stood. I squatted and touched the surface of the Pool with my stave. Ripples sprang out. The time-weed reacted instantly, opening its scores of little mouths. I laughed and looked up at my son. He was not laughing. "It is not a deep pool," I said.

"It is there I will lie?"

"Yes," I said. "There is nothing to fear." I lifted my stave and touched his chest with its dripping end. His chest was hard, like the stalks of the guardian-weed at night when the reef cannot be passed. His skin shivered as the liquid from the Pool dripped upon it. "We are the same," I said. It was foolish, like saying that ploaters fly, but it meant a great deal to me then to say it. "Like my father and I, we are the same, you and I; and we belong the one to the other."

Behind us, Morras moved swiftly, doing things among the banks and god-letters. He moved like his father.

"Always the same," said Porran. He squatted. He placed his

hand on my knee. I reached over and placed my palm full on his chest to feel the heart beating. His eyes were intent, serious. "Why are we always the same?"

I thought of my father's heart, buried in the dark. "Ask rather," I answered softly, "why the scion of the earlyvine is the same as the plant from which it is cut."

"The ploaters are not always the same," Porran said. "A ploater comes from the egg. The egg comes from the body of his father. Yet he has two fathers, and he is not like the father from whom the egg comes, nor is he like the other father, but he is like both of them. Why?"

It was the time for such discussions. I said, "The ploaters have no Pool. For the ploater-father to make a son he needs more strength than is in himself alone, so he must seek out another ploater, and together they are strong enough. It is not so with us. People have the Pool. It takes a man's strength and his flesh and from it gives him a son in his likeness."

Porran stared at the surface of the Pool, as though it were an enemy, as though he had not come from it in his little sack, dripping and squalling in the grasp of Pool-Knower. Among the timeweed there was a movement. I pointed. "See," I said, "the timeweed has woven already the birth-sack for your son." Longing for my father came sharp as an arrow. I put aside the stave and gripped Porran's shoulders with my hands and closed my eyes. He put his hand on my head and stroked my hair, hesitantly. I thought of Song-Knower's song, and the water invading my father's groin. I stood up, pulling him.

It was time. I placed my hand at the small of my son's back and ran my fingers up his spine. He shivered; his grip on my hair tightened. It is where the two of us like to be touched. I held him against me, his thighs inside mine. I rubbed my beard against his. The hair of our chests mingled, and his breath came quickly. I dropped my hands to his buttocks and touched where a father may not touch a son until Poolday, and as I touched him, I felt my father's touch again, and passion awoke within me.

Then he pulled away. "Father," he said. Behind him near the god-lettered wall, Morras stood motionless, his back to us. "Father, stop."

"Do not be afraid, Porran," I said. "I will be kind and the pain is quickly forgotten. Then you will go into the Pool and sleep. Come." I reached for him. He drew away.

"Father," Porran said, "I do not wish this."

"What?" I said. I do not know what was in my face, but it unnerved him. He took a step toward me.

"I do not wish to lie with you in this way."

"But it is your Poolday," I said. "Are you afraid? The pain is for a moment, and there is much pleasure; we are one, and afterwards I will put you into the Pool, where you will sleep. The Pool is kind; it feeds you. You awaken to the face of Pool-Knower, to my face, to the walls of your lodge. The Pool will have made your son; it will guard him; he will grow; Pool-Knower will come to us on the day and say, 'He is born.'"

I did not wish to say it at the lodge, with the others near. I glanced for Morras; I could not find him. "Father, listen. It is another I wish to be united with me. It is another I wish to have with me, to lower me into the Pool for the making of my son."

Clearly I heard his words and did not want them. "What is the matter with you?" I said. "My father is dead; you have no son; you have me. With whom could you wish to lie if not with your father? We are the same." I spoke as an adult to a child. When he spoke, his tone was the same.

"Try to understand," he said. "I have already lain with another in the Poolday way, and it was good."

I could not bear it. I retched, moving quickly so as not to foul the Pool. When I see Death-Father I will not be more filled with horror than I was at that moment. I wiped my mouth with the back of my hand, twin to my son's hand, twin to my father's hand, twin to his father's hand. Morras had moved; I heard a noise behind me, and seeing Porran's eyes, I turned. Yavan son of Morras stood near the entrance to the lodge, watching. The secret times came back to me then, my glimpses of Porran and Yavan, running out of the forest, sitting down at the shore the both of them, close and talking low. "Are you a farrow, which spreads its legs for any creature?" I said. Porran said nothing. I struck him across the mouth. His head snapped to one side; he held it there.

I reached and took hold of his chin and turned his face toward mine. "We are the same," I said. It was all I could do to touch him. "You cannot lie with another. I alone have the right of lowering you into the Pool. It is for fathers and sons. Would you break the stave of he-who-journeys?"

"I love you," Porran said. "You pleasure me. You care for me. But it is Yavan I want." He said it, and his eyes were the eyes of another.

I snatched up my stave and turned toward the son of Morras. He disappeared. His father stood where he had stood, backed by the god-letters. I raised my arms and shook them, helpless. There had been other instances, a very few. I turned back to Porran. "I will lower you into the Pool," I said. "If you do not go of your own will, I will make you go. Otherwise our sameness will be a lie, and our house will be filthied, and I will have no one to send me out on the long journey."

"That is all that concerns you," Porran said, with contempt.

"My father lowered me into the Pool," I said desperately. "Together we went to the white lodge when the tide was out. We lay together and united. He sang to me the Song of the Time. He lowered me with his strength into the Pool, and the time-weed bore me up; the dreams came, and then you." I was shaking, as was my son, both of us in the paleness with the storm, I realized, shaking the trees outside. The Pool's water was unruffled.

"You are selfish," said my son, "and you are old in your spirit." He pointed to Pool-Knower. "Ask Morras. Ask Yavan. They know. Sons should not have to stay with fathers, and fathers with sons. It is a custom that means nothing. The Pool does the begetting; it does not need two, only one it needs. Each may be joined to whom he wishes, and sons will be made all the same."

But we are the same, I said, only I did not say it. It was no longer light in the lodge. It seemed as black as the dark below the reef. Porran stood as tall as I. His voice was triumphant, and sad. He turned and walked past me and joined Yavan and Morras; together the three of them left the lodge. I stayed where I was. The storm roared. The rain came, and tapped the walls and ceiling.

My father was there, his stave weighing down my shoulder. He looked at me, his mouth open, shouting. I heard nothing. There was sea-weed in his beard.

I went out into the rain. It was like night. People scurried about, driving workbeasts and children to shelter. This surprised me; I had thought the storm to have been raging for many hours. I stopped the first man who came close, Tom son of Tom. "Have you seen my son?" I asked him. Thunder struck us. He shook his head; I moved on. I questioned each person I met, and each time the answer was the same. I began to feel that they were not speaking the truth, that the whole village knew and was glad. I continued, fighting the wind. I was still naked from the burial. The rain gathered on my chest and sluiced down my abdomen.

I had reached the lodge of Pool-Knower before I realized that that was where I had been heading. The door was shut tightly, as of course it ought to have been, given the storm. I hammered upon it with my fist. It slid open. Morras stood before me with the light of a fire behind him. In his hand he held his stave, pointed at me as though it were a knife that could cut me. His face was dead. He said, "Go away. Your son is not here."

"Fathers belong to sons, sons to fathers," I said to him. "Always. Always. Your father said this to me before my father lowered me into the Pool. It is a good teaching. With it, each one has another; there is meaning to our sameness, and no sorrow."

"Go away," Morras said.

"Where are they?" I asked.

"They have gone," he said. He was weeping. "My son also is gone, not yours alone."

"Where have they gone?" I asked.

"Jun," said Morras. He spread his hands, stave resting on the palms. "Have you never wished for any but your son?"

"It is one thing to wish," I said. "Where have they gone?"

The storm bellowed. A gust of wind blew rain against my back and spattered it on the floor about Morras's feet. Morras looked at me and said, "It is true, what Porran said. You are old in spirit. Go away." The door slid shut.

I turned from the lodge and held my stave close to me. The wood of it was hard and old, like the wood of which the lodges are fashioned, wood that does not burn and has no grain. Where it is found and how it is fashioned no man knows; this is wisdom of the First Fathers, and dead along the way. Unlike a lodge, a stave may be lost; therefore we hold them rarely, and rarely take them from the lodges. From the First Fathers the staves have been handed down, from father to son. On the day a son is taken from the Pool his father cuts for him from the forest a stave of common wood. It is his stave until his father dies; then he straps it to his father's body and takes his father's stave for his own.

Now Porran and Yavan will act as father and son, I thought, *and all will change.*

Therefore I knew that I would have to kill Yavan son of Morras. I stumbled in the rain and wind, moving for my lodge. The killing of a person is something that only Death-Knower may do, and that only when no healing may be found, as when a man must burn a whiteberry bush that has the rot. In the time of the Sixth Fathers, the son of Sand-Knower and the son of Beast-Knower had sought a joining. When this was discovered, the Fathers had gathered, pronounced them diseased, and when they refused to turn from their way, Death-Knower had drowned them. They are buried in the earth under the green mound at the western edge of the forest, out of sight of the sea. Now I thought, *I must go to Death-Knower; I must go to the Fathers.* But another thought came to me, that with Pool-Knower's word against me, vengeance would not be taken.

I see now that a madness was upon me, come of sorrow and pain. I could not reason, and I moved again to the lodge of Morras.

When he opened the door I hit him with my stave. He was surprised; he fell, and his cry was lost in the storm. I closed the door and sat on him. With my stave I pressed upon his neck until his face grew red. Then I said, "You will tell me where your son has gone."

"First Place," he said. He pulled at my arms, but I am stronger than Morras.

"By which path?" I asked.

"The oldest path," he said.

I must have struck him, for when I next knew reason I was standing with blood on my stave and Morras limp on the floor. His breathing was sure and the bleeding spare; I turned and left the lodge, closing the door. My mind was clear. I ran to my lodge. Everything was as I had left it when I had set out with Porran for the Pool. *He has been planning this,* I thought, *else the stores would have been lessened.* I took some of the dry pulse and the fish-chew, placed it in my bag, strapped my stave to my back, and set out into the rain. The oldest path lies to the west, and leads past the green mound. It is not forbidden, but it is avoided, as it is unlike all other paths, as the Place is unlike all other places. Neither is sought often. So I knew that was indeed where Porran and Yavan had gone.

I turned my back on the sea and the wind pushed me out of the village.

My father visited me three times that day and night. I am not given to vision; that is for Song-Knower. Yet I do not doubt that it was my father who came to me, and not merely memory made wild-edged by grief, as in the white-lodge. The first time he came to me it was as I toiled over the roughs, above the thornfruit plantings. The path begins there, marked with a post of the wood that does not burn. I had had the post in view for some time, but the wind had shifted, and I was fighting it again. I caught a gleam of white in the rocks; I bent to it. It was a shell, marked with the mark of the Pool-Knowers, a talisman or a keepsake of the son of Morras. I put it in my bag; I do not know why. When I looked for the post again I saw my father. He was huge and young, as I remember him from my childhood, and there was a light about him. In his hand he carried a bunch of earlyvine, flower, tendril, and root whipping in the wind. He was naked. He said, "My son, do not forget the law of the scion." He vanished, as visions do. I continued, reached the post, and climbed up a boulder to the oldest path.

The oldest path is fashioned of the same wood as the lodges, and like the lodges it does not weather. It stands above the ground the height of a man, and walking upon it one may look down at the land divided on either side. Fence-Knower says that it is not a path, but a wall, yet it has always been called a path, and it could be a barrier only to children and farrows. It is cool to the feet. I began to run, crouching nearly so as less to catch the wind; I moved in this way until the roughs smoothed out and fieldgrass lapped the base of the path. I stopped to rest, lying prone in the middle of the path. The storm roared around me like a father-beast protecting me, his son. I realized that my madness was passing; I no longer felt the village and the storm to be my enemies. But there was Yavan, and his father Morras; so I got up and went on.

I do not know how long I traveled before my father came to me again, but it must have been no little time, for dark not of the storm had begun to come to the sky. The path makes a wide curve toward the forest, not a straight line, so the grassland was still about me when I stopped. My father was standing in the path, like any man. The light was gone. He came up to me and put his arms around me. Our nakednesses met. I put my head on his chest; he held me. The storm continued, but it seemed not to reach us. I felt his hand on my hair, stroking it as Porran strokes it. "Father," I said. He raised my chin and kissed me; then he looked into my eyes. I could not bear his gaze; I lowered my head and clung to him fiercely. He kissed my cheek and his breath warmed my ear.

He said, "Jun, it is not Yavan you must kill."

Then he was gone, as before. I stood trembling. The storm had lessened in intensity, but still I stumbled as I walked on.

I reached the green mound about the middle of the first part of the night. By that time the storm had subsided, leaving wet sighing grass and a clear breeze behind it. The sky was yet overcast, and the moons were veiled. The mound rose to the left in a sudden hump. It seemed too old to be repulsive; its owners too long dead to inspire scorn. I wondered at the change in my feelings. I remembered, as a boy, calling Ren son of the old Net-Knower: "stupid as a Mounder" and stinging him to tears. My father had punished me. Now I looked at the mound and felt ashamed. *They wished one another, those two,* I thought. *Surely they could not have wished to wish. Surely they were ashamed, but could not leave off. Not even while they breathed in the sea.* I thought of Porran, loving me and wanting Yavan. *What lack of care did you find with me, my son?* I thought, as fathers always think when their children betray them. Then I saw what I had been seeing and not recognizing: two figures, flat in the grass against the top of the mound.

At first I did not know it was a vision. I saw Yavan and Porran lying together in the grass of the mound. I shouted and brandished my stave. They did not look up, and then I knew it to be a vision, for it was as though I were with them on the mound, watching a short way off. They were united, limbs strong in the patched dark of the afterstorm; I heard Porran gasp, and Yavan groan. They shifted, bending grass, turning their faces to the sky in joy. They were no longer Porran and Yavan. They were my father and the father of Morras. In horror I cried out, reaching. I saw my arm grown pale, and felt the touch of farrow-skulls at my chest. I moved forward; they did not know that I was there. I came up behind them and caught them by the hair of their heads. I yanked, forcing their gazes to meet mine. They lay frozen, coupled, terrified, my father and the father of Morras.

The grass moved and flowed like water. I took them and pushed them beneath it and held them. They struggled, but they were caught in their coupling. I saw my father's face shining pale, his mouth open, tongue distended; I laughed, and pushed him further down into the deep grass. The grass sucked at my wrists; I withdrew them, empty handed. They had disappeared, the two, and I stood on the oldest path, sick.

At dawn I came to the First Place, and found my son.

It is in the woods and it is surrounded by a wall that is made of stones. The path stops a distance from the wall, which is broken in many places and overgrown with forest things. Newborns are taken here. Pool-Knower stands within the circle of the walls and the father stands outside the circle of the walls. Song-Knower sings, and the child is handed through the wall to the father. One of the people, close friend to the father, acts as Greeter, and claps his hands, *clap,clap!* while the child is passed through. It is the only time the First Place is used for anything by people, unless they are fleeing. Why the First Place is not forbidden I do not know, for it is a holy place, the very oldest. It is here that the First Fathers came to rest when Sky-Father set them down. But there is nothing remarkable here, save for the ruined wall, which is not as old as the Place or the path, and within the wall, forest litter.

I dropped from the wall to the forest floor and immediately caught sight of Yavan. He was standing like his father at the Gate of the Newborn. The early light caught his hair, making it soft in the shadow. I could not see his face clearly. He said, "Porran," without turning, and in a moment my son joined him at the Gate. They stood together, so different. I thought of the two I had drowned. I said, "Why have you done this? Why have you gone the way of the Mounders when you have your fathers?"

"It is the way it should be," said Yavan.

"No," I said, gripping my stave. "Never has it been this way. You break the staves of your fathers and tread them into the mud."

"Do you hear him?" the son of Morras said to my son. "Tell him."

And Porran said, "You are wrong, Father. Your way is false. The way of the First Fathers was ours."

I stood stunned. "That is not true," I said.

"It is true," said the son of Morras. "I know. We found it written in the god-letters."

"The god-letters," I said, "the letters in the white lodge?"

"You know nothing," Yavan said. "You do not even know that there are other letters, many of them, carved into wood that does not burn, in the secret places beneath the Pool."

"It is true, Father," Porran said. "Yavan has showed me."

"He is lying about what he reads," I said. My son stood, staunch. "He is lying. The father of Morras himself told me that fathers and sons are meant for one another, and that any other way is diseased. Why would Pool-Knower say this if it were false?"

"He did not know," Yavan said. "My father found them."

"Found them?"

"Pool-Knowers are men only, Plant-Knower," said the son of Morras scornfully. "They do not see all or understand all. The First Fathers made the white lodge the strongest of all the lodges. The Pool is our life; without it, we could have no sons. So it is well-protected. Therefore within the lodge the Fathers placed that which they did not wish lost to time or accident. Among these things were the writings that Morras my father found."

"Mounder writings!" I spat in the shadow. Porran looked stricken, which pleased me.

Yavan shook his fist. "Mounder writings, then, yes!" To Porran he said, "I told you. It is no use. He will never believe us."

"He is my father, Yavan," Porran snapped. Yavan thrust my

son behind him and stepped closer to me, large in his anger.

"Listen, Plant-Knower," he said. "Time passes. Things are forgotten. What the First Fathers made and understood, the Third Fathers made and did not understand. Things were written, so people would not forget, but letters do not cry out with voices; they can be shut away where none may read. My father and I, we do what must be done in the white lodge to keep the time-weed from failing and the Pool from drying, but we do not understand what we do, Plant-Knower. We do what we are told. In the god-letters."

I could not reply. I heard Yavan say, "Pool-Father knew his sons' sons would forget, so you see that he was wise to have had written for us the things we need to know for our lives. And among these things is the truth about fathers and sons."

"And what is your truth?" I asked.

Porran answered, stepping forward again, his words an eager rush, eyes glinting. "They came from far away," he said. "The gods exiled them. They were like the workbeasts, Father. They had no strength to make sons alone. They joined with others. Some gave strength, others received strength, and adding to it their own strength bore sons within them."

"Like ploaters," I said. "Laying eggs."

"The bearing-Fathers were lost on the journey. The others were alone in the sea of the sky. Without the bearers, there could be no sons. It was then that they built the Pool."

"In the sea of the sky they built a Pool?" I asked. I laughed. Porran's face darkened.

"It is true," said Yavan. "There were Pools already, for small beasts they had taken with them into exile. They changed the Pools for people. They found this place, our home, and found the sea, found that it was much like the water in their Pools. They saw that they could make new Pools, here. They came. They made the oldest path and built the lodges. They brought their staves with them. They made the white lodge and the Pool. They planted in the way of the sea's flow the guardian-weed, which cleanses the waters and makes them fit for the Pool." He stopped for breath. "Do you see? Do you hear? Once it was not fathers and sons, always together, only fathers and sons. Once there were others, like the farrows and the ploaters. *They* are proof! *They are from the old home!"* He spoke like Morras, strong, sure. "A Pool-Knower came who must have hated the old way. He taught lies. Men feared that the old wisdoms would be lost without strictures. Fathers were bound to sons. But the First Fathers wished us to be with whomever we chose. The Pool begets all the same, and no one is unhappy." He stopped. His voice softened. "Do you see, Jun?"

"They built the Pool," I said, stupidly, "so that sons could be made from fathers without these others."

"Without these others," said Porran softly. "And such odd others, more different still from us than Morras is from you. So you see, Father, how can it be wrong for Yavan to lower me into the Pool?"

I did not intend to do then what I did. I took my stave and hurled it, and it struck Yavan son of Morras on the side of the head as my clod of mud had struck Ren Sand-Knower's son on the day my father punished me. He fell, with blood. Porran cried out, and went to him. I strode forward and gripped Porran by the hair. I pulled him from Yavan and cast him to the ground. I took Yavan by the throat and I squeezed his throat until he was dead. Porran tried to stop me; but I was strength, and blood, and fire. At night my head rings from the beating he gave it.

When Yavan was dead I dropped him and Porran left off striking me. I thought that he would fall to his knees and weep over Yavan as I had wept over my father's body; he did not. He had no tears. He looked at me, merely. He has my father's face, as have I. "Porran," I said. I could think of nothing more to say.

I slept. In my sleep I felt the scar in my side where the Pool had taken flesh from which to grow Porran. I felt it grow large, and ugly. The Pool gave it hands, and a knife, and it cut itself from my side where it had grown. And it sang, *"Full fathom five my father lies,"* with the voice of Morras.

I came to myself in the close gloom of my lodge. My father's stave was beside me. Porran was there, sponging my face, making no sound. At the back of the lodge, Death-Knower's form was an aged calm. Porran must have noticed the wits returning to me, for he uttered a cry and came close. There was no warmth in his eyes.

"We are the same," I said. He merely looked.

"The son of Morras is dead," said Death-Knower. "The Fathers have met. It is as it should be; you are released from blood-guilt. Porran your son has admitted his wrong in wishing Yavan for his father; he has asked to be cleansed."

"What of Morras?" I asked.

"He grieves," said Death-Knower. "We are satisfied that all that was done by Yavan was done without Pool-Knower's knowledge. He will give to the Pool something more of his flesh so that he may have another son to raise in the ways of Pool-Father. The wisdom will not be lost."

I glanced at my son, and knew that Death-Knower knew nothing, and knew that Morras had told nothing of the hidden god-letters or the Pool in the middle of the sea of the sky. "Porran," I said, and reached for his hand. He did not move. Like my father he sat, like me he sat, crushing the sponge in his fist. After a moment he turned to me.

"Father," said Porran, and the way he said it touched me cold like the current off the deep beyond the reef. There was a weight about his shoulders. Suddenly he did not look like me at all. "You may lower me into the Pool when you wish, that I may get a son for you." He said it as though he were building a wall with the words. Then he leaned over me, close, as though to kiss me on the mouth. Instead he whispered, so low not even Death-Knower could have heard him. "Do not expect me to look upon your face," he said.

Then he turned away, averting his eyes, and I knew what my father had tried to tell me, that it was not Yavan who had been my enemy after all. I cried out, and would have touched him again; but he sat, and the stillness of the way he sat told me that I would never be able to touch him any more. I knew why he had averted his eyes. It is unlucky to view the beginning of a journey, especially that which is the last. And as I watched him, sitting like one who sits in his boat while his father sinks down into the blackness of his grave, I realized that although it would be many years before my journey's end, it had begun.

Time Considered as a Helix of Semi-Precious Stones

Samuel R. Delany

When it first appeared in the sixties, some readers missed a lot of the sexual content in this story – and, more or less consequently, were baffled as to just what the story could be about. A post-Stonewall audience, however, will be likely to find that sex and sexual orientation play a central part in this elegant tale. Of course there must have been quite a few readers even back in those ancient days who savored every little nuance: "Time/Stones", as Delany abbreviates it, won both the Nebula and the Hugo for its year.

Lay ordinate and abscissa on the century. Now cut me a quadrant. Third quadrant if you please. I was born in 'fifty. Here it's 'seventy-five.

At sixteen they let me leave the orphanage. Dragging the name they'd hung me with (Harold Clancy Everet, and me a mere lad – how many monickers have I had since; but don't worry, you'll recognize my smoke) over the hills of East Vermont, I came to a decision:

Me and Pa Michaels, who had belligerently given me a job at the request of *The Official* looking *Document* with which the orphanage sends you packing, were running Pa Michaels' dairy farm, i.e., thirteen thousand three hundred sixty-two piebald Guernseys all asleep in their stainless coffins, nourished and drugged by pink liquid flowing in clear plastic veins (stuff is sticky and messes up your hands), exercised with electric pulsers that make their muscles quiver, them not half-awake, and the milk just a-pouring down into stainless cisterns. Anyway. The Decision (as I stood there in the fields one afternoon like the Man with the Hoe, exhausted with three hard hours of physical labor, contemplating the machinery of the universe through the fog of fatigue): With all of Earth, and Mars, and the Outer Satellites filled up with people and what-all, there had to be something more than this. I decided to get some.

So I stole a couple of Pa's credit cards, one of his helicopters, and a bottle of white lightning the geezer made himself, and took off. Ever try to land a stolen helicopter on the roof of the Pan Am building, drunk? Jail, schmail, and some hard knocks later I had attained to wisdom. But remember this o best beloved: I have done three honest hours on a dairy farm less then ten years back. And nobody has ever called me Harold Clancy Everet again.

Hank Culafroy Eckles (red-headed, a bit vague, six-foot-two) strolled out of the baggage room at the spaceport, carrying a lot of things that weren't his in a small briefcase.

Beside him the Business Man was saying, "You young fellows today upset me. Go back to Bellona, I say. Just because you got into trouble with that little blonde you were telling me about is no reason to leap worlds, come on all glum. Even quit your job!"

Hank stops and grins weakly: "Well. . ."

"Now I admit, you have your real needs, which maybe we older folks don't understand, but you have to show some responsibility toward. . ." He notices Hank has stopped in front of a door marked MEN. "Oh. Well. Eh." He grins strongly. "I've enjoyed meeting you, Hank. It's always nice when you meet somebody worth talking to on these damned crossings. So long."

Out same door, ten minutes later, comes Harmony C. Eventide, six-foot even (one of the false heels was cracked, so I stuck both of them under a lot of paper towels), brown hair (not even my hairdresser knows for sure), oh so dapper and of his time, attired in the bad taste that is oh so tasteful, a sort of man with whom no Business Men would start a conversation. Took the regulation 'copter from the port over to the Pan Am building (Yeah. Really. Drunk), came out of Grand Central Station, and strode along Forty-second towards Eighth Avenue, with a lot of things that weren't mine in a small briefcase.

The evening is carved from light.

Crossed the plastiplex pavement of the Great White Way – I think it makes people look weird, all that white light under their chins – and skirted the crowds coming up in elevators from the subway, the sub-sub-way, and the sub-sub-sub (eighteen and first week out of jail, I hung around here, snatching stuff from people – but daintily, daintily, so they never knew they'd been snatched), bulled my way through a crowd of giggling, goo-chewing school girls with flashing lights in their hair, all very embarrassed at wearing transparent plastic blouses which had just been made legal again (I hear the breast has been scene [as opposed to obscene] on and off since the seventeenth century) so I stared appreciatively; they giggled some more. I thought, Christ, when I was that age, I was on a God-damn dairy farm, and took the thought no further.

The ribbon of news lights looping the triangular structure of Communication, Inc., explained in Basic English how Senator Regina Abolafia was preparing to begin her investigation of Organized Crime in the City. Days I'm so happy I'm disorganized I couldn't begin to tell.

Near Ninth Avenue I took my briefcase into a long, crowded bar. I hadn't been in New York for two years, but on my last trip through ofttimes a man used to hang out here who had real talent for getting rid of things that weren't mine profitably, safely, fast. No idea what the chances were I'd find him. I pushed among a lot of guys drinking beer. Here and there were a number of well-escorted old bags wearing last month's latest. Scarfs of smoke gentled through the noise. I don't like such places. Those there younger than me were all morphadine heads or feeble-minded. Those older only wished more younger ones would come. I pried my way to the bar and tried to get the attention of one of the little men in white coats.

The lack of noise behind me made me glance back.

She wore a sheath of veiling closed at the neck and wrists

with huge brass pins (oh so tastefully on the border of taste); her left arm was bare, her right covered with chiffon like wine. She had it down a lot better than I did. But such an ostentatious demonstration of one's understanding of the fine points was absolutely out of place in a place like this. People were making a great show of not noticing.

She pointed to her wrist, blood-colored nail indexing a yellow-orange fragment in the brass claw of her wristlet. "Do you know what this is, Mr. Eldrich?" she asked; at the same time the veil across her face cleared, and her eyes were ice; her brows, black.

Three thoughts: (One) She is a lady of fashion, because coming in from Bellona I'd read the Delta coverage of the "fading fabrics" whose hue and opacity were controlled by cunning jewels at the wrist. (Two) During my last trip through, when I was younger and Harry Calamine Eldrich, I didn't do anything *too* illegal (though one loses track of these things); still I didn't believe I could be dragged off to the calaboose for anything more than thirty days under that name. (Three) The stone she pointed to . . .

". . . Jasper?" I asked.

She waited for me to say more; I waited for her to give me reason to let on I knew what she was waiting for (when I was in jail, Henry James was my favorite author. He really was).

"Jasper," she confirmed.

"—Jasper . . ." I reopened the ambiguity she had tried so hard to dispel.

". . . Jasper—" But she was already faltering, suspecting I suspected her certainty to be ill-founded.

"Okay. Jasper." But from her face I knew she had seen in my face a look that had finally revealed I knew she knew I knew.

"Just whom have you got me confused with, ma'am?"

Jasper, this month, is the Word.

Jasper is the pass/code/warning that the Singers of the Cities (who last month sang "Opal" from their divine injuries; and on Mars I'd heard the Word and used it thrice, along with devious imitations, to fix possession of what was not rightfully my own; and even there I pondered Singers and their wounds), relay by word of mouth for that loose and roguish fraternity with which I have been involved (in various guises) these nine years. It goes out new every thirty days; and within hours every brother knows it, throughout six worlds and worldlets. Usually it's grunted at you by some blood-soaked bastard staggering into your arms from a dark doorway; hissed at you as you pass a shadowed alley; scrawled on a paper scrap pressed into your palm by some nasty-grimy moving too fast through the crowd. And this month, it was: Jasper.

Here are some alternate translations:

Help!

or

I need help!

or

I can help you!

or

You are being watched!

or

They're not watching now, so *move!*

Final point of syntax: If the Word is used properly, you should never have to think twice about what it means in a given situation. Fine point of usage: Never trust anyone who uses it improperly.

I waited for her to finish waiting.

She opened a wallet in front of me. "Chief of Special Services Department Maudline Hinkle," she read without looking at what it said below the silver badge.

"You have that very well," I said, "Maud." Then I frowned. "Hinkle?"

"Me."

"I know you're not going to believe this, Maud. You look like a woman who has no patience with her mistakes. But my name is Eventide. Not Eldrich. Harmony C. Eventide. And isn't it lucky for all and sundry that the Word changes tonight?" Passed the way it is, the Word is no big secret to the cops. But I've met policemen up to a week after change date who were not privy.

"Well, then: Harmony. I want to talk to you."

I raised an eyebrow.

She raised one back and said, "Look, if you want to be called

Henrietta, it's all right by me. But you listen."

"What do you want to talk about?"

"Crime, Mr. . . ?"

"Eventide. I'm going to call you Maud, so you might as well call me Harmony. It really is my name."

Maud smiled. She wasn't a young woman. I think she even had a few years on Business Man. But she used make-up better than he did. "I probably know more about crime than you do," she said. "In fact I wouldn't be surprised if you hadn't even heard of my branch of the police department. What does Special Services mean to you?"

"That's right, I've never heard of it."

"You've been more or less avoiding the Regular Service with alacrity for the past seven years."

"Oh, Maud, really—"

"Special Services is reserved for people whose nuisance value has suddenly taken a sharp rise . . . a sharp enough rise to make our little lights start blinking."

"Surely I haven't done anything so dreadful that—"

"We don't look at what you do. A computer does that for us. We simply keep checking the first derivative of the graphed-out curve that bears your number. Your slope is rising sharply."

"Not even the dignity of a name—"

"We're the most efficient department in the Police Organization. Take it as bragging if you wish. Or just a piece of information."

"Well, well, well," I said. "Have a drink?" The little man in the white coat left us two, looked puzzled at Maud's finery, then went to do something else.

"Thanks." She downed half her glass like someone stauncher than that wrist would indicate. "It doesn't pay to go after most criminals. Take your big-time racketeers, Farnesworth, The Hawk, Blavatskia. Take your little snatch-purses, small-time pushers, housebreakers, or vice-impresarios. Both at the top and the bottom of the scale, their incomes are pretty stable. They don't really upset the social boat. Regular Services handles them both. They think they do a good job. We're not going to argue. But say a little pusher starts to become a big-time pusher; a medium-sized vice-impresario sets his sights on becoming a full-fledged racketeer; that's when you get problems with socially unpleasant repercussions. That's when Special Services arrive. We have a couple of techniques that work remarkably well."

"You're going to tell me about them, aren't you?"

"They work better that way," she said. "One of them is hologramic information storage. Do you know what happens when you cut a hologram plate in half?"

"The three dimensional image is . . . cut in half?"

She shook her head. "You get the whole image, only fuzzier, slightly out of focus."

"Now I didn't know that."

"And if you cut in half again, it just gets fuzzier still. But even if you have a square centimeter of the original hologram, you still have the whole image – unrecognizable but complete."

I mumbled some appreciative *m*'s.

"Each pinpoint of photographic emulsion on a hologram plate, unlike a photograph, gives information about the entire scene being hologrammed. By analogy, hologramic information storage simply means that each bit of information we have – about you, let us say – relates to your entire career, your overall situation, the complete set of tensions between you and your environment. Specific facts about specific misdemeanors or felonies we leave to Regular Services. As soon as we have enough of our kind of data, our method is vastly more efficient for keeping track – even predicting – where you are or what you may be up to."

"Fascinating," I said. "One of the most amazing paranoid syndromes I've ever run up against. I mean just starting a conversation with someone in a bar. Often, in a hospital situation, I've encountered stranger–"

"In your past," she said matter-of-factly, "I see cows and helicopters. In your not too distant future, there are helicopters and hawks."

"And tell me, oh Good Witch of the West, just how–" Then I got all upset inside. Because nobody is supposed to know about that stint with Pa Michaels save thee and me. Even the Regular Service, who pulled me, out of my mind, from that whirlibird bouncing towards the edge of the Pan Am, never got that one from me. I'd eaten the credit cards when I saw them waiting, and the serial numbers had been filed off everything that could have had a serial number on it by someone more competent than I: good Mister Michaels had boasted to me, my first lonely, drunken night at the farm, how he'd gotten the thing in hot from New Hampshire.

"But why" – it appalls me the clichés to which anxiety will drive us – "are you telling me all this?"

She smiled, and her smile faded behind her veil. "Information is only meaningful when shared," said a voice that was hers from the place of her face.

"Hey, look, I–"

"You may be coming into quite a bit of money soon. If I can calculate right, I will have a helicopter full of the city's finest arriving to take you away as you accept it into your hot little hands. That is a piece of information..." She stepped back. Someone stepped between us.

"Hey, Maud–"

"You can do whatever you want with it."

The bar was crowded enough so that to move quickly was to make enemies. I don't know – I lost her and made enemies. Some weird characters there: with greasy hair that hung in spikes, and three of them had dragons tattooed on their scrawny shoulders, still another with an eye patch, and yet another raked nails black with pitch at my cheek (we're two minutes into a vicious free-for-all, case you missed the transition. I did) and some of the women were screaming. I hit and ducked, and then the tenor of the brouhaha changed. Somebody sang "Jasper!" the way she is supposed to be sung. And it meant the heat (the ordinary, bungling Regular Service I had been eluding these seven years) were on their way. The brawl spilled into the street. I got between two nasty-grimies who were doing things appropriate with one another, but made the edge of the crowd with no more wounds than could be racked up to shaving. The fight had broken into sections. I left one and ran into another that, I realized a moment later, was merely a ring of people standing around somebody who had apparently gotten really messed.

Someone was holding people back.

Somebody else was turning him over.

Curled up in a puddle of blood was the little guy I hadn't seen in two years who used to be so good at getting rid of things not mine.

Trying not to hit people with my briefcase, I ducked between the hub and the bub. When I saw my first ordinary policeman, I tried very hard to look like somebody who had just stepped up to see what the rumpus was.

It worked.

I turned down Ninth Avenue and got three steps into an inconspicuous but rapid lope—

"Hey, wait! Wait up there. . ."

I recognized the voice (after two years, coming at me just like that, I recognized it) but kept going.

"Wait. It's me, Hawk!"

And I stopped.

You haven't heard his name before in this story; Maud mentioned *the* Hawk, who is a multi-millionaire racketeer basing his operations on a part of Mars I've never been to (though he has his claws sunk to the spurs in illegalities throughout the system) and somebody else entirely.

I took three step back towards the doorway.

A boy's laugh there: "Oh, man. You look like you just did something you shouldn't."

"Hawk?" I asked the shadow.

He was still the age when two years' absence means an inch or so taller.

"You're still hanging around here?" I asked.

"Sometimes."

He was an amazing kid.

"Look, Hawk, I got to get out of here." I glanced back at the rumpus.

"Get." He stepped down. "Can I come, too?"

Funny. "Yeah." It makes me feel very funny, him asking that. "Come on."

By the street lamp half a block down, I saw his hair was still pale as split pine. He could have been a nasty-grimy: very dirty black denim jacket, no shirt beneath; very ripe pair of black-jeans – I mean in the dark you could tell. He went barefoot; and the only way you can tell on a dark street someone's been going barefoot for days in New York is to know already. As we reached the corner, he grinned up at me under the street lamp and shrugged his jacket together over the welts and furrows marring his chest and belly. His eyes were very green. Do you recognize him? If by some failure of information dispersal throughout the worlds and worldlets you haven't, walking beside me beside the Hudson was Hawk the Singer.

"Hey, how long have you been back?"

"A few hours," I told him.

"What'd you bring?"

"Really want to know?"

He shoved his hands into his pockets and cocked his head. "Sure."

I made the sound of an adult exasperated by a child. "All right." We had been walking the waterfront for a block now; there was nobody about. "Sit down." So he straddled the beam along the siding, one filthy foot dangling above the flashing black Hudson. I sat in front of him and ran my thumb around the edge of the briefcase.

Hawk hunched his shoulders and leaned. "Hey. . ." He flashed green questioning at me. "Can I touch?"

I shrugged. "Go ahead."

He grubbed among them with fingers that were all knuckle and bitten nail. He picked two up, put them down, picked up three others. "Hey!" he whispered. "How much are all these worth?"

"About ten times more than I hope to get. I have to get rid of them fast."

He glanced down past his toes. "You could always throw them in the river."

"Don't be dense. I was looking for a guy who used to hang around that bar. He was pretty efficient." And half the Hudson away a water-bound foil skimmed above the foam. On her deck were parked a dozen helicopters – being ferried up to the Patrol

Field near Verrazano, no doubt. But for moments I looked back and forth between the boy and the transport, getting all paranoid about Maud. But the boat *mmmm*ed into the darkness. "My man got a little cut up this evening."

Hawk put the tips of his fingers in his pockets and shifted his position.

"Which leaves me uptight. I didn't think he'd take them all, but at least he could have turned me on to some other people who might."

"I'm going to a party later on this evening—" he paused to gnaw on the wreck of his little fingernail "—where you might be able to sell them. Alexis Spinnel is having a party for Regina Abolafia at Tower Top."

"Tower Top. . .?" It had been a while since I palled around with Hawk. Hell's Kitchen at ten; Tower Top at midnight—

"I'm just going because Edna Silem will be there."

Edna Silem is New York's eldest Singer.

Senator Abolafia's name had ribboned above me in lights once that evening. And somewhere among the endless magazines I'd perused coming in from Mars, I remembered Alexis Spinnel's name sharing a paragraph with an awful lot of money.

"I'd like to see Edna again," I said offhandedly. "But she wouldn't remember me." Folk like Spinnel and his social ilk have a little game, I'd discovered during the first leg of my acquaintance with Hawk. He who can get the most Singers of the City under one roof wins. There are five Singers of New York (a tie for second place with Lux on Iapetus). Tokyo leads with seven. "It's a two Singer party?"

"More likely four . . . if I go."

The inaugural ball for the mayor gets four.

I raised the appropriate eyebrow.

"I have to pick up the Word from Edna. It changes tonight."

"All right," I said. "I don't know what you have in mind, but I'm game." I closed the case.

We walked back towards Times Square. When we got to Eighth Avenue and the first of the plastiplex, Hawk stopped. "Wait a minute," he said. Then he buttoned his jacket up to his neck.

"Okay."

Strolling through the streets of New York with a Singer (two years back I'd spent much time wondering if that were wise for a man of my profession) is probably the best camouflage possible for a man of my profession. Think of the last time you glimpsed your favorite Tri-D star turning the corner of Fifty-seventh. Now be honest. Would you really recognize the little guy in the tweed jacket half a pace behind him?

Half the people we passed in Times Square recognized him. With his youth, funereal garb, black feet and ash pale hair, he was easily the most colorful of Singers. Smiles; narrowed eyes; very few actually pointed or stared.

"Just exactly who is going to be there who might be able to take this stuff off my hands?"

"Well, Alexis prides himself on being something of an adventurer. They might just take his fancy. And he can give you more than you can get peddling them in the street."

"You'll tell him they're all hot?"

"It will probably make the idea that much more intriguing. He's a creep."

"You say so, friend."

We went down into the sub-sub. The man at the change booth started to take Hawk's coin, then looked up. He began three or four words that were unintelligble through his grin, then just gestured us through.

"Oh," Hawk said, "thank you," with ingenuous surprise, as though this were the first, delightful time such a thing had happened. (Two years ago he had told me sagely, "As soon as I start looking like I expect it, it'll stop happening." I was still impressed by the way he wore his notoriety. The time I'd met Edna Silem, and I'd mentioned this, she said with the same ingenuousness, "But that's what we're chosen for.")

In the bright car we sat on the long seat; Hawk's hands were beside him, one foot rested on the other. Down from us a gaggle of bright-bloused goo-chewers giggled and pointed and tried not to be noticed at it. Hawk didn't look at all, and I tried not to be noticed looking.

Dark patterns rushed the window.

Things below the gray floor hummed.

Once a lurch.

Leaning once, we came out of the ground.

Outside, the city tried on its thousand sequins, then threw them away behind the trees of Ft. Tryon. Suddenly the windows across from us grew bright scales. Behind them girders reeled by. We got out on the platform under a light rain. The sign said TWELVE TOWERS STATION.

By the time we reached the street, however, the shower had stopped. Leaves above the wall shed water down the brick. "If I'd known I was bringing someone, I'd have had Alex send a car for us. I told him it was fifty-fifty I'd come."

"Are you sure it's all right for me to tag along then?"

"Didn't you come up here with me once before?"

"I've even been up here once before that," I said. "Do you still think it's . . ."

He gave me a withering look. Well; Spinnel would be delighted to have Hawk even if he dragged along a whole gang of real nasty-grimies – Singers are famous for that sort of thing. With one more or less presentable thief, Spinnel was getting off light. Beside us rocks broke away into the city. Behind the gate to our left the gardens rolled up towards the first of the towers. The twelve immense, luxury apartment buildings menaced the lower clouds.

"Hawk the Singer," Hawk the Singer said into the speaker at the side of the gate. *Clang* and tic-tic-tic and *Clang*. We walked up to the path to the doors and doors of glass.

A cluster of men and women in evening dress were coming out. Three tiers of doors away they saw us. You could see them frowning at the guttersnipe who'd somehow gotten into the lobby (for a moment I thought one of them was Maud because she wore a sheath of the fading fabric, but she turned; beneath her veil her face was dark as roasted coffee); one of the men recognized him, said something to the others. When they passed us, they were smiling. Hawk paid about as much attention to them as he had to the girls on the subway. But when they'd passed, he said, "One of those guys was looking at you."

"Yeah. I saw."

"Do you know why?"

"He was trying to figure out whether we'd met before."

"Had you?"

I nodded. "Right about where I met you, only back when I'd just gotten out of jail. I told you I'd been here once before."

"Oh."

Blue carpet covered three-quarters of the lobby. A great pool filled the rest in which a row of twelve foot trellises stood, crowned with flaming braziers. The lobby itself was three stories high, domed and mirror-tiled.

Twisting smoke curled towards the ornate grill. Broken reflections sagged and recovered on the walls.

The elevator door folded about us its foil petals. There was the distinct feeling of not moving while seventy-five stories shucked down around us.

We got out on the landscaped roof garden. A very tanned, very blond man wearing an apricot jump-suit, from the collar of which emerged a black turtleneck dicky, came down the rocks (artificial) between the ferns (real) growing along the stream (real water; phony current).

"Hello! Hello!" Pause. "I'm terribly glad you decided to come after all." Pause. "For a while I thought you weren't going to make it." The Pauses were to allow Hawk to introduce me. I was dressed so that Spinnel had no way of telling whether I was a miscellaneous Nobel laureate that Hawk happened to have been dining with, or a varlet whose manners and morals were even lower than mine happen to be.

"Shall I take your jacket?" Alexis offered.

Which meant he didn't know Hawk as well as he would like people to think. But I guess he was sensitive enough to realize from the little cold things that happened in the boy's face that he should forget his offer.

He nodded to me, smiling – about all he could do – and we strolled toward the gathering.

Edna Silem was sitting on a transparent inflated hassock. She leaned forward, holding her drink in both hands, arguing politics with the people sitting on the grass before her. She was the first person I recognized (hair of tarnished silver; voice of scrap brass).

Jutting from the cuffs of her mannish suit, her wrinkled hands about her goblet, shaking with the intensity of her pronouncements, were heavy with stones and silver. As I ran my eyes back to Hawk, I saw half a dozen whose names/faces sold magazines, music, sent people to the theater (the drama critic for *Delta*, wouldn't you know), and even the mathematician from Princeton I'd read about a few months ago who'd come up with the "quasar/quark" explanation.

There was one woman my eyes kept returning to. On glance three I recognized her as the New Fascistas' most promising candidate for president, Senator Abolafia. Her arms were folded, and she was listening intently to the discussion that had narrowed to Edna and an overly gregarious younger man whose eyes were puffy from what could have been the recent acquisition of contact lenses.

"But don't you feel, Mrs. Silem, that—"

"You must remember when you make predictions like that—"

"Mrs. Silem, I've seen statistics that—"

"You *must* remember" – her voice tensed, lowered till the silence between the words was as rich as the voice was sparse and metallic – "that if everything, *everything* were known, statistical estimates would be unnecessary. The science of probability gives mathematical expression to our ignorance, not to our wisdom," which I was thinking was an interesting second installment to Maud's lecture when Edna looked up and exclaimed, "Why, Hawk!"

Everyone turned.

"I *am* glad to see you. Lewis, Ann," she called: there were two other Singers there already (he dark, she pale, both tree-slender; their faces made you think of pools without drain or tribute come upon in the forest, clear and very still; husband and wife, they had been made Singers together the day before their marriage seven years ago), "he hasn't deserted us after all!" Edna stood, extended her arm over the heads of the people sitting, and barked across her knuckles as though her voice were a pool cue. "Hawk, there are people here arguing with me who don't know nearly as much as you about the subject. You'd be on my side, now wouldn't you—"

"Mrs. Silem, I didn't mean to—" from the floor.

Then her arms swung six degrees, her fingers, eyes, and mouth opened. "You!" Me. "My dear, if there's anyone I never expected to see here! Why it's been almost two years, hasn't it?" Bless Edna; the place where she and Hawk and I had spent a long, beery evening together had more resembled that bar than Tower Top. "Where have you been keeping yourself?"

"Mars, mostly," I admitted. "Actually I just came back today." It's so much fun to be able to say things like that in a place like this.

"Hawk – both of you –" (which meant either she had forgotten my name, or she remembered me well enough not to abuse it) "come over here and help me drink up Alexis' good liquor." I tried not to grin as we walked towards her. If she remembered anything, she certainly recalled my line of business and must have been enjoying this as much as I was.

Relief spread Alexis' face: he knew now I was *someone* if not *which* someone I was.

As we passed Lewis and Ann, Hawk gave the two Singers one of his luminous grins. They returned shadowed smiles. Lewis nodded. Ann made a move to touch his arm, but left the motion unconcluded; and the company noted the interchange.

Having found out what we wanted, Alex was preparing large glasses of it over crushed ice when the puffy-eyed gentleman stepped up for a refill. "But, Mrs. Silem, then what do you feel validly opposes such political abuses?"

Regina Abolafia wore a white silk suit. Nails, lips and hair were one color; and on her breast was a worked copper pin. It's always fascinated me to watch people used to being the center thrust to the side. She swirled her glass, listening.

"I oppose them," Edna said. "Hawk opposes them. Lewis and Ann oppose them. We, ultimately, are what you have." And her voice had taken on that authoritative resonance only Singers can assume.

Then Hawk's laugh snarled through the conversational fabric.

We turned.

He'd sat cross-legged near the hedge. "Look. . ." he

whispered.

Now people's gazes followed his. He was looking at Lewis and Ann. She, tall and blonde, he, dark and taller, were standing very quietly, a little nervously, eyes closed (Lewis' lips were apart).

"Oh," whispered someone who should have known better, "they're going to . . ."

I watched Hawk because I'd never had a chance to observe one Singer at another's performance. He put the soles of his feet together, grasped his toes, and leaned forward, veins making blue rivers on his neck. The top button of his jacket had come loose. Two scar ends showed over his collarbone. Maybe nobody noticed but me.

I saw Edna put her glass down with a look of beaming anticipatory pride. Alex, who had pressed the autobar (odd how automation has become the upper crust's way of flaunting the labor surplus) for more crushed ice, looked up, saw what was about to happen, and pushed the cut-off button. The autobar hummed to silence. A breeze (artificial or real, I couldn't tell you) came by, and the trees gave us a final *shush*.

One at a time, then in duet, then singly again, Lewis and Ann sang.

Singers are people who look at things, then go and tell people what they've seen. What makes them Singers is their ability to make people listen. That is the most magnificent over-simplification I can give. Eighty-six-year-old El Posado in Rio de Janeiro saw a block of tenements collapse, ran to the Avenida del Sol and began improvising, in rhyme and meter (not all that hard in rhyme-rich Portuguese), tears runneling his dusty cheeks, his voice clashing with the palm swards above the sunny street. Hundreds of people stopped to listen; a hundred more; and another hundred. And they told hundreds more what they had heard. Three hours later, hundreds from among them had arrived at the scene with blankets, food, money, shovels, and more incredibly, the willingness and ability to organize themselves and work within that organization. No Tri-D report of a disaster has ever produced that sort of reaction. El Posado is historically considered the first Singer. The second was Miriamne in the roofed city of

Lux, who for thirty years walked through the metal streets, singing the glories of the rings of Saturn – the colonists can't look at them without aid because of the ultraviolet the rings set up. But Miriamne, with her strange cataracts, each dawn walked to the edge of the city, looked, saw, and came back to sing of what she saw. All of which would have meant nothing except that during the days she did not sing – through illness, or once she was on a visit to another city to which her fame had spread – the Lux Stock Exchange would go down, the number of violent crimes rise. Nobody could explain it. All they could do was proclaim her Singer. Why did the institution of Singers come about, springing up in just about every urban center throughout the system? Some have speculated that it was a spontaneous reaction to the mass media which blanket our lives. While Tri-D and radio and newstapes disperse information all over the worlds, they also spread a sense of alienation from first-hand experience. (How many people still go to sports events or a political rally with their little receivers plugged to their ears to let them know that what they see is really happening?) The first Singers were proclaimed by the people around them. Then, there was a period where anyone could proclaim himself who wanted to, and people either responded to him or laughed him into oblivion. But by the time I was left on the doorstep of somebody who didn't want me, most cities had more or less established an unofficial quota. When a position is left open today, the remaining Singers choose who is going to fill it. The required talents are poetic, theatrical, as well as a certain charisma that is generated in the tensions between the personality and the publicity web a Singer is immediately snared in. Before he became a Singer, Hawk had gained something of a prodigious reputation with a book of poems published when he was fifteen. He was touring universities and giving readings, but the reputation was still small enough so that he was amazed that I had ever heard of him, that evening we encountered in Central Park (I had just spent a pleasant thirty days as a guest of the city and it's amazing what you find in the Tombs Library). It was a few weeks after his sixteenth birthday. His Singership was to be announced in four days, though he had been informed already. We sat by the lake till dawn while he weighed and pondered and agonized over the coming responsibility. Two years later, he's still the youngest Singer in six worlds by half a dozen years. Before becoming a Singer, a person need not have been a poet, but most are either that or actors. But the roster through the system includes a longshoreman, two university professors, an heiress to the Silitax millions (Tack it down with Silitax), and at least two persons of such dubious background that the ever-hungry-for-sensation Publicity Machine itself has agreed not to let any of it past the copy editors. But wherever their origins, these diverse and flamboyant living myths sang of love, of death, of the changing of seasons, social classes, governments, and the palace guard. They sang before large crowds, small ones, to an individual laborer coming home from the city's docks, on slum street corners, in club cars of commuter trains, in the elegant gardens atop Twelve Towers, to Alex Spinnel's select soirée. But it has been illegal to reproduce the "Songs" of the Singers by mechanical means (including publishing the lyrics) since the institution arose, and I respect the law, I do, as only a man in my profession can. I offer the explanation then in place of Lewis' and Ann's song.

They finished, opened their eyes, stared about with expressions that could have been embarrassment, could have been contempt.

Hawk was leaning forward with a look of rapt approval. Edna was smiling politely. I had the sort of grin on my face that breaks out when you've been vastly moved and vastly pleased. Lewis and Ann had sung superbly.

Alex began to breathe again, glancing around to see what state everybody else was in, saw, and pressed the autobar, which began to hum and crush ice. No clapping, but the appreciative sounds began; people were nodding, commenting, whispering. Regina Abolafia went over to Lewis to say something. I tried to listen until Alex shoved a glass into my elbow.

"Oh, I'm sorry . . ."

I transferred my briefcase to the other hand and took the drink smiling. When Senator Abolafia left the two Singers, they were holding hands and looking at one another a little sheepishly. They sat down again.

The party drifted in conversational groups through the

gardens, through the groves. Overhead clouds the color of old chamois folded and unfolded across the moon.

For a while I stood alone in a circle of trees, listening to the music: a de Lassus two-part canon programmed for audio-generators. Recalled: an article in one of last week's large-circulation literaries, stating that it was the only way to remove the feel of the bar lines imposed by five centuries of meter on modern musicians. For another two weeks this would be acceptable entertainment. The trees circled a rock pool; but no water. Below the plastic surface, abstract lights wove and threaded in a shifting lumia.

"Excuse me. . . ?"

I turned to see Alexis, who had no drink now or idea what to do with his hands. He *was* nervous.

". . . but our young friend has told me you have something I might be interested in."

I started to lift my briefcase, but Alexis' hand came down from his ear (it had gone by belt to hair to collar already) to halt me. Nouveau riche.

"That's all right. I don't need to see them yet. In fact, I'd rather not. I have something to propose to you. I would certainly be interested in what you have if they are, indeed, as Hawk has described them. But I have a guest here who would be even more curious."

That sounded odd.

"I know that sounds odd," Alexis assessed, "but I thought you might be interested simply because of the finances involved. I am an eccentric collector who would offer you a price concomitant with what I would use them for: eccentric conversation pieces — and because of the nature of the purchase I would have to limit severely the people with whom I could converse."

I nodded.

"My guest, however, would have a great deal more use for them."

"Could you tell me who this guest is?"

"I asked Hawk, finally, who you were, and he led me to believe I was on the verge of a grave social indiscretion. It would be equally indiscreet to reveal my guest's name to you." He smiled. "But indiscretion is the better part of the fuel that keeps the social machine turning, Mr. Harvey Cadwaliter-Erickson. . ." He smiled knowingly.

I have *never* been Harvey Cadwaliter-Erickson, but then Hawk was always an inventive child. Then a second thought went by, viz., the tungsten magnates, the Cadwaliter-Ericksons of Tythis on Triton. Hawk was not only inventive, he was as brilliant as all the magazines and newspapers are always saying he is.

"I assume your second indiscretion will be to tell me who this mysterious guest is?"

"Well," Alex said with the smile of the canary-fattened cat, "Hawk agreed with me that *the* Hawk might well be curious as to what you have in there," (he pointed) "as indeed he is."

I frowned. Then I thought lots of small, rapid thoughts I'll articulate in due time. "*The* Hawk?"

Alex nodded.

I don't think I was actually scowling. "Would you send our young friend up here for a moment?"

"If you'd like." Alex bowed, turned. Perhaps a minute later, Hawk came up over the rocks and through the trees, grinning. When I didn't grin back, he stopped.

"Mmmm. . ." I began.

His head cocked.

I scratched my chin with a knuckle. ". . . Hawk," I said, "are you aware of a department of the police called Special Services?"

"I've heard of them."

"They've suddenly gotten very interested in me."

"Gee," he said with honest amazement. "They're supposed to be effective."

"Mmmm," I reiterated.

"Say," Hawk announced, "how do you like that? My namesake is here tonight. Wouldn't you know."

"Alex doesn't miss a trick. Have you any idea *why* he's here?"

"Probably trying to make some deal with Abolafia. Her investigation starts tomorrow."

"Oh." I thought over some of those things I had thought before. "Do you know a Maud Hinkle?"

His puzzled look said "no" pretty convincingly.

"She bills herself as one of the upper echelon in the arcane organization of which I spoke."

"Yeah?"

"She ended our interview earlier this evening with a little homily about hawks and helicopters. I took our subsequent encounter as a fillip of coincidence. But now I discover that the evening has confirmed her intimations of plurality." I shook my head. "Hawk, I am suddenly catapulted into a paranoid world where the walls not only have ears, but probably eyes and long, claw-tipped fingers. Anyone about me – yea, even very you – could turn out to be a spy. I suspect every sewer grating and second-story window conceals binoculars, a tommygun, or worse. What I just can't figure out is how these insidious forces, ubiquitous and omnipresent though they be, induced you to lure me into this intricate and diabolical –"

"Oh, cut it out!" He shook back his hair, "I didn't lure–"

"Perhaps not consciously, but Special Services has Holographic Information Storage, and their methods are insidious and cruel– "

"I said cut it out!" And all sorts of hard little things happened again. "Do you think I'd–" Then he realized how scared I was, I guess. "Look, the Hawk isn't some small-time snatch-purse. He lives in just as paranoid a world as you're in now, only all the time. If he's here, you can be sure there are just as many of his men – eyes and ears and fingers – as there are of Maud Hickenlooper."

"Hinkle."

"Anyway, it works both ways. No Singer's going to – Look, do you really think *I* would–"

And even though I knew all those hard little things were scabs over pain, I said, "Yes."

"You did something for me once, and I–"

"I gave you some more welts. That's all."

All the scabs pulled off.

"Hawk," I said. "Let me see."

He took a breath. Then he began to open the brass buttons. The flaps of his jacket fell back. The lumia colored his chest with pastel shiftings.

I felt my face wrinkle. I didn't want to look away. I drew a hissing breath instead, which was just as bad.

He looked up. "There're a lot more than when you were here last, aren't there?"

"You're going to kill yourself, Hawk."

He shrugged.

"I can't even tell which are the ones I put there anymore."

He started to point them out.

"Oh, come on," I said too sharply. And for the length of three breaths, he grew more and more uncomfortable till I saw him start to reach for the bottom button. "Boy," I said, trying to keep despair out of my voice, "why do you do it?" and ended up keeping out everything. There is nothing more despairing than a voice empty.

He shrugged, saw I didn't want that, and for a moment anger flickered in his green eyes. I didn't want that either. So he said: "Look . . . you touch a person softly, gently, and maybe you even do it with love. And, well, I guess a piece of information goes on up to the brain where something interprets it as pleasure. Maybe something up there in my head interprets the information all wrong . . ."

I shook my head. "You're a Singer. Singers are supposed to be eccentric, sure; but—"

Now he was shaking his head. Then the anger opened up. And I saw an expression move from all those spots that had communicated pain through the rest of his features and vanish without ever becoming a word. Once more he looked down at the wounds that webbed his thin body.

"Button it up, boy. I'm sorry I said anything."

Halfway up the lapels, his hands stopped. "You really think I'd turn you in?"

"Button it up."

He did. Then he said, "Oh." And then, "You know, it's midnight."

"So?"

"Edna just gave me the Word."

"Which is?"

"Agate."

I nodded.

He finished closing his collar. "What are you thinking about?"

"Cows."

"Cows?" Hawk asked. "What about them?"

"You ever been on a dairy farm?"

He shook his head.

"To get the most milk, you keep the cows practically in suspended animation. They're fed intravenously from a big tank that pipes nutrients out and down, branching into smaller and smaller pipes until it gets to all those high-yield semi-corpses."

"I've seen pictures."

"People."

". . . and cows?"

"You've given me the Word. And now it begins to funnel down, branching out, with me telling others and them telling still others, till by midnight tomorrow . . ."

"I'll go get the—"

"Hawk?"

He turned back. "What?"

"You say you don't think I'm going to be the victim of any hanky-panky with the mysterious forces that know more than we. Okay, that's your opinion. But as soon as I get rid of this stuff, I'm going to make the most distracting exit you've ever seen."

Two little lines bit down Hawk's forehead. "Are you sure I haven't seen this one before?"

"As a matter of fact I think you have." Now I grinned.

"Oh," Hawk said, then made a sound that had the structure of laughter but was all breath. "I'll get the Hawk."

He ducked out between the trees.

I glanced up at the lozenges of moonlight in the leaves.

I looked down at my briefcase.

Up between the rocks, stepping around the long grass, came the Hawk. He wore a gray evening suit; a gray silk turtleneck. Above his craggy face, his head was completely shaved.

"Mr. Cadwaliter-Erickson?" He held out his hand.

I shook: small sharp bones in loose skin. "Does one call you Mr. . . . ?"

"Arty."

"Arty the Hawk?" I tried to look like I wasn't giving his gray attire the once-over.

He smiled. "Arty the Hawk. Yeah. I picked that name up when I was younger than our friend down there. Alex says you got . . . well, some things that are not exactly yours. That don't belong to you."

I nodded.

"Show them to me."

"You were told what–"

He brushed away the end of my sentence. "Come on, let me see."

He extended his hand, smiling affably as a bank clerk. I ran my thumb around the pressure-zip. The cover went *tsk*. "Tell me," I said, looking up at his head still lowered to see what I had, "what does one do about Special Services? They seem to be after me."

The head came up. Surprise changed slowly to a craggy leer. "Why, Mr. Cadwaliter-Erickson!" He gave me the up and down openly. "Keep your income steady. Keep it steady, that's one thing you can do."

"If you buy these for anything like what they're worth, that's going to be a little difficult."

"I would imagine. I could always give you less money–"

The cover went *tsk* again.

"– or, barring that, you could try to use your head and outwit them."

"You must have outwitted them at one time or another. You may be on an even keel now, but you had to get there from somewhere else."

Arty the Hawk's nod was downright sly. "I guess you've had a run-in with Maud. Well, I suppose congratulations are in order. And condolences. I always like to do what's in order."

"You seem to know how to take care of yourself. I mean I notice you're not out there mingling with the guests."

"There are two parties going on here tonight," Arty said. "Where do you think Alex disappears off to every five minutes?"

I frowned.

"That lumia down in the rocks" – he pointed towards my feet – "is a mandala of shifting hues on our ceiling. Alex," he chuckled, "goes scuttling off under the rocks where there is a pavilion of Oriental splendor–"

"And a separate guest list at the door?"

"Regina is on both. I'm on both. So's the kid, Edna, Lewis, Ann–"

"Am I supposed to know all this?"

"Well, you came with a person on both lists. I just thought. . ." He paused.

I was coming on wrong. Well. A quick change artist learns fairly quick that the verisimilitude factor in imitating someone up the scale is your confidence in your unalienable right to come on wrong. "I'll tell you," I said. "How about exchanging these" – I held out the briefcase – "for some information."

"You want to know how to stay out of Maud's clutches?" He shook his head. "It would be pretty stupid of me to tell you, even if I could. Besides, you've got your family fortunes to fall back on." He beat the front of his shirt with his thumb. "Believe me, boy. Arty the Hawk didn't have that. I didn't have anything like that." His hands dropped into his pockets. "Let's see what you got."

I opened the case again.

The Hawk looked for a while. After a few moments he picked a couple up, turned them around, put them back down, put his hands back in his pockets. "I'll give you sixty thousand for them, approved credit tablets."

"What about the information I wanted?"

"I wouldn't tell you a thing." He smiled. "I wouldn't tell you the time of day."

There are very few successful thieves in this world. Still less on the other five. The will to steal is an impulse towards the absurd and tasteless. (The talents are poetic, theatrical, a certain reverse charisma. . .) But it is a will, as the will to order, power, love.

"All right," I said.

Somewhere overhead I heard a faint humming.

Arty looked at me fondly. He reached under the lapel of his jacket and took out a handful of credit tablets – the scarlet-banded tablets whose slips were ten thousand apiece. He pulled off one. Two. Three. Four.

"You can deposit this much safely—"

"Why do you think Maud is after me?"

Five. Six.

"Fine," I said.

"How about throwing in the briefcase?" Arty asked.

"Ask Alex for a paper bag. If you want, I can send them—"

"Give them here."

The humming was coming closer.

I held up the open case. Arty went in with both hands. He shoved them into his coat pockets, his pants pockets; the gray cloth was distended by angular bulges. He looked left, right. "Thanks," he said. "Thanks." Then he turned and hurried down the slope with all sorts of things in his pockets that weren't his now.

I looked up through the leaves for the noise, but I couldn't see anything.

I stooped down now and laid my case open. I pulled open the back compartment where I kept the things that did belong to me and rummaged hurriedly through.

Alex was just offering Puffy-eyes another Scotch, while the gentleman was saying, "Has anyone seen Mrs. Silem? What's that humming overhead—?" when a large woman wrapped in a veil of fading fabric tottered across the rocks, screaming.

Her hands were clawing at her covered face.

Alex sloshed soda over his sleeve, and the man said, "Oh, my God! Who's that?"

"No!" the woman shrieked. "Oh, no! Help me!" waving her wrinkled fingers, brilliant with rings.

"Don't you recognize her?" That was Hawk whispering confidentially to someone else. "It's Henrietta, Countess of Effingham."

And Alex, overhearing, went hurrying to her assistance. The Countess, however, ducked between two cacti and disappeared into the high grass. But the entire party followed. They were beating about the underbrush when a balding gentleman in a black tux, bow tie and cummerbund coughed and said in a very worried voice, "Excuse me, Mr. Spinnel?"

Alex whirled.

"Mr. Spinnel, my mother. . ."

"Who are *you*?" The interruption upset Alex terribly.

The gentleman drew himself up to announce: "The Honorable Clement Effingham," and his pants leg shook for all the world as if he had started to click his heels. But articulation failed. The expression melted on his face. "Oh, I . . . my mother, Mr. Spinnel. We were downstairs at the other half of your party when she got very upset. She ran up here – oh, I told her not to! I knew you'd be upset. But you must help me!" and then looked up.

The others looked, too.

The helicopter blacked the moon, doffing and settling below its hazy twin parasols.

"Oh, please . . ." the gentleman said, "You look over there! Perhaps she's gone back down. I've got to" – looking quickly both ways – "find her." He hurried in one direction while everyone else hurried in others.

The humming was suddenly syncopated with a crash. Roaring now, as plastic fragments from the transparent roof clattered down through the branches, clattered on the rocks. . .

I made it into the elevator and had already thumbed the edge of my briefcase clasp, when Hawk dove between the unfolding foils. The electric-eye began to swing them open. I hit DOOR CLOSE full fist.

The boy staggered, banged shoulders on two walls, then got back breath and balance. "Hey, there's police getting out of that helicopter!"

"Hand-picked by Maud Hinkle herself, no doubt." I pulled the other tuft of white hair from my temple. It went into the case on top of the plastiderm gloves (wrinkled, thick blue veins, long carnelian nails) that had been Henrietta's hands, lying in the chiffon folds of her sari.

Then there was the downward tug of stopping. The Honorable Clement was still half on my face when the door opened.

Gray and gray, with an absolutely dismal expression on his

face, the Hawk swung through the doors. Behind him people were dancing in an elaborate pavilion festooned with Oriental magnificence (and a mandala of shifting hues on the ceiling). Arty beat me to DOOR CLOSE. Then he gave me an odd look.

I just sighed and finished peeling off Clem.

"The police are up there?" the Hawk reiterated.

"Arty," I said, buckling my pants, "it certainly looks that way." The car gained momentum. "You look almost as upset as Alex." I shrugged the tux jacket down my arms, turning the sleeves inside out, pulled one wrist free, and jerked off the white starched dicky with the black bow tie and stuffed it into the briefcase with all my other dickies; swung the coat around and slipped on Howard Calvin Evingston's good gray herringbone. Howard (like Hank) is a redhead (but not as curly).

The Hawk raised his bare brows when I peeled off Clement's bald pate and shook out my hair.

"I noticed you aren't carrying around all those bulky things in your pockets any more."

"Oh, those have been taken care of," he said gruffly. "They're all right."

"Arty," I said, adjusting my voice down to Howard's security-provoking, ingenuous baritone, "it must have been my unabashed conceit that made me think that those Regular Service police were here just for me—"

The Hawk actually snarled. "They wouldn't be that unhappy if they got me, too."

And from his corner Hawk demanded, "You've got security here with you, don't you, Arty?"

"So what?"

"There's one way you can get out of this," Hawk hissed at me. His jacket had come half-open down his wrecked chest. "That's if Arty takes you out with him."

"Brilliant idea," I concluded. "You want a couple of thousand back for the service?"

The idea didn't amuse him. "I don't want anything from you." He turned to Hawk. "I need something from you, kid. Not him. Look, I wasn't prepared for Maud. If you want me to get your friend out, then you've got to do something for me."

The boy looked confused.

I thought I saw smugness on Arty's face, but the expression resolved into concern. "You've got to figure out some way to fill the lobby up with people, and fast."

I was going to ask why, but then I didn't know the extent of Arty's security. I was going to ask how, but the floor pushed up at my feet and the doors swung open. "If you can't do it," the Hawk growled to Hawk, "none of us will get out of here. None of us!"

I had no idea what the kid was going to do, but when I started to follow him out into the lobby, the Hawk grabbed my arm and hissed, "Stay here, you idiot!"

I stepped back. Arty was leaning on DOOR OPEN.

Hawk sprinted towards the pool. And splashed in.

He reached the braziers on their twelve-foot tripods and began to climb.

"He's going to hurt himself!" the Hawk whispered.

"Yeah," I said, but I don't think my cynicism got through. Below the great dish of fire, Hawk was fiddling. Then something under there came loose. Something else went *Clang!* And something else spurted out across the water. The fire raced along it and hit the pool, churning and roaring like hell.

A black arrow with a golden head: Hawk dove.

I bit the inside of my cheek as the alarm sounded. Four people in uniforms were coming across the blue carpet. Another group were crossing in the other direction, saw the flames, and one of the women screamed. I let out my breath, thinking carpet and walls and ceilings would be flame-proof. But I kept losing focus on the idea before the sixty-odd infernal feet.

Hawk surfaced on the edge of the pool in the only clear spot left, rolled over on to the carpet, clutching his face. And rolled. And rolled. Then, came to his feet.

Another elevator spilled out a load of passengers who gaped and gasped. A crew came through the doors now with fire-fighting equipment. The alarm was still sounding.

Hawk turned to look at the dozen-odd people in the lobby. Water puddled the carpet about his drenched and shiny pants legs. Flame turned the drops on his cheek and hair to flickering copper and blood.

He banged his fists against his wet thighs, took a deep breath, and against the roar and the bells and the whispering, he Sang.

Two people ducked back into two elevators. From a doorway half a dozen more emerged. The elevators returned half a minute later with a dozen people each. I realized the message was going through the building, there's a Singer Singing in the lobby.

The lobby filled. The flames growled, the fire fighters stood around shuffling, and Hawk, feet apart on the blue rug by the burning pool, Sang, and Sang of a bar off Times Square full of thieves, morphadine-heads, brawlers, drunkards, women too old to trade what they still held out for barter, and trade just too nasty-grimy; where earlier in the evening, a brawl had broken out, and an old man had been critically hurt in the fray.

Arty tugged at my sleeve.

"What. . .?"

"Come on," he hissed.

The elevator door closed behind us.

We ambled through the attentive listeners, stopping to watch, stopping to hear. I couldn't really do Hawk justice. A lot of that slow amble I spent wondering what sort of security Arty had:

Standing behind a couple in a bathrobe who were squinting into the heat, I decided it was all very simple. Arty wanted simply to drift away through a crowd, so he'd conveniently gotten Hawk to manufacture one.

To get to the door we had to pass through practically a cordon of Regular Service policemen, who I don't think had anything to do with what might have been going on in the roof garden; they'd simply collected to see the fire and stayed for the Song. When Arty tapped one on the shoulder – "Excuse me please" – to get by, the policeman glanced at him, glanced away, then did a Mack Sennet double-take. But another policeman caught the whole interchange, touched the first on the arm, and gave him a frantic little headshake. Then both men turned very deliberately back to watch the Singer. While the earthquake in my chest stilled, I decided that the Hawk's security complex of agents and counter-agents, maneuvering and machinating through the flaming lobby, must be of such finesse and intricacy that to attempt understanding was to condemn oneself to total paranoia.

Arty opened the final door.

I stepped from the last of the air-conditioning into the night.

We hurried down the ramp.

"Hey, Arty . . ."

"You go that way." He pointed down the street. "I go this way."

"Eh . . . what's that way?" I pointed in my direction.

"Twelve Towers sub-sub-subway station. Look. I've got you out of there. Believe me, you're safe for the time being. Now go take a train someplace interesting. Good-bye. Go on now." Then Arty the Hawk put his fists in his pockets and hurried up the street.

I started down, keeping near the wall, expecting someone to get me with a blow-dart from a passing car, a deathray from the shrubbery.

I reached the sub.

And still nothing had happened.

Agate gave way to Malachite:

Tourmaline:

Beryl (during which month I turned twenty-six):

Porphyry:

Sapphire (that month I took the ten thousand I hadn't frittered away and invested it in The Glacier, a perfectly legitimate ice cream palace on Triton – the first and only ice cream palace on Triton – which took off like fireworks; all investors were returned eight-hundred percent, no kidding. Two weeks later I'd lost half of those earnings on another set of preposterous illegalities and was feeling quite depressed, but The Glacier kept pulling them in. The new Word came by):

Cinnabar:

Turquoise:

Tiger's Eye:

Hector Calhoun Eisenhower finally buckled down and spent three months learning how to be a respectable member of the upper middle class underworld. That is a long novel in itself. High finance; corporate law; how to hire help: Whew! But the complexities of life have always intrigued me. I got through it. The basic rule is still the same: observe carefully, imitate effectively.

Garnet:

Topaz (I whispered that word on the roof of the Trans-Satellite Power Station, and caused my hirelings to commit two murders. And you know? I didn't feel a thing):

Taafite:

We were nearing the end of Taafite. I'd come back to Triton on strictly Glacial business. A bright pleasant morning it was: the business went fine. I decided to take off the afternoon and go sight-seeing in the Torrents.

"...two hundred and thirty yards high," the guide announced, and everyone around me leaned on the rail and gazed up through the plastic corridor at the cliffs of frozen methane that soared through Neptune's cold green glare.

"Just a few yards down the catwalk, ladies and gentlemen, you can catch your first glimpse of the Well of This World, where over a million years ago, a mysterious force science still cannot explain caused twenty-five square miles of frozen methane to liquefy for no more than a few hours during which time a whirlpool twice the depth of Earth's Grand Canyon was caught for the ages when the temperature dropped once more to..."

People were moving down the corridor when I saw her smiling. My hair was black and nappy, and my skin was chestnut dark today.

I was just feeling overconfident, I guess, so I kept standing around next to her. I even contemplated coming on. Then she broke the whole thing up by suddenly turning to me and saying perfectly deadpan: "Why, if it isn't Hamlet Caliban Enobarbus!"

Old reflexes realigned my features to couple the frown of confusion with the smile of indulgence. *Pardon me, but I think you must have mistaken* . . . No, I didn't say it. "Maud," I said, "have you come here to tell me that my time has come?"

She wore several shades of blue with a large blue brooch at her shoulder, obviously glass. Still, I realized as I looked about the other tourists, she was more inconspicuous amidst their finery than I was. "No," she said. "Actually I'm on vacation. Just like you."

"No kidding?" We had dropped behind the crowd. "You are kidding."

"Special Services of Earth, while we cooperate with Special

Services on other worlds, has no official jurisdiction on Triton. And since you came here with money, and most of your recorded gain in income has been through The Glacier, while Regular Services on Triton might be glad to get you, Special Services is not after you as yet." She smiled. "I haven't been to The Glacier. It would really be nice to say I'd been taken there by one of the owners. Could we go for a soda, do you think?"

The swirled sides of the Well of This World dropped away in opalescent grandeur. Tourists gazed, and the guide went on about indices of refraction, angles of incline.

"I don't think you trust me," Maud said.

My look said she was right.

"Have you ever been involved with narcotics?" she asked suddenly.

I frowned.

"No, I'm serious. I want to try and explain something . . . a point of information that may make both our lives easier."

"Peripherally," I said. "I'm sure you've got down all the information in your dossiers."

"I was involved with them a good deal more than peripherally for several years," Maud said. "Before I got into Special Services, I was in the Narcotics Division of the regular force. And the people we dealt with twenty-four hours a day were drug users, drug pushers. To catch the big ones we had to make friends with the little ones. To catch the bigger ones, we had to make friends with the big. We had to keep the same hours they kept, talk the same language, for months at a time live on the same streets, in the same buildings." She stepped back from the rail to let a youngster ahead. "I had to be sent away to take the morphadine detoxification cure twice while I was on the narc squad. And I had a better record than most."

"What's your point?"

"Just this. You and I are traveling in the same circles now, if only because of our respective chosen professions. You'd be surprised how many people we already know in common. Don't be shocked when we run into each other crossing Sovereign Plaza in Bellona one day, then two weeks later wind up at the same restaurant for lunch at Lux on Iapetus. Though the circles we move in cover worlds, they *are* the same, and not that big."

"Come on." I don't think I sounded happy. "Let me treat you to that ice cream." We started back down the walkway.

"You know," Maud said, "if you do stay out of Special Services' hands here and on Earth long enough, eventually you'll be up there with a huge income growing on a steady slope. It might be a few years, but it's possible. There's no reason now for us to be *personal* enemies. You just may, someday, reach that point where Special Services loses interest in you as quarry. Oh, we'd still see each other, run into each other. We get a great deal of our information from people up there. We're in a position to help you, too, you see."

"You've been casting holograms again."

She shrugged. Her face looked positively ghostly under the pale planet. She said, when we reached the artificial lights of the city, "I did meet two friends of yours recently, Lewis and Ann."

"The Singers?"

She nodded.

"Oh, I don't really know them well."

"They seem to know a lot about you. Perhaps through that other Singer, Hawk."

"Oh," I said again. "Did they say how he was?"

"I read that he was recovering about two months back. But nothing since then."

"That's about all I know, too," I said.

"The only time I've ever seen him," Maud said, "was right after I pulled him out."

Arty and I had gotten out of the lobby before Hawk actually finished. The next day on the news-tapes I learned that when his Song was over, he shrugged out of his jacket, dropped his pants, and walked back into the pool.

The fire-fighter crew suddenly woke up; people began running around and screaming: he'd been rescued, seventy percent of his body covered with second- and third-degree burns. I'd been industriously trying not to think about it.

"*You* pulled him out?"

"Yes. I was in the helicopter that landed on the roof," Maud said. "I thought you'd be impressed to see me."

"Oh," I said. "How did you get to pull him out?"

"Once you got going, Arty's security managed to jam the elevator service above the seventy-first floor, so we didn't get to the lobby till after you were out of the building. That's when Hawk tried to—"

"But it was you who actually saved him, though?"

"The firemen in that neighborhood hadn't had a fire in twelve years! I don't think they even know how to operate the equipment. I had my boys foam the pool, then I waded in and dragged him—"

"Oh," I said again. I had been trying hard, almost succeeding, these eleven months. I wasn't there when it happened. It wasn't my affair. Maud was saying:

"We thought we might have gotten a lead on you from him, but when I got him to the shore, he was completely out, just a mass of open, running—"

"I should have known the Special Services uses Singers, too." I said. "Everyone else does. The Word changes today, doesn't it? Lewis and Ann didn't pass on what the new one is?"

"I saw them yesterday, and the Word doesn't change for another eight hours. Besides, they wouldn't tell me, anyway." She glanced at me and frowned. "They really wouldn't."

"Let's go have some sodas," I said. "We'll make small talk and listen carefully to each other while we affect an air of nonchalance; you will try to pick up things that will make it easier to catch me; I will listen for things you let slip that might make it easier for me to avoid you."

"Um-hm." She nodded.

"Why did you contact me in that bar, anyway?"

Eyes of ice: "I told you, we simply travel in the same circles. We're quite likely to be in the same bar on the same night."

"I guess that's just one of the things I'm not supposed to understand, huh?"

Her smiled was appropriately ambiguous. I didn't push it.

It was a very dull afternoon. I couldn't repeat one exchange from the nonsense we babbled over the cherry-peaked mountains of whipped cream. We both exerted so much energy to keep up the appearance of being amused, I doubt either one of us could see our way to picking up anything meaningful; if anything meaningful was said.

She left. I brooded some more on the charred phoenix.

The Steward of The Glacier called me into the kitchen to ask about a shipment of contraband milk (The Glacier makes all its own ice cream) that I had been able to wangle on my last trip to Earth (it's amazing how little progress there has been in dairy farming over the last ten years; it was depressingly easy to hornswoggle that bumbling Vermonter) and under the white lights and great plastic churning vats, while I tried to get things straightened out, he made some comment about the Heist Cream Emperor; that didn't do *any* good.

By the time the evening crowd got there, and the moog was making music, and the crystal walls were blazing; and the floor show – a new addition that week – had been cajoled into going on anyway (a trunk of costumes had gotten lost in shipment [or swiped, but I wasn't about to tell them that]), and wandering through the tables I, personally, had caught a very grimy little girl, obviously out of her head on morph, trying to pick up a customer's pocketbook from the back of a chair – I just caught her by the wrist, made her let go, and led her to the door daintily, while she blinked at me with dilated eyes and the customer never even knew – and the floor show, having decided what the hell, were doing their act *au naturel*, and everyone was having just a high old time, I was feeling really bad.

I went outside, sat on the wide steps, and growled when I had to move aside to let people in or out. About the seventy-fifth growl, the person I growled at stopped and boomed down at me, "I thought I'd find you, if I looked hard enough! I mean if I really looked."

I looked at the hand that was flapping at my shoulder, followed the arm up to a black turtleneck where there was a beefy, bald, grinning head. "Arty," I said, "what are . . . ?" But he was still flapping and laughing with impervious *gemütlichkeit*.

"You wouldn't believe the time I had getting a picture of you, boy. Had to bribe one out of the Triton Special Services Department. That quick change bit. Great gimmick. Just great!" The

Hawk sat down next to me and dropped his hand on my knee. "Wonderful place you got here. I like it, like it a lot." Small bones in veined dough. "But not enough to make you an offer on it yet. You're learning fast there, though. I can tell you're learning fast. I'm going to be proud to be able to say I was the one who gave you your first big break." His hand came away, and he began to knead it into the other. "If you're going to move into the big time, you have to have at least one foot planted firmly on the right side of the law. The whole idea is to make yourself indispensable to the good people; once that's done, a good crook has the keys to all the treasure houses in the system. But I'm not telling you anything you don't already know."

"Arty," I said, "do you think the two of us should be seen together here . . . ?"

The Hawk held his hand above his lap and joggled it with a deprecating motion. "Nobody can get a picture of us. I got my men all around. I never go anywhere in public without my security. Heard you've been looking into the security business yourself," which was true. "Good idea. Very good. I like the way you're handling yourself."

"Thanks. Arty, I'm not feeling too hot this evening. I came out here to get some air . . ."

Arty's hand fluttered again. "Don't worry, I won't hang around. You're right. We shouldn't be seen. Just passing by and wanted to say hello. Just hello." He got up. "That's all." He started down the steps.

"Arty?"

He looked back.

"Sometime soon you will come back; and that time you will want to buy out my share of The Glacier, because I'll have gotten too big; and I won't want to sell because I'll think I'm big enough to fight you. So we'll be enemies for a while. You'll try to kill me. I'll try to kill you."

On his face, first the frown of confusion; then the indulgent smile. "I see you've caught on to the idea of hologramic information. Very good. Good. It's the only way to outwit Maud. Make sure all your information relates to the whole scope of the situation. It's the only way to outwit me, too." He smiled, started to turn, but thought of something else. "If you can fight me off long enough and keep growing, keep your security in tiptop shape, eventually, we'll get to the point where it'll be worth both our whiles to work together again. If you can just hold out, we'll be friends again. Someday. You just watch. Just wait."

"Thanks for telling me."

The Hawk looked at his watch. "Well. Goodbye." I thought he was going to leave finally. But he glanced up again. "Have you got the new Word?"

"That's right," I said. "It went out tonight. What is it?"

The Hawk waited till the people coming down the steps were gone. He looked hastily about, then leaned towards me with hands cupped at his mouth, rasped, "Pyrite," and winked hugely. "I just got it from a gal who got it direct from Colette," (one of the three Singers of Triton). Then he turned, jounced down the steps, and shouldered his way into the crowds passing on the strip.

I sat there mulling through the year till I had to get up and walk. All walking does to my depressive moods is add the reinforcing rhythm of paranoia. By the time I was coming back, I had worked out a dilly of a delusional system: The Hawk had already begun to weave some security-ridden plot about me, which ended when we were all trapped in some dead-end alley, and trying to get aid I called out, "Pyrite!" which would turn out not to be the Word at all but served to identify me for the man in the dark gloves with the gun/grenade/gas.

There was a cafeteria on the corner. In the light from the window, clustered over the wreck by the curb was a bunch of nasty-grimies (à la Triton: chains around the wrist, bumblebee tattoo on cheek, high-heel boots on those who could afford them). Straddling the smashed headlight was the little morph-head I had ejected earlier from The Glacier.

On a whim I went up to her. "Hey?"

She looked at me from under hair like trampled hay, eyes all pupil.

"You get the new Word yet?"

She rubbed her nose, already scratch red. "Pyrite," she said. "It just came down about an hour ago."

"Who told you?"

She considered my question. "I got it from a guy, who says he got it from a guy, who came in this evening from New York, who picked it up there from a Singer named Hawk."

The three grimies nearest made a point of not looking at me. Those further away let themselves glance.

"Oh," I said. "Oh. Thanks."

Occam's Razor, along with any real information on how security works, hones away most such paranoia. Pyrite. At a certain level in my line of work, paranoia's just an occupational disease. At least I was certain that Arty (and Maud) probably suffered from it as much as I did.

The lights were out on The Glacier's marquee. Then I remembered what I had left inside and ran up the stairs.

The door was locked. I pounded on the glass a couple of times, but everyone had gone home. And the thing that made it worse was that I could see it sitting on the counter of the coat-check alcove under the orange bulb. The steward had probably put it there, thinking I might arrive before everybody left. Tomorrow at noon Ho Chi Eng had to pick up his reservation for the Marigold Suite on the Interplanetary Liner *The Platinum Swan*, which left at one-thirty for Bellona. And there behind the glass doors of The Glacier, it waited with the proper wig, as well as the epicanthic folds that would halve Mr. Eng's sloe eyes of jet.

I actually thought of breaking in. But the more practical solution was to get the hotel to wake me at nine and come in with the cleaning man. I turned around and started down the steps; and the thought struck me, and made me terribly sad, so that I blinked and smiled just from reflex; it was probably just as well to leave it there till morning, because there was nothing in it that wasn't mine anyway.

About the contributors

Marion Zimmer Bradley has been a science fiction/fantasy fan since her middle teens, and made her first sale as an adjunct to an amateur fiction contest in *Fantastic/Amazing Stories* in 1949. In 1952 she sold her first professional short story to *Vortex Science Fiction*. She has written everything from sf to Gothics, but is probably best known for her Darkover novels, of which there are now 19 in print (and two more in the works). The Darkover series also includes two anthologies of amateur fiction, *The Keeper's Price* and *Sword of Chaos*, as well as several short stories. Of special interest to gay readers is Bradley's non-sf novel about a three-generation circus family of trapeze flyers, *The Catch Trap*.

She currently lives in Berkeley with her younger son and foster daughter. Her hobbies are opera (including "lightwalking" at the S.F. Opera), book reviewing, and making clothes for her several Cabbage Patch and similar dolls.

Samuel R. Delany, called "the most interesting author of science fiction writing in English today" by *The New York Times Book Review*, was born in New York City in 1942. His science fiction novels include *Babel-17* and *The Einstein Intersection* (both winners of the Nebula Award), *Nova*, *Triton*, and the best-selling *Dhalgren*. His work also includes the Nevèrÿon fantasy series, the latest of which, *Flight from Nevèrÿon*, deals with aspects of the current AIDS epidemic, and short stories, two of which have also won Nebula Awards. He has published two collections of sf criticism, *The Jewel-Hinged Jaw* and *Starboard Wine*, as well as *The American Shore*, a book-length study of Thomas M. Disch's story "Angouleme." *Stars in My Pocket Like Grains of Sand*, 1984, is the first of a diptych of novels exploring a gay male love affair of the distant future.

Nicholas Fisk is a British writer whose career has included acting, illustrating, editing, publishing, advertising, and jazz music. His latest works include several sf novellas for young readers. Married, with two children, he has a wide range of personal enthusiasms and interests. He has 25 books in print.

Jewelle Gomez has had her work appear in *Conditions, Ikon, 13th Moon*, and *Essence*. She writes reviews for *The Village Voice*, Wellesley's *Women's Review of Books* and *Womanews*. The story "No Day Too Long" is part of her forthcoming collection, *The Gilda Stories*.

Rand B. Lee is the son of actress Kaye Brinker and the late Manfred B. Lee, co-author of the "Ellery Queen" detective novels. Mr. Lee's work has appeared in *Isaac Asimov's Science Fiction Magazine, Amazing Science Fiction Stories*, and several anthologies, including Donald Wollheim's *1984 Annual World's Best SF*. "Full Fathom Five" was his first published story.

Of Walt Liebscher his agent and friend Forrest J Ackerman writes: "In his youth he produced one of the best sci-fi fanzines of all time, *Chanticleer*. A thoroughly fey personality, he didn't give a damn who knew he was gay; in actuality, he was bisexual, and both men and women of hetero and homo persuasion loved him dearly. It is doubtful if he had any enemies. He was a great good friend of such writers as E.E. "Doc" Smith, Philip Jose Farmer and

Robert Bloch. A cruel stroke late in life partially paralyzed him but never got him down. He continued to write (and sell) stories, attend sf conventions (frequently as a Guest of Honor) and play his electric organ more inspirationally with one hand than most organists could with two." Though, sadly, he died before he could see *Worlds Apart* in print, Mr. Liebscher was delighted that his story was to be reprinted in a lesbian/gay anthology.

Elizabeth A. Lynn is an experienced science fiction writer who has twice won the World Fantasy Award. She has recently published her first children's novel, *The Silver Horse*. She is a black belt instructor of Aikido. She enjoys painting her house, taking in stray dogs, and feeding her cats.

Edgar Pangborn was born in 1909 in New York City. He was educated at Brooklyn Friends School, Harvard University and the New England Conservatory of Music. He saw music as a possible career at first but soon became more deeply committed to writing. His earlier stories were mysteries in the popular magazines of the 30s; later he described these efforts as "learning to write by writing." From 1939 to 1942 he had a try at subsistence farming in Maine. He served in the U.S. Army Medical Corps in the New Guinea and Philippines area from 1942 to 1945. After the war he settled to a career of free-lance writing, becoming more and more interested in the free-wheeling fantasy genre that is usually labeled "science fiction." He twice won the International Fantasy Award and is perhaps best known for the delightful novel, *Davey*. He died on February 1, 1976.

Joanna Russ, highly acclaimed writer and academic, is the person most directly responsible for the introduction of lesbianism and feminism into contemporary science fiction. Originally from

New York, she holds degrees from Cornell and Yale and has taught at several universities. She won the Nebula Award for her story "When It Changed" and the Hugo for "Souls." Her novels include *The Female Man, The Two of Them* and *On Strike Against God.* She is also noted for her incisive and original literary criticism, and for cutting-edge feminist essays such as those collected in *Magic Mommas, Trembling Sisters, Puritans and Perverts.*

James Tiptree, Jr. gives us this telegraphic synopsis of her life: "Born 1915, promptly traveled a lot, set up as a graphic artist, enlisted in AAF in World War II, worked as Photo Intelligence Officer; after was a spell of country business with husband-partner; then called back to then-new CIA to help set up photo intelligence shop. Got disgusted with CIA, returned to college, interested in psychology of perception. Ph.D. 1966, GWU, D.C. Health forced retirement from teaching, but did complete some research. Meanwhile sf stories were selling, so they changed from hobby to serious work. Ambitions: To learn to speak and write English, and do some more painting. Hobbies, chess (formerly), gardening, and koi. Sports (formerly) show jumping, or anything to do with horses."

With characteristic modesty, Tiptree omits mention of the awards her writing has received, among them the prestigious Nebula Award for her story "The Screwfly Solution," with another Nebula and a Hugo for "Houston, Houston, Do You Read?" Tiptree has also published stories under the pseudonym Raccoona Sheldon.

Camilla Decarnin is a radical feminist pervert living in San Francisco. Her writings on sex and other subjects (she grudgingly admits there *are* other subjects) have appeared in *The Advocate, Heresies, Plexus, Coming to Power, Yellow Silk, Riverside Quarterly, The Little Magazine, Inscape,* and other alternative and science fiction publications.

Eric Garber is the co-author of *Uranian Worlds: A Reader's Guide to Alternative Sexuality in Science Fiction and Fantasy* (G.K. Hall, 1983). He was the apprentice editor of the documentary film *Word is Out*. In 1978 he helped found the San Francisco Lesbian and Gay History Project. His current research is on the lesbian and gay subcultures in Harlem during the 1920s. He has presented a slide lecture on this subject across the country. He divides his time among work on a book about gay Harlem, reading musty paperback novels, and an occasional dinner party.

Lyn Paleo is the co-author of *Uranian Worlds: A Reader's Guide to Alternative Sexuality in Science Fiction and Fantasy* (G.K. Hall, 1983). She is a member of the San Francisco Lesbian and Gay History Project and the Women's AIDS Network. She has been a factory worker, drug abuse counsellor, sign language interpreter and AIDS health educator.

Other books of interest from
ALYSON PUBLICATIONS

☐ **SOCRATES, PLATO AND GUYS LIKE ME: Confessions of a gay schoolteacher,** by Eric Rofes, $7.00. When Eric Rofes began teaching sixth grade at a conservative private school, he soon felt the strain of a split identity. Here he describes his two years of teaching from within the closet, and his difficult decision to finally come out.

☐ **MURDER IS MURDER IS MURDER,** by Samuel M. Steward, $7.00. Gertrude Stein and Alice B. Toklas go sleuthing through the French countryside, attempting to solve the mysterious disappearance of their neighbor, the father of their handsome gardener. A new and very different treat from the author of the Phil Andros stories.

☐ **ONE TEENAGER IN TEN: Writings by gay and lesbian youth,** edited by Ann Heron, $4.00. One teenager in ten is gay; here, twenty-six young people tell their stories: of coming to terms with being different, of the decision how – and whether – to tell friends and parents, and what the consequences were.

☐ **DANCER DAWKINS AND THE CALIFORNIA KID,** by Willyce Kim, $6.00. Dancer Dawkins would like to just sit back and view life from behind a pile of hotcakes. But her lover, Jessica Riggins, has fallen into the clutches of Fatin Satin Aspen, and something must be done. Meanwhile, Little Willie Gutherie of Bangor, Maine, renames herself The California Kid, stocks up on Rubbles Dubble bubble gum, and heads west. When this crew collides in San Francisco, what can be expected? Just about anything. . . .

☐ **LEGENDE,** by Jeannine Allard, $6.00. Sometime in the last century, two women living on the coast of France, in Brittany, loved each other. They had no other models for such a thing, so one of them posed as a man for most of their life together. This legend is still told in Brittany; from it, Jeannine Allard has created a hauntingly beautiful story of two women in love.

☐ **WANDERGROUND,** by Sally Miller Gearhart, $7.00. Here are stories of the hill women, who combine the control of mind and matter with a sensuous adherence to women's realities and history. A lesbian classic.

THE ALEX KANE BOOKS:

☐ **No. 1: SWEET DREAMS,** by John Preston, $5.00. In this, the first book of the series, Alex Kane travels to Boston when he hears of a ruthless gang preying on gay teenagers; in so doing he meets his future partner, Danny Fortelli.

☐ No. 2: **GOLDEN YEARS,** by John Preston, $5.00. Operators of a shady nursing home think they can make a profit by exploiting the dreams of older gay men – but they haven't reckoned with the Alex Kane factor.

☐ No. 3: **DEADLY LIES,** by John Preston, $5.00. Kane goes after a politician who's using homophobia to advance his own political career.

☐ No. 4: **STOLEN MOMENTS,** by John Preston, $5.00. Kane takes on a tabloid publisher in Texas, who has decided that he can take advantage of homophobia to increase his paper's circulation.

☐ **REFLECTIONS OF A ROCK LOBSTER: A story about growing up gay,** by Aaron Fricke, $5.00. When Aaron Fricke took a male date to the senior prom, no one was surprised: he'd gone to court to be able to do so, and the case had made national news. Here Aaron tells his story, and shows what gay pride can mean in a small New England town.

☐ **COMING OUT RIGHT, A handbook for the gay male,** by Wes Muchmore and William Hanson, $6.00. The first steps into the gay world – whether it's a first relationship, a first trip to a gay bar, or coming out at work – can be full of unknowns. This book will make it easier. Here is advice on all aspects of gay life for both the inexperienced and the experienced.

☐ **BELDON'S CRIMES,** by Robert C. Reinhart, $7.00. In his grey suit and silk tie, David Beldon resembles thousands of other Wall Street stockbrokers – until a grisly murder forces him out of the closet and consequently costs him his job. He sues his former employer in what starts out as a simple anti-discrimination case, but unexpectedly grows into a media sensation. Even if Beldon ultimately wins his lawsuit, is he the victor – or victim – of this three-ring media circus?

☐ **DEAR SAMMY: Letters from Gertrude Stein and Alice B. Toklas,** by Samuel M. Steward, $8.00. As a young man, Samuel M. Steward journeyed to France to meet the two women he so admired. It was the beginning of a long friendship. Here he combines his fascinating memoirs of Toklas and Stein with photos and more than a hundred of their letters.

☐ **THE MEN WITH THE PINK TRIANGLE,** by Heinz Heger, $6.00. In a chapter of gay history that is only recently coming to light, thousands of homosexuals were thrown into the Nazi concentration camps along with Jews and others who failed to fit the Aryan ideal. There were forced to wear a pink triangle so that they could be singled out for special abuse. Most perished. Heger is the only one ever to have told his full story.

☐ **EIGHT DAYS A WEEK,** by Larry Duplechan, $7.00. Can Johnnie Ray Rousseau, a 22-year-old black singer, find happiness with Keith Keller, a six-foot-two blond bisexual jock who works in a bank? Will Johnnie Ray's manager ever get him on the Merv Griffin show? Who was the lead singer of the Shangri-las? And what about Snookie? Somewhere among the answers to these and other silly questions is a love story as funny, and sexy, and memorable, as any you'll ever read.

☐ **CHOICES,** by Nancy Toder, $7.00. This popular novel about lesbian love depicts the joy, passion, conflicts and intensity of love between women as Nancy Toder conveys the fear and confusion of a woman coming to terms with her sexual and emotional attraction to other women.

☐ **THE PEARL BASTARD,** by Lillian Halegua, $4.00. Frankie is fifteen when she leaves her large, suffocating Catholic family. Here, with painful innocence and acute vision, she tells the story of her sudden entry into a harsh maturity, beginning with the man in the fine green car who does not mourn the violent death of a seagull against his windshield.

☐ **GAY AND GRAY,** by Raymond M. Berger, $8.00. Working from questionnaires and case histories, Berger has provided the closest look ever at what it is like to be an older gay man. For some, he finds, age has brought burdens; for others, it has brought increased freedom and happiness.

☐ **IN THE TENT,** by David Rees, $6.00. Seventeen-year-old Tim realizes that he is attracted to his classmate Aaron, but, still caught up in the guilt of a Catholic upbringing, he has no idea what to do about it until a camping trip results in unexpected closeness.

☐ **THE HUSTLER,** by John Henry Mackay; trans. by Hubert Kennedy, $8.00. Gunther is fifteen when he arrives alone in the Berlin of the 1920s. There he is soon spotted by Hermann Graff, a sensitive and naive young man who becomes hopelessly enamored with Gunther. But love does not fit neatly into Gunther's new life . . . *The Hustler* was first published in 1926. For today's reader, it combines a poignant love story with a colorful portrayal of the gay subculture that thrived in Berlin a half-century ago.

To get these books:

Ask at your favorite bookstore for the books listed here. You may also order by mail. Just fill out the coupon below, or use your own paper if you prefer not to cut up this book.

\- - - - - - - - - - - - - - - - -

Enclosed is $_______ for the following books. (Add $1.00 postage when ordering just one book; if you order two or more, we'll pay the postage.)

1. ______________________________
2. ______________________________
3. ______________________________
4. ______________________________
5. ______________________________

name: ______________________________

address: ____________________________

city: ______________ state: ______ zip: ______

ALYSON PUBLICATIONS
Dept. B-87, 40 Plympton St., Boston, Mass. 02118